P9-EEH-208

Old Spain
and New Spain

Old Spain
and New Spain

The Travel Narratives
of Camilo José Cela

David Henn

Madison • Teaneck
Fairleigh Dickinson University Press

Associated University Presses
2010 Eastpark Boulevard
Cranbury, NJ 08512

The paper used in this publication meets the requirements of the American National Standard for Permanence of Paper for Printed Library Materials Z39.48-1984.

Library of Congress Cataloging-in-Publication Data

Henn, David.
Old Spain and new Spain : the travel narratives of Camilo José Cela / David Henn.
p. cm.
Includes bibliographical references and index.
ISBN 0-8386-4015-X
1. Cela, Camilo Josâ, 1916—Knowledge—Spain. 2. Cela, Camilo Josâ, 1916-Del Miäo al Bidasoa. 3. Cela, Camilo Josâ, 1916-Judâós, moros y cristianos. 4. Cela, Camilo Josâ, 1916-Primer viaje andaluz. 5. Cela, Camilo Josâ, 1916-Viaje el Pirineo de Lârida. 6. Cela, Camilo Josâ, 1916-Nuevo viaje a la Alcarria. 7. Spain—Description and travel. I. Title.
PQ6605.E44Z6865   2004
863'.62—dc22   2004043281

PRINTED IN THE UNITED STATES OF AMERICA

Contents

Preface

CAMILO JOSÉ CELA WAS BORN ON 11 MAY 1916 IN IRIA FLAVIA, A HAMLET adjacent to the Galician town of Padrón and which lies twenty kilometers southwest of Santiago de Compostela. He died, in Madrid, on 17 January 2002. In a literary career spanning nearly six decades, Cela published novels and short stories, travel books, poetry, criticism on literature and the plastic arts, dictionaries of eroticism and of scabrous usage, as well as countless essays and shorter pieces on a wide range of cultural and social matters. In 1956 he founded the literary magazine *Papeles de Son Armadans* [Papers of Son Armadans] and it quickly became a vehicle for the dissemination of creative and critical writing from within Spain and also from abroad. It was a point of contact with Spanish artists and intellectuals in exile, and a publication with a livelier and more independent approach than most of the cultural organs of 1950s Spain. Cela was the sole editor of this prestigious and handsomely produced magazine that he closed in 1979, four years after the death of General Franco, with the simple valedictory comment that it had served its purpose.

Yet the Galician author is still best known for three books that he published in the early part of his career: his first novel, *La familia de Pascual Duarte* [The Family of Pascual Duarte] (1942); his first travel book, *Viaje a la Alcarria* [Journey to the Alcarria] (1948); and his fourth novel, *La colmena* [The Hive] (1951). These works are now regarded as modern classics of Spanish literature. Cela continued writing travel narratives until the mid-1980s and fiction well into the 1990s, and in 1989 he was awarded the Nobel Prize for Literature. Although at the Stockholm ceremony the presentation address for the author included brief assessments of each of the principal novels he had published from the 1940s to the 1980s, there was just a passing reference to what were termed his "classic travel books of the 1940s and 1950s." This sidelining of what is undoubtedly the second most important part of Cela's creative output is typical of the general response to all but the first of his travel works.

Nonetheless, the award of the Nobel Prize stirred a new interest in Cela's writing, an interest that had begun to flag in the 1970s and 1980s as other, younger Spanish authors established themselves as the leading figures on the literary scene. The Nobel announcement of October 1989 brought about a scramble to produce new editions of Cela's works (mainly the novels), while outside the Spanish-speaking world old translations were reissued and new ones commissioned. There was also the customary flurry of scholarly activity, with homage volumes and conferences. But again, the focus was almost overwhelmingly on the author's fiction. When, occasionally, his travel writing was brought into play, it was nearly always with reference to the first and most famous work: *Viaje a la Alcarria* was frequently reconfirmed as "a classic" that was "beautifully written" and which exhibited the author's "magnificent powers of observation," and so on. Yet although many comments of this style were trotted out, there were no serious attempts at a reappraisal or sustained analysis of the work.

Cela's travel narratives, then, with the possible exception of the first to appear, have been inexcusably neglected. The purpose of the present study is to remedy this situation. After an opening chapter in which there is a discussion of a number of key issues connected with travel accounts of both foreign and domestic journeys, along with some preliminary observations on Cela's approach to travel writing, there follows a detailed look at the author's frequently expressed views on the purpose and benefits of traveling, and on the composition of the account of the journey. My aim here is to determine the extent to which the author develops a set of consistent thoughts or ideas (the term "theory" is possibly a little too grand) on the reasons for traveling and on the production of the travel narrative. Subsequently, I examine the evolution and constituents of Cela's travel writing by assessing each of his six travel books in turn and in order of publication.

While it is interesting to consider the degree to which these accounts reflect the author's stated views on traveling and writing up, my principal aim with each narrative is to show how Cela's travel books have been put together and what the outcome of this process appears to be. As a novelist, Cela usually comes across as a pessimistic observer and a skilled technician, with a keen ear for dialogue and a wonderful command of the language, rather than as a gifted creator of great dramas, characters, and settings. In his travel accounts, it is easy to discern the technician at work. But these narratives are not just composed of meticulously crafted, carefully positioned, and highly polished struts, nuts, and bolts. In social, cultural, or economic terms they reflect diverse aspects of distinct periods of postwar Spain. In addition, each account projects a strong sense of the geography of the areas visited, while collectively they present a picture of a changing Spain—from the tense and difficult times of the 1940s to the general prosperity, consumerism, ease, and even frivolity of the 1980s. These narratives will also be seen to reveal, in a variety of ways, the hand of Cela the novelist and literary artist.

Although my approach in this study is largely empirical, with a main focus on technical and thematic aspects of the six travel narratives, I have also drawn on a certain amount of theoretical material on travel writing that has come from critics of the genre as well as from practitioners. As will be seen, though, such material has normally been generated by meditations on *foreign* travel. The subject of *domestic* travel hardly figures in theoretical literature and this reveals a significant blind spot in the field of travel criticism. Finally, Cela has published many observations on journeying and the travel genre (his statements normally concern approach rather than significance), which furnish a good deal of useful material on the author's views on the activity of traveling and also on the process of recording the journey. His thoughts on the art of travel writing will be given some consideration in the last part of chapter 1 and will be assessed in detail in chapter 2.

Acknowledgments

DURING THE PERIOD THAT THIS BOOK WAS BEING RESEARCHED AND written, the staff of the main library of University College London gave me valuable help in locating particular editions of Cela's travel works, as well as related material, and for this I am extremely grateful. I should also like to express my gratitude to the staff of the British Library and to their colleagues at the British Library Newspaper Library, at Colindale.

Over the years I have received encouragement from a number of eminent colleagues in the United Kingdom and elsewhere for my work on Cela's fiction and travel literature, and I should especially like to express my gratitude for moments of moral (and sometimes practical) support from Professor Derek Gagen, of the University of Wales Swansea; Professor Ian Michael of the University of Oxford; Professor Donald Shaw of the University of Virginia; Professor Darío Villanueva of the Universidade de Santiago de Compostela; and the late Professor Roger Walker of Birkbeck College, University of London.

In the Department of Spanish and Latin American Studies at University College London, I have enjoyed many fruitful discussions on the travel genre with Professor Jason Wilson and he has, from time to time, provided me with useful leads on travel writing. In addition, I gained many insights into nineteenth-century Spanish travel writing from my former research student, Dr Gloria Muñoz-Martín. Also here at UCL, I have received much valuable and time-saving computing advice and assistance from Brigitte Picot. To these and other unnamed colleagues who have helped me in a variety of ways, I express my thanks. I must also acknowledge the debt I owe to my wife, Gill Briggs, for her incisive comments and observations, her patience with my grumpiness when work was not going well, and the way she has, during a number of holidays in Spain, cheerfully accompanied me to places, sometimes well off the beaten track, described in Cela's travel books.

In the following chapters I quote extensively from Cela's essays on travel writing and his six full-length travel narratives. I am extremely grateful to the Agencia Literaria Carmen Balcells, S.A., of Barcelona, for permission to reproduce the following: twenty-three lines from volume 10 of Cela's *Obra completa*, copyright 1978; 173 lines from *Viaje a la Alcarria*, copyright 1948; 119 lines from *Del Miño al Bidasoa*, copyright 1952; ninety-four lines from *Judíos, moros y cristianos*, copyright 1956; sixty-eight lines from *Primer viaje andaluz*, copyright 1959; sixty-six lines from *Viaje al Pirineo de Lérida*, copyright 1965, and seven lines from *Nuevo viaje a la Alcarria*, copyright 1986. I should also like to express my gratitude to the University of Wisconsin Press and Granta Books of London, publishers of the English version of *Viaje a la Alcarria*, the only one of Cela's travel books to have been translated into English—by Frances M. López-Morillas, and titled *Journey to the Alcarria* (1964 and 1990)—for permitting me to use my own translations of excerpts from the original of this travel narrative. All translations from Spanish are, unless otherwise indicated, my own.

Old Spain
and New Spain

1

Introduction: Contexts and Approaches in Travel Writing

PLACE AND APPROACH

As WAS NOTED ABOVE, DISCUSSIONS OF TRAVEL WRITING (AS WELL AS anthologies of the work of travel writers) deal almost exclusively with accounts of journeys to places beyond the borders of a writer's home country. This is no doubt a reflection of the fact that most travel works do, indeed, describe trips to and through foreign parts. It is also an indication that the records of such journeys satisfy the curiosity of a reading public eager for descriptions of other countries and societies or accounts of wonders revealed and perhaps challenges confronted in exotic or daunting environments.

Following on this, it comes as no surprise that the vast majority of critical assessments of travel writing focus on what might be termed the "abroadness" of the accounts discussed: the qualities of that "otherness" as shown in descriptions of places and features encountered—landscapes and towns, cultural delights or shocks, and sometimes the physical challenges involved in certain kinds of traveling or terrain. On this last point, Freya Stark, in a discussion of what leads some travelers to pit themselves against the harshest kinds of terrain, comments on the wilderness where "the magnitude of Nature is so apparent, the reality of her obstacles so visible."[1] Another highly successful practitioner of the art of travel writing, Colin Thubron, mentions "the traveler's tensions either of solitude and hardship or of specific goals" and also comments that curiosity is "a quality without which any travel book is dead."[2] Indeed, curiosity, although normally a far less dramatic aspect of travel writing than the "adventure theme," is frequently a fundamental feature of the traveler's motivation and behavior. It often explains why a particular journey was undertaken and why, once on that journey, the traveler pursues specific routes, goals, or interests. Furthermore, it will often account for the reader's decision to begin and persevere with the literary description of the journey.

But what the reader learns will not necessarily be pleasurable or exciting. In the context of overseas travel in the nineteenth century, Susan Sontag observes: "One of the recurrent themes of modern travel narratives is the depradations of the modern, the loss of the past: the report on a society's decline."[3] Paul Fussell, also dealing with foreign travel, pursues this same notion when he comments that part of the excitement of travel lies in the escape from "the constriction of the daily" and from "domestic identity," and goes on to add: "The traveler's escape, at least since the Industrial Age, has also been from the ugliness and racket of Western cities, and from factories, parking lots, boring turnpikes, and roadside squalor."[4] Fussell subsequently observes that the traveler-author may often be anxious to educate those who read his narrative: "The ideal travel writer is consumed not just with a will to know. He is also moved by a powerful will to teach. Inside every good travel writer there is a pedagogue—often a highly moral pedagogue—struggling to get out" (p. 15). In a similar vein, Percy Adams, comparing travel literature to didactic fiction, suggests that throughout the centuries "travelers with broad, inquisitive, or trained minds observed, read, listened, wrote, and then taught."[5]

But what was the thrust and substance of the instruction and information apparently contained in the work of so many travel writers? Susan Sontag begins her essay, "Model Destinations," with the statement: "Books about travel to exotic places have always opposed an 'us' to a 'them.'" Shortly after, she adds that "most classical and medieval travel literature is of the 'us good, them bad'—typically, 'us good, them horrid'—variety. To be foreign was to be anomalous, often represented as a physical anomaly." Sontag later notes: "The travel literature that can be understood as premodern takes for granted the contrast between the traveller's society and those societies defined as anomalous, barbaric, backward, odd." Then focusing on the nineteenth century, she comments that "modern travel literature starts when civilization becomes a critical as well as a self-evident notion—that is, when it is no longer so clear who is civilized and who is not" (p. 699).

Mark Cocker, however, addresses another kind of nineteenth-century travel narrative, the journey of exploration, observation, and the recording of discoveries and natural phenomena, when he suggests that "the classic Victorian travel book was a brisk, uncomplicated stream of empirical data."[6] Yet travel books are not simply observations on and records of different places and peoples, customs, flora, and fauna that are strange, even exotic, in the eyes of both traveler and reader. Nor are they just the logging of journeys and their attendant hardship and perils, and nor are they simply the mapping of routes through unfamiliar territory toward a specific location—or into the unknown. They are also narratives. Some of them may be rigidly methodical and heavily factual, but they are, nonetheless, narratives. Thus, when compared with certain flatter, scientific, or "factual" accounts, some narratives reveal much more of an artistic or literary structure and tone, perhaps with a far greater consciousness of style. Such "literary" accounts may also disclose a more pronounced sense of tension or include carefully developed and climaxed dramatic episodes, thereby showing the hand of a narrator who aims for the journey undertaken and the experiences involved to be translated into a work of literature that is both informative and enticing.

On this topic, Paul Fussell asserts that "the autobiographical narrative at the heart of a travel book will use many of the devices of fiction" and he goes on to note that travel narratives "can create suspense and generate irony by devices of concealment and foreshadowing" (p. 16). Similarly, Michael Kowalewski observes that "travel writing borrows freely from the memoir, journalism, letters, guidebooks, confessional narrative, and, most important, fiction."[7] Kowalewski also notes that travel writers continue to use "fictional devices" and emphasizes what he terms "the foregrounding of the narrator" (p. 13). Certainly, most travel narratives have an obvious protagonist who is normally carrying the narration in the first person. Furthermore, if the physical appearance of the author-narrator is known to the reader, then he or she will be easily visualized as the travel experiences are narrated. The author of a work of fiction, on the other hand, will probably not be so readily (if, in fact, at all) associated with the figure of a first-person narrator or with the disembodied voice involved in third-person narration.

Be that as it may, nearly all commentators on travel literature suggest that first-person delivery is the hallmark of travel works. Thus, Kowalewski talks of "firstperson nonfictional narratives that form the heart of the genre" (p. 7); Cocker makes the sweeping claim that travel books are "invariably narrated in the first person singular" (p. 4), while Fussell describes them as "a sub-species of memoir" and talks of their "autobiographical narrative."[8] Bill Buford sums up the genre in the following terms: "Travel writing is the beggar of literary forms: it borrows from the memoir, reportage and, most important, the novel. It is, however, pre-eminently a narrative told in the first person, authenticated by lived experience."[9]

Percy Adams does, nevertheless, point out that not all travel accounts have had first-person narrators, although he also mentions that third-person travel narratives, what he calls the "travel biography," are often the product of the rewriting or editing of earlier journals or are sometimes the record of a traveling companion (pp. 44, 163–64). But what Adams fails to acknowledge is that there also exists a good deal of "firsthand" travel writing in which the first-person narrative voice is kept to a minimum and in which the figure of the traveler is kept away from center stage. In such works, the narrator frequently, perhaps even constantly, adopts the role of observer or commentator and is continually referring, for example, to "they," "the people here," "the land here," and so on, thereby developing a kind of descriptive account or a social, geographical, anthropological, or historical commentary that may at times have a certain textbook tone to it. Nor does Adams make reference to the extremely unusual practice of a travel writer referring to himself or herself, as traveler-protagonist, in the third-person singular, the narrative method that Camilo José Cela adopts in all six of his travel books, calling himself "el viajero" [the traveler] in three of them and "el vagabundo" [the vagabond] in the others. This technique, which does not appear to be part of any Spanish tradition of travel narration, has recently been adopted by Cela's fellow Spaniard, Julio Llamazares. In the first two travel works published by the young novelist, *El río del olvido: Viaje* [The River of the Past: A Journey] (1990) and *Trás-os-Montes: (Un viaje portugués)* [Trás-os-Montes:(A Portuguese Journey)] (1998), he refers to himself throughout in the third person, as "the traveler."

However, this mode of travel narration, although very rare, is not confined to Spanish writing. In 1981, the Portuguese novelist José Saramago published an account of a lengthy journey (it took almost six months) that he made around his home country during the winter of 1979–80, *Viagem a Portugal* [Journey to Portugal]. In this work, Saramago narrates in the third person, constantly styling himself "o viajante" [the traveler].[10] More recently, Imogen Stubbs's "The Undiscovered Road" was included as one of eleven pieces in a collection of travel accounts by women writers. Although in the last couple of pages there is a switch to first-person narration, this ten-thousand-word narrative is almost entirely written in the third person, with the protagonist normally identified as "the mother" or "she."[11] The other ten travel pieces in the volume, all by different writers, are wholly narrated in the first person. One reviewer described most of the pieces as "excellent" and also commented: "Stubbs's Northumberland journey is ambitiously told in the third person, and is unexpectedly effective."[12] The implications for Cela's travel books of this "ambitious" narrative method will be discussed in chapter 2.

Finally, and to return to the issue of the influence of prose fiction on travel writing (an influence that has undoubtedly been reciprocated), it is clear that certain ploys of the writer of novels, such as selectivity, telescoping, pacing, varying material, building tension, and using dialogue and description for a variety of purposes (such as conveying information or creating dramatic impact) are constituents or even features of many travel narratives. Adams sums up by observing that, despite some differences: "Prose fiction and the travel account have evolved together, are heavily indebted to each other, and are often similar in both content and technique" (p. 279). Indeed, considering the extent to which, during the last 250 years, novelists from many countries have also left their mark as practitioners of travel writing, it comes as no great surprise to find that there is often a close relationship of structure and even substance between prose fiction and the travel genre.

DOMESTIC TRAVEL

In "The Undiscovered Road," Imogen Stubbs describes a journey, mainly by train, from London to Northumberland, the county of her birth. Julio Llamazares's first travel book, *El río del olvido*, narrates a journey made mainly on foot, and largely following the course of a river, to his home district in the highlands of León. So in each of these works there are two journeys being undertaken, one literal and one figurative: toward the place of the protagonist's geographical origins and also back to the past. Both protagonists have their memories jogged: they notice changes and perceive contrasts between the old and the new. And since both writers are describing scenes taking place within their own countries, and therefore within their own cultural frameworks, the things that catch their attention are much more mundane than the differences of physical environment, language, customs, food, and general notions of alterity—the "strangeness" that Claude Lévi-Strauss mentions in *Tristes Tropiques* (1955)[13] —that would presumably fascinate travelers to foreign or little-known regions. So what conclusions can be drawn about the purpose and subject matter of accounts of travel to or through areas of a writer's homeland?

Of course, such domestic works do not necessarily follow, as is the case with the homecoming journeys of Llamazares and Stubbs, the pattern of a trip back to one's roots and the past, with the reader steadily developing a picture of a protagonist's person and origins. Thus, J. B. Priestley's *English Journey* (1934) describes a tour of England in late 1933, at a time of severe economic depression—something that the author points out when his narrative is already well underway: "I am here, in a time of stress, to look at the face of England, however blank or bleak that face may chance to appear, and to report truthfully what I see there. I know there is deep distress in the country."[14] Hereafter, Priestley travels through much of England, visiting factories, fairs, markets, country villages, and modest homes in cities. He makes a good deal of comment on social and industrial matters, considers the effects on people of machinery and technology, and he fears for the future of some of the more appealing parts of the English countryside.

Also of the 1930s, George Orwell's *The Road to Wigan Pier* (1937) is the product of a two-month visit that the author made in February and March of 1936 to some of the most depressed areas of industrial Yorkshire and Lancashire. The work is a grittily social kind of travel writing, called by Philip Dodd "a variant on what has come to be known as the 'into Unknown England' travel book,"[15] but is probably more accurately and simply described as a grim documentary. In any case, only the first half of the book recounts Orwell's gloomy experiences in Wigan, Barnsley, and Sheffield, while the second part is largely a forthright discussion of Socialism, working-class conditions, and class divisions and attitudes.

In Spain, the kind of travel account that could most obviously be linked with the type of approach that Orwell takes in *The Road to Wigan Pier* has come from the novelist Juan Goytisolo, whose *Campos de Níjar* [Lands of Níjar] (1960) and *La Chanca* [The Chanca] (1962) examine and expose the poverty and social conditions that the author found in the late 1950s in the the province of Almería. Also in 1960, Antonio Ferres and Armando López Salinas, who were just beginning to establish themselves as writers of prose fiction, published *Caminando por las Hurdes* [Traveling around Las Hurdes]. In the brief prologue to this work, the authors describe their narrative as a contribution to the task of getting to know or understand Spain. They also praise the achievement of Cela's *Viaje a la Alcarria* and Goytisolo's *Campos de Níjar*, stating that their own work is an attempt to continue the process of describing how Spaniards live, think, and work, in order to understand the problems of contemporary Spain.[16] In *Caminando por las Hurdes*, which is narrated almost entirely in the third-person plural, with the two authors referred to as "the travelers," the reader is presented with a cheerless account of the backward and poverty-stricken district of Las Hurdes, some seventy-five kilometers to the southwest of Salamanca and which Luis Buñuel had shown in all its starkness in his 1932 documentary film, *Tierra sin pan* [Land without Bread].

In an essay written thirty years after Buñuel's film, Juan Goytisolo accused the writers of the so-called Generation of 1898 and, more recently, Cela, of portraying people simply as part of the landscape, in what he saw as an aesthetic approach to travel writing. Goytisolo also echoed the sentiments of Ferres and López Salinas by proclaiming the necessity, in this kind of literature, of showing human beings and the landscape in which they are born, work, suffer, and die. For Goytisolo, this was an important step toward confronting the reality of modern Spain and creating a committed, authentic art. Indeed, the novelist went on to note, with reference to rural Spain, that the standard of living in almost half of the Spanish provinces was barely above that in underdeveloped countries.[17] Later in the essay, Goytisolo reiterates the point when he observes that, unlike the 1898 writers and their present-day "epigones," foreign writers traveling in Spain do take an interest in the living conditions of the local people. Indeed, in this respect Goytisolo compares *Viaje a la Alcarria* with Gerald Brenan's *South from Granada* (1957) and suggests that whereas the English writer's book is imbued with social awareness, human interest, and a love for the land, this is not the case with Cela's first travel book (p.1054).[18]

Of course, Juan Goytisolo overlooks the fact that some writers of the 1898 generation did, on occasion, show an awareness of and even a concern for the straitened circumstances of the less fortunate citizens they came across during their travels around Spain. For example, Azorín (José Martínez Ruiz) described the poverty in the Lebrija area in a group of articles he published in *El Imparcial* in April 1905 and which were incorporated, under the unequivocal title "La Andalucía trágica" [Tragic Andalusia], in 1914 in the collection *Los pueblos* [The Communities]. In addition, Miguel de Unamuno, in his account of a journey through Las Hurdes in August 1914, and which was later published in *Andanzas y visiones españolas* [Spanish Adventures and Visions] (1922), noted the widespread hardship in the area. Indeed, this piece, in which the author soon mentions the impressive mountain scenery, his sense of being cut off from the outside world, and his feelings of excitement at entering what many supposed to contain primitive, isolated inhabitants, includes frequent references to the hardship and misery that marks the district and many of its inhabitants. However, Unamuno is not outraged by what he witnesses. While commenting on the unproductive terrain and wretched way of life of those who struggle to survive in such difficult circumstances, he can admire the hardiness and stoicism of such individuals, and note the large numbers of delightful, rosy-cheeked, bright-eyed children that he has seen in Las Hurdes. However, he also notes that, in the years to come, these youngsters will be ruined by "aquella terrible lucha por el miserable sustento" [that terrible struggle for a miserable livelihood].[19] Hereafter, Unamuno mentions the squalid villages and hovels where so many of the inhabitants live, the hard, stony ground, and the grim appearance of the local people. Yet these observations on social conditions are unusual in Unamuno's travel pieces. In general, Goytisolo is right when he suggests that in their journeys the 1898 writers were much more interested in the aesthetic and even mystical qualities of the landscape and its inhabitants, or in the evocation of historical characters, moments, or processes, than in the socioeconomic plight of the people living in the areas they traveled through.

CELA'S TRAVEL NARRATIVES

In an interview that he gave not long after being awarded the Nobel Prize for Literature, Cela was asked if, in his travel works, he was continuing Unamuno's enterprise of journeying through the rural areas in order to appreciate what Unamuno had termed the "intrahistory" of Spain. Cela's response was that he did not know, but that it was possible. However, he then added that the 1898 writers only knew Spain "page by page," whereas he knew it "step by step." He went on to suggest that their journeys had always been very short and were almost always unfinished. On the other hand, Cela noted, the 1898 authors were talented enough to produce superb literary accounts of these trips.[20] Here, though, it should be pointed out that in *Por tierras de Portugal y de España* [Through the Lands of Portugal and Spain] (1911) Unamuno observes: "No, it was not through books or writers that I learned to love my country: it was through traveling around it, through devotedly visiting its far-flung places."[21]

But whatever the accuracy of Cela's pronouncement on the wayfaring stamina of the 1898 travelers, the fact remains that the first indication of his "step by step" knowledge of Spain came with the magazine publication in June and July 1946 of the early chapters of the account of his recent visit to the Alcarria district. The Spanish Civil War had ended on 1 April 1939 and the 1940s was a decade of hardship for many of the people of the country. Having noted the special historical circumstances at the turn of the century that prompted writers such as Azorín, Pío Baroja, Antonio Machado, and Unamuno to focus their attention at a time of crisis on the landscapes and inhabitants of rural Spain, the critic J. M. Castellet sees Cela as renewing this process during another period of adversity.[22] Yet while *Viaje a la Alcarria* captures, to some extent at least, the atmosphere of postwar Spain and the deprivation experienced by a substantial number of its people, Cela's first travel book is certainly not the kind of hard-hitting exposé of poverty and despair that Goytisolo or Ferres and López Salinas were to produce a dozen or so years later. Indeed, in the early 1960s Goytisolo stressed that the travel writer must always familiarize himself with the socioeconomic and historical circumstances of the area he is going to describe: if he does not do this, he commented, "he will see nothing."[23] On the same occasion that he made these observations, the Catalan writer went on to make it absolutely clear that, unlike Cela and (presumably) the 1898 travelers, he does his research before setting out and subsequently aims to produce a *documentary* work: "For me, unlike Cela and his predecessors, travel literature requires preparatory research and should be documentary literature" (p. 232).

Cela, on the other hand, claims that in his travel books he refrains from editorializing or interpreting. The latter, he believes, is a task for the reader. Nor, apparently, does Cela embark on his travels armed with the kind of preliminary material proposed by Goytisolo. But of course, what Philip Dodd describes as "domestic travellers" will often carry with them "kinds of knowledge which are unavailable to the traveller abroad, however well-informed" (p. 130), and it is quite obvious, especially in some of Cela's later travel works, that he does take along the road with him a good deal of cultural, historical, or geographical knowledge. Indeed, some of this influences the routes he takes and some of it is deployed in transit in comments, thoughts, and questions. But what must also be recognized is that a significant amount of detailed material on cultural and other matters will certainly have been included subsequently, at the time of the composition of final drafts of the accounts. Nevertheless, in his early observations on travel writing, Cela was constantly anxious to state that his role as traveler-writer was simply to observe and to record. Yet over the years, and with successive travel books, it becomes increasingly clear that his method is much more than a transparent and unadorned technique of seeing things and reporting them as they are.

Much earlier in the century, José Ortega y Gasset had used an appealingly simple subtitle for two of his travel essays, "Tierras de Castilla: Notas de andar y ver" [Lands of Castile: Notes of Traveling and Seeing] (1911) and "De Madrid a Asturias, o los dos paisajes: Notas de andar y ver" [From Madrid to the Asturias, or the Two Landcapes: Notes of Traveling and Seeing] (1915). However, these two pieces consist of much more than Ortega just traveling and recording what he saw. His notion of "seeing" involves the acts of observing, meditating, speculating, and digressing, for these essays are sprinkled with pronouncements of many different kinds. So, in the 1911 essay he muses: "From time to time it is useful to take a long look at the dense groves of the past: there we learn true values—not in today's market."[24] In the 1915 piece he notes: "Spain is a mental construction of ours" (p. 555). In addition, these essays contain digressions on, for example, modern cities, the countryside, or the act of traveling. Likewise, Cela's travel books increasing come to include narratorial opinion and comment on matters both trivial and weighty. Indeed, in the prefatory material to his last published travel work, *Nuevo viaje a la Alcarria* [New Journey to the Alcarria] (1986), which appeared when Cela had shown for almost four decades that his travel accounts were much more than unadorned records of journeys made, the Galician author seems to be acknowledging Ortega's term (and possibly his approach) when he refers to travel narratives as "libros de andar y ver" [books of traveling and seeing].[25]

Between 1948 and 1986 Cela published six travel books. After *Viaje a la Alcarria* came *Del Miño al Bidasoa* [From the Miño to the Bidassoa] (1952), *Judíos, moros y cristianos* [Jews, Moors and Christians] (1956), *Primer viaje andaluz* [First Andalusian Journey] (1959), *Viaje al Pirineo de Lérida* [Journey to the Lérida Pyrenees] (1965), and then, finally, *Nuevo viaje a la Alcarria*. These narratives describe, or purport to describe, journeys made around or through specific areas of Spain. In the chapters that follow, I shall first of all consider Cela's views on the genre of travel writing and then examine each of his travel books in turn. Two chapters are devoted to *Viaje a la Alcarria* and one to each of the other five works. The reason that substantial extra attention is paid to Cela's first travel book is because it is the author's best known and most widely acclaimed travel work, as well as being, despite its apparent simplicity, probably his most intriguing travel narrative. Furthermore, I have sought to use *Viaje a la Alcarria* as a kind of generic template for the subsequent consideration of the five later works.

As was mentioned earlier, most essays and books on travel writing seem to assume that travel narratives are exclusively the record of travelers' experiences in foreign places. In fact, one critic has not only compared domestic travel writers unfavorably with what she terms "their more exotic colleagues," but has gone on to dismiss accounts of home travel as merely "a form of travel writing."[26] On the other hand, the novelist and travel writer, Paul Theroux, talks of "the most difficult of all travel subjects: the journey near home."[27] Indeed, what needs to be acknowledged is that for the domestic travel writer to develop an interesting narrative about people and places with which the reader is already partly or wholly familiar is probably much more of a challenge than it is for him or her to generate interest out of material dealing with, for example, perilous foreign journeys or encounters with fascinating societies and locations. This is a challenge that Cela accepts.

There is one final point that needs to be made at this stage. Throughout the following chapters I use the versions of Spanish place-names that Cela employs in his travel narratives and not the forms that are used in the Basque, Catalan, or Galician languages. So, for example, I write San Sebastián, Lérida, or La Coruña. This is solely in order to be consistent with usage in Cela's travel works and is certainly not intended as any kind of political or linguistic gesture on my part.

2

Cela's Views on Travel and Travel Writing

THE AUTHOR'S THOUGHTS ON TRAVEL NARRATIVES

ON 10 JULY 1946, LESS THAN A MONTH AFTER HIS RETURN FROM THE Alcarria and just at the time when the first three chapters of the account of the trip were being published in the magazine *El Español*, Cela published an article entitled "Los libros de viajes" [Travel Books] in the newspaper *Patria*. This piece, approximately eight hundred words in length and written shortly *before* the Alcarria visit, is the author's first statement on the travel genre. During the next twenty or so years, in articles and prefatory essays, Cela made many observations on travel literature (principally his own) and related matters, ranging from thoughtful considerations on approach and content to the briefest of passing comments. In order to determine whether or not Cela's thoughts on travel and travel writing can be regarded as constituting a coherent corpus, and also in an attempt to plot the evolution and consider the consistency of the author's views, this chapter will examine many of the numerous relevant observations that he has made over the years.

Cela's article in *Patria* opens with the assertion that, generally speaking, there are three kinds of prose narrative that the Spanish creative genius does not handle well: the epistolary style, memoirs, and travel books. After referring to this last form as "los libros del andar y el deambular" [books about traveling and wandering],[1] the author states that it is now a forgotten genre in Spain and also makes the questionable assertion that travel books are not intimately related to any other kind of literary work. Cela goes on to assert that "el libro de viajes es, sin más, contar a la gente a la pata la llana lo que se ve" [the travel book is simply about telling people what is seen], and suggests that it is for this reason that the travel book (or at least, this kind) is not understood by those who will not accept its contents at face value. Indeed, this idea that travel literature should simply be a presentation of what is, or was seen, is immediately reinforced as he draws on the much used (and thoroughly inadequate) standby, Stendhal's mirror. In fact, Cela ventures that the French writer's notion of fiction as a mirror journeying along the highway would be more apt for travel books (X, 228). But, in any case, the author acknowledges that this approach is not widely adopted and goes on to suggest that there is a certain similarity between many travel books and the reports of foreign correspondents (X, 228–29). Thus, he claims that there are few travelers and even fewer correspondents "que se limitan a dejar constancia de lo que ven" [who restrict themselves to recording what they see] (X, 229).

Then, in the central section of the article, Cela expounds on the kinds of intrusion that, in his opinion, subvert travel literature. In the first place, he asserts that history and scholarship "suelen ser los dos cuerpos extraños más frecuentes que se fijan, para desvirtuarlos, sobre los libros de viajes" [are the two most common foreign bodies that attach themselves to, and distort, travel books]. The author then refers to the discipline that, in the ensuing years, he will frequently associate with his travel narratives—geography: "El viajero no suele ver que sólo la geografía puede ser, en determinadas y concretas ocasiones, su auxiliar" [The travel writer tends not to realize that, on certain and specific occasions, only geography can be of assistance to him]. Next, he holds forth on what the travel writer must avoid when it comes to recording a trip. Again, the editorializing journalist is presented as the model to avoid:

> Igual que el corresponsal, que en vez de contar, dogmatiza, y en lugar de dar versión de primera mano de los hechos y las noticias de las cuales pueda ser testigo, se obstina en escribir editoriales y artículos de fondo, así el viajero suele caer en la tentación—y ¡ay!, en el peligro—de hacer sociología, o economía política, o ensayo, de lo que sólo debe ser literaria exposición de aquello que pasa ante sus ojos. (X, 229)

> [Just like the correspondent who, instead of recounting, dogmatizes, and instead of giving a firsthand version of the events and news that he witnesses, persists in writing editorials, so the travel writer usually succumbs to the temptation—and, oh, the danger—of creating sociology, or political economy, or an essay out of what should just be the literary presentation of what is happening before his eyes.]

Interpretation, Cela insists, is a task for the reader: "Ignoran muchos viajeros—y muchos corresponsales—que la interpretación histórica, o sociológica, o económica, o política, del dato escueto que ellos deben aportar, es cosa, no suya, sino de los demás" [A lot of travel writers—and many correspondents—are oblivious to the fact that the historical, sociological, economic, or political interpretation of the bare facts that they should convey is something for others, not them, to engage in] (X, 229).

In the last paragraph of "Los libros de viajes," Cela mentions that he is planning to produce a travel book. However, the literary enterprise he indicates here is rather grander in scope and vaguer in content than the material subsequently revealed in *Viaje a la Alcarria*. He suggests that what he has in mind is "un libro de viajes por ese mosaico de paisajes, razas y costumbres que llamamos España" [a book about travels through that mosaic of landscapes, races, and customs that we call Spain] (X, 230). Next, the author signals the rather sentimental goals at the heart of his approach and concludes the article with a poetic flourish that sits uneasily with earlier comments on the altogether more mundane "seeing and telling" method of travel narration:

> Fuera de las estadísticas y de los censos, al margen de las historias locales y los índices de las bibliotecas de los conventos y los ayuntamientos, este divagador de los viajes cree que lo que hay que reseñar es lo que falta, aquello de lo que nadie — ¿por tan poco lucido, quizás? — se ha querido ocupar: el olor del corazón de las gentes, el color de los ojos del cielo, el sabor de las fuentes de las montañas y de los manantiales de los valles. (X, 230)

> [Besides the statistics and the censuses, apart from the local stories and the catalogs of the libraries of monasteries and town halls, this relater of travels believes that what has to be reported is what is missing, the things – is it because they are so insignificant? – that nobody has botherd with: the smell of people's hearts, the color of the sky's eyes, the taste of spring water on the mountainside or in the valleys.]

Despite the rather cloying nature of these final lines of "Los libros de viajes," the article largely deals with the role of the travel writer and his duty to transmit, rather than interpret, the everyday reality that he comes across. During the following years, Cela reiterated this notion a number of times, consistently presenting it as central to his approach to the travel genre. Indeed, when in December 1947 he wrote the material for the dedication of *Viaje a la Alcarria* — to Gregorio Marañón — Cela made three main points concerning the method and the credo that had apparently governed his first travel book. In the first place, he notes that during his trip around the Alcarria *"fui siempre apuntando en un cuaderno todo lo que veía"* (italics in original) [*I was constantly jotting down in a notebook everything I saw*]. He also states that he planned to describe what he had seen, for his account is geography rather than fiction: *"Pensaba contar lo que hubiera visto (porque este libro no es una novela, sino más bien una geografía)"* [*I intended to relate what I had seen (for this book is not a novel, but rather a geography book)*]. And finally, Cela asserts that geography requires fact and veracity, since it is a like a "science."[2]

A few years later, in his note to the second edition (1952) of *Viaje a la Alcarria*, Cela reiterates that in his work he has recorded things as they were, or as he perceived them, and again insists that travel books should avoid judgments and interpretation:

> En el *Viaje a la Alcarria*, como en casi todo lo mío, salvo en algunas páginas muy de los primeros tiempos de andar yo en este oficio, las cosas están contadas un poco a la pata la llana y tal como son o como se me figuraron. En esto de los libros de viajes, la fantasía, la interpretación de los pueblos y de los hombres, el folklore, etc., no son más que zarandajas para no ir al grano. Lo mejor, según pienso, es ir un poco al toro por los cuernos y decir 'aquí hay una casa, o un árbol, o un perro moribundo', sin pararse a ver si la casa es de éste o del otro estilo, si el árbol conviene a la economía del país o no y si el perro hubiera podido vivir más años de haber sido vacunado a tiempo contra el moquillo.[3]

> [In *Viaje a la Alcarria*, as in almost all my travel writing, except for a few pages I wrote very early on, things are related without frills and just as they were or how they appeared to me. In this business of travel writing, fantasy, the interpretation of peoples and individuals, and folklore, etc., are simply distractions that stop you getting to the point. To my way of thinking, the best thing is to take the bull by the horns and say "here is a house, or a tree, or a dying dog," without stopping to consider whether the house is this or that style, whether or not the tree is useful for the economy of the country, or whether the dog would have lived longer if it had been inoculated against distemper.]

Then in the following paragraph, as if to emphasize the notion of the travel book as just a document of record, Cela states that he regarded *Viaje a la Alcarria* as simply a "cuaderno de bitácora" [log book] (IV, 512), a term that he was to repeat eight years later when he wrote a prologue to the Harrap edition that appeared in 1961.[4]

The fourth edition of *Viaje a la Alcarria* appeared in 1954. In the note to this edition Cela maintains his position with regard to the documentary nature of the work and repeats the point that imagination should play no part in travel narratives: "El escritor viajero cumple con reflejar lo que ve y con no inventar. Para inventar ya están otras esquinas de la literatura" [The writer-traveler should just show what is seen and not make things up. Invention belongs in other kinds of literature].[5] And here again he asserts that the travel writer should maintain a purely descriptive role. There should be no editorializing, the reader should be left to make the inferences, and above all there should be no falsification:

Pues bien: retratando al hombre y a su paisaje, sin meterse en camisa de once varas y en berenjenales que le lleven a sacar conclusiones filosóficas, morales o políticas (que ya sacará el lector, si quiere y acierta), el escritor viajero ya hace bastante. Y, sobre todo, ni se mixtifica él, ni mixtifica nada. (IV, 515)

[So then: portraying man and his landscape, without poking his nose where it does not belong or getting into pickles that lead him to reach philosophical, moral, or political conclusions (which the reader will come to, if he wants to and knows what he is doing), the writer-traveler is doing quite enough. But above all, he must not falsify, not falsify anything.]

However, with the prologue to *Judíos, moros y cristianos* (1956), Cela suggests that this latest travel work will be rather more subjective than the previous two, *Viaje a la Alcarria* and *Del Miño al Bidasoa*, and indicates that in this new travel account objective, mechanical description may have been overlaid by a rather more personal flavor. Thus the vagabond's journey "no será mucha más cosa que un viaje sentimental, corazonal, como se dice en los tangos" [will not amount to much more than, as they say in tangos, a sentimental, heart-tugging journey].[6] The author then goes on to stress that didacticism has no place in travel literature and is, in any case, pointless: "Los viajes didácticos o educativos suelen ser plúmbeos e insoportables. Además, y para colmo de males, con ellos no se aprende nada" [Didactic or educational journeys are usually leaden and unbearable. Besides, and to cap it all, you learn nothing from them]. In addition, and presumably stemming from the more subjective approach adopted, it is noted that this new travel work will contain only a limited amount of facts and figures: "En este libro no aparecerán demasiados datos, porque este libro no es una tesis doctoral" [There are not too many facts in this book, since it is not a doctoral dissertation] (V, 129). He adds that, in any case, such information can be readily located in countless other books.

So what is Cela's stated intention with *Judíos, moros y cristianos*? It seems to be something that harks back to the closing lines of his first essay on travel literature, the *Patria* piece of ten years earlier. This new travel book is apparently intended to provide those interested in Old Castile with: "En vez del dato, el color; en lugar de la cita, el sabor, y a cambio de la ficha, el olor del país; de su cielo, de su tierra, de sus hombres y sus mujeres, de su cocina, de su bodega, de sus costumbres, de su historia, incluso de sus manías" [In place of facts, the color; instead of a reference, the taste; and in exchange for an index card, the smell of the country: of its sky, of its land, of its men and women, of its cuisine, its wine cellars, its customs, its history, and even of its strange ways]

(V, 129–30). In other words, Cela is aiming to convey, but presumably through description, the feel and the flavor of an area.

In view of the fact that these sentiments revealed in the prologue to *Judíos, moros y cristianos* are unmistakably reminiscent of those expressed at the end of the *Patria* article, it would be reasonable to conclude not that Cela suddenly rediscovered the need to capture and convey certain intangible yet inherent qualities in the people and places he visited, but rather that this could well have been a constant quest, one which is found lurking beneath the descriptive realities of all his travel books. On the other hand, there exists the possibility that Cela's Castilian travel book is, indeed, somewhat more concerned with innate regional or national characteristics than those that preceded it. Nevertheless, in October 1963, in an introductory essay to *Viaje al Pirineo de Lérida*, published in *ABC* a few days before that newspaper began serialization of the work, Cela commented: "Al viajero ya se le van cansando las piernas de caminar el santo suelo de la dura y pagana España" [Now the traveler's legs are getting tired from walking the sacred soil of harsh, pagan Spain].[7] So here, it is now suggested that the author's travels may well have been concerned with more than just seeing and documenting people, places, and objects, and may even have involved a notion of pilgrimage.

CELA'S REASONS FOR TRAVELING

This last quotation, with its suggestion that Cela was beginning to feel a little too old for all this tramping around, also raises the question of why, in the previous seventeen or eighteen years, he should have engaged so often in this activity. Certainly during the period spanning the publication of his first travel book to the mid-1960s, Cela offered, in a variety of sources, explanations for why he decided to undertake his journeys around Spain. From time to time he mentions the pleasure of travel for its own sake and the pleasure of learning, and he also indicates that he travels to find peace and solitude. But the most frequent indication as to why Cela makes his journeys seems to be connected with his apparent rejection of city life.

As was mentioned in the introduction, Paul Fussell has observed that since the advent of the Industrial Age the traveler has sought to escape from "the ugliness and racket of Western cities,"[8] and Cela has frequently suggested that cities are best fled from and thereafter avoided. Furthermore, it is worth recalling that in January 1946, five months before he wrote the early chapters of *Viaje a la Alcarria*, Cela delivered a preliminary draft of his fourth novel, *La colmena*, to the office of the censor. In this work, with its largely bleak portrayal of life in 1943 Madrid, the narrator at one point refers to the capital as "ese sepulcro, esa cucaña, esa colmena" [that tomb, that greasy pole, that hive].[9] A few months later, in the opening chapter of *Viaje a la Alcarria*, as the impending trip is being planned, the traveler-to-be announces that he will skirt the cities of the Alcarria district, "como los buhoneros y los gitanos, igual que el jabalí y el gato garduño" [just like peddlers and gypsies, just like the boar and the wild cat) (IV, 33). Yet the rapidity with which he changes his mind in order not to miss the sight of a town's young ladies out for a mid-afternoon stroll suggests that his apparent aversion to cities might not be deep-seated. On the other hand, in the first half of chapter 2, as the traveler makes his way through the early morning darkness of Madrid and heads for the Atocha rail station, the impression is clearly given that the city is a gloomy place, with its squalor and suffering, and from which the traveler is escaping into the countryside.

The contrast between the city and the countryside is focused on in several of the many newspaper articles that Cela wrote in the years following the publication of his first travel book. Indeed, in "Visita de la ciudad" [Visitor from the city] (*Arriba*, 25 July 1950), the writer, in his summer quarters at Cebreros and away from the city where he normally lives, reveals an ambivalent attitude to the metropolis: "El escritor, que habitualmente vive en la ciudad, aún se pasma, gracias a Dios, ante la ciudad, ese invento que, a veces, nos enerva y quisiéramos destruirlo con un inmenso petardo" [The writer, who normally lives in the city, still marvels, thank God, at the city, that invention that at times enervates us and which we would like to destroy with a huge bomb].[10] He goes on to compare the technological advantages of city life with the fragrant and heavily symbolic fecundity of rural areas, mentioning "los amables bienes mecánicos de la ciudad—hermosos, sin duda, pero horros y huérfanos de los aromas de las tierras del pan y de las fuentes del vino" [the pleasing mechanical benefits of the city—which are no doubt wonderful, but which lack and are deprived of the aromas of the wheat-growing, wine-producing lands] (X, 29–30).

Elsewhere, in "Otra vez la ciudad" [Back in the city] (*La Vanguardia*, 27 September 1950), Cela twice refers to the metropolis as a monster but nevertheless concludes that for professional reasons he must resign himself to the urban environment and comply with what he terms "las circunstancias de la ciudad" [the circumstances of the city].[11] And in "El campo, la ciudad, el campo . . . , esa margarita" [The Countryside, the City, the Countryside . . . , that Daisy] (*La Vanguardia*, 16 November 1950), the writer refers to "la libertad del campo" [the freedom of the countryside] and compares and contrasts this with "la concreta cárcel de la ciudad" [the actual prison of the city].[12]

In 1952, in the note to the second edition of *Viaje a la Alcarria*, Cela refers to the city as a tedious environment, implies that it poses a certain threat, and describes his first travel book as simply "el cuaderno de bitácora de un hombre que se aburría en la ciudad, cogió el morral y salió al campo" [the log book of a man who was getting bored in the city, grabbed his knapsack and headed for the countryside] (IV, 512). Then, in the fourth edition (1954), the author makes the point that no vagabond worth his salt enters a city, adding: "Las ciudades se bordean. Quienes se meten en ellas no son escritores viajeros ni vagabundos: son ensayistas, que es peor" [Cities should be skirted. Those who enter them are not writer-travelers or vagabonds: they are essayists, which is worse] (IV, 515).

Nine years later, the introductory essay to the newspaper publication of *Viaje al Pirineo de Lérida* sees Cela waxing lyrical on the delights of travel and life in the countryside, and then making what is by now the expected contrast: "El viajero piensa que la vida a contrapelo, la vida de las ciudades y los escalafones, es un pecado triste y aburrido, una atadura puesta por el diablo para mejor gobernar las almas prisioneras" [The traveler thinks that life against the grain, life in cities and on registers, is a sad and boring sin, a tether tied by the devil in order to exert greater control over captive souls] (VI, 381). Later in 1963, in the preliminary essay to the fourth volume of his *Obra completa*, the author suggests that the principal characteristic of the city is hatred, in the guise of envy, and from which the countryside provides a refuge. Thus the vagabond "se lavó el odio, se desnudó del odio en la ciudad, y se echó al monte, igual que un bandolero, para ejercitarse en las solitarias mañas que estrangulan al odio como a un conejo" [washed away hatred, stripped off his hatred in the city and took to the hills, like a brigand, to enjoy the solitary skills that choke hatred as if it were a rabbit].[13] One further point concerning the city is made in this essay: the open road has brought a great deal of peace to the traveler, whereas, and by now this statement will come as no surprise, "las ciudades y los ciudadanos le negaron su paz" [cities and their inhabitants have denied him peace] (IV, 11).

In the twenty or so years after the publication of *Viaje a la Alcarria*, Cela made a number of other comments on his reasons for traveling and on the advantages to be derived from travel. He referred, for example, to the "mucha paz" [great peace] that he encountered on the highways (IV, 11) and also observed that traveling "calma los nervios y aplaca las inclinaciones" [calms the nerves and soothes one] (IV, 519). Consonant with such sentiments is the remark that the author makes in the prefatory note to the third edition (1961) of *Del Miño al Bidasoa*, stating that on the road "la soledad, lejos de ser un castigo, suele entenderse como una bendición de Dios" [solitude, far from being a punishment, is seen as a blessing from God].[14]

However, on an altogether different note, Cela also suggests, in an article published in the magazine *Destino* (28 December 1957), the pleasure of travel (specifically walking) for its own sake. The title of this article, "Andar por andar y, de paso, ver" [Walking for the Sake of Walking, while at the Same Time Seeing] is presumably a nod of acknowledgment to Ortega y Gasset. In any case, the title is particularly appropriate considering that, as Cela bemoans the gradual disappearance of the pastime of walking the roads and looking about, he should conclude the piece with a reference to the threat that hitchhiking (and also, no doubt, the motor car) poses to what he terms "las honestas inclinaciones del andar por andar y, si se tercia y a nadie ofende, mirar un poco lo que pasa" [the honorable occupation of walking for the sake of walking and, if the occasion arises and nobody is offended, having a little look at what is going on].[15] Furthermore, in the 1963 essay, "Con la mochila al hombro y una paz infinita en el corazón" [With your Knapsack over your Shoulder and an Infinite Peace in your Heart], Cela also comes up with the notion of the road that has to be traveled "because it is there" and because of the unalloyed pleasure that this pursuit affords: "Sí; el camino se hizo para ser caminado, no para ir a lado alguno sino por el mero y angélico placer de caminarlo" [Yes, indeed; the road was made to be traveled, not to get to some particular place but for the simple, angelical pleasure of traveling it] (IV, 11).

In the *Destino* article of December 1957, the author had also noted the following: "Teórica—y oficialmente—se viaja por dos razones primordiales: el conocimiento y la evasión" [Theoretically—and officially—one travels for two basic reasons: knowledge and escape] (X, 525). For Cela, the suggestion of travel as escape or flight is presumably to be seen as escape from the city, rather than from the family or a difficult home environment that Freud indicates in his essay on the Acropolis.[16] But concerning the idea of travel as some kind of quest for knowledge, Cela goes on to indicate that this is the case provided that the traveler is prepared to confront and absorb the eventualities that present themselves during the course of the journey.

On a number of occasions, Cela makes the association between traveling and learning, or the acquisition of wisdom, and in the closing paragraphs of *Viaje a la Alcarria* the narrator comments that the traveler has learned many things and, no doubt, still has much to learn. Some eighteen months after the publication of this work, the author produced a newspaper article entitled "Mensaje a los vagabundos" [Message to Vagabonds], a piece inspired by a congress of vagabonds being held in the United States. In this article, he touches on the issue of learning through travel and in so doing fondly recalls one of the most memorable characters he encountered during his trip around the Alcarria:

> Caminando por los caminos de España todos hemos aprendido más que en lado alguno. Y el escritor, que no puede guardar buen recuerdo de ninguno de sus maestros, piensa, con una gratitud sin límite, en el viejo mendigo del camino de Brihuega a Masegoso, el dueño del asnillo Gorrión, que tantas cosas buenas le enseñó.[17]

> [By walking the roads of Spain, we have all learned more than from any other source. And this writer, who has no good memories of any of his teachers, thinks, with boundless gratitude, of the old beggar on the road from Brihuega to Masegoso, who owned the little donkey, Gorrión, and who taught him so many good things.]

Finally, in September 1965, in another essay suggesting that his traveling days are probably a thing of the past, Cela indicates that his *learning* days are certainly over. However, he stresses that he is not being arrogant when he states this:

> El vagabundo supone que son pocas las enseñanzas que, a estas alturas, pudiera ya el camino brindarle. No es que entienda que se las sabe todas — presuntuoso supuesto que está muy lejos de dar por bueno — sino que sospecha, con mayor sencillez, que ya no le cabría, en la esponjita de su sesera, más ciencia de la que, poca o mucha, lleva aprendida.[18]

> [The vagabond reckons that, at this stage, there is little that the road can now teach him. It is not that he thinks he knows everything — that would be a presumptuous assumption and a very unwise one — but that he simply suspects that in the small sponge of his brain there is room for no more knowledge than the little, or plenty, that he has already acquired.]

Despite the fact that, for Cela, learning is apparently as much a by-product of travel as one of its motivations, the author is nevertheless tantalizingly secretive on what, specifically, he has learned during the course of his journeys around Spain. Has travel given him insights into his country and its culture, into his fellow Spaniards, and even into his own character? On this issue he remains remarkably coy and is presumably leaving it to the reader to deduce the substance and significance of what he may have learned from his travels.

MAKING THE JOURNEY AND WRITING UP

Over the years, Cela has also addressed himself to the issue of how to approach the activity of traveling and has constantly stressed the need for flexibility once the journey is underway. Indeed, this point is recognized in the first chapter of *Viaje a la Alcarria* when the would-be traveler muses on distances to be covered, how much walking to do at a stretch, and which part of the day is best for making ground. But even here, the neophyte acknowledges that plans do go astray: "Después, sobre el terreno, todos estos proyectos son papel mojado y las cosas salen, como pasa siempre, por donde pueden" [Later, on the road, all these plans are just scraps of paper and, as is always the way, things turn out however they will] (IV, 31). And when a few days later he sets out, the observation is made: "El viajero tiene su filosofía de andar, piensa que siempre, todo lo que surge, es lo mejor que puede acontecer" [The traveler has his philosophy of walking; he firmly believes that whatever comes about is the best thing that could happen] (IV, 36).

This notion of traveling and waiting to see what turns up is reiterated in a lengthy article that Cela published in 1949 and in which the author reveals his desire to make a journey around La Mancha. He indicates that he has believed in this take-things-as-they-come approach for a number of years and, furthermore, he suggests that he travels with an open mind and is unwilling to allow himself to become burdened with facts, statistics, and so on. Thus Cela the traveler seeks "lo que la suerte quiera enseñarle" [whatever chance will reveal to him].[19] He goes on to confess that he really enjoys what he terms "esta manera un tanto anárquica de caminar, esta forma de andar a lo que caiga, a lo que salte, o a lo que Dios quiera" [this somewhat anarchic approach to traveling, this way of seeing how things turn out, what turns up, or what God wills] (X, 583).

A few years later, in the prologue to *Judíos, moros y cristianos*, the same point is again made, although this time with the added qualification that the freedom to wander hither and thither might not be total:

Naturalmente, el vagabundo, a pesar de todas sus teorías, después, ya sobre el camino, andará, como siempre hace, un poco a la buena de Dios, otro poco por donde le apetezca, y siempre no más que por donde le dejen. (V, 128)

[Naturally, and despite all his theories, once on the road the vagabond always travels to some extent at random, sometimes where he fancies, and only where he is allowed to go.]

And towards the close of the prologue, he suggests that perhaps the most salutary concern that the traveler can have is "la de echarse al camino completamente despreocupado y a lo que salga" [that of taking to the road completely unconcerned and ready for whatever turns up]

(V, 131). In 1957, a year after these words were written, Cela also made the point in the article "Andar por andar y, de paso, ver," that it was best to travel alone. Here he rejects gregariousness and adds that "la manada va contra la esencia misma del viaje" [a crowd goes against the very essence of traveling] (X, 525). Such views do, of course, tie in with the author's stated quest for peace and solitude in the travel experience and also suggest that he is drawing a distinction between the traveler and the tourist.

With the publication in 1959 of *Primer viaje andaluz* Cela returned to the subject of what it was that determined where he traveled and the experiences garnered in the process. In the introduction to his fourth travel book, the author makes the frivolous assertion that his feet do the thinking and then adds: "En el camino, a los pies les nace una brújula entre los dedos, un minúsculo ingenio que sirve para aconsejar" [On the road your feet acquire a compass needle between the toes, a tiny device that serves to advise you].[20] The kind of uncertainty and spontaneity apparently provided by the march of such wondrous feet is also mentioned in a further preliminary essay written for the first edition of *Primer viaje andaluz*. However, here the author also proposes the altogether more commonplace, and generally more acceptable, notions of Providence and chance as the determining factors in the traveler's roaming: "El vagabundo hace sus singladuras a la buena de Dios y a la que caiga" [The vagabond does his day's traveling according to how things turn out or what turns up].[21]

And when should the accounts of these journeys be put together? From time to time in Cela's travel books the reader is informed that the traveler is taking notes or jotting down thoughts, although there is never any suggestion that this is an organized or lengthy process. In fact, the early chapters of Cela's first travel work were composed within days of his return from the Alcarria, whereas chapters 6 to 11 were not written until eighteen months later, and once again at considerable speed. Some twenty years earlier, the novelist and travel writer, Azorín, advised against rushing travels into print. In his article "Los viajes" [Travels], published in 1927, he suggested that there should be a substantial delay between the journey and its transformation into literature in order to allow the important features to emerge: "So let time pass by, in the depths of one's mind, doing its work, classifying and refining reality. Afterwards, when the essential features have surfaced, let us set about writing, simply, our impressions of what was observed."[22] However, this was certainly not the method that Azorín had adopted in his early years when, for example, the articles that later constituted *La ruta de Don Quijote* [Don Quixote's Route] were written in La Mancha in March 1905, sent to Madrid, and published within days in *El Imparcial*.

On this occasion, though, he had newspaper deadlines to meet and was therefore in no position to indulge in a lengthy process of maturation or distillation.

Cela, too, was presumably under some journalistic pressure when he returned from the Alcarria trip in June 1946. However, the fact that he crossed swords with the powers-that-be at *El Español* after submitting five chapters (three of which were quickly published) brought to a halt the rapid composition of his account of the journey. In fact, not one of Cela's four travel narratives that appeared in the 1950s and 1960s was written soon after the completion of the journey described. Indeed, this would not have been possible in the case of *Del Miño al Bidasoa, Judíos, moros y cristianos,* and *Primer viaje andaluz* since, as the author has admitted, these works are composite offerings incorporating trips taken at various periods. And even in the case of the one travel book published in the 1960s, *Viaje al Pirineo de Lérida,* this did not appear in print until seven years after Cela had made the journey on which it is based. Indeed, he acknowledges this fact in the essay published in October 1963 in *ABC* to mark the beginning of the newspaper's serialization of the work. In this same piece, Cela addresses the question of delayed composition and comes to the following bland conclusion:

> Este libro no hubiera sido el mismo de haberse escrito sobre la marcha o inmediatamente después de la marcha. El viajero no piensa que haya acertado dejando pasar el tiempo; tampoco se atrevería a confesarse errado. (VI, 379)

> [This book would not have been the same if it had been written during the journey or immediately after the trip. The traveler does not think that he was right to allow such a delay; nor would he dare confess that he was wrong.]

And while in December 1963 the author referred to *Viaje a la Alcarria* as *perhaps* his most "simple, immediate, and direct work,"[23] it should be noted that the account of Cela's return trip around the Alcarria in June 1985, *Nuevo viaje a la Alcarria,* was published within nine months of the visit, thus making it the most "immediate" record of any of his journeys.

There remains one distinctive, technical aspect of Cela's travel books that merits careful consideration: this is the constant use of third-person narrative and the concomitant projection of Cela the author as "the traveler" or "the vagabond." This method obviously runs counter to the standard, first-person presentation that is associated with travel works. Yet on only one occasion has Cela commented on this distinctive feature of his travel literature. In the introductory essay to the first of his travel books to appear in the *Obra completa*, Cela briefly suggests that third-person narration gives objectivity, distance, and even veracity to the traveling protagonist. Thus he makes reference to: "El vagabundo—que ahora habla de él como de otro hombre, objetivándose en la distanciadora y persuasiva tercera persona" [The vagabond—who is now talking about himself as if he were someone else, objectifying himself in the distancing and persuasive third person] (IV, 10).

The employment of such a narrative strategy in a genre which, on the face of it, is a personal, factual recounting of a journey, may or may not sit comfortably with the reader. Yet at the same time, this technique certainly invites consideration of its artistic advantages and drawbacks, and these will be discussed subsequently. However, for the moment it should be mentioned that Cela's proclivity for referring to himself in the third person is not confined to his travel books. In 1957 he published *Cajón de sastre* [Odds and Ends], a collection of over 140 articles and assorted pieces, nearly all of which were first published in newspapers and magazines between 1945 and 1954. Setting aside the specialized section entitled "Balada del vagabundo sin suerte" [Ballad of the Luckless Vagabond], half of the twenty pieces of which use third-person projections of Cela as "the vagabond," "the traveler," and even "the wayfarer," well over a third of the remaining articles present Cela referring to himself as either "the writer" or "the chronicler." However, there are no instances of such usage predating the publication of the early chapters of *Viaje a la Alcarria* in June and July 1946. Yet within a few months of the Alcarria journey Cela would, from time to time, refer to himself in the third person in journalistic pieces, and by 1950 this technique was commonplace in his newspaper and magazine articles. Cela continued the practice throughout the 1950s and, during his stewardship of the literary magazine *Papeles de Son Armadans* (1956–79), he frequently referred to himself in the pages of that publication as "el director" [the editor].

For most of his literary career, Cela was a prolific essayist who was seldom bashful about expressing his opinions, especially on literature and cultural matters in general. Consequently, it comes as no surprise to see that during the twenty or so years that followed his June 1946 trip to the Alcarria, Cela had a good deal to say about travel and travel writing, particularly his own. These articles and opinions on traveling and the composition of travel accounts petered out in the mid-1960s, presumably because the author, then around the age of fifty, had decided that he would probably undertake no more wayfaring, and possibly because he had also lost interest in the travel genre. Although Cela's many observations on traveling and travel narratives might not constitute a comprehensive set of positions on travel and the associated genre, they nevertess provide an interesting collection of ideas that can be usefully borne in mind when the author's travel accounts are examined.

3

The Approach to the Alcarria

IN HOLY WEEK OF 1891, THE NOVELIST EMILIA PARDO BAZÁN TOOK THE train from Madrid in order to make brief visits to the nearby cities of Alcalá de Henares, Guadalajara, and Sigüenza. No sooner had she reached Guadalajara on the Thursday morning than it occurred to her to hire a carriage so that she could indulge in a "tempting excursion" to the Alcarria district. Pardo Bazán had in mind the historic towns of Pastrana, Hita, and Cogolludo. However, she was soon to lament her ignorance of local topography when she discovered that the nearest of these towns was some six leagues from Guadalajara. Realizing that any such visit would involve an overnight stay, she promptly abandoned her project.

Consequently, the author spent the whole of Maundy Thursday in Guadalajara. The first thing that Pardo Bazán records doing during the rest of that day was to attend mass in the church of Santa María de la Fuente. Then, having chanced to meet the Civil Governor of Guadalajara, an old friend of her father, she was taken on a tour of the city's principal historic buildings. Most of the author's account of the day is given over to a detailed and enthusiastic description of the splendors of the Palacio del Infantado, the ancestral home of the Mendoza family but which was at that time used as an orphanage. However, in marked contrast to Pardo Bazán's report on the architectural and artistic delights of the palace is her distressed and angry account of the fate of the Capilla de los Urbinas. Once part of the sixteenth-century church of San Miguel, by 1891 the chapel was being used to keep carts and, the author indignantly conjectures, perhaps even served as a stable. Through the straw, mud, and filth on the floor she could make out the coat of arms of one of the family tombstones. Having also visited the Pantheon of the Osunas and the castle, the Galician writer concludes her account of the historical attractions of Guadalajara with the following observation: "Journeys around Spain are, generally speaking, visits to the dead. The dead inspire most of our impressions, for our history is written on tombstones."[1]

Pardo Bazán then moved on to Sigüenza, to spend part of Good Friday in that city, before returning to Madrid in the late afternoon. It is not clear whether she ever managed to visit the Alcarria. However, at the end of the account of her Holy Week excursion the novelist still had the subject very much in her mind, musing on the mellifluous fragrances of the district famed for its honey and on the possibility of one day evoking in Pastrana the shade of the town's most tragic resident, the Princess of Eboli.

One June morning fifty-five years later, Pardo Bazán's fellow Galician, Camilo José Cela, spent about three hours in Guadalajara before heading on foot for the Alcarria. As the traveler made his way from the rail station into the center of the city, he is described, in the sparest of terms, crossing the Henares River, walking past a barracks and being looked at by a group of soldiers sitting in the doorway, and then disappearing into a bar. The bar bears a delightful name: "El viajero entra a refrescar en una taberna que tiene un hermoso nombre. La taberna se llama: Lo mejor de la uva" [The traveler stops to have a drink at a bar with a lovely name. The bar is called: The Best of the Grape] (IV, 49). The observation that the bar has "a lovely name" immediately raises the question of when, precisely, in the evolution of the travel book this judgment was made. Is it the opinion of the traveler on the day (6 June 1946) or that of the author at the time of the composition of this chapter (17 June 1946)?[2]

After his drink in the bar, the visitor leaves his traveling gear in a café, goes to send a telegram to his wife, notes the time (9:10 A.M.), and returns to the café, where he buys newspapers, has a short, inconsequential chat with the five-year-old newspaper boy, and then reads while he has his second breakfast of the day. Subsequently, the traveler goes for a stroll around the city center: not, apparently, so that he can take in the sights but simply because he needs to get to a bank. Such a desire seems to be completely in keeping with the low-key, prosaic activities and descriptions that mark, thus far, his stay in Guadalajara. But then the reader is suddenly made witness to a graphic and dramatic juxtaposition:

El palacio del duque del Infantado está en el suelo. Es una pena. Debía ser un edificio hermoso. Es grande como un convento o como un cuartel. Por el centro de la calle pasa un tonto con una gorra de visera amarilla y la cara plagada de granos. Va apresurado, jovial, optimista. Va muerto de risa, frotándose las manos con regocijo; es un tonto feliz, un tonto lleno de alegría. (IV, 50)

[The palace of the Duque del Infantado has fallen down. It is a shame. It must have been a beautiful building. It is as big as a monastery or a barracks. A simpleton goes down the middle of the street, wearing a yellow peaked cap and with his face covered in spots. He is hurrying, cheerful, and optimistic. He is laughing his head off, happily rubbing his hands; he is a happy simpleton, a simpleton full of cheer.]

Thus the palace that had so captivated Pardo Bazán in 1891 and the description of which had formed the core of her account of Guadalajara is now presented as a pile of rubble that is described in four short, simple, almost childlike utterances. The destruction of this building in the early weeks of the Spanish Civil War is regarded by Hugh Thomas as one of the four greatest artistic losses suffered by Spain during that conflict.[3] Sacheverell Sitwell, who states that the façade was still standing in April 1948, whereas the interior was a "melancholy ruin," goes even further than Thomas, terming the destruction of the palace "the most dreadful artistic casualty" of the war.[4] Yet the traveler in *Viaje a la Alcarria* makes no allusion to either the circumstances or the cultural significance of this loss. Indeed, the reader's attention is immediately drawn to the presence of the simpleton and more consideration is given to his appearance and manner than was afforded to a palace that was once of national importance.

It is certainly legitimate to be at least a little intrigued by the brief, almost matter-of-fact response to the ruined building. Moreover, it is tempting to make the association war-destruction-insane behavior, and so on. But what emerges during the course of *Viaje a la Alcarria* is that Cela's traveler is rarely willing to dwell on the past, either distant or immediate. He is not, to paraphrase Pardo Bazán, looking for the dead or seeking history in the inscriptions on tombstones. Nor is he, it would seem, undertaking what Michel Butor terms a "pilgrimage" to "those places that speak, that tell us of our history and ourselves."[5] In Guadalajara, Cela shows his traveler indulging in mundane activities (walking into town, going for a drink, sending a telegram, buying newspapers, talking with a small boy, reading the papers over breakfast) but also reveals him witnessing two sights (the ruined palace, the happy, hurrying simpleton) which, although they might provoke the reader to ponder implications, elicit no more than a fleeting and minimal response from the traveler. Indeed, he is only really seen to assert himself as a protagonist when he indulges in a few playful lies at a local saddlery, in the scene that closes the second chapter. Yet this lighthearted vignette should give the reader cause for thought. If, as is admitted, the traveler is capable of embellishment and fibbing, would the reader not be wise to treat the whole of his account with caution? Can the narrator always be relied upon to inform the reader, as he does on this occasion, of instances when words deliberately distort reality? Perhaps a little harmless fun concerning the purchase of a leather crownpiece for a mule supposedly intended as a gift for his wife's uncle, a priest, should not be given undue weight. Yet the inscription on the incongruous item — which so neatly closes chapter 2 with details of place and date: "Casa Montes. Guadalajara, 6 de junio de 1946" [Casa Montes. Guadalajara, 6 June 1946] (IV, 52) — was apparently requested to prove when and where the traveler acquired the crownpiece.

While the brief Guadalajara episode (though untypical of the work as a whole, in that it takes place in a city) does give some indication of descriptive scope and narrative approach, it also marks an important stage in the account. It signals the end of the preliminary phase of *Viaje a la Alcarria* (the decision to travel, to which area, how to move around, and the excursion through and out of Madrid), which will now be succeeded by the description of the traveler enjoying the freedom of the open road as he makes his way into and thence around the Alcarria district. However, before the narrative is followed into the Alcarria, some consideration needs to be given to the important material contained in the work's *Dedicatoria* (Dedication) and also to the opening, preparatory chapter.

A DEDICATION

Cela set out for the Guadalajara section of the Alcarria in the early hours of 6 June 1946 and completed his tour on 14 June, returning to Madrid the following day. On 16 June he began writing up the notes he took during the trip. In the next ten days the author drafted the first five chapters and delivered them to the weekly magazine, *El Español*. The short chapter 1 was published on 22 June and chapters 2 and 3 appeared between 29 June and 13 July. However, Cela then fell out with those running *El Español* and, he informs us, only managed with some difficulty to obtain the return of chapters 4 and 5. The remaining six chapters were composed, again at considerable speed, in the last week of 1947 in order to meet the deadline set by the publisher, Revista de Occidente. The dedication was also written at this later stage and Cela's first travel book was published in March 1948 with the prefatory heading, *Las botas de siete leguas* [*The Seven-League Boots*].[6]

Cela's account of his trip to the Alcarria is dedicated to Dr Gregorio Marañón (1887–1960), a distinguished medical man who was also a renowned cultural historian, biographer, and sociologist. In fact, with this dedication, Cela is repaying a debt. Marañón had written a lengthy prologue to the fourth edition of *La familia de Pascual Duarte*, which was published in May 1946, shortly before Cela set out for the Alcarria. In addition, Marañón's biography of Philip II's secretary, Antonio Pérez, which was published in 1947, provided its own connection with the Alcarria district in the person of Ana Mendoza de la Cerda, Pérez's lover and fellow conspirator. She was born in Cifuentes and became the notorious and fascinating Princess of Eboli, who was to die imprisoned in Pastrana in 1592. Yet it is not Marañón's prologue to *La familia de Pascual Duarte* or this historical link (both are unmentioned in the *Dedicatoria*) that make this preliminary document such a significant prelude to the narrative of *Viaje a la Alcarria*.

In the first place, the dedication is considerably more extensive than what Gérard Genette describes as "the modern form of a simple mention of the dedicatee."[7] In fact, it is a six-hundred-word address that is much more in keeping with the kind of substantial, epistolary dedication that saw its heyday in the eighteenth century, when an author often sought favor and protection from some eminent figure. For example, in 1760 Laurence Sterne dedicated *Tristram Shandy* to William Pitt, the Elder, at the time perhaps the most powerful politician in Britain. However, the two hundred words of Sterne's dedication reveal nothing of the content of the novel. Cela's address to Gregorio Marañón, also couched in the epistolary format, is initially a statement of the young writer's debt to a distinguished literary figure. Yet it is soon transformed into a brief assessment of the Alcarria and its inhabitants, a summary of the content of the work, and an indication of the author's approach to travel writing. In effect, the dedication becomes a preface and in some ways a conclusion, but principally it tells the reader what to expect and also what not to expect from the account.

After the somewhat florid opening paragraph of acknowledgment and gratitude, Cela comments simply and directly on the Alcarria district, the people he encountered there, and his own response to the inhabitants and the place:

La Alcarria es un hermoso país al que a la gente no le da la gana ir. Yo anduve por él unos días y me gustó. Es muy variado, y menos miel, que la compran los acaparadores, tiene de todo: trigo, patatas, cabras, olivos, tomates y caza. La gente me pareció buena; hablan un castellano magnífico y con buen acento y, aunque no sabían mucho a lo que iba, me trataron bien y me dieron de comer, a veces con escasez, pero siempre con cariño. (IV, 27. Italics in original.)

[The Alcarria is a lovely area that people do not want to visit. I walked around there for a few days and I liked it. It is very diverse and, except for honey, which is bought up by profiteers, it provides everything needed: wheat, potatoes, goats, olive trees, tomatoes, and game. The inhabitants are fine people; they speak magnificent Castilian, with a good accent, and although they did not know too much about what I was doing there, they treated me well and gave me food to eat, sometimes just a little, but always with kindness.]

A little later, having given the dramatic news that in one of the villages he was locked up for a day and a night, Cela mentions his technique as traveler-observer, the ordinariness of what he saw, and his disciplined and honest approach to travel writing:

Por la Alcarria fui siempre apuntando en un cuaderno todo lo que veía, y esas notas fueron las que me sirvieron de cañamazo para el libro. No vi en todo el viaje nada extraño, ni ninguna barbaridad gorda—un crimen, o un parto triple, o un endemoniado, o algo por el estilo—, y ahora me alegro, porque, como pensaba contar lo que hubiera visto (porque este libro no es una novela, sino más bien una geografía), si ahora, al escribirlo, me caigo pintando atrocidades, iban a decir que exageraba y nadie me había de creer. En la novela vale todo, con tal de que vaya contado con sentido común; pero en la geografía, como es natural, ya no vale todo, y hay que decir siempre la verdad, porque es como una ciencia. (IV, 28)

[In the Alcarria I was constantly jotting down in a notebook everything I saw, and these notes served as the canvas for the book. In the whole trip I did not see anything strange nor anything really shocking—a murder, the birth of triplets, somebody possessed, nothing like that—and I am happy about this because, since I intended to relate what I had seen (for this book is not a novel, but rather a geography book), if when I wrote it I started describing awful things, people would say I was exaggerating and nobody would believe me. In the novel anything goes, provided it is told in a sensible way; but with geography, as you would expect, you cannot put what you like and you always have to recount the truth, since it is a kind of science.]

The dedication accompanying the text of *Viaje a la Alcarria* therefore becomes a statement of response to a place, of approach to a literary genre, and also a bare summary of the content of a particular work. Travel works, like novels, sometimes contain prefatory observations written by the author and which give a sense of the work, of its content, and possibly its conclusions. Such introductory material may be short or lengthy, vague or specific. Thus, V. S. Pritchett's *Marching Spain* (1928) contains a thirteen-line preface that is rather poetic in tone and contains only the briefest of factual references. The first half of the preface reads as follows:

A strange country draws from the heart strange cries, strange assertions, the fitness and worth of which time alone can test. In my march across Spain from Badajoz to Leon, which this book describes, I have recorded only what then I heard from the people, from the land's voice, and from my own heart.[8]

Here Pritchett seems to be asking a potential reader to become involved with the strangeness of both a place and the writer's response. The second half of the preface asks for the reader's sympathetic understanding and interpretation. Although the fact that this was the author's first book might account for the diffident, even imploring tone of the preface, it cannot excuse its vagueness. There is little to persuade the browser of 1928 to take the plunge, whereas later generations of readers would presumably engage with the work on the basis of Pritchett's subsequently established reputation.

Gerald Brenan's *The Face of Spain* (1950) reveals an altogether different approach to preliminary material. In a preface that is over seven pages long, the author quickly establishes his credentials as an observer and interpreter of Spain:

In my youth I had spent some six or seven years in Andalusia. When I married we bought a house near Málaga and from it we watched the confusion and horror of the opening phases of the civil war. Then, on our return to England, my wife wrote an account of our experiences, while I produced two large books—one on Spanish history and politics and the other (now in the press) on Spanish literature.[9]

Brenan goes on to state that his return to Spain in 1949, after an absence of thirteen years, was intended to answer certain questions concerning the nature of Spain and its culture and civilization. However, he found himself reluctantly dragged into political and social considerations, the reflections of which become an important feature of his account, and he spends the remaining three-quarters of his preface on an assessment of the plight of contemporary Spain and a discussion of the possible solution to this unhappy state of affairs. Here Brenan's diagnosis and prognosis, which are balanced and thoughtful, are a reassertion of his expertise and also an attempt to steer his readers toward an equally thoughtful interpretation of the material presented.

The early pages of the preface to *The Face of Spain*, a book obviously intended for an English-speaking, primarily British readership, is peppered with statements and expressions that prepare the reader for a bleak social view of the Spain of 1949. Thus Brenan indicates his conclusion by observing that "the picture that emerges is a depressing one;" he then mentions "widespread corruption;" adds that "severe inflation has reduced the middle and lower middle classes to great straits and the agricultural labourers to starvation," and a little later notes "the terrible

poverty and misery one sees in Spain today" (pp. 10–11). Such observations are consistent with other views of the plight of Spain as the
1940s, the so-called "years of hunger," drew to a close. However, not
everyone was afflicted. Raymond Carr and Juan Pablo Fusi Aizpurua
point out that "in the Spain of the forties where prices were rising faster
than wages, where meat and leather shoes were luxuries to the lower
paid and underemployed, poverty was made more painful by the conspicuous waste of the fortunate few."[10] Paul Preston, on the other hand,
sees this hardship in even more graphic human terms. Having mentioned, in the context of the industrial unrest of May 1947, the "appalling living conditions of the working class" and also the mass migration
of rural laborers into the industrial cities, Preston subsequently alights
on the complacent tone of Franco's address to the nation of 31 December 1948, which gave prominence to the notion that the worst of Spain's
economic problems were now behind her:

> Franco's self-congratulation suggested that he was oblivious to the fact that,
> in working class districts of major towns, people in rags could be seen hunt-
> ing for scraps. Outside Barcelona and Málaga, many lived in caves. Most
> major cities had shanty towns on their outskirts made of cardboard and cor-
> rugated iron huts where people lived in appallingly primitive conditions.
> The streets were thronged with beggars. State medical and welfare services
> were virtually non-existent other than the soup kitchens provided by the
> Falange. Hardship, malnutrition, epidemics, the growth of prostitution, the
> black market, corruption were consequences of his regime's policies which
> inevitably did not figure in the Caudillo's optimistic survey.[11]

Despite all this, the dedication that precedes the text of *Viaje a la Alcarria* does no more than hint, in its transition into preface, at the possible hardship encountered in the Alcarria district in June of 1946. Of
course, it could have been that this area was spared the widespread social and economic deprivation that blighted Spain in the 1940s. And
while there are indications in the early, Madrid section of the work of
the kind of poverty that both Brenan and Preston mention, this facet of
the book is certainly not heralded in the dedication. This is perhaps because Cela was mindful of the censor or of the sensibilities of Dr Marañón, or simply because he chose to allow his readers to see and judge
for themselves. Certainly, the dedication is no enthusiastic or enticing
invitation for the reader to hurry into the text: the one dramatic, intriguing incident referred to is an unpleasant occurrence with slightly
comic overtones (the traveler's brief imprisonment in a disagreeable
place) that will not, it is made clear, figure in the account. In addition,
the author's assertion that he saw nothing out of the ordinary during
the whole of his trip is also something of a damper. Or is the author

of *La familia de Pascual Duarte* simply aiming to allure through ironic understatement?

INTRODUCING A TECHNIQUE AND A TRAVELER

In the opening pages of *The Old Patagonian Express* (1979), Paul Theroux denounces those travel books that start "in the middle of things," by projecting the reader into "a bizarre place without having first guided him there."[12] The American author then gives three examples of this technique and goes on to state that his usual question, unanswered by most travel books, is "How did you get there?" He then expands: "Even without the suggestion of a motive, a prologue is welcome, since the going is often as fascinating as the arrival" (pp. 11–12). Theroux has in mind accounts of foreign travel, as he quickly confirms: "From the second you wake up you are headed for the foreign place." He immediately mentions Kenya, suggesting the "rivetting book" that could have been written "about the sea journey from Southampton to Mombasa" (p. 12). So the the preliminary journey, what might be termed the geographical prologue, is regarded by Theroux as an important feature of a travel narrative: unless, he suggests, the traveler chooses to be whisked to the designated country by a jet aircraft—what he disparagingly refers to as a "carpeted tube" (p. 13).

Compared to the visits to far-flung places that Theroux has in mind, Cela's first travel book is a short, local affair. Pastrana, where the account of the trip comes to an end, is only one hundred kilometers from Madrid. So, in terms of travel writing traditions and practice, in June 1946 Cela spent a week and a half almost on his doorstep. Yet the Alcarria district does not come into view until well into the third chapter, and before that point in the narrative the author provides a good deal of fascinating preliminary material that goes well beyond the scope of even Theroux's concerns.

The opening chapter of *Viaje a la Alcarria*, "Unos días antes" [A few days earlier], serves to introduce both the intending traveler and a technique—especially the author's projection of himself as the "viajero" or traveler-figure and the concomitant use of third-person narration. As was mentioned in chapter 1, literary critics of the travel genre constantly suggest that the one thing that travel books do have in common is their narrative mode: delivery in the first-person singular. However, chapter 1 of *Viaje a la Alcarria* immediately confronts the reader with an altogether different narrative approach that will mark the remainder of the work: third-person narration in the present tense. The first two paragraphs of this chapter, with their strong visual quality, introduce the traveler-to-be and also reveal the omniscient capacity of the third-person narrator:

> El viajero está echado, boca arriba, sobre una chaise-longue forrada de cretona. Mira, distraídamente, para el techo y deja volar libre la imaginación, que salta, como una torpe mariposa moribunda, rozando, en leves golpes, las paredes, los muebles, la lámpara encendida. Está cansado y nota un alivio grande dejando caer las piernas, como marionetas, en la primer postura que quieran encontrar.
>
> El viajero es un hombre joven, alto, delgado. Está en mangas de camisa fumando un cigarrillo. Lleva ya varias horas sin hablar, varias horas que no tiene con quién hablar. De cuando en cuando bebe un sorbo—ni pequeño ni grande—de whisky o silba, por lo bajo, alguna cancioncilla. (IV, 29)

> [The traveler is stretched out, on his back, on a cretonne-upholstered chaise longue. He looks absentmindedly at the ceiling and lets his imagination wander. It flits, like a clumsy, dying butterfly, gently touching the walls, the furniture, and the burning lamp. He is tired and feels a great relief as he allows his legs to flop, like those of a marionette, into the position they first encounter.
>
> The traveler is young, tall, and slim. He is in his shirtsleeves and smoking a cigarette. He has not spoken for several hours, for during that time he has had nobody to speak to. Now and then he takes a sip—neither a small one nor a large one—of whiskey, or quietly whistles a ditty.]

About a third of all the paragraphs in this short, opening chapter begin with the words "El viajero" [The traveler] and this is a pattern that will be repeated throughout the work. The poet and travel writer, Ted Walker, who in the 1980s followed some of Cela's tracks around the Alcarria and had long been fond of the work that inspired this shadowing, observes of the narrative presentation in *Viaje a la Alcarria*: "The book's objectivity—a strange device in a travel book—is increased by its having been written in the third person, Cela alluding to himself throughout (and this can become wearisome) as 'the traveller.'"[13]

Whether or not Cela's employment of this method of narration does come to weary the reader, or whether the reader becomes accustomed or even inured to this technique, is obviously a matter of individual response to the text. But what is particularly interesting is that while, almost without exception, critics of this and Cela's other travel works comment at the outset on the highly unconventional mode of narrative presentation (although none—as far as I know—has joined Walker in expressing reservations on the matter), rarely do they pause to consider the implications of this technique.

So what is achieved with this narrative method? In the first place,

Cela the writer, who was responsible for the final draft of the narrative, distances himself, at least to some extent, from the traveler who made the journey, had the experiences, and took the notes. From an artistic point of view this is both legitimate and laudable, since it is an honest and realistic approach. Unless a traveler undertakes the whole literary composition during the course of the journey (something which, for a variety of practical and even artistic reasons, can hardly be expected), then the person who writes the final version of the account is already removed chronologically and geographically from the person who did the traveling. This applies even in the case of the early chapters of *Viaje a la Alcarria* which, as was noted earlier, were written up within a few days of Cela's return to Madrid. It is, of course, much more relevant to the last six chapters, drafted some eighteen months later.

Commenting on the specific issue of the role of the traveler and that of the writer, the travel writer Jonathan Raban points out what he regards as the inadequacy of himself as traveler and note taker, and the frustration that this causes him as the individual who subsequently attempts to compose the account of the journey. Having made a solo voyage, in the spring and summer of 1996, from Seattle to Juneau, Alaska, and back, Raban observed some ten or so months later:

> Home, at this desk, seated at this typewriter, I find myself wading through the notebooks with familiar irritation. If the man who wrote them had been hired by me as my researcher, I'd sack him for gross neglect of duty.
>
> My dim-bulb alter ego. The notebooks expose him as short-sighted and long-winded by turns. Bogged down in the quotidian details of his adventure, he can't see the wood for trees. He travels, but can't remember why he's travelling. He's short of wit, and rarely passes up an opportunity to whine. He asks all the wrong questions (when he remembers to ask any questions at all). He's at his worst when trying hardest to "write:" I have to skip page after page of phoney lyricism in search of one memorable fact.

Then, recalling a row between two women that took place in a bar in Prince Rupert, British Columbia, and realizing that "the traveler" made no note of this little drama, Raban emphasizes what he sees as the distinction between the man on his travels and the man at his desk: "Why didn't he write about them? Why didn't he listen to the row more closely? Because, in our ill-matched duo, he's the traveller and I'm the writer, and the two are chalk and cheese."[14]

So, the role of the author as drafter and editor, although dependent on and presumably inspired by the role of the author as traveler, observer, and note taker, is somewhat different from that of the wayfarer. In his study in Madrid, Cela, who by 1946 had already published three novels and a volume of poetry, would have practiced his craft as a writer on his notes of the Alcarria journey and shaped the material by pruning and embellishing, thereby engaging in a second level of mediation of his travels of June 1946.

In one sense, then, the narrative presentation of *Viaje a la Alcarria* involves a distance between author and traveler that first-person narration does not allow. Furthermore, the combination of third-person narration and the almost constant use of the present tense serves to bring the reader, figuratively speaking, to the side of the narrator. This permits what Roger Fowler terms "a community of viewpoint between narrator and reader."[15] From this viewpoint, the reader and narrator together witness the traveler who is given a presence and a physicality that a traveler employing first-person narration seldom reveals. In a restricted space, for example the room in the opening chapter, the traveler-to-be is at the center of narrative focus and his presence dominates the scene. On the open road or in a village, the traveler is almost constantly seen in the middle ground or in the foreground—as part of a setting and part of an environment.

This framing of the traveler-protagonist does, however, start to break down toward the close of *Viaje a la Alcarria*, as does the consistency of use of the present tense. With the last chapter, the Pastrana episode, and despite the restrictions of third-person narration, the traveler is becoming quite noticeably transformed into the concerned voice and opinion giver that the reader would associate with the traditional, first-person narrator of a travel work. Perhaps by this stage, wearying of the self-imposed restraint of having his traveler-figure engage in little more than seeing and reporting, Cela decided to lift the restriction when he encountered a suitable cause for indignation. Or quite possibly, the author's grip on his approach loosened as, writing up the final stage of his account in the last day or two of 1947, he hurried to meet a publisher's deadline.

It is of course noteworthy that Cela's first three novels—*La familia de Pascual Duarte* (1942), *Pabellón de reposo* [Rest Home] (1944), and *Nuevas andanzas y desventuras de Lazarillo de Tormes* [New Adventures and Misfortunes of Lazarillo de Tormes] (1944)—all eschewed third-person narration. In fact, it was not until *La colmena* (1951) that the author employed this narrative method in a full-length work of fiction. Given that a first draft of *La colmena* was submitted to the censor in January 1946, a mere six months before the Alcarria trip and the publication of the early chapters of the travel book, it is possible that the unconventional narrative approach that Cela adopted with the Alcarria account was the result of his switch to and satisfaction with the almost total employment of third-person narration in *La colmena*.

Understandably, some readers may find the narrative method that

Cela adopts for *Viaje a la Alcarria* irksome and, given the traditional, memoir form of travel books, contrived. Indeed, the opening chapter of the work soon reveals a possibly jarring aspect of the author's narrative approach. Alone in his study, the intending traveler is reduced to talking to himself as he ponders over and then reveals his plans:

> El viajero habla despacio, muy despacio, consigo mismo, en voz baja y casi como si quisiera disimular.
> — Sí, la Alcarria. Debe ser un buen sitio para andar, un buen país. Luego ya veremos; a lo mejor no salgo más; depende. (IV, 30)

> [The traveler talks slowly, very slowly to himself, and quietly, almost as if trying not to be heard.
> "Right, the Alcarria. It should be a good place for walking, a good area. Afterwards, we'll see; I probably won't do it again; it all depends."]

This somewhat clumsy, although of course realistically plausible device of having the traveler talk to himself is employed throughout most of the short, first chapter until, near the end, the reader is allowed access to his thoughts.

Following on from this last point, one important aspect of Cela's narrator-traveler relationship needs to be clarified. Although for long stretches of the Spaniard's travel books the reader might be lulled into assuming that the narrator is some kind of shadowy figure or disembodied voice who moves along with the traveler, revealing his thoughts and commenting on his actions, the author has occasionally confirmed in his travel works that it is in fact the traveler who, at one remove, is narrating his own experiences. For example, in the prologue to *Judíos, moros y cristianos* Cela talks about the vagabond having attempted to compose "his book" in a particular way (V, 130). Then, in *Primer viaje andaluz*, where the traveler is once again labeled "the vagabond," details are given of certain atrocities committed during the Carlist Wars. Despite the horrifying incidents that it describes, the reference is brisk and almost matter-of-fact. However, it is immediately followed by the statement: "Quede claro que el vagabundo escribe lo que antecede con el mismo dolor con que lo aprendió" [Let it be understood that the vagabond has written the above with the same pain with which he learned of it].[16] Thus, once again it is confirmed that it is the traveler who is doing the narrating and who is also responsible for the composition of the account. So, although Cela the author consistently seeks to distance himself from his traveler-figure, he does, now and again, acknowledge the intimacy and, indeed, unity of the relationship between author, narrator, and traveler.

Perhaps in the early pages of *Viaje a la Alcarria* the author is shaking down his technique. Be that as it may, chapter 1 is a rather heavily contrived preparatory episode in which the relaxed protagonist, surrounded by maps, decides to go to the Alcarria and (no doubt Paul Theroux would approve) gives a disarmingly simple motive: it ought to be a good place to walk and a pleasant stretch of country. Hereafter, the intending traveler chooses which part of the district to visit, delights in the thought of keeping his route relatively flexible, and then plans the practical approach to covering the area while at the same time recognizing the folly of trying to be too precise:

> —Etapas ni cortas ni largas, es el secreto. Una legua y una hora de descanso, otra legua y otra hora, y así hasta el final. Veinte o veinticinco kilómetros al día ya es una buena marcha; es pasarse las mañanas en el camino. Después, sobre el terreno, todos estos proyectos son papel mojado y las cosas salen, como pasa siempre, por donde pueden. (IV, 31)

> ["Stages that are neither too short nor too long, that's the secret. Walk a league and then rest for an hour, another league and another hour, and so on. Twenty or twenty-five kilometers a day is a good stretch; it means spending the mornings on the road. Later, once the journey's underway, all these plans are just scraps of paper and, as is always the way, things turn out however they will."]

In addition, he decides to skirt the towns but then, somewhat impishly, changes his mind: " —O no, no las bordearé. Las ciudades hay que cruzarlas, a media tarde, cuando las señoritas salen a pasear un rato" ["No, I won't skirt them. It's best to pass through cities in mid-afternoon, when the young ladies are out for a stroll"] (IV, 33).

Yet this opening chapter of decision and planning was written immediately *after* Cela's return from the Alcarria and is therefore of some interest for being a prelude and a plan composed after the event. The chapter also serves as an introduction to the protagonist and as a kind of implicit presentation of his credentials. So, he is revealed to the reader as "un hombre joven, alto, delgado" [a tall, slim, young man] (IV, 29). (Here, it is worth pausing to consider the effect if this description had been conveyed by a first-person narrator. The reader would surely have flinched a little in response to a perceived hint of narcissism). The author then proceeds to compose a picture of a young fellow (in June 1946 Cela had just turned thirty) who, seen in his solitude, smokes and drinks far into the night as he considers where to travel and how to approach the trip. On the one hand, the intending traveler exudes seriousness of purpose with his many annotated maps, measurements, notes and other documents, and also with his walking boots and new flask at the ready. Yet at the same time he quickly changes his mind about skirting towns and settles instead for passing through them in mid-afternoon so that he can catch sight of respectable young ladies. He is, after all, a young man.

The traveler is also a writer: "Sobre la mesa, cientos de cuartillas en desorden dan fe de muchas horas de trabajo" [Strewn about on the desk, hundreds of sheets of paper bear witness to many hours of work] (IV, 29–30). Indeed, an extremely important part of the picture presented in the opening chapter of *Viaje a la Alcarria* is that of an individual who, it is implied, is qualified to write about the area he plans to visit. In other words, it is here that the credentials of the traveler are revealed and his authority suggested, even though the protagonist does not mention or think about the task of reporting his trip or even what to report. This matter of competence is, of course, touched on in the dedication. But it should be recalled that this "preliminary" document was written eighteen months after the publication of the first chapter.

One other point concerning the portrayal of the traveler is worth mentioning. Not only is he a writer: he also appears to be a serious reader. Reference is made to the pile of novels on the carpet and to the presence of bookshelves, from which he absentmindedly removes a copy of Manuel Murguía's *Historia de Galicia*. Setting aside the fact that this extensive study was published in five volumes (1865–1913), what is particularly interesting is that Murguía, the husband of Rosalía de Castro, was one of the leading figures of the Galician regionalist movement that developed in the closing decades of the nineteenth century.[17] This mention of such a champion of regionalism and, indeed, the possible allusion to the whole regionalist issue is perhaps a touch audacious in view of what Carr and Fusi Aizpurua describe as "the suppression of 'separatism'" that followed General Franco's victory (p. 12).

But then, after the protagonist has leafed through a few pages of the Murguía, it is pointed out, and again this is somewhat intriguing, that one of the books shelved next to it is Ernest Hemingway's first novel, *The Sun Also Rises* (1926).[18] This work, set mainly in Spain, has a strong sense of place and movement, and also reveals the sparse, objective, reporting style that was to become such a feature of Hemingway's later fiction. Indeed, notwithstanding the obvious difference in narrative mode and the American writer's employment of the past tense, Cela's descriptive method in *Viaje a la Alcarria* is quite often reminiscent of that revealed in the following, typical piece of description from *The Sun Also Rises*:

> The road came out from the shadow of the woods into the hot sun. Ahead was a river-valley. Beyond the river was a steep hill. There was a field of

buckwheat on the hill. We saw a white house under some trees on the hill-side. It was very hot and we stopped under some trees beside a dam that crossed the river.[19]

Yet, if the passing reference to Hemingway's novel invites some speculation on a possible literary influence on the young Spanish writer, what is even more fascinating is the fact that Cela chooses to single out a novel by an author who was in bad odor with the Franco regime. During the civil war, Hemingway had spent a good deal of time in Spain as a reporter and was certainly not a neutral observer. He constantly expressed pro-republican sympathies and also became involved in a number of activities, in Republican Spain and abroad, aimed at assisting the struggle against the Nationalists.[20] Not surprisingly, Hemingway's novel about the war, *For Whom the Bell Tolls* (1940), was banned in Spain. So, too, was his treatise on bullfighting, *Death in the Afternoon* (1932). However, the aimlessness and debauchery that marks much of *The Sun Also Rises* was apparently deemed acceptable by the authorities. Indeed, a translation of this work was published in Spain in 1948.[21] It is possible that, with the mention of the Hemingway novel, Cela is being a little showy or trendy, or simply indulging in a touch of bravado. But what should also be allowed is that at this preliminary stage of the narrative the author is, in addition, asserting his independence of taste, opinion, and view.

SETTING OUT

Earlier it was mentioned that many novelists have written travel works and that commentators on the travel genre have frequently indicated and discussed differences and similarities exhibited by the two narrative forms. Yet in the dedication to *Viaje a la Alcarria*, Cela, already a successful young novelist, attempts to make a clear distinction between what prose fiction allows and what, in his opinion, travel literature requires. Having stated that *Viaje a la Alcarria* is not fiction but basically a work of geography, he goes on to suggest that the novel is a thoroughly permissive genre. This is followed by a rather po-faced declaration that equates travel literature, geography, truth, and science (IV, 28). Such an assertion, somewhat undermined by the lighter moments of the opening chapter, is later followed by the gentle literary tease that opens chapter 2, the episode of departure: "La del alba sería . . . No; no era aún la del alba: era más temprano" [It was around daybreak . . . No, it was not yet daybreak: it was earlier] (IV, 35).

Cela's use of the words "La del alba sería," which begin chapter 4 of part 1 of *Don Quixote* and present the eponymous hero joyfully setting forth from the La Mancha inn at which he had been "dubbed" knight, are obviously laden with associations concerning a journey, ideals, adventure, equipment, and so on. But the denial and correction that immediately follow the Cervantine borrowing are presumably intended to serve as a clear pointer to the reader that fact, not fiction, reality, not illusion are the currency of this work. Yet, this reminder of the *Quixote* also has other resonances. Thus, in the opening chapter of *Viaje a la Alcarria* the traveler mentions in passing the possibility of a trip to La Mancha (this reference does not, however, occur in the first edition), while the preliminary considerations and departure of Cela's traveler do in some respects, in terms of parallels as well as contrasts, recall Azorín's setting out from Madrid at the beginning of *La ruta de Don Quijote* [Don Quixote's Route].

In March 1905, while working as a journalist for *El Imparcial*, Azorín was sent to La Mancha at the time of the tercentenary of the publication of the first part of *Don Quixote*. The fifteen articles that he wrote during his trip were published between 4 March and 25 March in the newspaper and appeared shortly afterwards in book form, entitled *La ruta de Don Quijote*, with each article corresponding to a chapter. The opening chapter, "La partida" [The Departure], serves to announce and anticipate his trip. Like the first chapter of *Viaje a la Alcarria*, it presents the traveler-to-be as a practicing writer. Yet whereas Cela's chapter introduces an individual who, although physically tired, can still concern himself enthusiastically with the practicalities of the chosen trip (maps, measuring, a geography book, distances to be covered, and so on), Azorín's opening chapter evinces an altogether different concern and spirit. He is a world-weary person confronted with an uncertain itinerary and yet one more literary task to fulfill: "¿Dónde iré yo, una vez más, como siempre, sin remedio ninguno, con mi maleta y mis cuartillas?" ["Where will I go, yet again, as always, without any choice, with my suitcase and my writing-paper?"].[22] It is as if he is a perpetual, weary slave to the act of writing: "Y yo, entristecido, resignado con esta inquieta pluma que he de mover perdurablemente y con estas cuartillas que he de llenar hasta el fin de mis días . . ." ["And I, saddened and resigned, with this restless pen that I have to move everlastingly and with these sheets of paper that I must fill until the end of my days . . ."] (p. 79).

The second chapter of *La ruta de Don Quijote*, "En marcha" [Setting out], and that of *Viaje a la Alcarria*, "El camino de Guadalajara" [On the way to Guadalajara] both present the protagonist leaving his home in Madrid (Azorín, in fact, has lodgings), heading for the Atocha station, and then catching the train for an initial destination: in the case of

Azorín, it is Argamasilla de Alba. Both men get up in the dark and, in the opening phase of each chapter, both comment on the strangeness of the city at this time of day. Azorín's statement, though, is generic in character:

> Esta es la hora en que las grandes urbes modernas nos muestran todo lo que tienen de extrañas, de anormales, tal vez de antihumanas. Las calles aparecen desiertas, mudas; parece que durante un momento, después de la agitación del trasnocheo, después de los afanes del día, las casas recogen su espíritu sobre sí mismas, y nos muestran en esta fugaz pausa, antes que llegue otra vez el inminente tráfago diario, toda la frialdad, la impasibilidad de sus fachadas, altas, simétricas, de sus hileras de balcones cerrados, de sus esquinazos y sus ángulos, que destacan en un cielo que comienza poco a poco, imperceptiblemente, a clarear en lo alto . . . (p. 81)

> [This is the hour when great modern cities show us everything about them that is strange, abnormal, perhaps even antihuman. The streets appear deserted, silent; it seems that for a moment, after the day's exertions, after the nighttime activity, the houses reveal their own presence and show us in this fleeting pause, before the imminent daily bustle resumes, all the coldness, all the impassivity of their tall, symmetrical façades, of their rows of closed balconies, of their corners and edges that stand out against a sky that, high above, is gradually, imperceptibly, beginning to lighten . . .]

Yet despite this passage of observation and contemplation, Azorín narrates at a generally rapid pace. At the beginning of the second chapter, and within the space of half a dozen lines, he has been woken by his landlady, has got up, dressed, and gone out to the street. A hackney carriage speeds him to Atocha and then, after two pages of description of the rail station and his fellow passengers, Azorín is on his way.

Cela's account of the departure from the city is much more slow-paced and is crammed with detail. For instance, the Galician author devotes as much space to describing the period from when his traveler rises and eventually gets to Atocha as Azorín does to the whole of his journey from the lodging house to Argamasilla de Alba. Despite a couple of descriptive pauses, Azorín's chapter of departure appears designed to get the reader to Argamasilla with the minimum of fuss and delay. Cela, on the other hand, uses his second chapter to convey a generally somber view of the city, to give further indications of his traveler's character and purpose, and also to reveal a process of transition from city to countryside, and from the ominous darkness of the early hours to the light of morning.

When Azorín set out, his description focused on the absence of people in contrast to the bustling activity of other times of the day. However, as Cela's traveler makes his way through the streets of Madrid he evokes the *presence* of the inhabitants behind the closed windows and blinds of the houses, the contrasting fortunes of the residents, and the probable difficulty of guessing people's nature or fate from the appearance of where they live:

> Las casas tienen las ventanas cerradas y las persianas bajas. Detrás de los cristales— ¡quién lo sabe!—duermen su maldición o su bienaventuranza los hombres y las mujeres de la ciudad. Hay casas que tienen todo el aire de alojar vecinos felices, y calles enteras de un mirar siniestro, con aspecto de cobijar hombres sin conciencia, comerciantes, prestamistas, alcahuetas, turbios jaques con el alma salpicada de sangre. A lo mejor, las casas de los vecinos venturosos no tienen ni una sola matita de yerbabuena o de mejorana en los balcones. A veces, las casas de los vecinos ahogados por la desdicha, señalados con el hierro cruel del odio y la desesperación, presumen de un balcón de geranios o de claveles rompedores, gordos como manzanas. (IV, 36)

> [The houses have their windows closed and their blinds pulled down. Behind the windows—who knows!—the men and women of the city are enjoying the sleep of the cursed or of the blessed. There are houses that have all the appearance of sheltering happy folk as well as whole streets with a sinister look, as if they contain people without a conscience: shopkeepers, moneylenders, procurers, or dim-witted thugs with blood-spattered souls. The homes of the fortunate probably do not have a single mint or marjoram plant on their balconies. Sometimes the homes of those overwhelmed by misfortune, or marked by the cruel branding-iron of hatred and desperation, display balconies full of geraniums or hefty carnations, as big as apples.]

This passage of description and speculation (which would fit quite unobtrusively into certain sections of *La colmena* and which is hardly consonant with notions of simply "seeing and describing") has a focus completely different from that of Azorín's picture of the sleeping city's streets and dwellings.

Moreover, as Cela's traveler walks toward the station the somber and subjective tone of the previously cited extract is continued as the first light of day is noticed. Azorín describes this moment in terms of the stark yet striking effect of dawn on the urban and industrial landscape. His picture is powerful and impressive, but then the scene is immediately abandoned and succeeded by his sudden arrival at the station, and the posing of a lame question:

> Ya en el horizonte comienza a surgir un resplandor mate, opaco; las torrecillas metálicas de los cables surgen rígidas; la chimenea de una fábrica deja escapar un humo denso, negro, que va poniendo una tupida gasa ante la

claridad que nace por oriente. Yo llego a la estación. ¿No sentís vosotros una simpatía profunda por las estaciones? (pp. 81–82)

[Now on the horizon a dull, opaque glow begins to appear; the pylons carrying electric cables rise rigidly; a factory chimney gives off dense, black smoke that lays a thick gauze in front of the light appearing in the east. I reach the station. Do you not feel a great fondness for stations?]

Cela, on the other hand, continues with a subjective approach that involves the use of pathetic fallacy, as the dawn reluctantly reveals itself over the city. The traveler then gradually lowers his gaze, shortens his perspective, and once again indicates a measure of compassion and concern, as he sentimentally muses on a large group of stray cats in the park:

El día fuerza por levantarse, cauto, desconfiado, sobre los cables más altos, sobre las últimas azoteas de la ciudad, mientras los gorriones recién despiertos chillan, en los árboles del parque, como condenados. En el parque también, sobre la yerba, la república de los gatos cimarrones, dos docenas de gatos sin fortuna, sin amo, dos docenas de gatos grises, malditos, sarnosos; de gatos que, sin un sitio al lado de ningún hogar encendido, deambulan en silencio, como aburridos presos sin esperanza o enfermos incurables, dejados de la mano de Dios. (IV, 37)

[The day strains to rise, cautiously, mistrustfully, over the highest cables and rooftops of the city, while on the trees in the park the recently awoken sparrows squawk like condemned men. Also in the park, on the grass, is the republic of stray cats: two dozen luckless, ownerless cats, two dozen grey, wretched, mangy cats; cats that, with no fireplace to sit beside, wander around in silence, like bored prisoners without hope or like the incurably ill, abandoned by the hand of God.]

Setting aside the question of whether the use here of terms such as "condemned," "republic," or "prisoners without hope" might allude to the contemporary political situation, what does emerge as Cela's traveler makes his way through the city is a suggestion of personal involvement that yet again belies the stated, neutral intention of simply observing and reporting. Indeed, his compassion surfaces once more when he notices a child rummaging through garbage:

Al paso del viajero levanta la frente y se echa a un lado, como disimulando. El niño ignora que las apariencias engañan, que debajo de una mala capa puede esconderse un buen bebedor; que en el pecho del viajero, de extraño, quizá temeroso aspecto, encontraría un corazón de par en par abierto, como las puertas del campo. El niño, que mira receloso como un perro castigado, tampoco sabe hasta qué punto el viajero siente una ternura infinita hacia los niños abandonados, hacia los niños nómadas que, rompiendo ya el día, hurgan con un palito en los frescos, en los tibios, en los aromáticos montones de basura. (IV, 40).

[As the traveler goes by, the child looks up and moves aside, as if doing nothing. The child does not know that appearances are deceptive, that a poor coat can hide a good nature; that beneath the traveler's strange, perhaps frightening aspect he would find a heart that is as big as the countryside. Nor does the child, who has the mistrustful look of a whipped dog, realize how much the traveler feels a boundless compassion for abandoned children, for homeless children who, at the break of day, poke around with a stick in the fresh, warm, aromatic piles of garbage.]

The dolefulness of this scene is compounded immediately afterwards with mention of the sorry state of the sheep being led to the slaughterhouse. But whereas here, in a much shorter passage, the narrator avoids any direct, emotional statement, he can at the same time make an observation that indicates both the callousness of his fellows and his own cynicism: "Los dos hombres que las conducen les pegan bastonazos, de cuando en cuando, por entretenerse quizás" [From time to time, the two men leading them along hit them with their sticks, perhaps to amuse themselves] (IV, 40). In any case, this casual, tagged-on comment concerning the possible motive for the two men's actions is a brief but striking example of the traveler interpreting what he sees, rather than simply reporting it.

On his way to Atocha, and a little before coming across the boy scavenging in the pile of garbage, the traveler had recalled Antonio Machado's poem "He andado muchos caminos" [I have traveled many highways] (*Soledades* [Solitudes], 1899–1907) and then recited all but the opening stanza. The ailing Machado had fled from Spain at the end of the civil war and died shortly afterwards in France. Although most of his poetry was still published in Spain in the 1940s, Machado's republican sympathies and his civil-war writing ensured that his work was regarded with hostility in right-wing quarters. In this respect, Cela's choice of Machado's poem could be rather pointed. Indeed, over the years the Galician author consistently referred to Machado in terms of esteem and affection, and pays particular homage to him in *Judíos, moros y cristianos*. But in any case, the choice of this poem seems especially apt for a travel writer concerned with Spain and contemplating the journey to be made. In fact, in chapter 1 of *Marching Spain*, as he traveled by train to Southampton, V. S. Pritchett reflected on the first and penultimate stanzas of the same poem.

In *Viaje a la Alcarria*, Cela's use of all but the opening stanza of "He andado muchos caminos" (two of the lines in the first stanza address travel by sea and have presumably been deemed inappropriate for a short, overland trip to a nearby district) is much more thoughtful than Pritchett's restricted selection and altogether effusive conclusion.[23] Cela's traveler divides his version of the poem in two, trusting that when he returns he will have the courage to convey the unpalatable truths about people suggested in the first part of the poem. Yet he also believes, or hopes, that his account will come to reflect the other side of people that is indicated in the second part of Machado's poem.

Subsequently, the traveler's arrival at the Atocha station is marked not by a sense that he has reached the point of departure and therefore of escape, but rather that, having negotiated the Stygian gloom of the city's arteries, he has now entered the halls of Hades:

> El viajero, mientras busca su tercera, piensa que anda por un inmenso almacén de ataúdes, poblado de almas en pena, al hombro el doble bagaje de los pecados y las obras de misericordia. (IV, 41)

> [While he looks for his seat in third class, the traveler imagines that he is walking through a huge warehouse full of coffins, inhabited by souls in torment who are carrying over their shoulders the double baggage of their sins and their acts of charity.]

Yet the station is really more a symbol of purgatory than a latter-day hall of Hades. It is a place of transition, both a terminus and a point of departure. Here the traveler boards his train and experiences the dimness of the unlit carriages and then the brief plunge into total darkness: "Se apagan las luces del andén y la oscuridad es ya absoluta" [The platform lights go out and everything is pitch black] (IV, 42). This is shortly followed by the train pulling out and emerging from the station's opaque canopy into the early light of day.

The daylight first reveals movement: that of another train running beside the traveler's, before it heads off along a different route. After describing the fleeting visual recognition between the occupants of the two trains, which becomes both a point of contact and separation, the narrator briefly digresses on the way in which the passengers of one train are always a little envious of those of another that comes into view. He then focuses once more on the transition from darkness to light and notes the striking, rosy hue of the sky. Next, in antithetical relation to the startling and imposing morning sky, the narrator's perspective immediately switches to the train as it makes its way through the industrial landscape of rail tracks, piles of coal, and sidings with steam engines lying idle, some out of service and others withdrawn for the scrap heap. The latter have the appearance of "caballos muertos en la batalla y puestos a secar al sol" [horses killed in battle and left to dry out in the sun] (IV, 42). This animal imagery and also the notion of parching are straightaway followed by the description of the plight of a wagon load of cows and mention of the fate that awaits them:

> En un vagón sin enganchar, en un vagón solitario, se agolpan docena y media de vacas negras, de largos cuernos y ubre peluda y escasa, que esperan estoicamente la hora de la puntilla y del ancho cuchillo de sangrar. El viajero piensa que los animales estarán muertos de sed, sin saber demasiado a ciencia cierta que es lo que les pasa. (IV, 42–43)

> [In an uncoupled wagon, a solitary wagon, a dozen and a half black cows with long horns and scrawny, hairy udders are crowded together, stoically awaiting the moment of the slaughterer's knife. The traveler thinks that the animals are probably dying of thirst and know little about what is happening to them.]

This description of the animals, displaced from their rural habitat and now en route to the urban slaughterhouse, is a reminder of his earlier encounter with the sheep being callously herded through the center of Madrid on their way to the abattoir.

As the traveler's train passes the final points, signals, and network of tracks beyond the station, and thereby largely leaves behind the mechanical reminders of the city's presence and control, the sun finally appears over the horizon. Here, on the outskirts of Madrid, there is the first indication of the proximity, and tranquility, of the countryside:

> El campo está verde y crecido; no parecen los alrededores de Madrid. Entre dos sembrados, un campo sin cuidar, un campo de amapolas meciéndose, suaves, a la ligera brisa de la mañana. (IV, 43)

> [The countryside looks green and flourishing. Between two fields of crops there is an uncultivated field, a field of poppies swaying gently in the light, morning breeze.]

It is at this stage that the traveler moves away from the window and takes a seat, and from here until the arrival in Guadalajara the narrative perspective constantly switches between activity in the carriage and exterior scenes or incidents. During this time, the traveler gradually becomes more animated, even humorous, and takes part in the occasional desultory conversation.

The solitary and somber figure who had made his way through the streets of Madrid a little earlier now becomes part of the disparate community of travelers within the confines of the train. Indeed, after his first, unsuccessful attempt at the lottery, the sudden announcement of which had shattered the silence in the carriage, he feels the desire to play once more in order to make a good impression with his fellow passengers. The narrative subsequently moves between descriptions of passengers leaving or joining the train, shows scenes at various stations and in the surrounding areas, focuses from time to time on the traveler's concerns and activities, and reveals glimpses of pleasant countryside. Finally, as the train is about to pull into Guadalajara, he is seen to refrain from joining in the hustle and bustle of alighting passengers. He reveals a certain composure and also reasserts his individuality by getting off last. The second stage of his journey is now complete.

SOME CRITICAL ASSESSMENTS OF *VIAJE A LA ALCARRIA*

After the brief pause in Guadalajara, Cela made his way on foot to the Alcarria district and spent the next nine or so days traveling around the towns and villages of the area. Forty years later, in the first of the two dedications in *Nuevo viaje a la Alcarria*, the author stated that during the Alcarria trip of June 1946 he had become acquainted with what he terms "las honestas delicias campesinas que encerraba el país" [the wholesome, rural delights of the area] (p. 9). However, such a cheery summary of his experiences of the first trip is not entirely reflected in the account and is almost completely out of kilter with the response of critics to the general tone and content of the work. Indeed, over the years *Viaje a la Alcarria* has normally been presented as a grim portrayal of a particularly difficult period in contemporary Spanish history, the 1940s, as well as an implicit condemnation of the first decade of the Franco regime. Certainly, the narrative was appropriated by opponents of Franco as a consummate work of literature that provided a sobering testimony to the aftermath of war and the plight of many Spaniards in the postwar period.

Viaje a la Alcarria is sometimes seen as a kind of rural companion piece to *La colmena*. However, one of the first critics to make this comparison, the novelist Arturo Barea, also indicates what he sees as significant contrasts. Barea, who fled Spain in 1938, wrote a ten-page introduction to the English translation of *La colmena*,[24] yet spent a third of this discussing Cela's first travel book. In the opening lines of his introduction, Barea describes himself as an "anti-Franco refugee" and also refers to Cela as belonging to Spain's "ruling caste, having fought on the winning side in the Civil War" (p. 7). Subsequently, Barea begins his appraisal of Cela's first travel book with a reference to Gerald

Brenan's *The Literature of the Spanish People* (1951) and the "note of hunger" that Brenan identifies in Spanish prose fiction from the Middle Ages to the eighteenth century. Barea asserts that Cela has sounded this note "when writing of Franco's own Spain until it rings like a tolling bell in a small book which, for me at least, is a masterpiece" (p. 13).

The exiled writer then goes on to comment on the presentation, content, and style of the work:

> On the face of it, this is the diary of a journey through an almost deserted hill district in New Castile where Moorish castles and renaissance palaces are crumbling in shrunken little towns, while the villages on the bleak hilltops go hungry and the villages in the valley can afford to be gay because their soil has water and so they are certain of their daily bread. Cela put down what he saw, in a beautiful, terse, limpid language. (p. 13)

Hereafter, though, Barea does not focus on the contrasting fortunes of the inhabitants of the Alcarria that the travel book presents but stresses a pervasive hardship and certain qualities revealed by the folk of the area, and which were not, apparently, to be found in their urban counterparts. Thus he refers to "a starving district" (p. 13) and also observes that "in men and women worn down by poverty, neglect and loneliness," Cela encountered "a simple strength and resilience he had missed in the capital" (p. 14). Barea also sees Cela as enunciating a common response to the plight of those depicted in both *La colmena* and *Viaje a la Alcarria*: "As in *The Hive*, bitter reactions and a desperate sentimentality lie behind Cela's taut descriptions of his journey in the Alcarria" (p. 14). Furthermore, he reiterates his belief that in the travel book the Galician writer acknowledges the moral fiber of rural inhabitants, whereas in the novel he exposes the character deficiences of city dwellers: "Like other Spanish writers from Miguel de Unamuno down, Cela seems incapable of finding unspoilt, genuine and strong people anywhere else than in the immutable hills and plains, least of all in Madrid" (pp. 14–15). As was mentioned previously, Barea notes that Cela indicates the contrasting fortunes of the inhabitants of the Alcarria (a valid point of comparison with *La colmena* that the exiled writer fails to spot) and also stresses that, despite the social and economic hardship that afflicts so many of these rural inhabitants, Cela still manages to convey their innate and praiseworthy qualities. However, Barea's rather sentimental slant (people maintaining their dignity, in spite of extremely difficult personal circumstances) could well have stemmed from his aversion to the Franco regime and his concern for the plight of ordinary Spaniards.

A few years later, in a brief article that Américo Castro wrote in 1959 while correcting the proofs of the second edition of *Hacia Cervantes*

[Toward Cervantes] and which was subsequently appended to that study, Castro considered *Viaje a la Alcarria* in the context of the picaresque tradition. In this piece he makes no mention of social conditions or human qualities that the work might reveal, and instead focuses on the individuality and quest of Cela the traveler. Castro sees freedom and movement as being at the heart of the narrative: "The traveler moves around in search of open spaces, of villages unthreatened by urban expansion and which have fields alongside. The highways are of more interest than where he stops during the traveling day."[25] At the same time he suggests that Cela was not seeking some kind of tranquil idyll but instead confronts the reader with "marginalized individuals, with those who have been ejected by the society of people living comfortable lives" (p. 387). In addition, Castro labels Cela's style as "prosified poetry" (p. 388).

In an article written three years after these comments, J. M. Castellet, described by one critic as a "leading dissident" of the 1950s,[26] judges Cela's first travel book in terms of its sociopolitical and socioeconomic thrust, with comments such as: "*Viaje a la Alcarria* is one, I am inclined to say the only one, of Cela's books that most harshly shows things, denounces countless things, . . . putting an accusing finger in the wound, in the open sore, of the Spain of those years" (p. 14), and: "The Alcarria is presented to us as a wretched area, with towns that are gradually falling down, and with its desolate, tiny, and abandoned villages" (p. 16). Subsequently in his article, Castellet again stresses the critical stance of *Viaje a la Alcarria*. He deems it to be more pronounced in this narrative than in the author's later works and, toward the end of his assessment, he acknowledges the continuing validity and force of Cela's first travel book: "Here is the book—fourteen years on, still vivid and topical—and accusing, cutting, bitter, cruel, and tender" (p. 19).

While Castellet viewed *Viaje a la Alcarria* as a work that was "characteristic of the period" (p. 18), Alonso Zamora Vicente, writing at almost exactly the same time as the Catalan critic and much more a voice of the literary establishment, also gives a pessimistic, although very different kind of appraisal of the book. Thus, after listing the various kinds of ordinary people encountered in the work, he refers to the pretensions and the decline of the towns visited by the traveler. Zamora Vicente then returns to the theme of decline and decay when he mentions how *Viaje a la Alcarria* talks of the rare books and old buildings that are ruined through ignorance and neglect, and indicates how Spaniards feel the weight of a glorious past that they are incapable of reviving. And just to ensure that the "1898" drift of his assessment is not lost on the reader, he closes by suggesting that Cela's first travel work recalls some of the essays of Unamuno and Azorín.[27]

The American critic Robert Kirsner, also writing in the 1960s, takes a completely different tack, more akin to that of Castellet, and vigorously pursues an approach that sees *Viaje a la Alcarria* as testimony to a grim and chaotic aftermath to the civil war. He states that "in the cruel reality of the nineteen forties, disorder reigns in La Alcarria,"[28] and then dramatically refers to "the chaos of contemporary conditions" and "the chaos that exists throughout Spain" (p. 103). Furthermore, Kirsner asserts that the shadow of the recent war is central to an understanding of *Viaje a la Alcarria*, noting: "The visible scars and the unhappy memories of a Civil War constitute the ironic theme of Cela's peregrinatory memoirs" (p. 109). Nevertheless, Kirsner still manages to see positive features in the outlook of the local people: "Pride will not permit the inhabitants to face the horror of the present. It is pride—often grotesque in nature—that sustains the dignity of the starving Spaniard" (p. 102).

Writing from the perspective of the late 1970s, Paul Ilie, like Kirsner, regards the tone of Cela's travel book as acerbic, but grants that there are frequent moments in which a more emollient approach is revealed.[29] And while Ilie mentions "the grinding poverty of rural life" (p. 256) or the "silent pain that permeates the whole of the book" (p. 263), he sees the journey that Cela describes principally in terms of a personal quest to understand self, Spain, and "Spanishness." Thus Ilie believes that the traveler goes to rural areas to seek permanence and continuity of values, but above all to seek himself and answers to questions posed by the recent war: "He jots down the basic problems caused by the disastrous fratricide: those concerning the nature of being Spanish and the national values that this represents" (p. 253).

A rather different note is sounded by José María Martínez Cachero who, a dozen years later in a volume of essays celebrating Cela's receipt of the Nobel Prize for Literature, focused not on any personal or cultural quest of the traveler, but instead on the differentness, backwardness, ignorance, and even quaintness of the inhabitants of the Alcarria:

> The Spain offered here is, of course, another Spain, different from the Spain of the capital city and the urban life from which the traveler comes. Many of its characteristics suggest that it is a human space anchored in the past, with a mentality that (or so it would seem) might appear strange, even exotic, and which in the context of certain attitudes and individuals inspires a deep respect, but which, more often, provokes hilarity.[30]

In the same collection, Robert Kirsner also acknowledges the humorous side of Cela's first travel book but in addition stresses the grim context framing this humor, suggesting that in *Viaje a la Alcarria* "the humorous aspect is often evident within the frightening vision of a terrorized world."[31] And while in another essay published at the same time Kirsner refers to this period as "a sad, disrupted period,"[32] he goes on to propose that it is not the distressing situation that dominates the narrative. According to the critic, *Viaje a la Alcarria* is less a lament for a community than "a tribute to the perennial, indomitable Spanish spirit" (p. 42).

In the introduction to his edition of *Viaje a la Alcarria*, José María Pozuelo Yvancos describes Cela as a "novelist-traveler,"[33] and contrasts the Galician writer's approach to travel literature with what he sees as the metaphysical thrust of Unamuno's travel accounts, noting that in this genre Cela writes "like a novelist and with the enthusiasm of the novelist who is interested in characters and their surroundings, in order to look anti-metaphysically, at ground level, at the reality he comes across" (p. 26).

Finally, it is worth considering a disparate collection of assessments of *Viaje a la Alcarria* offered in the last few years by travel writers and book reviewers. In the mid-1980s, as part of a journey around Spain, Ted Walker retraced sections of Cela's trip to the Alcarria. This enterprise was partly inspired by what Walker describes as his "longstanding affection" for Cela's first travel book (p. 222), a work that he terms "an unpretentious and concise account, mostly without subjective comment, of the people he encountered and the things that he saw in the places he passed through" (p. 221). In 1991, another British writer, Michael Jacobs, embarked on a comprehensive tour of Spain as it prepared for the 1992 Olympics and the quincentenary celebrations of Columbus's first voyage to the New World. In a stimulating and sometimes iconoclastic account of the nation and its cultural heritage and attitudes, Jacobs describes a visit to Brihuega, Trillo, and Pastrana. During the course of this brief trip, he brings together the accounts of Cela's visits of 1946 and 1985 and, when he stops to see the gardens at the Real Fábrica de Paños [Royal Textile Factory] in Brihuega, Jacobs discovers that Nico, the present gardener, is the man who had accompanied Cela around the garden in 1985 and also the son of the gardener Cela had encountered almost forty years earlier. But just as fascinating as this connection is the way in which Nico's attitude to Cela casts an interesting light on a local perception of the famous author's approach to travel writing—which in turn elicits Jacobs's opinion on what he sees as the weakness of the Cela technique:

> Nico had the makings of a perceptive literary critic. In a single sentence he pinpointed the failings of Cela's method as a travel-writer, failings common to anyone who hopes to capture the character of a particular place on the

basis of transient meetings with picturesque types: "Cela would just spend a night in a village, go into a shop or bar, meet up with the village idiot or some deformed unfortunate, and—there you have it, the whole village summed up. Look at how he describes Brihuega. Who are the people he meets here? Why, there's that imbecile Julio Vacas. And then there's that stutterer who can't tell him the name of the fountain."[34]

Cela's receipt of the Nobel Prize led to a flurry of reissues of long ignored translations of his works, including the only English version of *Viaje a la Alcarria*,[35] which had first appeared in the United States in 1964. Indeed, the American reissue, published by the Atlantic Monthly Press and not by the original publisher, the University of Wisconsin Press, gives the work the anodyne subtitle, *Travels Through the Spanish Countryside*. Presumably this is to make clear to prospective American readers that the work does not have a Spanish-American (or even southern United States) setting rather than to entice them to purchase an account of an idyllic country ramble. However, in an extensive review of five translations of Cela's works, including *Journey to the Alcarria*, Sarah Kerr initially gives the impression that she has fallen for the subtitle, referring to the Alcarria work as "a small travel sketch."[36] Subsequently, though, she devotes some thoughtful and detailed attention to Cela's approach in this travel book.

In the first place, Kerr states that Cela is not seeking "a personal, historical interpretation" of Spain, its people, or its culture (p. 36). Indeed, she suggests that *Journey to the Alcarria* is "about moving through places and not understanding them" and that it is a work in which Cela "prefers strictly recording the present to reflecting on more cosmic matters." Kerr also notes that "the traveler is drawn to pitiful people, lonely children and deformed idiots whose external tics he relates rather than their intimacies." Concerning the civil war's influence on the work, the reviewer comments: "Usually too, whenever the war comes up he tries to divert the talk." A little later she observes: "The obsession with eternal things seems motivated by an almost complete blockage of interior feeling, a small version, perhaps, of the entire country's inability to discuss the war except in muddled symbols." Overall, Kerr sees the tone of *Journey to the Alcarria* as one of "deep melancholy" (p. 37).

In a brief newspaper review of *Journey to the Alcarria* and three other Spanish works in translation, John Butt also mentions the tone of the book and offers an explanation: "Factual and quiet in its sadness, it gives a touching picture of a land traumatised by Civil War, sunk in despair yet surviving on patience and human kindness."[37] However, in another review of the work, Harry Eyres suggests that Cela was *not* trying to probe the wounds caused by the civil war. He sees *Journey to the Alcarria* as an "apparently impartial, almost impassive book" and goes on to comment: "Extreme poverty gripped much of the country, but Cela seems to regard it as part of the landscape: something to be wondered at, not a social ill to be cured. What occupy him most are the basic sensations of his simple life."[38] And, in a journalistic piece describing how, in the summer of 1993, he retraced a good part of Cela's itinerary of 1946, James Wilson calls this travel narrative "simple, funny and imbued with nostalgia." He also claims that it is marked by a consciousness of the war and the fact that the author and the country have changed: "The sense that things would never again be the same pervades the book, on both a personal and national level. Spain seemed changed for good; the civil war casts a long shadow over *Journey to the Alcarria*."[39]

Cela's first travel book has provoked an abundant and constant critical response, and the foregoing assessments are indicative of the scope and tenor of critical opinions of this travel account. It is, of course, true that critics from different periods and backgrounds will tend to propose distinct interpretative readings of works of art. Even so, in the case of *Viaje a la Alcarria* critical responses have largely focused on the perceived socioeconomic thrust of the work. In addition, there has been a good deal of agreement in respect of the tone of the account and a considerable amount of attention has been paid to its historical and political weight. Within these areas of focus a few critics have, with regard to a number of specific features of the work, offered conclusions that might be described as debatable or even erroneous. It now remains to examine *Viaje a la Alcarria* in the light of Cela's stated views on travel and the practice of travel writing, with reference to his comments in the opening parts of the travel narrative, and also in conjunction with the already discussed critical assessments of the work.

4

Capturing the Present in Cela's
Geography of the Alcarria

SOME PRELIMINARY POINTS

IN HIS FIRST TRAVEL BOOK, CELA VISITED A SMALL, REASONABLY WELL-known area of his own country, a place that was a few hours away from Madrid. He was not, apparently, looking for anything in particular in the Alcarria district. Michael Kowalewski suggests that there are two kinds of travel account within one's homeland: the author may be "celebrating the local and unfamiliar or—in a long tradition of social exploration—exposing and investigating conditions at home that most would prefer to ignore" (p. 13). Certainly, *Viaje a la Alcarria* contains precious little material that suggests Cela's interest in "celebrating" colorful, fascinating, or impressive aspects of society in the Alcarria district. Rather, the critical consensus would be that with this work the author was simply portraying life in a small area at a time of much hardship and uncertainty.

In chapter 1 it was pointed out that in his *English Journey*, J. B. Priestley acknowledges that late 1933 was a "time of stress" in England. He goes on to add: "I know there is deep distress in the country" (pp. 61–62). Cela makes no such appraisal of the Spain of June 1946, despite the fact that economic conditions in the country would have been considerably worse than those of Priestley's England of thirteen years earlier. Thus, with reference to Spain of the mid-1940s, Paul Preston talks of "the appalling living conditions of the working class" (p. 569) and also observes that "Spanish industrial cities were flooded at this time by rural labourers fleeing the countryside" (p. 569n). Carr and Fusi Aizpurua note the domestic and industrial consequences of the shortage of electricity and also describe and account for the enfeebled state of Spanish agriculture: "By the late forties electrical power was in short supply: factories and homes suffered frequent cuts. Above all, agricultural production stagnated" (p. 50). They subsequently observe that: "Throughout the 1940s Spain was poor, an economy, in the words

of Professor Sardá, in which there was neither consumption nor production. These were the 'years of hunger'" (p. 52). Finally, with reference to the period 1939–51, Ramón Tamames states that whereas the
rest of Western Europe was aided in its postwar recovery by the Mar-
shall Plan (1948–52), Spain, on the other hand, whose request for Mar-
shall aid was rejected in 1948, "suffered a long, post-war period of
poverty."[1] Indeed, Tamames later refers to the collapse of agriculture in
the 1940s and points out that only the import of produce from Argentina managed to mitigate "the country's hunger" (p. 470).

THE PORTRAYAL OF NATURE

Although Cela would no doubt associate himself with Priestley's aim
"to report truthfully" (p. 62) what was seen, he makes no declaration
in the dedication to *Viaje a la Alcarria*, or in the text of the work, concerning the condition of contemporary Spain. Indeed, the epigraph of
the book, taken from the opening lines of one of the early poems of
the American writer, William Cullen Bryant (1794–1878), suggests that
Cela's first travel work will reveal or proclaim the writer's affinity for
Nature. Thus:

> To him who in the love of Nature holds
> Communion with her visible forms, she speaks
> A various language.

However, Cela's epigraph does not mention the title of the poem from
which these lines are taken. It is "Thanatopsis," an eighty-one line,
blank-verse poem which, as the title indicates, is a meditation on death,
although a comforting meditation. Cela slightly truncates the opening
three lines, presumably to focus on the notion of the individual com-
muning with Nature. Bryant's poem goes on to indicate the radiance of
Nature and its restorative powers and then, perhaps intriguingly for
those seeking a significant motive for Cela's trip to the Alcarria, lines
14–15 contain an invocation that, when assailed and dispirited by
thoughts of death, the individual should "Go forth, under the open sky,
and list / to Nature's teachings."[2] The poem subsequently proclaims the
solace of the fellowship that death involves and ends with the poet
counseling that death be approached with dignity, calm, and trust.
    Cela has given no indication of why he turned to this particular poem
for his epigraph or whether, for instance, he was familiar with the
American's travel writing. Bryant visited much of Europe and published the accounts of his journeys in a series of letters. Between Sep-

tember and December of 1857 he made his way through Spain, from Irún to Málaga, and there embarked for Oran. During his Spanish journey Bryant spent some time in the capital and then headed south for Aranjuez and La Mancha. So it appears that he did not, unfortunately, make the acquaintance of the Alcarria district.[3]

Regardless of the degree of Cela's familiarity with Bryant's work, the fact remains that he chose for his epigraph to *Viaje a la Alcarria* lines that signal to a reader (or censor) familiar with English that this travel book will foreground the writer's relationship with, and perception of, Nature's "visible forms."[4] So, to what extent is this the case and in what measure might other concerns surface or be alluded to during the course of this travel narrative?

With Guadalajara behind him and at last on the open road, the traveler stops for a nap. At first, though, he engages in a close-up study of some of Nature's more minuscule creatures and also takes in other, more distant features of the location and area:

Se tumba a dormir la siesta, bajo un árbol. Por la carretera pasa, de vez en cuando, alguna bicicleta o algún coche oficial. A lo lejos, sentado a la sombra de un olivo, un pastor canta. Las ovejas están apiñadas, inmóviles, muertas de calor. Echado sobre la manta, el viajero ve de cerca la vida de los insectos, que corren veloces de un lado para otro y se detienen de golpe, mientras mueven acompasadamente sus largos cuernos, delgaditos como un pelo. El campo está verde, bien cuidado, y las florecitas silvestres—las rojas amapolas, las margaritas blancas, los cardos de flor azul, los dorados botones del botón de oro—crecen a los bordes de la carretera, fuera de los sembrados. (IV, 59)

[He stretches out beneath a tree to have a siesta. From time to time a bicycle or an official car passes along the road. In the distance, sitting in the shade of an olive tree, a shepherd is singing. His sheep are huddled together, still, and dying of heat. Sprawled on his blanket, the traveler watches the insect life close up, as they scurry in all directions and suddenly stop, while rhythmically moving their long feelers, as fine as hairs. The countryside is green and well tended, and small wild flowers—red poppies, white daisies, blue-flowered thistles, and golden buttercups—are growing at the side of the road, away from the fields of crops.]

Hereafter, such descriptions of the natural environment (which often incorporate references to the appearance or intervention of human beings) are relatively infrequent and brief. For example, the following morning as the traveler makes his way from Torija to Brihuega, he notes:

A la legua larga de Torija aparecen los robles, sueltos al principio, formando manchas más tarde. Un pastor camina sin prisa detrás de las ovejas, por la ladera de una loma. No se oye más que el piar de las golondrinas y el canto de las alondras. (IV, 70)

[A good league from Torija, oak trees appear, scattered at first and later in groves. Along the side of a hillock, a shepherd walks unhurriedly behind his sheep. All that can be heard are twittering swallows and the song of the skylarks.]

And shortly after:

Dos conejos miran para el viajero, un instante, moviendo las orejas, sentados sobre el rabo, y huyen después, veloces, a esconderse detrás de unas piedras. Un águila vuela trazando círculos, no muy lejos. Una mujer, subida en un burro, se cruza con el viajero. (IV, 71)

[Two rabbits, sitting on their scuts, look at the traveler for a moment, moving their ears, and then scamper away to hide behind some rocks. Not far away, an eagle is circling in the sky. A woman riding a donkey passes the traveler, going in the opposite direction.]

A similar descriptive formula is used when, in the late afternoon of the following day, the traveler leaves Brihuega and ponders where to head for:

Por poniente cruzan, lentas, alargadas como culebrillas, unas nubecitas rojas, de bordes precisos, bien dibujados. Dicen que las nubes de color de fuego, a la puesta del sol, presagian calor para el día siguiente. El río corre rumoroso, rápido, por la vega, y a su orilla silban los pajaritos de la tarde, croan las últimas ranas de la tarde. Se está fresco, sentado al borde de la carretera, a la sombra de un olmo, después de un día caluroso en el que se han caminado algunas leguas y se ha pateado, de un lado para el otro, un pueblo grande y recién descubierto. Cruza, con su vuelo cortado, un caballito del diablo. Pasan dos chicas jóvenes subidas en un burro manso, castrado, que anda despacio, con la cabeza inclinada hacia adelante. (IV, 99)

[Some small, red clouds, elongated like snakes, with sharp, clearly defined edges, slowly make their way across the western sky. They say that when there are fire-colored clouds at sunset it means a hot day to come. The river runs swiftly, babbling, across the meadow, and at its banks the evening birds are singing and the last frogs of the day are croaking. It feels cool, sitting beside the road in the shade of an elm, after a hot day in which a few leagues have been covered and in which a large, newly discovered town has been tramped through from one end to the other. A dragonfly, with its darting flight, appears. Two young girls go by on a docile, castrated donkey that walks slowly with its head hanging forward.]

So here the focus moves from distant clouds, to the river, to the seated traveler, to the passing dragonfly, and thence to the two girls riding the donkey.

Another facet of Cela's approach in *Viaje a la Alcarria* is that he avoids panoramic descriptions of landscape and, instead, restricts his occasional bucolic scenes to what might be termed small-scale Nature. Such scenes usually come with the indication that at least part of the land is put to productive use. Sometimes, too, people are witnessed working the land. Nowhere in the narrative is there a better example of this, developed with the customary simple, uncluttered style, than at the beginning of chapter 6, as the traveler leaves Cifuentes, walking along by its river:

> Hace algo de fresco y se camina a gusto. Sobre el río se extiende una tenue cinta de niebla casi imperceptible. Vuelan los estorninos y los vencejos; una urraca blanca y negra salta de piedra en piedra mientras una alondra silba sobre los sembrados. El vientecillo de la mañana corre sobre el campo, y el aire está limpio, lúcido, transparente, diáfano.
>
> No más remontado un zopetero, Cifuentes desaparece. El camino va entre choperas aisladas, no muy tupidas. Entre el camino y el río verdean las huertas de tomates. Al otro lado, el terreno aparece otra vez seco, duro, de color pardo. En el terreno seco se ven rebaños de ovejas blancas y ovejas negras —mejor, castaño oscuro—, todas revueltas, y en el de agua se ven mujeres y niños trabajando la tierra. (IV, 119–20)

> [It is quite cool and pleasant walking along. A faint, almost imperceptible ribbon of mist hangs over the river. Starlings and swifts are flying around; a black-and-white magpie hops from stone to stone while above the fields of crops a lark sings. The light, morning wind moves across the countryside and the air is clean, clear, transparent, diaphonous.
>
> Once a slope has been climbed, Cifuentes disappears from view. The road runs between scattered and not very dense poplar groves. Separating the road from the river are green fields of tomatoes. On the other side, the land once again looks dry, hard, and drably colored. On the dry land there are herds of white sheep and black ones —in fact, dark brown— all jumbled together, and on the irrigated land women and children are working in the fields.]

In the following chapter, as the traveler makes his way to the Tetas de Viana, a rather rugged, unkempt kind of landscape is described. After a lengthy enumeration of the kinds of vegetation present, the description then dwells on the clarity of the light, the Tagus River and, finally, the reminder of human presence, this time in the form of the leprosarium. The focus of attention moves back and forth, and a keen visual awareness is maintained:

En el monte de la Dehesa la vegetación es dura, balsámica, una vegetación de espinos, de romero, de espliego, de salvia, de mejorana, de retamas, de aliagas, de matapollos, de cantueso, de jaras, de chaparros y de tomillos; una vegetación que casi no se ve, pero que marea respirarla. No hace todavía calor aunque el día se anuncia bueno. El aire es transparente. El Tajo, que de cerca es un río turbio y feo, desde lejos parece bonito, muy elegante. Viene haciendo curvas y se ve desde muy lejos, siempre rodeado de árboles. La leprosería aparece a su orilla en primer término. (IV, 142)

[On the high ground of Dehesa, the vegetation is hardy and fragrant, consisting of thorn bushes, rosemary, lavender, sage, marjoram, broom, gorse, spurge flax, Arabian lavender, rock roses, dwarf oak, and various kinds of thyme; vegetation that can hardly be seen but the smell of which causes light-headedness. Even though it promises to be a fine day, it is still not hot. The air is clear. The Tagus, which close up is a muddy, unattractive river, looks pretty and very elegant from a distance. It has many bends and can be seen from a long way off, always lined with trees. The leprosarium is on one of its banks, in the foreground.]

Shortly thereafter, a brief descriptive passage reveals a different kind of picture, one that seems to aim for action and effect, and which presents the traveler as both spectator and participant:

Marchando por la Entrepeña el viajero ve una hermosa decoración, una decoración teatral de grandes piedras abruptas y peladas y de árboles muertos, partidos por el rayo. Una rapiña vuela con un gazapo entre las garras. Un lagarto inmenso, un lagarto verde, amarillo y rojo, sale huyendo desde los mismos pies del viajero. (IV, 143)

[Walking through the Entrepeña, the traveler witnesses a beautiful scene, a theater set with great, sheer, bare stones and dead trees, cleft by lightning. A bird of prey flies by with a young rabbit in its claws. A huge lizard, a green, yellow, and red lizard flees from the very feet of the traveler.]

Yet this kind of desolately dramatic picture is altogether untypical of the twenty or so brief descriptions of the natural (or seminatural) physical environment found in *Viaje a la Alcarria*. But what needs to be borne in mind here is that the trip to the Tetas de Viana involves the traveler's only encounter in the Alcarria district with the wilderness type of landscape. Elsewhere, the descriptions of the natural environment are in keeping with the kind of small-scale, charming scenes witnessed from the side of a road or the banks of a river: fields, trees, flora, reptiles, insects, and so on, and frequently with scudding or wispy clouds surmounting the picture.

All in all, the descriptions of Nature to be found in *Viaje a la Alcarria* are infrequent and invariably brief, ranging from a couple of lines to eight or ten at the most. They also tend to focus on what is close by or in the middle distance. Although the traveler occasionally gazes afar, to a starry sky, the clouds, or distant mountains, he soon shortens his perspective so as to focus on more immediate and less majestic presences. In fact, most of the descriptions of Nature in the account are cozy and even intimate, and seem to be in proportion to the modest temporal and geographical scope of the work as a whole. Overall, it would appear that Cela has the eye and approach of a miniaturist rather than the soul or technique of a traveler engaging in profound and extensive communion with Nature.

THE HUMAN IMPRINT AND PRESENCE

In view of the author's comments on his approach to travel writing, it is hardly surprising that *Viaje a la Alcarria* should reveal an interest in physical and human geography that easily outweighs the narrative's limited treatment of what might be termed the manifestations and delights of Nature. The traveler rarely abandons the beaten track and the account becomes an almost constant reminder of the presence of the road: the road as a means of getting from one village or town to the next, as the location for company or communication with another wayfarer, as a vantage point from which to see and describe others going their way or doing their work, or as a place from which to take in surroundings or more distant sights. Rivers may sometimes accompany roads or come into view, but they are simply presented as part of the setting rather than as modes of communication between one place and another.

Occasionally, though, the narrator becomes somewhat carried away with the geography of road networks and river systems, lapsing into what is at best a kind of mechanical verbal mapping, and at worst a guidebook style:

> El camino va, desde la salida de La Puerta, con el Solana a la izquierda; a la altura de Cereceda, que queda detrás de la Peña del Tornero, se cruza un puentecillo y el río sigue paralelo hasta que cae en el Tajo, dejando a Mantiel al sur, a una legua de Cereceda, otra de Chillarón del Rey y dos de Alique y de Hontanillas, todo por sendas de herradura. (IV, 154)

> [After leaving La Puerta, the road has the Solana River to its left. Opposite Cereceda, which is behind the Tornero crag, one crosses a small bridge and the river stays parallel to the road until it joins the Tagus, with Mantiel to the south, a league from Cereceda, Chillarón del Rey is a league farther on,

and two more leagues beyond are Alique and Hontanillas, all reached by bridle paths.]

Or, shortly after, and this time with a little more variation in perspective:

> Al borde del camino se ven zarzales, matas de espino y flores de cornicabra. Por el sur aparece ahora el monte Aleja y por el norte el terreno llamado de la Nava. Poco después se cruza el Tajo y se camina a su orilla durante media hora. Al cabo de este tiempo sale de la carretera un ramal que va a Durón y a Budia y que llega, más arriba, hasta Brihuega e incluso sale, más arriba todavía, a la carretera general de Zaragoza. Siguiendo la orilla del Tajo va el camino de Sacedón, con un ramal a Pareja, a orillas del arroyo Empolveda [*sic*]. (IV, 154–55)

> [At the side of the road there are brambles, clumps of hawthorn, and flowers of the wild fig tree. To the south, Mount Aleja can now be seen and to the north the land called the Nava. Shortly after, one crosses the Tagus and walks along its bank for half an hour. After this time, a road branches off the highway and goes to Durón and Budia, and farther up goes as far as Brihuega, and even farther on joins the main road to Zaragoza. Continuing alongside the Tagus, the road goes to Sacedón, with a turn-off to Pareja, on the banks of the Ompolveda.]

However, the sense of geography that Cela reveals in *Viaje a la Alcarria* is not solely concerned with road networks, river systems, and other features of the natural landscape such as nearby trees, surrounding crags, or distant hills. Throughout the account of the Alcarria trip, there is a constant awareness of the human imprint on the countryside that goes beyond descriptions of the presence and destinations of roads and tracks. The traveler is often concerned with the use to which land is put and the reader is frequently presented with a picture of people working that land or on their way to tend it. In other words, the human and economic geography of the area is noticed and indicated. During the traveler's train journey attention is drawn to crops growing on the outskirts of the capital, to the young wheat growing near San Fernando de Jarama, and to the plowing taking place at Azuqueca. But obviously, signs of agricultural activity do not necessarily indicate productive land, nor an adequately fed society, and it is only with the traveler's arrival in the Alcarria district and contact with the local people, combined with the closer narrative view of the landscape, that the travel book reveals any sense of the condition and activities of the *alcarreños*.

In chapter 2, making his way through the gloomy streets of central Madrid, the traveler mused on the probable contrasting fortunes of the sleeping residents of the shuttered houses. Subsequently, he saw some graphic indications of urban hardship. Yet the scenes in the train and the signs of activity along the route to Guadalajara give no impression that such distress is widespread. Indeed, this particular section of the narrative, with its presentation of people engaging in work or in leisure pursuits and generally going about their business, reveals a largely positive view of social conditions and activities. However, once the traveler reaches the Alcarria district, the poorer towns, villages, and inhabitants are contrasted with the more comfortable or even prosperous situations of places and people in the same area.

When he first sets foot in the Alcarria, there are indications of austerity and shortages that inconvenience the traveler, or simply catch his attention. Thus, he finds that there is no red wine available in Taracena and also reveals that the *parador* in Torija has no wine at all: it has to be sent for. Indeed, at the *parador*, where the traveler spends his first night on the road, it transpires that the availability of electricity is restricted to certain periods of the day, and that even when the current is flowing it is feeble and largely useless, gaining no adequate strength until the end of the night (IV, 68).

However, shortages of wine and an unreliable electricity supply are, in most respects, secondary concerns in times of hardship. The availability of food must be a principal measure of comfort in any society and, from time to time, Cela indicates the lack of adequate provisions in some places. So, for example, there appears to be precious little food in La Puerta (IV, 149), while in the area around Casasana the crop yield is varied but small (IV, 193). However, the traveler generally finds food and often eats well. But he does, of course, have the wherewithal to pay for his meals. Regardless of this, it is clearly indicated in *Viaje a la Alcarria* that some parts of the district offer, at best, a precarious existence. Indeed, from time to time the traveler is informed by the people he meets of the contrasting fortunes of the locals. So, the carter from La Puerta tells him:

> —En Budia encontrará usted de todo; todos estos pueblos son muy pobres; aquí no hay más que para los que estamos, y no crea usted que sobra. Budia es un pueblo muy rico; allí el que más y el que menos maneja sus cuartos.
> — ¿Y Cereceda?
> —Como nosotros; Cereceda es también muy pobre. (IV, 153–54)

> ["You'll find everything you want in Budia. All these villages are very poor; here there's only just enough for those of us who live here. Believe me, there's nothing to spare. Budia is a very rich village; there every single inhabitant looks after his money."

"And Cereceda?"
"Like us, Cereceda's also very poor."]

On other occasions, it is the traveler who makes the observation or allusion: for example, describing El Olivar as "un pueblo miserable" [a wretched village] (IV, 165); pointing out that Alhóndiga is an adobe village (IV, 219); mentioning the poorly dressed girls in Casasana (IV, 191), and the ramshackle (but very clean) schoolhouse in the same place (IV, 194).

Whatever the state of people and places, though, the determining factor is always seen to be the productivity of the land. Time and again, the contrast is made between prosperous towns and villages in fertile areas and, nearby, unproductive terrain with settlements that show obvious signs of want. The lie of the land is what matters here, as is guessed by the traveler and explained to him by the shepherd he comes across near El Olivar:

El viajero hace como que no oye y se pone a hablar de lo bueno que debe ser el terreno de orillas del río.
—Sí, señor, ¡ya lo creo! Ese terreno sí que es bueno; aquí, ¿sabe usted?, lo pobre es la sierra; en cuanto que usted baja hasta el llano ya empieza a encontrarse un terreno muy alegre, muy agradecido. (IV, 167)

[The traveler pretends he does not hear and starts talking about how good the land down by the river must be.
"Yes, indeed! That land's good; but here, up in the hills, it's very poor. As soon as you go down to the plain you start to find some really lovely, productive land."]

In fact, throughout *Viaje a la Alcarria* there are many indications that poverty is the plight of the unfortunate minority and certainly not the norm in this society. For example, on the third day of the trip, when the traveler enters Cifuentes, it is described as "un pueblo hermoso, alegre, con mucha agua, con mujeres de ojos negros y profundos, con comercios bien surtidos" [a fine, cheerful town, with plenty of water, well-stocked shops, and women with deep, black eyes] (IV, 107). Shortly after, reference is made to the green, cultivated land by the river, thereby accounting for and complementing the cheerful and prosperous character of the town that is regarded as the capital of the Alcarria (IV, 109). The following day, as the traveler passes through Gárgoles, the narrative contains a succint observation that sums up the town's business and the character of its inhabitants: "Gárgoles es un pueblo huertano, con el terreno bien trabajado y la gente aplicada a su labor" [Gárgoles is an agricultural town, with well-cultivated land and hard-

working people] (IV, 127). And while Gárgoles is presented as a relatively prosperous place, when the traveler moves on to Trillo he finds
that the land there is even better for agriculture.

By this midway stage in the account, Cela has established a picture
of the Alcarria as an area of contrasting social and economic fortunes.
Hereafter, the traveler finds ample indications of this dichotomy: prosperous Budia, as was mentioned earlier, is apparently surrounded by
poor villages; the soil around Casasana requires back-breaking effort if
the locals are to eke out an existence; the people of Córcoles, though,
are enjoying a good standard of living. Similarly, the land around
Sacedón is busy and productive, and the well-being of the town is contrasted with the misfortune of other places and gratefully acknowledged
by one of the locals:

> — ¡Aquí sí que hay riqueza!
> — Sí, eso parece.
> — ¡Vaya si la hay! En Sacedón no es como en otros pueblos, aquí, quién
> más quién menos, todos se van a dormir con la panza llena. (IV, 204)

> ["Things are certainly prosperous here!"
> "It looks like it."
> "Really prosperous! Sacedón isn't like other places; here everybody goes
> to bed with a full belly."]

Cela's social and economic "geography" of the Alcarria, then, shows
areas of plenty and others of want. The district is presented largely in
terms of fertile, low-lying tracts of land supporting an industrious, comfortable population, while elsewhere, stretches of unproductive terrain
are inhabited by people who are required to graft if they are to maintain
some kind of modest subsistence or even stave off hunger. Thus, the
author provides a balanced account of how the inhabitants of the Alcarria were faring in June 1946 and certainly avoids suggesting that the
area was either largely poor or predominantly rich. And while Arturo
Barea at first acknowledges this even-handed approach in the travel
book, he later appears to allow his political leanings to influence his
assessment of the social content of the work when he talks of "a starving
district" (p.15). Even more surprising, though, is Robert Kirsner's assertion that "disorder reigns in La Alcarria."[5] Indeed, there is sufficient
evidence in the text to indicate that Cela is describing a generally well
organized system of agricultural production that is in the care of an orderly, busy workforce. Finally, for one other typical comment on the
apparent social conditions of the *alcarreños*, it is worth recalling Paul
Ilie's reference to "the grinding poverty of rural life" (p. 256).

I have returned to some of these assessments of the socioeconomic thrust of *Viaje a la Alcarria* in order to illustrate the way in which most critics have imposed a reading on the work that seems to stem from the following perception: the 1940s were years of hardship in Spain (and they certainly were for many), therefore Cela's book must be a grim reflection of that hardship. Such an assessment or interpretation is not supported by the evidence of the text. It would, for example, be equally inaccurate to claim that *La colmena* shows that the inhabitants of 1943 Madrid were poverty-stricken. Indeed, what that novel and *Viaje a la Alcarria* have in common is that both works suggest the contrasting fortunes of a group of inhabitants of a particular place. But whereas in *La colmena* there are frequent, close-up views of those in need as well as those living in comfort, in *Viaje a la Alcarria* the technique is rather different. Here, the traveler usually finds food, and often eats well. A good number of other people encountered in the work also seem to be eating adequately or even well. On the other hand, there are occasional indications of deprivation and also mentions of shortages.[6] But the principal difference of presentation of the "two societies" revealed in *La colmena* and *Viaje a la Alcarria* is that whereas in the novel Cela often dwells on hardship, in the travel account his approach is simply to touch on it from time to time.

CONTACTS AND COMPANIONSHIP

Cela's first travel book, though, is far from being just a series of observations on the social and economic conditions of a group of country dwellers and a portrayal of the physical features of the Alcarria. The narrative also keeps a constant focus on the traveler himself. Throughout the work he is gradually developed as an individual who expresses curiosity and concern and who often reveals a pleasure-loving streak. He enjoys looking at young women, meeting and talking with local "characters," and communicating with ordinary folk, young and old. The traveler also derives obvious pleasure from moments or periods of companionship that occur during the course of his journey. In other words, he is far from being some kind of wandering automaton who merely witness and records scenes and incidents, and he is certainly not a loner jealously protecting his solitude.

The traveler's rapid reversal of his initial planning decision to avoid cities and his determination, instead, to make his way through them at a time when the local young ladies should be out taking a stroll, suggests less the dedication of a serious wayfarer than the cheerful confidence of a young man in his prime. He enjoys watching the girls who

pass by as he makes his way to Taracena (1V, 59), while his verbal encounter in Brihuega with the attractive and apparently coquettish Mer-
che suggests an approach on his part and an awareness on hers (IV,
77). A little later, the traveler passes some cheerful, thigh-slapping
young females and subsequently he pauses to watch and muse on a
group of girls doing the washing. In fact, it is the same time of day, mid-
afternoon, that in the opening chapter the traveler-to-be had associated
with young ladies taking the air. Here, although the social class involved and the activity are different, the traveler's sentimental commitment is undiminished:

> El sol está en la media tarde. Hay un momento en que el viajero ve hermosas
> a todas las mujeres. Se sienta sobre una piedra y mira, lleno el corazón de
> pesar, para un grupo de ocho o diez muchachas que lavan la ropa. (IV, 79)

> [The mid-afternoon sun is shining. At certain times the traveler regards all
> women as beautiful. He sits on a stone and, with a rueful heart, looks over
> at a group of eight or ten girls washing clothes.]

Then, as the traveler gazes for the last time at the clothes-washing girls,
he moves off, resigned to his role as spectator. Shortly after, he comments to a local that there are plenty of attractive young women in the
town (IV, 81), while a few days later, in Pareja, he notes that *all* the
women there are very pretty (IV, 178).

Yet good-looking females do not always inspire such an enthusiastic
response, and an encounter shortly before the traveler enters Brihuega
provokes, instead, a sense of drama and mystery:

> Una mujer, subida en un burro, se cruza con el viajero. El viajero la saluda,
> y la mujer ni le mira ni le contesta. Es una mujer joven, pálida y hermosa,
> vestida de luto, con un pañuelo sobre la cabeza y unos grandes, profundos
> ojos negros. El viajero se vuelve. La mujer va inmóvil, dejándose llevar del
> trote del burro entero, poderoso. Podría pensarse que es una muerta sin
> compañía, que va sola a enterrarse, camino del cementerio. (IV, 71)

> [A woman riding a donkey, passes the traveler going in the opposite direc-
> tion. The traveler greets her, but she does not look at him or answer. She is
> young, pale, and beautiful, and dressed in mourning, with a scarf over her
> head and great, deep, black eyes. The traveler turns around. The woman
> moves away, motionless, carried forward by the sturdy, uncastrated don-
> key's trot. It almost seems as if she is a solitary, dead woman, on her way to
> the cemetery to bury herself.]

During his trip around the Alcarria, then, the traveler is not simply a
detached recorder of what he sees: he has varying interests in the inhab-

itants of the district and, occasionally, seeks to create some dramatic focus for the reader. Furthermore, from time to time he strikes up relationships that result in company for him and even companionship. Certainly, the traveler by no means strives for the solitude suggested by Cela as one of his principal reasons for taking to the road. Indeed, what needs to be acknowledged at this stage is that Cela was, in fact, accompanied during his trip to the Alcarria.

The title page of the first edition of the travel book states that the photographs contained in the work (fifty black-and-white plates) were taken by Karl Wlasak, and in a note to the *Obra completa* edition of *Viaje a la Alcarria* Cela mentions that he traveled with Wlasak and Conchita Stichaner (IV, 171). This does, of course, raise some fundamental issues regarding the content and authenticity of the narrative. For a start, there is no mention in the text that Cela had company with him and there are no clues to this, apart from the photographs in the first edition and the title-page mention of the photographer. Subsequent editions carried neither these photographs nor, understandably, the acknowledgment and so, until the revealing note in the 1965 edition, most readers would have assumed that Cela made his journey unaccompanied.

The narrative unambiguously indicates that the traveler usually eats, beds down, and travels around on his own, except when he finds a traveling companion. Nobody the traveler comes across suggests that he is in company and nor does he proffer this information. Furthermore, the reader privy to the disclosure in the 1965 footnote might reasonably wonder whether Cela's traveling companions followed the whole of the route, whether they slept under the stars with him when he slept out, whether they were locked up with him when he was detained, and so on.[7] Yet, setting aside these questions, the unavoidable and significant point is that in his narrated version of the trip Cela has chosen not to reveal what is an important factual aspect of his journey and has, instead, employed the narrative device of presenting a solitary traveler. And it is this apparently lone figure who makes and carries the contact with the various people he encounters in the course of his visit to the Alcarria.

In much of the early part of the account, the solitude of the traveler is emphasized: he is alone in his study and is a solitary spectator as he makes his way through the city to the Atocha station. Aboard the train, though, he becomes increasingly aware of those around him and soon partakes in the small talk and activity generated by his fellow travelers. However, it is not until the traveler has left Guadalajara and found himself on the open road that he begins to indicate the simple pleasure to be derived from even the briefest of company or even the slightest indications of companionship. His contact and conversation with the young, redheaded boy serve as a prelude to a series of largely pleasurable encounters and sympathetic companions that mark the trip around the Alcarria. Thus, when the carter, Martín Díaz, and the traveler meet on the road to Torija they begin with a comradely drink and a smoke, and subsequently Díaz offers to share his food (IV, 62–63). A little later, when the pair part company in Torija, the traveler watches the carter head for Trijueque with a just hint of affection (IV, 66).

But it is of course with the old man, Jesús, and his ancient donkey, Gorrión, that the traveler exhibits the most striking example of companionship to be found in *Viaje a la Alcarria*. At first impressed by the poor yet dignified bearing of Jesús, the traveler is also intrigued by this fellow wanderer and muses on him as one of a breed, crisscrossing the countryside in the Brihuega area (IV, 94–95). However, admiration and curiosity are soon transformed into a bond when the old man and the traveler come across each other a little later and together head for Cifuentes. The fact that the traveler's heart leaps when he catches sight of Jesús and his donkey is a clear indication of his strength of feeling and desire for his company (IV, 101). They share a smoke and a drink, and soon bed down in the open, side by side and under the traveler's blanket. (One might be excused for wondering, at this point, where Stichaner and Wlasak were.) The old man and the traveler regard sharing each other's body warmth under a blanket as confirmation of the bond of friendship and by the time the two wayfarers reach Cifuentes they have several times been referred to as friends. In Cifuentes the traveler presents the donkey with a saddlecloth and the traveler gives public acknowledgment of the relationship between himself and the old fellow when, out of earshot of Jesús, he describes him as "un antiguo amigo mío" [an old friend of mine] (IV, 113).

Another indication of the traveler's feeling for his companion comes when the former hesitates for a moment when Jesús asks him if he will be moving on from Cifuentes. Subsequently, when the traveler bids him farewell there is an unmistakable note of sadness (IV, 113). Hereafter, although the traveler occasionally makes his way in company, the fraternal and emotional chord struck by his brief period with Jesús is not repeated in the remainder of the narrative. The day after their parting, as he makes his way along the road to Gárgoles, he journeys for a while with a rather dotty and slightly menacing peddler, and later has a brief encounter with a sympathetic shepherd, Roque. But on the other hand, when young Quico takes the traveler to the Tetas de Viana there is little sense of fellowship revealed between the two: they tend to communicate as guide and visitor, and when Quico's task is safely accomplished the traveler bids him farewell in a businesslike manner (IV, 148).

There remain two other characters with whom the traveler does strike an obvious rapport: Martín, the salesman, and the Mayor of Pastrana. The young, affable Martín, whom the traveler had first encountered in Trillo, helps the wayfarer find food and a bed in Budia, and the same again in Sacedón, where the two men continue to develop a certain jovial and youthful camaraderie. Then, in the final stage of the journey, when the traveler arrives at Pastrana, he and the local mayor apparently experience an immediate, mutual affinity: "Al cabo de un rato de conversación, se dan cuenta de que son amigos" [After a brief conversation, they realize that they are friends] (IV, 229). This is soon followed by an explanation, obviously given with hindsight, of the appeal of the man who, in the final phase of the Alcarria trip, takes the traveler under his wing, gives him his time and hospitality—and in some ways transforms the visitor into a tourist:

> Don Mónico es un hombre inteligente y cordial, más bien grueso, algo bajo, lector empedernido, conversador ameno y según propia confesión, poco aficionado a escribir cartas. Don Mónico es un alcalde antiguo, que rige el pueblo en padre de familia y que tiene un sentido clásico y práctico de la hospitalidad y de la autoridad. (IV, 229)

> [Don Mónico is an intelligent, friendly man, rather stout, shortish, an avid reader, a good conversationalist and, by his own admission, not very fond of writing letters. Don Mónico is a mayor of the old school, who runs the town like a father of the family and who has an old-fashioned and practical sense of hospitality and authority.]

Thus, having left the bosom of his family when he set out on his trip, the traveler completes the journey as very much the welcome guest of the dignitaries of the community of Pastrana. In between, the narrative presents the traveler making a variety of social contacts and with varying degrees of intimacy. However, only occasionally does it show him experiencing the solitude that Cela gives as one of his reasons for taking to the open road. Indeed, *Viaje a la Alcarria* reveals at least as much interest in people as it does in place. The author shows examples of the destitute, the demented, the physically sick, the eccentric, as well as of the fortunate, the healthy, the friendly, and the well adjusted. Collectively, the narrative reveals the poor, the comfortably off, people working the land, or simply those going about their daily routine. And although some unpleasant characters and incidents do, from time to time, inject a few disturbing moments into the account, the overall picture that emerges is one of a society in which people are generally inoffensive and, quite often, affable and helpful.

EXPRESSIONS OF THE PAST

A noticeable feature of Cela's first travel book is that the account of the trip to the Alcarria pays little attention to the monuments of the past, historical buildings, be they in the countryside or in the town. In his essay "Notas del vago estío" [Notes of a Wandering Summer], in which Ortega y Gasset describes a car journey he made from Madrid to Spain's northern coast in the late summer of 1925, the philosopher observes:

> Landscape by itself, without any buildings, is mere geology. The township or village is too human; I would call it too civil, or artificial. The cathedral and the castle, on the other hand, are both Nature and history. They resemble natural outgrowths from the rocky bed of the earth and, at the same time, their deliberate lines possess a certain human meaning. Thanks to them, the landscape is intensified and is transformed into a setting. Stonework, without ceasing to be stone, is laden with electric, spiritual drama.[8]

However, when it comes to venerable piles in *Viaje a la Alcarria* what emerges is that Cela rarely finds time for the description of the relics of past ages and only occasionally focuses on the human associations of historic buildings.

In effect, the relatively few references that are made to architectural features of the Alcarria indicate that while an old building might catch the passing traveler's eye, it rarely arouses his interest. Indeed, when he does come across some ancient monument, the traveler often makes a point of rapidly switching his attention to far less imposing sights. This technique is illustrated early in the narrative, in Guadalajara, when the sorry state of the palace of the Duque del Infantado is noted, regretted, its former splendor acknowledged, its size commented on (all in three lines), and this is immediately supplanted by the picture of a cheerful simpleton passing by. Later, another unexpected juxtaposition, of an altogether different kind, occurs when the traveler enters Torija:

> Desde esta entrada tiene un gran aspecto, con su castillo y la torre cuadrada de la iglesia. Desde la pared de una casa, un letrero advierte: A Algora, 39 kilómetros. A Zaragoza, 248. Es un letrero azul con grandes letras en blanco. (IV, 65)

> [From this way into the town, it looks wonderful, with its castle and the square tower of the church. From the wall of a house a sign advises: To Algora, 39 kilometers. To Zaragoza, 248. It is a blue sign with large, white letters.]

Thus one sight or detail, and perhaps the anaphora emphasizes this, seems to be just as important as another. And when, approaching Brihuega, the traveler stops at what he mistakenly takes to be the Ibarra Palace, the focus soon switches from the tumbledown building to the overgrown gardens and a pair of animals there:

El palacio de Ibarra es un caserón semiderruido, con un jardín abandonado, lleno de encanto; parece un bailarín rendido, cortesano y enfermo, respirando el aire saludable de los campesinos. El jardín está ahogado por la maleza. Una cabra atada a una cuerda dormita, rumiando, tumbada al sol, y un asnillo peludo retoza coceando al aire como un loco. (IV, 71)

[The Ibarra Palace is a semi-derelict, old house, with an abandoned garden full of charm; it resembles an exhausted ballet dancer, refined and ailing, breathing the healthy air of the countryside. The garden is overgrown with weeds. A goat, tied with a rope, is dozing, chewing away, stretched out in the sun, and a small, shaggy donkey is frisking around, kicking the air like a maniac.]

Brihuega itself, on the other hand, presents a far more imposing and enduring sight than the nearby palace: "Brihuega tiene muy buen aire, con sus murallas y la vieja fábrica de paños, grande y redonda como una plaza de toros. . . . Parece una ciudad antigua, con mucha piedra, con casas bien construidas y árboles corpulentos" [Brihuega is very impressive, with its ramparts and the old textile factory, which is big and round, like a bullring. . . . It looks like an old city, with lots of stonework, well-built houses, and massive trees] (IV, 73). Hereafter, though, and until the traveler reaches Pastrana, there are just sporadic references to dilapidated buildings that he comes across. In these he shows only the slightest of interest.

For most of the narrative it is clear that, with very few exceptions, the traveler regards old buildings as simply unexciting aspects of the landscape or, close up, as backdrops for human or other animal activity, or even sites revealing the relentless triumph of rampant Nature. Little concern is shown for the history or artistic merit of such monuments. Indeed, this appears to be confirmed as the traveler's bus nears Tendilla and he spots what are described as "unas ruinas corrientes" [some run-of-the-mill ruins]. This dismissal is then immediately followed by the observation that "el viajero no sabe si serán históricas, lo que sí sabe es que le parecieron poco interesantes" [the traveler does not know if they are historic, but what he does know is that they did not look very interesting] (IV, 220). Yet, the confession of such sentiments, unsurprising in view of the traveler's previous attitude to ancient stones, will come to be seen as something of an ironic prelude to the final chapter of *Viaje a la Alcarria*, where, for the first time in the account, he takes an extensive and involved interest in a small town and its history.

Cela spent the last two nights of his Alcarria trip in Pastrana. Arriving at nightfall, he decided to postpone his exploration of the place until the following morning. Then, when he set foot in the Plaza de la Hora the next day, the reader is informed that "la primera sensación que tuvo fue la de encontrarse en una ciudad medieval" [the first sensation that he experienced was that of finding himself in a medieval city] (IV, 231). It is tempting to see this use of a verb in the preterite, in a work that is almost completely composed in the present tense and largely concerned with immediate impressions, as signaling the beginning of the traveler's first real journey into the past. However, it should be borne in mind that the paragraph before, describing the conversation of the previous evening, as well as most of the second half of the preceding chapter, had already made extensive use of past tenses. In any case, this late deviation from present-tense narration could indicate no more than a lapse provoked by the hasty composition of the second half of the book.

In Pastrana, the traveler is confronted by a blend of decaying grandeur, neglect, local and national vandalism, and also by what he sees as the dangers of an obsession with past glories. On the first day of his trip, he had, in passing, expressed his regret at the sorry state of the palace of the Duque del Infantado in Guadalajara. Now in Pastrana and nearing the end of his journey, the traveler is saddened by the condition of the Ducal Palace, where the Princess of Eboli was imprisoned and later died. Yet here, where the final act of one of the most bizarre episodes in Spanish political history took place, what is brought to the attention of the reader is not a historical drama but how the rather prosaic intrusion of the State and the depredations of the local rustics have taken their toll on this site:

El palacio da pena verlo. La fachada aún se conserva, más o menos, pero por dentro está hecho una ruina. En la habitación donde murió la Eboli—una celda con una artística reja, situada en la planta principal, en el ala derecha del edificio—sentó sus reales el Servicio Nacional del Trigo; en el suelo se ven montones de cereal y una báscula para pesar los sacos. La habitación tiene un friso de azulejos bellísimos, de históricos azulejos que vieron morir a la princesa, pero ya faltan muchos y cada día que pase faltarán más; los arrieros y los campesinos, en las largas esperas para presentar las declaraciones juradas, se entretienen en despegarlos con la navaja. (IV, 231–32).

[The palace is a very sad sight. The façade is still intact, more or less, but inside everything is in ruins. In the room where Eboli died—a cell with an ornate grille, located on the first floor, in the right wing of the building—the National Wheat Service has set up its office; there are piles of cereal on the floor and scales for weighing the sacks. The room has a wainscot of beautiful tiles, of historic tiles that witnessed the death of the princess, but now a lot of them are missing and with each passing day more will disappear; during their lengthy waits to present sworn declarations, the muleteers and the peasants entertain themselves by prising them loose with their knives.]

In many ways, this description of the neglect and abuse of a site of historical and artistic importance echoes Pardo Bazán's sorry account, in 1891, of the state of Guadalajara's Capilla de los Urbinas. Having experienced the splendor of the palace of the Duque del Infantado, the author of *Los Pazos de Ulloa* [The Manor of Ulloa] was in for a rude shock when she arrived at the chapel of the Urbina family:

> From the palace we went up to the castle, but not without first stopping at the chapel of the Urbinas, a little architectural delight that is now unfortunately used as a store for carts and possibly as a stable. Cobwebs cover at will the delicate stucco decorations and stretch their dusty curtain over the frescoes, while outside, one of the small turrets which form part of the original Mudejar architecture has collapsed. On the ground, through the straw, mud, and rubbish, the coat of arms of the Urbinas, an oak tree, can still be seen, embossed on a tombstone.[9]

Cela, for his part, sheds his customary detachment and becomes indignant when he considers the plight of the palace in Pastrana:

> El viajero no sabe de quién será hoy este palacio—unos le dicen que de la familia de los duques, otros que del Estado, otros que de los jesuitas—, pero piensa que será de alguien que debe tener escasa simpatía por Pastrana, por el palacio, por la Eboli o por todos juntos. (IV, 232)

> [The traveler does not know who owns this palace nowadays—some say the family of the Dukes, others the State, others the Jesuits—but he thinks that it must belong to someone who has precious little fondness for Pastrana, for the palace, for the Princess of Eboli, or for the whole lot of them.]

Furthermore, his response to the state of the Ducal Palace marks the beginning of a series of reflections in which the traveler reveals an outspoken impatience with current attitudes and practices. With regard to Pastrana's famous fifteenth-century tapestries, which had been removed to Madrid, apparently for safekeeping, and which had remained in the capital despite the protestations of the townsfolk,[10] the traveler voices a protest that includes unmistakable anticentralist sentiments:

> El viajero piensa que este es un pleito en el que nadie le ha llamado, pero piensa también que con esto de meter todas las cosas de mérito en los

museos de Madrid, se está matando a la provincia que, en definitiva, es el país. (IV, 233)

[The traveler thinks that this is really none of his affair, but he also thinks that this business of putting everything worthwhile in the Madrid museums is killing the provinces which, in the end, are the country.]

But the provinces losing their artistic treasures was not, seemingly, a new problem or issue. In her essay "El viaje por España" [Traveling around Spain] (1895), Pardo Bazán had also expressed concern at the vast amount of the country's art that ended up in the antique shops, private collections, and aristocratic residences of Madrid. She suggested that one might imagine that "in the rest of Spain there will be hardly anything left worth seeing, for everything will have been mopped up, removed and exploited for the benefit of the capital."[11] A little later she makes the point that, for aesthetic reasons, works of art are best left in the environment in which and for which they were produced, and the author goes on to emphasize that such artifacts are seen at their finest "in their natural setting, against the background that best suits them" (p. 91). Cela's rationale, however, is somewhat different: perhaps less aesthetic and possibly more political. Thus, he continues with his protest:

Las cosas están siempre mejor un poco revueltas, un poco en desorden; el frío orden administrativo de los museos, de los ficheros, de la estadística y de los cementerios, es un orden inhumano, un orden antinatural; es, en definitiva, un desorden. El orden es el de la naturaleza, que todavía no ha dado dos árboles o dos montes o dos caballos iguales. (IV, 233)

[Things are always best a little jumbled up, in a bit of disorder; the cold, administrative order of museums, of filing cabinets, of statistics, and cemeteries, is an inhuman, anti-natural order; it is, in short, disorder. Order is what is provided by Nature, which has yet to create two identical trees, hills, or horses.]

Yet the suggestion that things are best left as they were and where they were, free from the order imposed by categorization and relocation is soon tested when the Convento del Carmen, now a Franciscan house, is visited. The friar who shows the traveler around admits that the natural history museum there is in disarray and lays the blame for this on the actions of the communists during the civil war. At which the visitor notes to himself that seven years have passed since the end of the conflict. And when he enters the dusty, disorganized museum the traveler pointedly observes:

Es una tristeza, pero una tristeza que, probablemente, se podría arreglar en un mes metiendo allí a un perito que fuese colocando las cosas en su sitio, y a una criada con una escoba en la mano. (IV, 238)

[It is a sad mess, but a mess that could probably be sorted out in a month if they brought in an expert to put things where they belong and a maid with a broom.]

That morning, when the traveler first set foot in the Plaza de la Hora, he felt as if he were in a medieval city. During the course of the same day he had become increasingly aware of the presence and weight of Pastrana's past and its ecclesiastical tradition. By the end of the visit to the Franciscan monastery, what had become abundantly clear to the visitor was the way in which, in this town, the burden of the past had diverted the attention of the people and sapped their will to deal with day-to-day needs. Having by this stage of the narrative clearly cast off the self-imposed shackle of being a neutral observer, the traveler quotes the words of Eustoquio García Merchante, which lament the lost, glorious, martial past of Pastrana. However, he rejects the erstwhile parish priest's hyperbole and nostalgia. In so doing, he responds in a measured way with regard to the situation of Pastrana, and somewhat more forcefully (and daringly, in view of the regime's promotion of the glories of the Golden Age) with respect to Spain as a whole:

El viajero cree que don Eustoquio exagera. Pastrana, sin vigías, ni aires marciales, ni espíritu guerrero, ni Edad Media, es una ciudad como todas las ciudades, bella como pocas, y que sube y baja, crece o se depaupera, según los hados se le muestren propicios o se le vuelvan de espaldas. En Pastrana podría encontrarse quizás la clave de algo que sucede en España con más frecuencia de la necesaria. El pasado esplendor agobia y, para colmo, agosta las voluntades; y sin voluntad, a lo que se ve, y dedicándose a contemplar las pretéritas grandezas, mal se atiende al problema de todos los días. Con la panza vacía y la cabeza poblada de dorados recuerdos, los dorados recuerdos se van cada vez más lejos y al final, y sin que nadie llegue a confesárselo, ya se duda hasta de que hayan sido ciertos alguna vez, ya son como un caritativo e inútil valor entendido. (IV, 239)

[The traveler believes that Don Eustoquio is exaggerating. Pastrana, without its watchtowers, military airs, warrior spirit, and Middle Ages, is a city just like any other; more beautiful than most and which rises and falls, grows or withers, depending on whether the Fates are kind to it or turn their back on it. Perhaps there can be found in Pastrana the key to something that is happening in Spain more often than it should. The glories of the past weigh heavy and, in the end, sap the will of the people; and without will, so it would seem, they just concern themselves with past grandeur and fail to address present-day problems. When your belly is empty but your head is full of golden memories, the golden memories become increasingly distant and, in the end, without anyone admitting it, you even doubt their validity; yet they remain a comforting and useless token.]

REFLECTIONS OF THE PRESENT?

Until the final chapter of *Viaje a la Alcarria,* the narrator-protagonist maintains an almost total, studied detachment in the face of a number of strange or unpleasant encounters and sights on the journey. It is left to the reader to assess implications or draw conclusions. Such a procedure allows for the reader's response to, for example, indications of hardship in Madrid or in the Alcarria, the assault on the beggar at the Alcalá de Henares rail station and the mirth that this provokes, or the schoolgirl in Casasana who learns by rote and has no idea of the meaning of the words she spouts. In this last instance the traveler could be exposing poor educational practice or possibly alluding to something rather more sinister: political propaganda masquerading as education. On the other hand, the indications of people working in fields, or coming from or going to their work, or otherwise going about their business seem to suggest an industrious, responsible, and orderly society— which, of course, has room for a few eccentrics or characters who choose to live on the margins. Or all this could imply a society that is controlled, or cowed, or both.

Certainly, the narrative contains a good number of references to the presence of soldiers and members of the Civil Guard, and there is no doubt that uniforms would have been a prominent feature in Spain of 1946. Indeed, Paul Preston notes that forty-five percent of the Spanish budget for that particular year "was dedicated to the apparatus of repression, the police, the Civil Guard and the Army" (p. 549). And when, outside Durón, the traveler is asked by two Civil Guards to produce his papers or when, a little later, it is mentioned that sometimes the paramilitaries stop trucks, should such material be regarded as a reminder of the visible presence and the power of the authoritarian state? If so, such interpretations need to be counterbalanced by the fact that the traveler, a stranger, is stopped on a lonely road at nightfall and that the Civil Guards turn out to be friendly and helpful. Also, it appears that trucks are being checked apparently as part of an attempt to intercept black-market goods. Elsewhere, young Civil Guards are presented as being mainly interested in flirting with the local girls. Consequently, in the account, military or paramilitary uniforms are not obviously indicated as clothing callous brutes who are the ruthless tools of a totalitarian regime. But on the other hand, it is unlikely that the censor would have allowed Cela to get away with any such portrayal.

In the final chapter of *Viaje a la Alcarria*, the technique of seeing and recording, and of generally refraining from comment or commitment is, in a number of telling instances, jettisoned. Should, therefore, the Pastrana judgments be seen as simply a specific, localized response to what the traveler describes as a rather sleepy town. Or, should some of the opinions expressed in chapter 11 be regarded as having broader, political implications that might persuade the reader to reconsider some of the seemingly casual observations and encounters that took place earlier in the narrative?

There is no easy answer to these questions. Indeed, it is possible to see the traveler as quietly and frequently endorsing order and authority. For example, the traveler's enthusiastic portrayal of the mayor of Pastrana, obviously composed with hindsight, first presents him as an affable, cultured man and then, with reference to his administrative functions, as an old-style, benevolent paternalist and a worthy scion of the public officials of former ages (IV, 229). A few days earlier, the traveler had described the way in which the mayor of La Puerta was treated with great deference by the local people and went on to note that: "El alcalde de La Puerta está en todo, no se le escapa detalle, es un alcalde ejemplar" [The mayor of La Puerta is involved in everything, not a single detail escapes his attention, he is an exemplary mayor] (IV, 155).

Are these expressions of the protagonist's regard simply a response to the hospitality and concern displayed by the chief dignitaries of La Puerta and Pastrana, or is Cela indicating his esteem for efficient and caring figures of authority in contemporary Spain? And does his account tend to promote a picture of a generally orderly society in the Alcarria, perhaps exemplified in the closing pages of the narrative in the inhabitants of Zorita de los Canes? Here, according to the deputy mayor of Pastrana, who is a physician, the locals are extremely responsible when it comes to getting vaccinated. The traveler then proceeds to give a physical description of these bright and likeable villagers: they are, apparently, fair-haired and blue-eyed, tall and well built. The girls have neat, plaited hair and are very clean and healthy looking, with fair skin and rosy cheeks. This kind of detailed account of people's appearance is unusual in *Viaje a la Alcarria*, and the traveler leaves with a glowing comment on this small community that is presented as the epitome of good order and civic pride: "Zorita es un pueblo que vive en familia y en paz y en gracia de dios" [Zorita is a village that lives as a family, peacefully and in God's grace] (IV, 243). Do these people perhaps represent an ideal that the regime is striving for and should this idyllic picture thus be taken at face value? Or is the author injecting a note of irony here?

While the largely disciplined communities and groups of people that are seen throughout much of the narrative tend to elicit little more than bland passing comments from the traveler, the Pastrana episode does, of course, include observations that could be interpreted as thinly disguised criticism of the kind of order imposed by centralizing policies and the bureaucratic mentality. Moreover, when Pastrana and Spain are depicted as being beguiled by past glories and distracted from present-day problems, it requires no great stretch of the imagination to regard this as an allusion to the government's vigorous promotion of the spirit and values of the era of the foundation of modern Spain and the subsequent imperial and cultural glories. As Carr and Fusi Aizpurua observe:

> It was the splendours of this imperial past that the new regime wished to inherit and continue: the artistic achievements of the Golden Age; the architecture of Philip II's monastery-palace, the Escorial; the plastic tradition of the Castilian religious sculptors of the sixteenth century; the neo-classical poetry of the Renaissance and the passionate spirituality of the Spanish mystics. (p.107)

With his arrival in Pastrana, the traveler does, in a manner of speaking, enter the past. In different ways, the city reminds him of Toledo and Santiago de Compostela. But it also alerts him to the perils of a society being seduced by the glories of yesteryear and possibly sees him alluding to the complicity of the regime in this seduction. Yet this and other oblique references to conditions and attitudes in contemporary Spain are rare in a narrative that studiously avoids dealing explicitly with the recent past or with present issues. Certainly, with regard to events of the previous ten or so years, there are a few, scattered references to the period of the Second Republic and to the Spanish Civil War. But these are just asides and allusions rather than anything detailed or substantial, and are presented in quite a safe, noncontroversial way.

Concerning what was happening in Spain in 1946, and particularly during the first half of June, the narrative contains little more than general suggestions and the occasional specific reference. So, there are sporadic indications of an economic situation in which hardship, shortages of basic commodities, and the attendant black market were facts of life for some of the people that the traveler came into contact with. There are also mentions of the inadequacy of the electricity supply. But all these things would have been general manifestations of what Preston terms the "disastrous economic performance" of this period (p. 559). What *Viaje a la Alcarria* rarely conveys are specific matters of local interest. Setting aside observations on the quality of the land or on the economic situation of the inhabitants, there are only a few exceptions to this approach: shortly before he reaches Brihuega the traveler notices pools of water in a field and this prompts one of the locals to comment on the recent wet weather (IV, 72), while in the closing stages of the narrative reference is made to a flood-damaged main road and also to the widespread flooding (IV, 225). Elsewhere, and this time with regard to flooding by design, local people discuss the reservoirs that are to be created on the Tagus and Guadiela Rivers. While there is an acknowledgment that this scheme will entail the disappearance of certain areas beneath the waters, the traveler indicates no particular interest (IV, 217). But overall, and here the Pastrana episode provides the most memorable exception, the account of the Alcarria trip scarcely focuses on local matters. The traveler takes more interest in enjoying his food and drink, in finding a bed for the night, in observing attractive young women, or getting pleasure out of good company than he does in reporting issues closely affecting the inhabitants of the area. Indeed, the only features peculiar to the Alcarria that appear to be of special interest to the traveler are the nicknames that he so carefully gathers.

National events or concerns are even more thoroughly bypassed in the narrative. It is almost as if Cela had taken a decision not to refer to what was happening elsewhere in Spain nor, in fact, mention international developments, some of which, in the year after the end of World War II, were directly or indirectly relevant to the future of Spain. The traveler buys and reads newspapers in Guadalajara and there is mention that one of the salesmen in Trillo is reading *Nueva Alcarria*, while his colleague, Martín, is seen in Sacedón looking at the Guadalajara edition of *El Alcázar* and commenting that it gives good local coverage. Yet, there is never any indication of the stories being carried in the press. It is of course possible that from 6 June, the day of Cela's departure for the Alcarria, until his return ten days later, no published stories were deemed worthy of comment by any of the characters included in the narrative, or, that any responses to newspaper stories from the traveler or overheard by him were not worth recording in the account. To be sure, the report on 9 June on the front page of *Arriba*, the organ of the Falange, that the Barcelona trade fair, the Feria de Muestras, had opened the previous day would hardly have been a conversation starter. But the following day, Real Madrid's three-to-one victory over Valencia in the final of the Copa del Generalísimo, which was played in Barcelona, received extensive newspaper coverage. Yet in Cela's narrative, the match and its result generated not a single comment from anyone he came across in the Alcarria.

The Spanish press of the first half of June 1946 also carried a great deal of foreign material, including reports on 5 June of the inauguration of Juan Perón as President of Argentina; frequent stories on the Italian general election, the republican victory there and the subsequent exile of King Umberto II, and mention of the trial of General Jodl at the Nuremberg International Military Tribunal. Also stemming from the recent European war, on 8 June the Victory Parade that had been held in London was given front-page treatment in *Arriba*. However, the most significant foreign story carried by Spanish newspapers concerned an issue with clear domestic implications: the discussions at the United Nations on whether or not Franco's Spain was a threat to world peace and the related debates on the proposed diplomatic boycott of the country. Indeed, on 1 March, in response to the execution of ten opponents of the Franco regime, France had closed her border with Spain and cut all economic ties. So when, in Brihuega, the traveler and Julio Vacas comment that they do not know much about what is happening in France (IV, 90), it is possible that this is an allusion to current difficulties between the two countries.

Yet France was far from being Spain's most pressing international problem. In New York, at the end of April, a subcommittee of the United Nations had been established to consider the allegation by the Polish member of the Security Council that Spain was endangering world peace. The subcommittee's report, published on 31 May, concluded that Spain was "a potential threat to international peace and security" and also recommended that all members of the General Assembly should sever contacts with the country.[12] However, on 4 June, the monarchist daily *ABC* correctly assessed the reaction of Britain and the United States in a story headlined "The Proposed Diplomatic Isolation of Spain Does Not Appear to Have the Support of the Anglo-Saxons" (p. 15). In fact, the two Western allies ensured that when the report was discussed in June at various sessions of the Security Council most of its teeth were removed, with Spain being put on a kind of international probation rather than being the object of immediate action. As Paul Preston observes:

Its recommendations were toned down by both the United States and British representatives but it was decided rather feebly that, since the subcommittee had shown that the Franco regime constituted a potential threat to world peace, the Spanish question should be subject to constant vigilance by the Security Council. This effectively signified a recognition that no measures were likely to be taken against Franco. (pp. 559–60)

But while the Spanish press was giving extensive coverage to the hostility of eastern bloc countries and the helpful attitude of the United States and Britain, the Franco regime was, Preston points out, "working frantically to persuade the Spanish people that Spain was the victim of an international siege" (p. 559). Nevertheless, despite all the press reports of what was going on abroad at a particularly delicate phase in Spain's recovery and in the Franco regime's survival, the traveler and the people he meets and talks to in the Alcarria (including those of some standing) appear oblivious to the specter of foreign disapproval of, or even interference in, Spain's domestic affairs.

Consistent with his perception of the travel book as principally a work of geography, Cela shows, for most of the time, what he sees and he normally refrains from probing or seeking to explain. He attempts neither to address the past, which in June 1946 would loom most vividly in the shape of the recent civil war, nor to understand the wider issues of a present that largely resulted from the legacy of that conflict. Instead, Cela limits his focus to a small area seen within the span of a week and a half, and thereby offers a restricted and immediate present and a small-scale view of roads, rivers, fields, towns, and villages. Against this almost totally undramatic background, the author reveals a traveler and the people he comes across—people who are largely concerned with their immediate situation: whether it be with regard to work, food, illness, pleasure, or discomfort. In effect, in *Viaje a la Alcarria* Cela almost entirely avoids any direct address of leading issues and instead composes what largely amounts to a picture of the simple pleasures provided by Nature, by a meal or a glass of wine, by a conversation, or by the publication details of an old book, all interspersed with the mundane comforts, banalities, and trials of daily life. Consistent with the message of the dedication that precedes his account, he provides a low-key, sedately paced, and unexciting narrative. Yet, on occasion it can provide quietly lyrical moments or present itself as a travel work that is often intriguing for its allusions as well as its silences.

5

Fact and Fiction: *Del Miño al Bidasoa*

A Strange Opening

Whereas *VIAJE A LA ALCARRIA*, WITH ITS EARLY PAGES OF RUMINA-
tion, preparation, and setting out, amply complies with Paul Theroux's
plea for some kind of preliminary material in travel works, *Del Miño
al Bidasoa: Notas de un vagabundaje* (1952) starts in exactly the kind of
way—pitching "the reader in a bizarre place without having first
guided him there" (p. 11)—that so irks the American writer. Indeed,
the opening sequence of Cela's second travel book could not be more
strange, as the reader is confronted with the sight of the traveler walking along a country lane and carrying an empty coffin on his head. The
location is the Galician municipal district of As Neves, the southern
boundary of which is the Miño River. The occasion is the festival of
Santa Marta de Ribarteme (29 July), one of the oldest and best know
Galician pilgrimages, and whose celebration centers on the village
church of San José de Ribarteme, some ten kilometers north of the
banks of the Miño.

In her travel book, *Spain's Magic Coast: From the Miño to the Bidassoa*
(1965), Nina Epton devotes most of the opening section on Galicia to a
description of the picturesque rituals involving those who have come
either to thank Santa Marta de Ribarteme for health restored or to pray
to her for a cure. Epton observes:

> The original feature of this particular *romería*, or picnic-pilgrimage, which
> we were anxious to witness, consists of *ofrecidos* (people who have made a
> vow either to petition or to thank Saint Martha), who place themselves in
> open coffins during the procession that takes place after high Mass on the
> Saint's feast day. The coffins are carried by relatives or friends.[1]

However, Cela's traveler, in this work referred to as "the vagabond," is
carrying his own coffin since, as the reader is informed, he has no
friends or relatives.[2] As Epton's account indicates, some of those attend-
ing the pilgrimage carry hired, empty coffins on their heads (p. 7).[3]

In the opening, four-page section of *Del Miño al Bidasoa*, the traveler presents himself as a genuine pilgrim who is in search of "la salud perdida" [his lost health] (IV, 255). In his essay "Travel and Writing," Michel Butor declares that the term "pilgrimage" originally signified "the journey to the tomb of a saint, next to the spot of a vision, an oracular site; one carries his question there and expects a response, a curing of the body or soul" (p. 61). Certainly, Cela's vagabond is this kind of traveler-pilgrim in the opening section of the narrative. Furthermore, the following section sees him on the next phase of his apparent pilgrimage, on the road to Santiago de Compostela, "a pedir al apóstol que acabe de curar el mal que comenzara a sanar Santa Marta de Ribarteme" [to ask the Apostle to complete the cure of the illness that St Martha had started to heal] (IV, 256). But even the journey to the shrine of St James is interrupted by a brief stop in Padrón (the author was, of course, born in the adjoining hamlet, Iria Flavia), so that the vagabond can now pray for his soul as well as for his unnamed illness.

The third and final section of the opening chapter sees the vagabond briefly in the streets of Santiago, intending to give thanks to St James for keeping him alive, and then in the cathedral, where he offers a "confusa y piadosa oración" [confused and pious prayer] (IV, 261) before leaving for lunch and subsequently making his way out of the city. Chapter 2 begins with the vagabond heading southwest, along the road to Orense but still behaving more like a pilgrim than an observant or curious traveler. He says a prayer in the monastery of San Lorenzo de Carboeiro, later visits the sanctuary of Nuestra Señora de la Peña de Francia and also looks for the monastery of Osera. Then, when he gets to Orense and bumps into his cousin Benitiño do Chao as he crosses the Roman bridge into the city, he goes to say prayers with him in the cathedral. Hereafter, though, the sense of religious pilgrimage that marks the first five sections of *Del Miño al Bidasoa* almost totally disappears.

The last part of chapter 2 begins with the sudden arrival of the traveler and his cousin in La Coruña. No description has been given of their journey from Orense to the northern port and no indication of the route taken or the time involved. All that the reader is told is that the two men arrived by truck. There then follows a brief mention of some of the well known areas and features of the city and its coast, an indication of La Coruña's geographical location on the northwestern coast of Galicia, and a pointer to its overseas connections.

The first two chapters of *Del Miño al Bidasoa*, apart from suggesting the act of travel as a kind of religious pilgrimage and also indicating the vagabond's family contacts in Galicia, are a fragmented account, lacking both geographical and temporal continuity, of what seem like random journeys and episodes. Thus the narrative, having opened in a country lane in the vicinity of San José de Ribarteme, subsequently switches to Padrón (some seventy kilometers to the north) and then the following section begins with the traveler walking the streets of Santiago de Compostela (twenty kilometers northeast of Padrón). Fortunately, the subsequent section gives some sense of the process of travel, as the vagabond takes his leave of Santiago and begins the walk to Orense, 110 kilometers to the southeast, and on the banks of the Miño. Yet although in this opening section of the second chapter the descriptions of place and movement are rather sparse, at least it is possible for the reader to trace the route taken by the vagabond. After his arrival in Orense, and the chance meeting with cousin Benitiño, a brief section is then devoted to some of the city's principal attractions and a little of its history before, in the next section, both men are seen reaching La Coruña. So, the narrative suddenly switches from one end of Galicia to the other, without a word of description dedicated to the nature of the landscape between Orense and the northern port—a distance of some 180 kilometers—and no indication of how the trip was made, save mention of the two cousins' arrival at La Coruña in a truck.

Chapters 1 and 2, then, which account for almost a tenth of the travel work, constitute a rather bizarre and disjointed opening that gives a somewhat whimsical account of the vagabond's appearances in various parts of southern and northwestern Galicia. The protagonist is seen as an odd character who is altogether removed from the family man/writer/Cela figure of the opening stages of *Viaje a la Alcarria*. Indeed, the vagabond of *Del Miño al Bidasoa* is presented in the first two chapters as: someone who, seemingly, has no friends or family (IV, 253); who is a sailor from a family of sailors (IV, 267), and who is a self-styled career vagabond (IV, 259, 260). Moreover, although the scene in Padrón is an obvious reminder of the figure of the author, it is noteworthy that in Cuco's tavern the vagabond is received by the owner as a *friend* of "Don Camilo" (IV, 257). In effect, these first two chapters give no sense of a motive or strategy for the journey indicated in the title. Instead, they present a confusing indication of who the vagabond might be and reveal a turbulent narrative that covers three of the four Galician provinces in a sporadic and helter-skelter way, with the vagabond giving no systematic account of travels or landscape and shooting back and forth like a peregrinating pinball.

However, as soon as Cela's vagabond leaves La Coruña the whole character of the account changes. It becomes a travel work with logical sequences, some awareness of physical surroundings, and an increasingly clear sense of narrative development in the remaining eighteen chapters, as the vagabond makes his way east, toward the French border and the River Bidassoa. But why this change in approach after the altogether strange and disjointed first two chapters of the travel book? The answer is simple and also largely explains why there is no prejourney material indicating motive, purpose, or route. *Del Miño al Bidasoa* is not the record of one single journey. What Cela has done, and he later acknowledges this, is to reuse and adapt material describing a trip that he had previously taken and the account of which had already been published. A large part of that material, in modified form, has been coupled, at the point where chapter 3 begins, to the fragmented account presented in the first two chapters.

In a three-page essay written in December 1963 as the preface to the *Obra completa* edition of *Del Miño al Bidasoa*, Cela mentions that during July and August of 1948 he was assigned by the Madrid newspaper, *Pueblo*, to visit a number of holiday hostels for workers, located in various parts of Spain. Between 4 September and 6 November of that same year twenty-eight articles by Cela were published in *Pueblo* under the general heading, "Y así veranean los trabajadores. La vuelta a España de un novelista" [How Workers Spend their Summer Vacations: A Novelist's Tour of Spain].[4] In the same essay, Cela makes the following observations concerning the composition of *Del Miño al Bidasoa*: "Las crónicas que publiqué en *Pueblo*, amén de otras experiencias que fui anotando por el camino y sumadas a más previas o posteriores andaduras, fueron la base de este libro, su cañamazo y también su materia prima" [The chronicles that I published in *Pueblo*, as well as other experiences that I jotted down during the trip and blended with earlier or later rambles, formed the basis of this book, its canvas as well as its raw material] (IV, 247–48). Cela's second travel book is, then, a conflation of parts of the first thirteen of these newspaper pieces and some other journeys and jottings.

The reason that not all of the articles published in *Pueblo* were drawn on for the travel narrative is simply connected with the extensive geographical setting of the twenty-eight reports. For these articles, in which the author refers to himself throughout as "el viajero" [the traveler], Cela and his driver set out from where the author was living in the summer of 1948, Cebreros in the province of Avila,[5] and the first five published pieces relate the trip as far as the city of León. The sixth piece begins in Ponferrada (with no account of the drive from León) and it is in this same article that Galicia is reached, followed by the description of a rapid progress through Orense and then on to Vigo.

Although in all but two of the first thirteen newspaper articles, Cela describes the visits he makes to the workers' holiday hostels (the one on the Sardinero in Santander apparently consisted of two floors of a palace), commenting on the occupants and the facilities available, most of the material in these newspaper pieces narrates journeys, sights and scenery, as well as observations on local matters, both prosaic and historical. Thus, as Cela makes his way across southern Galicia he remarks on some handsome scenery, has a coffee and relaxes in Orense, and describes the port of Vigo and its surroundings. When he moves on, the following day, the author takes in various aspects of the Ría de Vigo, comments on the rail viaduct above Redondela, has nothing of note to say about Pontevedra (which is dealt with in a handful of lines) and, still heading north, he reports on road systems, landscape, rivers crossed, people going about their business, and then reaches Padrón. Here the author mentions Rosalía de Castro and some other famous local figures before passing through his birthplace on the northern edge of the town, an experience that, not unexpectedly, evokes childhood memories. Finally, with a couple of lines employed to describe how Santiago is seen in the distance and then left behind, the author's car reaches and bypasses La Coruña, but not without some comments on the impressive sight of the city and its surroundings.

In fact, this car journey from Orense to La Coruña could have served as the framework for the opening sections of *Del Miño al Bidasoa*. It covers, in a logical sequence, the principal cities and many of the significant towns of southern and western Galicia, following an orthodox, unexciting route. Yet, the author has not reworked this material for the opening two chapters of his second travel book and this is puzzling, especially in view of the fact that with chapter 3 of *Del Miño al Bidasoa* (which begins with the vagabond taking his leave of La Coruña) and throughout the rest of the work, Cela reuses—either verbatim or with slight modifications—a substantial part of the *Pueblo* pieces.

RECYCLING A JOURNEY

The first thirteen of the *Pueblo* articles (published 4–20 September 1948 and reprinted in the fourth volume of the author's *Obra completa*), are described by Cela as "el huevo" [the source] (IV, 248) of *Del Miño al Bidasoa* and total approximately twenty-three thousand words. Around thirty percent of this material is incorporated in the travel book. However, the first seven *Pueblo* pieces have practically no connection with the content and geographical scope of chapters 1 and 2 of *Del Miño al Bidasoa*. Indeed, as has been mentioned, it is only with the third chapter of this work, which opens with the vagabond heading away from La Coruña, that his route begins to trace that taken by Cela, in his chauffeur-driven car, as he skirted La Coruña in the summer of 1948. Thus, at just over the halfway point of the thirteen pieces, the eighth *Pueblo* article begins: "Atrás ya La Coruña" [With La Coruña now behind us] (IV, 581). Subsequently, from this stage in the newspaper articles, Cela incorporates in his second travel book around sixty percent of the eighth to thirteenth *Pueblo* reports. Sixty percent is clearly a hefty proportion of the last half dozen newspaper pieces. However, to put things into some kind of perspective, about seven thousand words of *Pueblo* material are spliced into chapters 3 to 20 of the travel book and this borrowed and recycled material amounts to about fifteen percent of the total wordage of these chapters.

By comparing the two texts, it is a straightforward task to identify the borrowings from the *Pueblo* pieces. The length of the many transplanted extracts ranges from a dozen words to as many as 250. Only two of chapters 3 to 20 appear to be entirely free of previously published matter and a further five chapters contain repeated lines amounting to a mere thirty to 130 words in each. On the other hand, several chapters include sizeable chunks of *Pueblo* material: some two thousand words in chapter 16, or over one third of the whole chapter, while around a quarter of chapters 3 and 8, and over one-fifth of chapter 4 draw on the 1948 pieces. Elsewhere, the borrowings are noticeable but not especially substantial: thus about one-tenth of the material in chapters 5, 9 14, 15, and 18 is recycled from the *Pueblo* articles.

In the previous two paragraphs I have used expressions such as "recycled material," "borrowings," "transplanted extracts," and "sizeable chunks," and it needs to be stressed that Cela has both *reused* and *reworked* passages from the 1948 newspaper pieces. Thus in chapter 3, where the author first begins to splice in parts of the *Pueblo* articles, there are some twenty borrowings—ranging in length from a couple of lines to a dozen or so. In the following chapter, the number of borrowings is ten: most are quite short (between two and six lines) with the exception of a twenty-five-line passage (IV, 296–97), and so on, throughout most of *Del Miño al Bidasoa*.

Quite frequently, the very short transfers have been made with only the change of a word or two, as in the following example from chapter 3:

Pueblo article	*Del Miño al Bidasoa*
Villalba es un pueblo subido en una colina. (IV, 582)	Villalba es un pueblo grande subido en una colina. (IV, 276)
[Villalba is a town set on a hill.]	[Villalba is a large town set on a hill.]

At other times, a few more words are inserted, to add a touch more descriptive detail and possibly to heighten the literary effect:

Pueblo article

Por Goiriz, un paisano de zuecos y en bicicleta lleva el paraguas a la espalda, colgado del cuello de la chaqueta. (IV, 582).

[Going through Goiriz, a local wearing clogs and riding a bicycle carries an umbrella on his back, hanging from the collar of his coat.]

Del Miño al Bidasoa

Por Goiriz, entre vetustos castaños de Indias, un paisano de zuecos y en bicicleta lleva el negro y cumplido paraguas a la espalda, colgado del cuello de la chaqueta. (IV, 277)

[Going through Goiriz, between ancient horse chestnut trees, a local wearing clogs and riding a bicycle, carries a large, black umbrella on his back, hanging from the collar of his coat.]

On other occasions, a particular scene is subjected to substantially more reworking and additional of detail. Thus, the vagabond's arrival in Villalba is dealt with as follows in the two versions:

Pueblo article

Como al día siguiente es fiesta, las calles comienzan ya a engalanarse; quizás, por la misma razón, un loco hace unas piruetas inverosímiles en medio de la carretera, ante la indiferencia de todos; se ve en seguida que es un loco que ha abusado de sus habilidades, que ya acostumbró a todo el mundo a que lo vean dar saltos mortales. Por los caminos se acercan a Villalba los campesinos que van a la feria, con un cerdo color de rosa atado a una pata. (IV, 582)

[As there is a festival the next day, the streets are already beginning to be decked out; perhaps, for the same reason, a simpleton is performing strange-looking pirouettes in the middle of the road, to which everyone is

Del Miño al Bidasoa

Como al día siguiente es fiesta—no importa qué fiesta—, las calles de Villalba comienzan a engalanarse. Quizás por la misma razón, un loco bien parecido da unos saltos mortales increíbles en medio de la carretera, sin que nadie le haga caso; en seguida se echa de ver que el loco es un loco que se prodigó, un loco que ha abusado de sus mañas, sus ingenios y sus habilidades, un loco que ya acostumbró a todo el mundo a contemplar—e incluso a olvidar—sus difíciles artes de saltimbanqui.

Por los caminos que traen hasta Villalba se acercan, despacios y solemnes, los campesinos que van a la feria arreando una vaca marela o llevando un cerdo color de rosa atado de una pata. (IV, 277)

[As there is a festival the next day—it does not matter which festival—the streets of Villalba are beginning to be decked out. Perhaps for the same reason, a good-looking simpleton is performing some incredible, mortal leaps indifferent; straight away you can see that he is a simpleton who has overexposed his talents, who has got everyone used to seeing him make mortal leaps. The peasants who are coming to the festival are making their way along the roads, with pink pigs tied by their legs.]

in the middle of the road, without anyone paying him any attention; straight away you notice that the simpleton is a simpleton who has been overenthusiastic, a simpleton who has overexposed his skills, his creativity, and his talents, a simpleton who has got everyone used to watching—and also forgetting—his tricky acrobatic feats.

The peasants who are coming to the festival are making their way, slowly and solemnly, along the roads that lead into Villalba, driving long-horned cows or bringing pink pigs tied by their legs.]

From the above it is clear that the *Pueblo* passage has been quite extensively reworked in order, presumably, to give the scenes more detail, more drama, and more visual impact. Above all, this last example reveals an *artistic* revision of the original passage—from the already attention-catching *Pueblo* version to the more colorful, more informative, and more literary, travel-book account of the scene.

However, it should be noted that Cela does not always engage in this degree of reworking when he extracts material from the newspaper chronicles. For example, the memory of an anecdote associated with the Galician town of Betanzos, followed by a few general comments and a small, descriptive detail, is taken from the *Pueblo* account and reused with just minor modifications:

Pueblo article

El viajero, cada vez que pasa por Betanzos, no lo puede evitar, se acuerda de aquel acto de propaganda electoral en el que el candidato a diputado, asomándose al balcón del ayuntamiento, preguntaba con voz tonante a la multitud:

— ¡Betanceiros!, ¿qué queredes?

— ¡Que suba o pan e que baixe a caña!

— Pois cando chegue a Madrid xa falarei con premura.

— ¡ Viva Premura!

Betanzos es un pueblo ilustre, anti-

Del Miño al Bidasoa

El vagabundo, cada vez que pasa por Betanzos, y ya lleva pasadas unas cuantas en su vida, no puede evitar el acordarse de aquel acto de propaganda electoral en el que el candidato a diputado, asomándose al balcón del ayuntamiento, preguntaba con voz tonante a la multitud:

— ¡Betanceiros! ¿Qué queredes?

— ¡Que suba o pan e que baixe a caña!

— Pois cando chegue a Madrid, xa falarei con premura.

— ¡Viva Premura!

guo, lleno de historia. La peluquería de señoras Avelina cuelga su marca sobre el noble granito de una fachada con blasón. (IV, 581–82)

Betanzos es un pueblo ilustre, antiguo, rebosante de tradición, lleno de historia. La peluquería de señoras Avelina cuelga su marca sobre el noble granito de una fachada con blasón. (IV, 273–74)

[Each time the traveler goes through Betanzos, he cannot help but remember that election campaign in which the prospective deputy, standing on the town-hall balcony, asked the crowd in a thundering voice:
"Citizens of Betanzos! What do you want?"
"Bread to go up and cane-spirit to come down!"
"Well, when I get to Madrid I shall speak with expedition."
"Long live Expedition!"
Betanzos is an illustrious, ancient town, full of history. The ladies' hairdressers, Avelina, has its sign hanging from the noble granite of a façade with a coat of arms.]

[Each time the vagabond goes through Betanzos, and he has been through there a few times in his life, he cannot help but remember that election campaign in which the prospective deputy, standing on the town-hall balcony, asked the crowd in a thundering voice:
"Citizens of Betanzos! What do you want?"
"Bread to go up and cane-spirit to come down!"
"Well, when I get to Madrid I shall speak with expedition."
"Long live Expedition!"
Betanzos is an illustrious, ancient town, brimming with tradition, full of history. The ladies' hairdressers, Avelina, has its sign hanging from the noble granite of a façade with a coat of arms.]

And while this extract from the *Pueblo* piece constitues the whole of the newspaper account of Betanzos, in *Del Miño al Bidasoa* the author adds a further 250 or so words on the town's churches, its two rivers, and its history.

But not all the material taken from the *Pueblo* articles and reused in the travel book deals with incidents, anecdotes, or descriptions of place. Occasionally, there are passages of meditation or even editorializing that find their way, with little change, from the 1948 publication to that of 1952. So, in the eleventh of the newspaper reports, as the traveler enters the province of Vizcaya en route to Bilbao and the French border, he notes the industrialization of certain areas and muses on this phenomenon. Here, the lengthy *Pueblo* passage is heavily drawn on for both content and tone in the opening passage of chapter 16 of the travel narrative:

Pueblo article
Por Somorrostro aparece la industria; la industria es algo que tiene escasa

Del Miño al Bidasoa
Por Somorrostro aparece la industria. El vagabundo piensa que la industria

defensa, algo que hay que tolerar porque es necesaria, pero nada más.

Daría mucho qué pensar—quizás demasiado que pensar—el intentar esclarecer si es mejor vivir más tranquilo, pero menos cómodo, sin industria, o más intranquilo, pero menos incómodo, con ella. Las dos posturas tienen evidentemente sus apologistas y sus detractores, y los dos grupos tienen también, como siempre pasa, su parte de razón. El viajero, que es, gracias a Dios, un viejo europeo occidental, antepone el sosiego al confort, aunque sabe bien que sus ideas están llamadas a ser no más cosa que históricas piezas de museo y que el mundo, cada día que pasa más próximo a su aburrido final, tiende hacia la nevera eléctrica y al aspirador de polvo y la televisión, aun a trueque de no cejar ni un solo instante en su estúpido ajetreo.

En Nocedal un grupo de niños juega, no demasiado divertido, con unos palitos al borde de la carretera; cuando el viajero pasa les dice adiós con la mano y los niños ponen un gesto de sorpresa, le miran, pero no le contestan. Eran unos niños extraños los niños de Nocedal; unos niños serios, de aire pensativo, llenos de responsabilidad y, probablemente, de proyectos para el futuro. (IV, 603–4)

es algo que tiene escasa defensa, algo que hay que tolerar porque es necesario y útil para los demás, pero no por ninguna otra razón. El vagabundo, entre vivir sin industria, más tranquilo pero menos cómodo, o con ella, menos incómodo y más desasosegado, piensa que es mejor lo primero. Si no, no sería vagabundo: sería, en vez, perito agrícola, o registrador de la propiedad, o ferretero.

El vagabundo piensa también que las dos posturas tienen, evidentemente, sus defensores y sus enemigos, y que a ninguno de los dos puntos de vista les falta, como siempre pasa, su parte de razón. La verdad es que los hombres no han conseguido todavía una sola idea que no tenga ninguna razón; a la humanidad le falta aún mucho camino por andar.

El vagabundo, que es, sin haber tenido en ello arte ni parte, un viejo occidental, antepone, ¡y qué le va a hacer!, la calma a la mecánica, aunque sabe bien que sus ideas, si es que esto son ideas, están llamadas a ser no más cosa que históricas y enmohecidas piezas de museo; el mundo, cada día que pasa más cercano a su aburrido final, tiende hacia las máquinas y las estadísticas, aun a trueque de olvidar los bellos nombres de las estrellas, la delicada color de las florecillas silvestres y el sabor del aire cuando Dios amanece sobre el campo abierto. ¡Qué le vamos a hacer!

En Nocedal un grupo de niños no consigue divertirse mientras juega con unos palitos al borde de la carretera. Cuando el vagabundo pasa, sonríe, casi como un patriarca pobre, y les dice adiós.

—Adiós . . .

Los niños, cuando el vagabundo los saluda, ponen un gesto de sorpresa, le miran como si fuera un ser caído de otros mundos, y no le contestan. Son unos niños extraños estos niños de Nocedal; unos niños serios y conservadores, unos niños de aire pensativo, llenos de responsabilidad y, probablemente, de proyectos para el futuro. (IV, 429–30).

[In Somorrostro, industry comes into view; industry is something that there is precious little defense for, something that has to be tolerated because it is necessary, but that is all. It really would set you thinking—perhaps thinking too much—to try to figure out if it is better to live more peacefully, but less comfortably, without industry, or more anxiously, but less uncomfortably, with it. The two stances obviously have their proponents and their opponents, and the two sides will both be, as is always the case, right to some extent. The traveler, who is, thank Heaven, an old western European, prefers calm to comfort, even though he knows only too well that his ideas are destined to be nothing more than old museum pieces and that the world, every day that it moves a little closer to its dreary end, tends toward the electric refrigerator, the vacuum cleaner, and television, even at the cost of not pausing for an instant in its foolish, constant activity.

In Nocedal a group of children are playing with some sticks, without really enjoying themselves, by the side of the highway; when the traveler goes by he waves at them and the children, looking surprised, watch him but do not respond. The children of Nocedal were strange children; serious, pensive-looking children, full of responsibility and, probably, plans for the future.]

(In Somorrostro, industry comes into view. The vagabond thinks that industry is something that there is little defense for, something that has to be tolerated because it is necessary and useful for others, but not for any other reason. If a choice has to be made between living without industry, more peacefully but less comfortably, or with it, less uncomfortably and more uneasily, the vagabond thinks that the former is better. If he did not, he would not be a vagabond: instead he would be an agricultural expert, a property recorder, or an ironmonger.

The vagabond also thinks that the two stances obviously have their defenders and their enemies, and that neither viewpoint, as is always the case, is entirely lacking in sense. The truth is that human beings still have not conceived a single idea that is wholly without reason; humanity still has a long way to go.

The vagabond, who is, without having had any say in the matter, an old westerner, prefers, and what else can he do!, tranquillity to machinery, although he knows only too well that his ideas, if indeed they are ideas, are destined to be nothing more than old and rusty museum pieces; the world, every day that it moves a little closer to its dreary end, tends toward machines and statistics, even at the expense of forgetting the beautiful names of the stars, the delicate color of small wild flowers, and the taste of the air when God brings dawn to the countryside. What can we do about it!

In Nocedal a group of children
cannot quite manage to enjoy themselves as they play with some sticks
by the side of the highway. When the
vagabond goes by he smiles, almost
like a poor patriarch, and greets them.
"Hello . . ."
When the vagabond greets them
they appear surprised, looking at him
as if he had fallen out of the sky, and
do not answer him. They are strange,
these children from Nocedal; serious,
conservative, full of responsibility
and, probably, of plans for the future.]

A comparison of these two substantial extracts (the *Pueblo* passage of
some 220 words has been developed to about 340 words in the travel
book) reveals not just the easily visible, word-for-word transfers or
expansions from the newspaper piece. There is also a little more sentimentality and poetic style in the later account. But the most noticeable
difference between the two passages is the way in which the traveler-
figure is given more prominence in the second version. The two-para-
graph *Pueblo* passage begins and continues for a while with the disembodied voice of a narrator indulging in a simple exercise of narratorial
meditation. In fact, it is not until the halfway point of the first paragraph
(after about eighty words) that the focus is brought clearly on to what
the traveler thinks about the pros and cons of industralization. Indeed,
the term "traveler" is used only twice during the *Pueblo* passage, the
second time being in the last paragraph as the issues of tranquillity and
progress/industralization are left behind in the opening paragraph. The
second paragraph is used to reveal a picture, a physical presence of the
traveler passing through Nocedal and waving from his car at a group
of rather serious-looking youngsters, and then reflecting on them once
they have disappeared from view.

In the travel-book version it is made clear almost immediately that
thoughts on industry, progress, a tranquil life, and so on, are those of
the vagabond and not the ruminations of a detached narrator. Indeed,
the term "vagabond" is introduced after a mere half dozen words of the
passage and is subsequently used a further six times. Granted, this is in
a passage now some 50 percent longer than the *Pueblo* version, yet the
important point of difference is that in *Del Miño al Bidasoa* the vagabond's presence and philosophizing are foregrounded to a much greater
degree than in the newspaper account. The passage in the travel book

is much more concerned with projecting what the *vagabond* thinks about the relevant issues than, as looks to be the case in the somewhat more objective *Pueblo* version, with the issues themselves. Also, toward the end of the first paragraph the wayfarer presents himself as a kind of "career vagabond" and in so doing contributes to a certain distancing that takes place throughout most of the narrative between the rough and ready wanderer and the lurking figure of Cela, the professional writer.

Finally, comment should be made on two slight differences between the versions of the above passage that are apparently generated by the fact that the protagonist moves around by car in the *Pueblo* pieces, whereas he is frequently presented as walking from place to place in the travel book. In the 1948 passage, he waves, from his car, to the group of children in Nocedal, leaves them behind, and then thinks about them. However, in the version of this insignificant event found in *Del Miño al Bidasoa*, the now *walking* vagabond has the opportunity to *say* "hello" to the youngsters (thus the wave from the car of 1948 is transformed into a spoken greeting in 1952) and reflect on how they appear at the moment he looks at them. In addition, this encounter with the group of children provides the opportunity for an allusion to the apparently straitened circumstances of this individual who is walking the roads of northern Spain. Indeed, in *Del Miño al Bidasoa* the vagabond is no longer the responsible (yet humorous), observant, chauffeur-driven writer of the *Pueblo* chronicles. He has now been transformed into a hard up (yet hedonistic) and roguish vagabond making his way across the north of Spain—most of the time in the company of a down-at-heel French peddler.

Traveling Companions

In a rather bland assessment of *Del Miño al Bidasoa*, Alonso Zamora Vicente suggests that the work reveals certain character types (pompous and sentimental returned migrants, fussy, bourgeois, Spanish holidaymakers) as well as giving a more general view of people, landscape, and Nature (p. 95). However, he makes no mention of the striking presence of the Frenchman, Dupont. In contrast, José María Martínez Cachero notes the way in which the vagabond and Dupont become not only partners and companions on the road but also, he suggests, co-protagonists of the narrative (p. 127). And when Robert Kirsner refers to the vagabond-Dupont relationship, he is reminded of an earlier literary twosome. Thus, after stating that *Del Miño al Bidasoa* "recalls in spirit" the wanderings of Don Quixote, he goes on to propose a kind of

Quixote-Sancho relationship between the vagabond and Dupont, but one based on equality and in which the two men "serve each other."[6] In fact, the cover of the first edition of the travel work (which shows two men walking along, side by side, one slim and the other shorter, stockier, and carrying toy windmills), if alluding to nothing else, certainly implies that the partnership is central to the narrative.[7]

Although Cela has stated a number of times that he travels to find peace and solitude, *Del Miño al Bidasoa* clearly does not reveal such an intention achieved. The frantic opening scenes and hectic pace of the first two chapters, and the gathering speed with which the vagabond crosses northern Spain, all seem far removed from any notion of tranquillity attained through the contemplation of, or communion with Nature. And as for travel as the route to solitude: from the beginning of the work, with the vagabond in the company of a variety of fellow pilgrims, his trip from Orense to La Coruña with cousin Benitiño, and then the subsequent journey across most of the northern regions in the company of Dupont, there is precious little opportunity (and no expressed desire on the part of the vagabond) for the solitary existence. Indeed, the central narrative feature—from both a dramatic and structural point of view—of *Del Miño al Bidasoa* is the relationship between Cela's wayfarer and the French peddler.

In chapter 5, when the vagabond finds himself in the Asturian town of Navia (the birthplace of Ramón de Campoamor), he comes across the Frenchman, selling his paper windmills. From this point in the work and throughout the remaining chapters, the two men are seen together for most of the narrative and gradually develop a partnership and a bond that comes to dominate the account until the poignant moments of their parting on the penultimate page. Although from time to time Dupont disappears from view, occasionally parting company from the vagabond for a brief period, the experiences and conversations of the two men give a firm narrative direction to *Del Miño al Bidasoa*. Moreover, their exploits and relationship generally overshadow other considerations that might be more readily associated with travel literature, such as scenery, social and economic matters, or the cultural and historical features of the route followed. These two men of the road soon strike up a friendship and fraternal bond, frequently referring to each other as "hermano" [brother]. But they not only make easy company on the road, they also go hungry together, get tired together, sleep rough together, get drunk or beg together, and share odd jobs. Then, as they prepare to go their separate ways at the end of the narrative, their sadness at the prospect of parting is marked by a gradual inability to know what to say to each other.

In fact, it is altogether ironic that the banter and conversations of the two men should dry up toward the end of their association, since so much of the last fifteen chapters of *Del Miño al Bidasoa* is devoted to their observations on or discussions of, for example, food, Spaniards who migrate to the New World, sailing ships, songbirds, groups of young women they come across, their respective friends in Santander, the behavior of vacationers, ghost ships, local wars, the kinds of fish to be found in a particular river, the charms of the poet Gabriel Celaya, or the life of a fisherman. And then there are other, more basic matters to discuss, such as when to stop for a while, when to eat, or where to find a drink. From the above list it is apparent that Dupont and the vagabond spend little or no time discussing matters that might be expected to figure prominently in a travel work, such as aspects of landscape, features of towns and villages, the presence or lack of crops, local people and local customs, appearances of prosperity or poverty, and so on. Overwhelmingly, their observations and conversations are simply the stuff of small talk. With the exception of the comments on Gabriel Celaya, the two men's exchanges consist of light and entertaining observations as they move along the highway, pause over a drink, or stroll around a town or village.

In a discussion of Eric Newby's classic travel work, *A Short Walk in the Hindu Kush* (1958), Mark Cocker refers to Newby as "the traveller as comic anti-hero" (p. 141). And while there are certainly frequent moments of humor and light relief in Newby's account of his arduous journey, the perils of Nuristan provide a sobering reminder of the task confronting the Englishman and his companions. The vagabond and Dupont, on the other hand, are largely presented as comic antiheroes in a much more congenial setting. The problems they encounter are not mountains or bandits, but normally involve comfort and hunger. And although the two men usually fail to perform as recorders of people and places, they function instead as a pair of eccentric, rather roguish, and altogether affable characters with the appearance and behavior of near down-and-outs. In fact, it comes as no surprise when they are turned away from a respectable hotel in Santander.

In the *Pueblo* articles there is no indication of Cela striking up a close relationship with his driver, Gregorio, and certainly no material that portrays the two men as companions. Gregorio is significant for his general invisibility and there is no suggestion that Dupont is any kind of bizarre projection of Cela's driver of 1948. However, once the author had decided to revamp the *Pueblo* version of the journey, put his traveler on foot (for most of the time, at any rate), and portray him as a somewhat eccentric vagrant (but with certain literary connections), then it may have been that Dupont was intended as a foil and counterbalance to this kind of traveler-figure, or perhaps just a suitable companion for him.

Yet the dramatic core to the travel account provided by the partnership of the vagabond and Dupont is a *fictitious* one. At the end of the narrative the Frenchman is acknowledged as an invention of the author. The first edition contains a "Censo de personajes" (pp. 237–55), an inventory of people seen or mentioned in the work. Some ninety people on this list, including Dupont, are indicated as being "personajes de ficción" [fictitious characters]. In fact, most of the approximately 220 names listed belong to historical figures—monarchs, soldiers, explorers, saints, and writers—nearly all of whom are just mentioned in passing. Apart from Dupont, other fictitious characters indicated include many minor players: old men, women, children (including those at Nocedal), drivers, priests, bar owners, and so on, as well as the vagabond's supposed cousin, Benitiño do Chao.

Juan Goytisolo has acknowledged that his first travel narrative, *Campos de Níjar*, is in fact a conflation of several trips that he made to the province of Almería in the late 1950s.[8] In her study of this work, Abigail Lee Six observes: "Juan Goytisolo never went on the journey described in *Campos de Níjar*. To that extent, the work is a fiction. On the other hand, he has been, at different times, to all the places he describes. To that extent, the text is factual."[9] Lee Six then proceeds to discuss, with reference to descriptive technique and character presentation, the whole issue of fact and fiction in this kind of text and she suggests that *Campos de Níjar* resides in the "blurry crossover area" that exists between "a novel based heavily on personal experience and a non-fictional memoir with its inevitable element of poetic licence" (pp. 61–62).

Yet, while both Cela and Goytisolo later came to reveal that *Del Miño al Bidasoa* and *Campos de Níjar* were composite narratives, Cela was also prepared to make it known at the end of the first edition of this particular travel book that the second most important character in the work (and whose actions and words are massively intertwined with those of the protagonist) was a creature of the author's imagination. Indeed, the foregrounding of the traveler that so strikingly marks *Viaje a la Alcarria* is now taken a significant stage further in *Del Miño al Bidasoa* with the narrative double act that dominates the development of the work. However, the fact that one of these two characters is entirely fictitious (while the vagabond himself has a number of fictitious touches about him) reopens the issue of whether this partly reconstituted narrative, with an invented central character, should really be classed as a travel book. Indeed, in the closing moments of *The Great Railway Bazaar* (1975), Paul Theroux confronts the issue of factual accounts and fictional creations. He observes: "The difference between travel writing and fiction is the difference between recording what the eye sees and discovering what the imagination knows." He then muses on how, had he been so inclined, he might have fictionalized and dramatized certain moments or aspects of his travels to and through Asia.[10]

Certainly, in the introduction to the first edition of *Del Miño al Bidasoa* Cela expressed no doubts about the genre of the work he was presenting to his readers. His opening words are as follow: "He aquí, lector amigo, otro libro de viajes, otras páginas nómadas, otras visiones y otras andanzas a través de los paisajes españoles" [Here you have, dear reader, another travel book, more nomadic pages, more visions of and adventures through Spanish landscapes] (IV, 535). This is, of course, a very relaxed use of the term "travel book." However, recognizing that *Del Miño al Bidasoa* is, for a variety of reasons, a hybrid creation, it now remains to consider other aspects of the construction and content of the work.

TRAVELING AT SPEED AND PAUSING

The leisurely pace that marks most of *Viaje a la Alcarria* is largely absent from Cela's second travel narrative. The hectic comings and goings of the first two chapters of the work are followed by an altogether rapid progress across northern Spain that not only traces the route of the car journey recounted in the *Pueblo* articles, but often reflects the speed, descriptive sketchiness, and even some of the omissions of the newspaper pieces. For example, when, having reached the Asturias, the vagabond of *Del Miño al Bidasoa* accepts a car ride outside Castropol, a nearby castle is quickly noted and three villages are passed through without a word of description. Nonetheless, the travel-book version still reveals some minor but colorful additions to the original:

Pueblo article	*Del Miño al Bidasoa*
A la izquierda, sobre un altozano, está el castillo de los Pardos, con sus torres almenadas. Por Barres, por Serantes y por Rapalcuarto, el viajero marcha detrás de una furgoneta que no quiere dejarle paso. (IV, 585)	A la izquierda, subido en un altozano, está el castillo de los Pardo, con sus torres almenadas y sus sangrientos recuerdos.
	Por Barres, por Serantes y por Rapalcuarto, el coche en el que viaja, o flota, el vagabundo, que hoy se siente poderoso como un diputado, marcha detrás de una furgoneta que no quiere cederle el paso. (IV, 296).

[To the left, on a hillock, is the castle of the Pardo family, with its crenellated towers. Through Barres, Serantes, and Rapalcuarto, the traveler is stuck behind a van that will not let him pass.]

[To the left, up on a hillock, is the castle of the Pardo family, with its crenellated towers and bloody memories.

Through Barres, Serantes, and Rapalcuarto, the car in which the vagabond is traveling, or floating, for today he feels as important as a deputy, is stuck behind a van that will not let him get past.]

Some thirty kilometers along the road, in Navia, the vagabond joins up with Dupont and, following the route of the *Pueblo* account, they head inland to the mountains where, on the outskirts of Salas, they begin a truck ride that takes them first of all to Nava. The distance between Salas and Nava (via the Asturian capital, Oviedo) is some seventy kilometers, and in the relevant *Pueblo* piece there is absolutely no description of this stretch of road, its features, or surroundings. The reason for this lack of data is simply that Cela ate very well in Salas and slept for the whole of the journey. In the corresponding part of *Del Miño al Bidasoa*, the author avoids having to include travel description in this section of the supposed truck journey by resorting to the same excuse. So, in Salas, Dupont and the vagabond eat a wonderful meal. The latter then falls asleep in the cab of the vehicle and does not wake until they reach Nava:

Pueblo article
El viajero, a quien había invadido el sueño del justo bien nutrido, no se despierta hasta La Nava [*sic*]. Atrás dejó la capital y quince pueblos. A veces, una comida hecha a gusto es un anestésico de primera. (IV, 588).

Del Miño al Bidasoa
Con el dulce meneo y la difícil digestión, el vagabundo se durmió como un infante con la conciencia tranquila. Cuando hubo de despertarse, al cabo de mucho tiempo, el camión había dejado atrás la capital y otros quince pueblos. A veces, una comida hecha a gusto es un anestésico de primera, mejor incluso que el anís. (IV, 324).

[The traveler, who had succumbed to the sleep of the just and well fed, does not wake until Nava. Behind him lay the capital of the region and fifteen towns and villages. At times, a fine lunch is a first-class anesthetic.]

[With the gentle swaying and all the necessary digesting, the vagabond fell asleep like a babe with a clear conscience. When he woke up, a good while later, the truck had left behind the regional capital and another fifteen towns and villages. At times, a fine lunch is a first-class anesthetic, even better than anisette.]

Yet though the relative haste with which in the *Pueblo* account Cela crossed from La Coruña to the French border (a matter of some five or six days) is often reflected in *Del Miño al Bidasoa*, not everything in the 1952 account is bustle and brevity of description. Indeed, the work is marked by constant changes of pace. Movement is regularly punctuated by narrative pauses which take a variety of forms. There are, for example, occasional lengthy passages describing activities or locations. So, whereas in the *Pueblo* account the *fiesta* in Nava is dealt with in eight lines, it takes up the whole of section 22 (three pages) in the travel book. Here, Dupont is seen selling his stock of windmills and then adjourning with the vagabond and the truck driver to a noisy, lively bar where the proceeds from the sale are spent on wine. Later, the picturesque resort and fishing port of San Vicente de la Barquera, allotted seven rather bland lines in the *Pueblo* version, is dealt with in four leisurely pages that touch on aspects of the appearance and history of the place, and then see the vagabond and Dupont ensconced in a bar. Here, they are engaged in conversation by the inquisitive owner (who apparently ends up telling them a story about a red shark, but which the vagabond cannot remember) and also consume a considerable amount of wine.

In the *Pueblo* account, Santander is covered in just over two pages, half of this material describing the visit to the workers' holiday residence. It is observed that Santander is, along with Cádiz, San Sebastián, and La Coruña, one of the loveliest cities in Spain. In *Del Miño al Bidasoa* this judgment is repeated, but with the Basque resort omitted from the list. However, in view of this glowing opinion of the attractiveness of Santander it is surprising to find that in the ten or so pages of the travel book that are dedicated to following the two companions around the city, there are just a couple of paragraphs of description of the place. Dupont and the vagabond spend most of their time talking about colorful friends who live there. Castro-Urdiales, on the other hand, a small resort more than seventy kilometers to the east and the presence of which is barely mentioned in the *Pueblo* version, is now accorded half a dozen pages. These deal with aspects of the town's location, its history, its fine local water and wine, its hard-working inhabitants, splendid young boys and girls, and the fact that the locals play *pelota* and skittles. All these observations are followed by a description of the two wanderers undertaking a casual job in return for a memorable quantity of food and drink (IV, 420–26).

Elsewhere, the pace of the narrative slows in order to give historical notes or background. So, Llanes (which receives two lines in the *Pueblo* account) has parts of its history mentioned as well as the names of a number of its illustrious sons (IV, 343–45), while Guetaria (nine lines in the *Pueblo* version) is presented largely in terms of its destruction in the 1830s, during the first Carlist War, the damage it sustained in hostilities in 1597 and 1638, and its fame as the birthplace of the first circumnavigator, Juan Sebastián Elcano. And here, too, material on local information and associations is then followed by the traveling companions deciding to sample local beverages, this time Guetaria's famous *chacolí* wine and its cider (IV, 469–71).

In other parts of *Del Miño al Bidasoa*, the motion of the journey is brought to a halt by sometimes lengthy sections of narrative that deal with the obsessions or biographies of quirky characters supposedly encountered by the two wayfarers. Thus, the interest in nicknames that is something of a feature of *Viaje a la Alcarria* resurfaces in the second travel work when practically the whole of section 29 (one of the three longest sections in the book) is given over to (the fictitious) Don Ferreol, a bizarre character who devotes himself to collecting nicknames. Copious examples of these dominate, to the point of tediousness, the long description of the encounter between him, the vagabond, and Dupont (IV, 352–62). Elsewhere, when the companions arrive in Torrelavega (a town that merits nine lines in the *Pueblo* chronicle) most of the material on their stay there involves the account given by a bar owner, Tristán Balmaseda (another invented character), of the tribulations suffered throughout his life. His tale is patiently heard by the visitors, who gratefully accept the wine that Balmaseda plies them with (IV, 381–88). Finally, toward the end of the narrative, comes the lengthy story of the (fictitious) restaurant owner, Fermín Cuartango, now married for the fourth time and the father of twenty-four children, precisely six from each marriage (IV, 435–42).

Del Miño al Bidasoa also includes other digressions that slow the narrative pace by bringing the geographical progress to a series of regular halts. Such pauses include the disquisition on the newspaper, *Las Riberas del Eo* (IV, 284–85), which draws heavily on the *Pueblo* account (IV, 584); the altogether surreal episode in Navia, where the vagabond holds a conversation with the statue of the poet Ramón de Campoamor (IV, 302–4) —here a three-line reference to the monument in the *Pueblo* version (IV, 587) is expanded into a three-page fantasy; the frivolous dream sequence in the restaurant in Salas (IV, 318–21); Dupont's tales of ghost ships (IV, 413–16); the christening party in Guipúzcoa that the two men gatecrash and where they eat and drink superbly well and are even given money to help them on their way (IV, 447–51), and the incident in Usúrbil when they find money in the road and bluff their way out of returning it to its rightful owner (IV, 478–80). This last episode, like the account of the christening party, is largely a comic sketch with a distinctly picaresque flavor. Indeed, these and other incidents or digressions found in *Del Miño al Bidasoa* provide occasional and usually lighthearted diversions from the road and travel in what is, in any case, a work that is generally light in tone. Such episodes, together with the frequent scenes in which the two travelers are presented as enthusiastically eating and drinking their way across northern Spain, reveal the author constantly altering the pace and movement of his narrative.

THE PICTURE OF NORTHERN SPAIN

There are three striking aspects of Cela's remodeling of the relevant *Pueblo* articles into chapters 3 to 20 of *Del Miño al Bidasoa*. These are the introduction in chapter 5 of Dupont; the transformation of the traveler-figure of *Viaje a la Alcarria* from a purposeful, generally serious young writer with a job to do, into a rather eccentric, devil-may-care vagabond leading a somewhat precarious existence and, finally, the inclusion of a massive amount of dialogue in the travel book.

Whereas the *Pueblo* pieces contain only occasional snatches of direct speech, usually a couple of lines in length, *Del Miño al Bidasoa* is, in contrast, heavily laden with dialogue. This is largely because of the introduction of Dupont and the subsequent lengthy exchanges between the two companions. In addition, the narrative contains many conversations between the wayfarers and the people they come across during the course of their travels. Cela often transforms sights, incidents, or scenes in the *Pueblo* version by dramatizing them (and presumably indulging in a degree of fictionalizing) and gives much of this material a certain immediacy by the use of direct speech. Thus the arrival at Campoamor's statue in the newspaper pieces (IV, 587) is developed into the bizarre conversation in the travel book (IV, 302–4); or one line in the *Pueblo* version mentions a church clock in Otur (IV, 587) and this is subsequently transformed into an eight-line conversation (IV, 310–11), while the passing mention of a pony and trap in the original (IV, 587) serves as the inspiration for a tale of mischief and humor that contains a good deal of dialogue and in which it seems that Cela has been unable to resist showing his novelistic hand (IV, 312–14).

Indeed, *Del Miño al Bidasoa* is, in a variety of ways, a novelized version of the *Pueblo* articles. With the appearance of Dupont, a character is introduced who very soon becomes one of the two leading players. All the while, the vagabond is steadily developed as a blend of eccentric, beggar, down-and-out, hedonist, and wag—someone with a rather puzzling background but who also has important literary connections, such as Alvaro Cunqueiro and Gabriel Celaya. Dupont and the vagabond become involved in a number of scenes and episodes that have all the flavor of fiction and throughout much of the work their partnership dominates the narrative and distracts from those features normally associated with the travel genre: the description of people and places. Yet, despite this fictional dressing that is given to the *Pueblo* material, the narrative is still interspersed with a number of descriptions of places and monuments. And while some of these passages are borrowed, with modifications, from the original newspaper articles, others appear to consist of material created for the travel-book version of the journey. (Some of this could, of course, be "old" material that the *Pueblo* account had no room for.)

Earlier, it was pointed out that in the *Pueblo* version the speed of the car journey is reflected in the way that towns and villages are often hurriedly passed through with only the barest of mentions, and that such descriptive haste and sketchiness is frequently transferred to the travel book. Yet, as was also mentioned previously, there are occasions when places given only the briefest of reference in the newspaper accounts are, in *Del Miño al Bidasoa*, described in terms of their location, history, or distinctiveness. But even in such cases, the author normally avoids attempting any kind of sharp, detailed depiction, preferring instead to convey general impressions of a particular locality.

Good examples of how a considerable expansion of *Pueblo* material does not necessarily involve precise description of appearance, or architecture, or other physical features can be found in the treatment of Llanes and, later, Laredo. The Asturian coastal town of Llanes is dealt with in one line in the *Pueblo* version, as "un pueblo, hermoso, limpio y veraniego" [a beautiful, clean, and summery town] (IV, 593). However, it is introduced in the travel book as "un pueblo hermoso y limpio, histórico y veraniego, marinero y, como la cebolla, con siete capas de humor y de retranca" [a beautiful and clean, historic and summery, seafaring town and, like an onion, with seven layers of humor and guile] (IV, 342), and is subsequently described in three pages. Nevertheless, there is absolutely no indication as to why the town should be considered "beautiful" (for example, no reference is made to the town's attractive mansions, its seventeenth-century castle, or fifteenth-century church) or wherein resides the place's "humor and guile." On the other hand, the insertion of the adjective "historic" in the travel-book description is certainly justified, as the reader is regaled with a good deal of information about local history.

Laredo, in Cantabria, which in the *Pueblo* account merits no more than "Laredo, con su cumplida playa de a legua, parece unido a Santoña" [Laredo, with its huge, league-long beach, appears to be joined to Santoña] (IV, 599), is, like Llanes, given much more attention in the travel work. However, half of the eight pages set in Laredo are concerned with Dupont's tales of ghost ships and there is nothing in the other, descriptive material that addresses the enticing introductory comment: "Laredo es un pueblo hermoso" [Laredo is a beautiful town] (IV, 409). In fact, the two companions are unimpressed as they wander the old part of the town until, bored, they head for the beach. So, once again, there is no attempt to paint any kind of detailed picture of a place that is introduced with an accolade.

What clearly emerges from any consideration of the descriptive material in Cela's second travel book is that the author is not given to indulging in much depiction of churches, castles, houses, streets, or towns. Furthermore, his descriptive accounts of landscapes traveled through or seen in the distance are infrequent and brief, although where they do occur they often reveal a simple charm. Material devoted to flora and fauna is even skimpier. However, where the author does reveal a good measure of descriptive enthusiasm, and this might be expected after *Viaje a la Alcarria*, is in his quite frequent detailing of river systems and road networks. But once again his approach is geographical and factual rather than pictorial. For what Cela seems to want to do with the roads and rivers of northern Spain is not capture appearance or characteristics, but instead give information on where they come from and go to. In effect, he is attempting to show how these roads and rivers would look on a map. It is with this kind of material that the author displays his attention to detail (and not, for example, in attempts to describe a church or a village) and it is also here that he most literally adheres to the notion of a travel book as principally an exercise in geography.

However, even the detailing of river systems can occasionally be given a certain lyrical touch. As the vagabond and Dupont make their way along the Asturian coast, they come to Ribadesella, where the sight of the local river conjures up a brief account, with poetic touches, of some of the tributaries of the Sella River:

> El Sella viene del monte de Ponga, después de beberse de un sorbo al Piloña. El Aguamía nace en la peña de Santianes. Y el Vega, con sus aguas claras cantarinas y bucólicas, rompe en la sierra de la Serolina y se ahoga en la ancha mar, bajo el puente de piedra por el que pasa, casi como un suspiro, el camino real. (IV, 335)

> [The Sella comes from the Ponga range of mountains, after quaffing in one go the Piloña. The Aguamía rises in the crag of Santianes. And the Vega, with its clear, babbling, bucolic waters, springs forth in the Sierra of Serolina and when it moves through the stone bridge over which the highway passes, almost like a sigh, it is engulfed in the open sea.]

Here there is no portrayal of the Sella itself and, apart from the reference to the qualities of the waters of the Vega and to the stone bridge, this kind of information could have been gleaned from a map or from a guide to the rivers of northern Spain. Furthermore, this is not material that has been transferred from the *Pueblo* articles. Rather, like the detailed account of the course of the Urola River, in Guipúzcoa (IV, 466), it has been inserted in the travel book more as a disquisition from the vagabond. The lengthier account of the wanderings of the Deva River (also in Guipúzcoa) is similarly presented as some kind of fluvial discourse from the vagabond. But at least on this occasion the material has, as a kind of tailpiece, a paragraph on some of the species of fish found in the river (IV, 456–57).

Overall, Cela's second travel book contains a good deal of information on river systems but very little description of individual rivers. There is, for example, no indication of the splendor of the Miño in southern Galicia nor, in the closing chapter, any mention of the appearance of the Bidassoa. Indeed, in the final pages the Bidassoa is seen not in terms of its geographical or narrative significance, but rather in the context of the tributaries that join it shortly before it disappears into the sea (IV, 492) and, at the other end of its course, as a name that ceases to exist in the mountains around Santesteban (IV, 496).

Since roads lack the vitality, organic growth, and usually the romance of rivers, it comes as no surprise to find that when, from time to time, roads or road systems are featured in *Del Miño al Bidasoa* they are normally presented in the practical terms of route and destination: a means of getting to certain places, even when they are not traveled but are simply acknowledged and passed by. So, as the vagabond and Dupont move away from the Asturian coast and head inland toward Salas, a smaller road than the one they are traveling is noted in a bare, factual, but also detailed manner:

> A una legua de Cortina, el camino que cruza la carretera lleva, por un lado y bordeando la sierra de las Ontedas, hasta Cudillero, en la mar y al sudeste del cabo Vidio, y por el otro y metiéndose por las sierras de Adrados y de Monteoscuro, hasta Tineo pasando por Paredes y Villatresmil. (IV, 315)

> [A league from Cortina, the road that crosses the highway goes, in one direction and skirting the Sierra de las Ontedas, as far as Cudillero, on the coast and to the southeast of Cape Vidio, and in the other direction through the Sierras of Adrados and Monteoscuro, and, passing through Paredes and Villatresmil, as far as Tineo.]

This kind of mechanical mention of roads not traveled, but the destinations of which are logged, is found elsewhere, with the same equally dull effect. At other times, though, routes that have noteworthy historical and cultural associations are sometimes signaled:

Antes de llegar a Zumaya la carretera tiene un ramal que va a Cestona, al pie del monte Erchina, y a Azpeitia, no lejos del santuario de San Ignacio de Loyola; de Azpeitia sale una desviación que va hasta Tolosa pasando por Régil, a la sombra del monte Hernio, con sus canteras de jaspe y sus recuerdos de fray Domingo de Herquicia, mártir en el Japón, y de Paulino Uzcudun. (IV, 465)

[Before reaching Zumaya, a branch road leaves the highway and goes to Cestona, at the foot of mount Erchina, and to Azpeitia, not far from the sanctuary of St Ignatius Loyola; from Azpeitia there is detour that goes to Tolosa via Régil, in the shadow of Mount Hernio, with its jasper quarries and memories of Friar Domingo de Herquicia, who was martyred in Japan, and Paulino Uzcudun.]

Once again, this passage is not based on material in the *Pueblo* version, despite the fact that the paragraphs that enclose it in *Del Miño al Bidasoa* draw heavily on the newspaper account.

Cela's second travel book contains noticeably more description of road and river systems than *Viaje a la Alcarria*, presumably because of the vastly greater physical and geographical scope involved in the northern journey. But an even more striking difference between the two narratives is the amount of material (descriptions and observations) dedicated to the respective landscapes. Setting aside accounts of river systems and the occasional view of coast and sea, *Del Miño al Bidasoa* contains relatively few references to the natural environment. From time to time there are brief descriptions of a changing landscape, of surrounding countryside, or hills and mountains in the distance. These are normally given in an unadorned, matter-of-fact way and stand in marked contrast to the rare attempts at poetic depiction, such as the passage that comes as the two companions head east, away from Bilbao. On this occasion, the piece is a close adaptation of the *Pueblo* version (IV, 608):

Entre las acacias del bosque se ven, de cuando en cuando, algunas verdes y relucientes manchas de húmedos praderíos y un tierno y susurrante pinar acompaña al vagabundo durante una legua de camino, sobre poco más o menos.

La humedad va en aumento, se ven hilillos de agua, temblorosas venas de agua por todas partes y, al pie de los árboles, crecen el suave musgo, el amoroso helecho, el césped de terciopelo y el tímido y medicinal culantrillo. (IV, 444)

[Through the acacias there can be seen, from time to time, green and glistening patches of damp meadowland, and a delicate, rustling pinewood accompanies the vagabond along the road for more or less a league.

The dampness increases: there are trickles of water, tremulous veins of water everywhere and, at the foot of the trees, soft moss, tender ferns, velvety grass, and delicate, medicinal maidenhair are all growing.]

The descriptive material dedicated to agricultural scenes and landscapes is even scarcer than that allotted to the natural environment and, when it is introduced, invariably amounts to a couple of lines or so. The probable explanation for this paucity of material describing the natural scenery (in one of the most attractive parts of Spain) or the agricultural imprint (on one of the most productive areas of the country) is that in 1948 Cela had traveled through at speed and so had little time for meditating on landscape or composing careful descriptions. But whatever the reason, the fact is that in the narrative the agricultural content amounts to little more than occasional snippets. Typical in length and tone are: "Liendo, a la derecha de la carretera, cría sus coliflores y sus praderas a la gallarda sombra del Mojón de Laya" [Liendo, to the right of the highway, tends its cauliflowers and meadows in the elegant shadow of the Mojón de Laya] (IV, 418); "Guetaria tiene una pequeña huertecilla con la que se va arreglando y algo de viñedo, de pomarada y de cereal" [Guetaria has a small area of arable land that is being tidied up, and some vineyards, apple orchards, and cereals] (IV, 469), and, in the closing pages: "En el valle de Santesteban de Lerín, se cultiva el maíz, la remolacha y el tabaco" [In the valley of Santesteban de Lerín, they grow sweet corn, beetroot, and tobacco] (IV, 495). Such brief observations, the almost total absence of focus on people working in the fields, or going to or coming from work, as well as the lack of comment from local inhabitants on agricultural matters, mark a real difference from the prominent treatment given to such sights and opinions in *Viaje a la Alcarria*.

Finally, it is worth noting that as the vagabond and his companion move into and across the Basque country, the narrative reveals an understandable awareness of the impact of industry on the people and landscapes of this part of the north. The province of Vizcaya is referred to as "Bilbao y un montón de fábricas una detrás de otra" [Bilbao and a stack of factories, one after another] (IV, 427), but is also seen in terms of excessive prosperity and order: "En Vizcaya hay demasiada riqueza a la vista, demasiada industria y mucho más orden del necesario" [In Vizcaya there is too much wealth on display, too much industry, and more order than is necessary] (IV, 427). Shortly thereafter, as the narrative moves into the outskirts of Bilbao and thence into the city, these preliminary observations are followed by an awareness of the presence of industrial and urban landscapes: a leaden sky, chimneys belching black smoke, unbreathable air, heavy traffic, noise, crowds of people, and uniformity, all of which bring the vagabond to reflect wistfully on the delights of the countryside (IV, 429–33).

The scenes in and around Bilbao (almost wholly based on the newspaper articles of 1948) reveal an industrialized, urbanized, rather hectic, and unappealing way of life. However, the picture of Bilbao and its hinterland presented in *Del Miño al Bidasoa* should not be interpreted as simply an indication of vigorous industrial progress and its associated social and aesthetic costs in rapidly modernizing, midcentury Spain. According to Ramón Tamames, until 1950 industrial growth was slow on account of inadequate supplies of power and shortages of cement, steel, and nonferrous metals. He points out that things only began to change in the following years, largely because of American aid and access to credit facilities from some European countries (p. 406). On the same subject, Raymond Carr and Juan Pablo Fusi Aizpurua point out that "by 1948 industrial production had just passed 1929 levels; by 1951 the national income had climbed back to the levels obtaining before the Civil War" (p. 52). Thus the brief period enclosed by the *Pueblo* pieces and Cela's second travel book was principally a time of painstaking catching-up and slow recovery.

Yet there is no attempt in *Del Miño al Bidasoa* to reflect the economic difficulties facing many Spaniards and precious little focus on the inhabitants of northern Spain. Whereas *Viaje a la Alcarria* contains indications of hardship and even destitution, the second travel work pays hardly any attention to the badly off and instead presents an almost constant series of impressions of people free of social and economic problems. And although, when the vagabond reaches the outskirts of Bilbao, mention is made of pollution, gloom, and crowds, at the same time there is the recognition that factories can mean prosperity. Indeed, the picture painted throughout most of the narrative is of a pleasant northern Spain, dotted with appealing towns and villages, and inhabited by apparently contented, helpful people. There are also, from time to time, comments on the prosperity and well-being seen in certain parts: the elegant jewelry shops and well-dressed nannies pushing expensive baby carriages in Navia; attractive houses and magnificent villas in Las Arriondas and on the outskirts of Torrelavega; well-dressed people in Santander; comfortably off holidaymakers in Laredo, and signs of prosperity throughout Vizcaya and also in Guipúzcoa.

Overall, *Del Miño al Bidasoa* radiates a general sense of well-being. Towns and villages appear to be clean and tidy; food and drink are readily available, and there are no signs of hunger (apart from the occasional pangs suffered by the two companions). There are busy coastal resorts, people are usually friendly, and carefree, cheerful young girls ride around on their bicycles. And while many of the indications of the pleasant state of things in those areas of northern Spain that are seen are drawn from the *Pueblo* articles, much supplementary material reinforcing the notion that everything is fine is incorporated into the travelbook version of the journey. Unlike *Viaje a la Alcarria*, *Del Miño al Bidasoa* gives an altogether sanitized and almost overwhelmingly comfortable view of Spain of the early 1950s.

CONCLUSION

With the first travel book, *Viaje a la Alcarria*, it is probably quite difficult for the reader not to be constantly mindful that the traveler-figure is the young Cela who sets out to visit, explore, and write about the area visited. Once the journey is underway there is no direct acknowledgment to the reader or to those encountered in the Alcarria (at least, none that is recorded) that the traveler is the author of *La familia de Pascual Duarte*. Indeed, during the trip there are only a couple of references to the fact that things are being jotted down, that the traveler is gathering material, and that this material is going to become an account of the Alcarria journey. Nevertheless, it is relatively easy for the reader to accept that the traveler is the thirty-year-old Cela and to picture him as such. The photograph that was used as the frontispiece for the first edition of *Viaje a la Alcarria*, a close-up view of the author sitting at the roadside and taking notes, would certainly remind the reader who the wayfarer was, or at least show what he looked like.

In *Del Miño al Bidasoa*, on the other hand, the traveler-figure, now termed "vagabond," is distanced from the author in a variety of ways. The individual first encountered on a country road in southern Galicia, and last seen rambling through the mountains of Navarre, is frequently likened to some kind of eternal wanderer. He is also portrayed as a down-at-heel wayfarer. The most striking narrative difference between the newspaper chronicles of 1948 and the travel book of four years later is the way in which the bland, responsible, chauffeur-driven protagonist is transformed into the eccentric, hard-up vagabond who makes his way across the north of the country.[11] In the travel account, he relies on finding the occasional odd job in order to make ends meet, sings for alms in Mondoñedo, catches fish and sells them in Ribadeo, while in other places he sometimes begs for money. Elsewhere, the vagabond and Dupont scrounge or are simply given food or drink, and on a number of occasions they are regarded as and treated like tramps.

On top of all this, it is suggested that the vagabond has no family, that he is a sailor from a family of sailors, and is no more than a *friend* of "Don Camilo."[12] But on the other hand, it is acknowledged that he is from the same place in Galicia as Cela and it is also revealed that this apparently hard-up wayfarer has some impressive literary connections. He is, it transpires, acquainted with Alvaro Cunqueiro (IV, 279); he and Dupont spend a night in San Sebastián in the flat of *their* friend, Gabriel Celaya (IV, 481–87), and in the closing pages of the work, as the two companions head for the home of Ricardo Baroja, both Ricardo and his brother, Pío Baroja, are described as friends of the vagabond (IV, 493).[13]

The traveler-figure of *Del Miño al Bidasoa*, then, is a colorful, distorted, and partly disguised projection of Cela. By the same token, this second travel book is an extended, embellished, and heavily fictionalized version of the *Pueblo* account. The seat of this fictionalization is to be found with the introduction of the Frenchman, Dupont. His subsequent relationship with the vagabond, the experiences, conversations, observations, and the growing affinity between the two men, all give rise to a lighthearted tone and sentimental focus that come to dominate the narrative.

6

Past and Present: *Judíos, moros y cristianos*

IN THE LENGTHY PROLOGUE TO THE FIRST EDITION OF *JUDÍOS, MOROS y cristianos: Notas de un vagabundaje por Segovia, Avila y sus tierras* [Jews, Moors and Christians: Notes of Wanderings through Segovia, Avila and their Lands] (1956), Cela refers (through the voice of his traveler-figure, once again a "vagabond") to the "agreeable disorder" of the material in this work. He justifies the structure of the account on the grounds that editorial constraints forced him to omit much of the original material and that it is, in any case, impossible to travel the length and breadth of Old Castile all in one go (V, 130). Earlier in the prologue the author describes various interpretations of the scope of Old Castile and also proposes his definition of the region: the provinces of Burgos, Soria, Segovia, Avila, Valladolid, and Palencia (V, 123–24).

In this third travel book, however, Cela makes no attempt to cover the whole of the area. The eight chapters of *Judíos, moros y cristianos* relate a journey through parts of the provinces of Segovia, Burgos, Valladolid, and Avila. But the bulk of the work is given over to an account of travels in the provinces of Segovia and Avila, with tours of the city of Segovia (about three-quarters of chapter 4) and the city of Avila (almost half of chapter 5) serving as the two central pillars of the narrative. The terrain covered is extensive. Mainly on foot, but occasionally transported by cart, car, truck, and train, the vagabond passes through much of an area about 250 kilometers in length that lies, transversely, to the west and north of Madrid: incorporating both flanks of the Sierra de Gredos and the northwestern slopes of the Sierra de Guadarrama and the Sierra de Ayllón, from Barco de Avila in the province of Avila to Aranda de Duero in the province of Burgos. The maximum breadth of the area covered is approximately one hundred kilometers: from the pass of Navacerrada, northwest to the town of Medina del Campo. Overall, the vagabond appears to complete a journey of around eight hundred kilometers.

Although for parts of the trip his feet do not touch the road, this is still an impressively extensive narrative coverage of the heartland of Old Castile. The number of days taken over the journey appears to be just under fifty, not including the two-week break that the vagabond has in Cebreros at the end of the trip, resting and seeing old friends before catching the train back to Madrid. All in all, then, *Judíos, moros y cristianos* purports to be the account of a journey of about seven weeks (a long period when compared to the other travel works) through an extensive area of impressively varied geographical scope: with the vagabond describing cities, towns, and hamlets, following rivers, and even hiking across the Sierra de Gredos.

However, it transpires that the journey described in Cela's third travel book is a conflation of a number of trips made in Old Castile during the late 1940s and early 1950s. Certainly, in the prologue to the first edition the author quietly gives the impression that his book is the account of a single journey, although he does, perhaps, drop a small hint when he suggests that nobody would consider traveling the whole of Old Castile in one session (V, 130). Nevertheless, it is not until the narrative is over that the framing dates of the gathering of material are revealed. Here, Cela indicates that the travels in the provinces of Segovia and Avila took place between 1946 and 1952 (no mention is made of the timing of any trips through the provinces of Burgos or Valladolid). He adds that writing up was completed in September 1955 (V, 479).

So what the author has done to create his third travel work is to merge a number of excursions that took place in the late 1940s and early 1950s into a largely seamless tour of a sizeable part of Old Castile. Quite understandably, Cela has made no attempt to give an exact chronological setting for his account. He does, however, insert several indicators that the journey described in *Judíos, moros y cristianos* appears to take place during high or late summer of 1951 or 1952 (V, 285, 292), or in 1953 (V, 389). The approximate setting therefore locates the third travel book (but not in any precise way) in the early 1950s. This was a time when signs of slow economic recovery were accompanied by diplomatic activity that led to a Cold-War inspired rapprochement between Spain and the United States, resulting in the signing in September 1953 of defense and economic aid agreements.[1] Yet, the focus of this travel narrative is not on the social and economic conditions of contemporary Spain: such considerations constitute an almost inconsequential part of the work's content. Nevertheless, the title *Judíos, moros y cristianos*, with its evocation of a far-off age of religious and cultural differences, and of conflict and conquest, would have had clear cultural and political resonances for many Spaniards of the 1950s.

PAST CONFLICTS AND PRESENT POLEMICS

Cela's first two travel books reveal no obvious, overarching theme. However, with *Judíos, moros y cristianos* the author uses his main title to indicate a subject of historical and cultural weight—and of much polemical potential. In the prologue to the work, Cela suggests that Old Castile is not a *natural* region: instead, he terms it "a historical entity" (V, 125). From this it might be expected that the settings, buildings, vestiges, and even the debris of history (as well as, of course, the associated events and players) will emerge as the stuff of this travel book. However, the main title signals a concern with historical matters less tangible but far more controversial than the site of a battle, the location of a famous event, or the presence of a castle.

In 1948, the distinguished academic, Américo Castro, who had been teaching in the United States since 1937 (mostly at Princeton University, from where he retired in 1953) published in Buenos Aires *España en su historia: Cristianos, moros y judíos* [Spain in her History: Christians, Moors and Jews]. In the prologue to this 650-page study, Castro announces his rejection of the thesis that the concept of "Spain" and "Spanishness" can be applied to Roman Spain and Visigothic Spain. He also refuses to accept that the presence of Muslims and Jews in the Iberian peninsula was simply an "unwelcome presence," an "annoying, 800-year interlude," and that after 1492 (the date of the conquest of Granada and the expulsion of the Jews) Spain returned to its "eternal essence." He, too, had once subscribed to this widespread view of Spanish historical development, but he is no longer able to do so: "*No. When I now talk about 'Spanishness,' this notion is present in my consciousness with an appearance and form whose sense I cannot discern before the year 711*" (italics in original).[2] Thereafter, and throughout the remainder of his monumental study, Castro constructs the thesis that Spain, as a historical and cultural entity, began to emerge in the centuries that followed the Muslim invasion of 711. He proposes that during this period the inhabitants of the peninsula gained a growing consciousness of their presence as a people and also engaged in a gradual blending—brought about through conflicts, tensions, and proximity—of Christian, Muslim, and Jewish groups. As a corollary of all this, Castro goes on to suggest that with the final defeat of the Muslims in 1492 and the expulsion of the Jews in the same year, the religious and cultural combination that had nourished the development of modern Spain was tragically destroyed.

As was noted above, in his prologue to *España en su historia* Castro acknowledged that he was rejecting the prevailing orthodoxy. Indeed, in 1947 Ramón Menéndez Pidal had published an essay entitled "Los españoles en su historia" [The Spaniards in their History], intended as the introduction to the first volume of his *Historia de España* [History of Spain], and in which he suggests similarities between "Roman Spain" and "Hapsburg Spain," and even refers to the two periods in question as the "most brilliant moments of unified Spain."[3] Given this kind of view of the history of the Iberian peninsula, it comes as no surprise to learn that the ideas of Castro were regarded as cultural "heresy,"[4] and that he was marginalized by the academic establishment.[5] Moreover Castro's views were not simply providing material for lofty (although heated) academic debates. As was acknowledged in a newspaper article to mark the twenty-fifth anniversary of Castro's death, in the Spain of the 1940s and 1950s his theories came into conflict with the regime's promulgation of notions of Spain's national destiny and the country's racial purity:

> When Américo Castro undertook . . . the reassessment of the peninsula's past and questioned the supposed age-old essence of our culture, what he was denouncing above all else was an idea that was not regarded at the time as just an idea, and that was the survival since time immemorial of the inde- structible essence of Spanishness, the ethnic purity of the nation.[6]

Castro went on to develop his thesis in *La realidad histórica de España* [The Historical Reality of Spain], which was published in Mexico City in 1954 and, not surprisingly, incurred a largely hostile response from the academic establishment in Spain. However, the most vigorous and detailed rebuttal of Castro's ideas came from another exiled historian, Claudio Sánchez-Albornoz, with his hefty *España, un enigma histórico* [Spain: A Historical Enigma] (1956) and then *Españoles ante la historia* [Spaniards and their History] (1958).[7]

Cela states that he first met Américo Castro in Majorca in the sum- mer of 1957,[8] and his son indicates that the historian became a regular visitor to the family home on the island.[9] Just over a year before he made the acquaintance of Castro, Cela began to publish *Papeles de Son Armadans*, which frequently included the work of exiled creative writers and scholars. In its early years, the journal contained a number of pieces by and about Américo Castro, and the May 1965 issue (no. 110) marked the historian's eightieth birthday by including tributes from a dozen luminaries, among them Dámaso Alonso, Rafael Lapesa, Pedro Laín Entralgo, and Julián Marías.

In his introduction to this collection, Cela reveals his affection and admiration for Castro. Indeed, in the early 1960s the Galician author had described himself to Robert Kirsner as "a humble disciple" of the historian.[10] This comment was made in response to the observation by

Kirsner (whose book on Cela is dedicated to Américo Castro) that Cela's 1959 essay, "Sobre España, los españoles y lo español" [On Spain, the Spaniards, and Spanishness], "smacked" of Castro—as indeed it does, and with due acknowledgments. In fact, this six-thousand-word piece begins with a reference to the "noble pages" of *España en su historia* and then includes a sixty-word extract from the prologue to the work. This quotation concerns Castro's assertion of the distinctiveness of Spain and the irreducible Spanishness of, among others, Cervantes, Goya, and Falla.[11] Throughout the remainder of this presentation of Cela's idea on Spain and Spanishness, the writer does little more than outline the essence of Castro's views as expounded in *España en su historia* and *La realidad histórica de España*. At the same time, he makes the occasional reference to the work of, among others, Menéndez Pidal, Sánchez-Albornoz, and Ortega y Gasset.

But at the heart of Cela's assessment of the cultural and psychological evolution of the Spanish people are reaffirmations of Castro's principal theses. Thus, Cela states that the concept of Spain and Spanishness only begins to take shape, and then very crudely, when the Muslims defeated the Visigoths on the banks of the Guadalete River in 711. Before then, he claims, this land that had in varying degrees been occupied by Phoenicians, Celts, Romans, and so on, still did not possess that certain essence that made it Spain (p. 228). According to Cela, Spain is the product of "the living together, the fighting, the reciprocal destruction, and the fusion of three races—this is a somewhat confusing term in Spanish history—and three religious groups: Christians, Moors, and Jews" (p. 229). Subsequently, he suggests that although Christians and Muslims fought with each other during the course of the centuries, there were also lengthy periods of "peaceful and fruitful co-existence" (p. 230). Meanwhile, he notes that the Jews, who were not involved in the conflict between Muslims and Christians, were living in both communities, developing their skills in science and administration, and also refining their religious, philosophical, and ethical approaches to life. It was, according to Cela, from the simmering (and occasional faster cooking) of these various ingredients that what can be called "Spain" emerged (p. 231).

"Sobre España, los españoles y lo español" was first presented as a lecture in Valencia in April 1959, three and a half years after Cela finished composing *Judíos, moros y cristianos*. Consequently the lecture cannot be regarded as having influenced thematic aspects of the third travel book. Instead, it provides a detailed confirmation of Cela's acceptance of Américo Castro's theories on the fundamental importance of the interaction of Christian, Muslim, and Jewish cultures in the forging of Spain and Spanishness. Furthermore, by giving his third travel book a main title that so clearly echoed the subtitle of Castro's monograph of 1948 Cela was no doubt seen as presumably indicating his adherence to Castro's propositions and this would certainly have ruffled some establishment feathers. Indeed, it is worth noting Pío Rodríguez's observation, made in the context of an assessment of the "Movimiento Nacional" [National Movement]: "Against the democratic principle of diversity Fascism has always advanced the principle of spiritual, racial and national unity."[12] Also, it should be pointed out that Cela's third travel book is the only one of the six with a main title that indicates a theme rather than a journey. It now remains to examine the way in which *Judíos, moros y cristianos* addresses the subjects mentioned in that title and also explores and develops other matters.

THE FORGING OF MODERN SPAIN

In his study of the work of Américo Castro, Julio Almeida suggests that the historian, deeply affected by the Spanish Civil War, was engaging in a kind of personal therapy when he meditated on the origins of Spain (p. 107). In the opening essay of *Cuatro figuras del 98* [Four Figures of 1898], a lecture first delivered in February 1952, Cela states that the 1898 writers had a common denominator in their examination of a closed, inward-looking Spain, a country that was alone and with nothing more to contemplate than its old, enfeebled, and lacerated body (p. 19). Half a century after Spain's disastrous war with the United States in 1898 and a few years beyond the strife of the civil conflict of 1936–39, it seems that Cela's excursions around Old Castile were also an attempt to understand the nature of Spain and Spanishness through the lens of the historic heart of the country. It is also possible that these journeys (and maybe some of the others) were the author's quest for some sort of personal therapy through observation, reflection, and narration. But whatever the validity of this notion, there is little doubt that the journey described in *Judíos, moros y cristianos* is a kind of pilgrimage through parts of the heartland of Spain.

It was pointed out in chapter 3 that Michel Butor proposes the notion of secular pilgrimages that are the result of psychological and cultural quests: "The pilgrimage becomes a journey to those places that speak, that tell us of our history and ourselves" (p. 61). In *Judíos, moros y cristianos*, the vagabond follows a route rich in historical and cultural associations (and also notable for its geographical features) that brings him, in the last chapter, which is called "Donde mejor o peor, se fundó España" [Where, for Better or Worse, Spain was Founded], to his apparent destination, the site of the famous stone bulls of Guisando. It was here, in September 1468, that Henry IV of Castile, known as "The Impotent," recognized his seventeen-year-old half sister, Isabella, as heir to the crown of Castile.[13] The vagabond's view of this momentous act is short and simple: "Sin el encuentro de los toros de Guisando, España no hubiera sido España" [Without the meeting at the bulls of Guisando, Spain would not have been Spain] (V, 468). Subsequently, the point is reiterated: "El vagabundo piensa que la carne de lo que hoy es España fue parto de la reina Isabel" [The vagabond thinks that the flesh of what nowadays is Spain was the creation of Queen Isabella] (V, 469). Also, as the vagabond looks at the four stone bulls, "tan pobres, tan mudos, tan recoletos" [so poor, so silent, so isolated], he sees them as a "bitter image" of Spain (V, 469). So, having made his way to the spot that he regards as the place of the political birth of modern Spain, the vagabond couples the historic importance of the site with the suggestion of the bulls' reflection or reminder of a melancholy and suffering nation.

The young Isabella on whom the vagabond had reflected when he reached the bulls of Guisando could fairly be regarded by an informed reader of *Judíos, moros y cristianos* as a pivotal historical figure whose reign witnessed the ending of one great epoch in Iberian history and the beginning of developments of great national and international moment. And yet the period that stretched from the Muslim invasion of 711 to the fall of Granada in 1492 and the expulsion of the Jews in that same year receives only occasional, and usually brief, mentions in this travel work. Granted, the subtitle of the book indicates that the focus will be on the presence of Jews, Muslims, and Christians in the provinces of Segovia and Avila. However, during the course of the narrative there are no more than about three dozen references to the Muslim and Jewish presence in these parts of Old Castile and to the interaction between the peoples of the three great religions that was deemed by Castro to have had such a marked effect on the development and character of Spain.

From time to time there are mentions of battles in Old Castile between Muslims and Christians, and of struggles that took place in other parts of the peninsula. For example, reference is made to the terrible battle for San Esteban de Gormaz, which made the waters of the Douro run red (V, 165); the beggar in Roa recounts how the town was fought over, razed, taken, rebuilt, lost, and regained (V, 187); there is a description of the struggles for Sepúlveda (V, 241–42), and in Segovia mention is made of the street in which the two knights who led the successful attack on Muslim-held Madrid, had their homes (V, 291). As the vagabond wanders around Avila, there are references to the tug-of-war that left the city flattened and vulnerable until, after the capture of Toledo in 1085, it was repopulated with Spaniards from all parts of the peninsula (and also with French people) and its massive walls and towers were constructed in the last decade of the eleventh century (V, 334–35). Finally, there are several references to Alfonso VIII's great victory at Las Navas de Tolosa, in the province of Jaén, in 1212.

Also scattered throughout the narrative are reminders of other aspects of the Muslim presence or the Jewish legacy in Old Castile. But again, such allusions are surprisingly few and seldom lead to any kind of considered observations. Brief indications of long-gone Muslim or Jewish communities are given in the context of a poor hamlet such as Alquité, "con su nombre moro, su miseria cristiana" [with its Moorish name and Christian poverty] (V, 154) and where "moro" [Moor], it is revealed, is the local name for an unbaptized baby (V, 154, 157). In the Segovia section there is a reference to an image of the Virgin Mary being hidden from "las iras moras" [the Moorish fury] (V, 266); a brief, uninformative look at parts of the city's old Jewish quarter (V, 284–85); mention of what was once the Moorish quarter, and of the fact that the church of San Millán was built by Muslim craftsmen (V, 289).

Of rather more dramatic impact are occasional accounts of intolerance, cruelty, and persecution. In chapter 1, as the vagabond moves through the villages of the community of Ayllón, he condemns the racism of St Vincent Ferrer, who used to preach in the area and persuaded the king to make Jews and Muslims identify themselves by the color and markings of the clothing they wore (V, 162). There is mention of the execution of Jews in fifteenth-century Sepúlveda for apparently murdering children (V, 242) and a little later the vagabond recounts the story of how the Jews of Segovia condemned to death one of their own young women whom they had found guilty of committing adultery with a Christian. However, the beautiful Esther was saved from a horrifying death by the intervention of the Virgin Mary and was soon baptized, taking the name of Mary (V, 264). Another legend, this time showing the Jews of Segovia in a rather more scheming light, tells how a group of them attempted to adulterate a consecrated communion wafer by cooking or boiling it. Miraculously, it not only survived but also demonstrated some impressive aerodynamic feats that caused much consternation in the ranks of the leading Jews of the city (V, 275). Perhaps the principal point that emerges from these and other legends or stories recounted in *Judíos, moros y cristianos* is that while Christians and Muslims are indicated as having constantly attempted to assert their superiority by doing battle with each other, the relationship between Christians and Jews, obviously not adversarial in the military sense, was one that seemed to express itself in persecution by one side and subterfuge on the other, with a good deal of mutual suspicion and intolerance in between.

But in any case, the historical element in Cela's third travel book goes well beyond a concern with the military tussles between Christians and Muslims or the treatment of Jews living in Christian communities. The author's observation that Old Castile is a historical rather than a natural entity is reinforced in the narrative of *Judíos, moros y cristianos* with frequent references to various aspects, events, protagonists, and monuments of peninsular history—from pre-Roman times to the twentieth century. Yet, the twentieth century receives only scant attention. Although there are a couple of general, fleeting references to the civil war (but no mention of military actions in the area) and a few other allusions to events or incidents of the first half of the century, Cela seems content to more or less close the historical record with the nineteenth century, with the War of Independence and the Carlist conflicts.

Throughout this work, the main historical references are, as might be expected, associated with a site (natural or man-made) or a place (a building or a town). Occasionally, though, the author makes space for rather more developed tranches of historical narrative, normally in connection with the growth and fortunes of a town or city. One of the most striking examples of this occurs in Roa, where a local beggar provides the vagabond with a detailed account, virtually a catalog, of dates and facts relating to the town's involvement with wars, monarchs, warlords, generals, famous prisoners, and destruction, from the tenth century to the nineteenth century (V, 186–94). Elsewhere, there can be found a brisk account of various struggles for Sepúlveda, from the Middle Ages to the time of the French occupation (V, 241–43), a brief two paragraphs on aspects of the history of the Alcázar of Segovia (V, 283–84), and, somewhat surprisingly, just a few fragments on the rise of the city. Avila, however, is afforded slightly more generous treatment, with the acknowledgment of a certain confusion over details of its early history, an outline of its fortunes in the battles between Christians and Muslims, and an account of the building of the city walls at the end of the eleventh century (V, 332–36). Then, after the vagabond had walked around the outside of the walls before entering the city, a further page is given over to Avila's history, this time to events of the fourteenth and fifteenth centuries, before the admission is made that the narrator "no se siente con fuerzas para ensamblar los mil grajos dispersos de la historia de Avila" [does not feel that he has sufficient strength to gather together the countless scattered rooks that make up the history of Avila] (V, 339). In effect, and despite the historical importance of a city such as Avila, Cela declines to develop a detailed history of the place. However, by refraining from such a course of action he does at least avoid falling into the trap of having his travel book weighed down by too much historical ballast.

All in all, then, *Judíos, moros y cristianos* contains a relatively modest amount of historical narrative. There are, as has been mentioned, plenty of passing references to the events or characters of history and quite frequent snippets concerning historical incidents, episodes, or developments. However, the moment that provides the historical climax to the whole work is the picture that is evoked of the scene at the bulls of Guisando, in 1468, when Henry IV recognized Isabella as his heir. This meeting between the half-siblings is acknowledged by the vagabond as a moment of supreme significance. And yet this climactic point in Cela's travel narrative (the symbolic end of his journey around Old Castile, the vagabond's arrival at his ultimate place of pilgrimage, an isolated spot that witnessed a turning point in history) almost comes out of the blue. Earlier in the journey there were a handful of brief references to the dynastic struggle known as the War of the Beltraneja: an atrocity committed; a castle associated with supporters of Isabella, or another fortress that had flown the standard of the child princess known as Joan of Beltraneja. And when, in the closing stages of his journey the vagabond reaches Mombeltrán, he reflects with a certain mischievous humor on the presumed impregnation of Henry's queen by the favorite, Beltrán de la Cueva, and which produced in 1462 the Princess Joan and gave rise to the ensuing dynastic conflict (V, 448–49).

A few pages later, when the vagabond reaches the site of Guisando, he sees in his mind's eye the famous encounter of 19 September 1468, with Princess Isabella of Castile accompanied by the Archbishop of Toledo, the Bishops of Burgos and Coria, loyal noblemen, and two hundred horsemen making their way from Cebreros, a dozen kilometers away. The imagined scene is narrated in a heavily contrived manner, with an alternation and contrast between the heady affairs of state on that far-off, momentous day and, almost five hundred years later, the picture of Nature and its creatures oblivious to the significance of the location. After the description of Isabella's escort, the narrative continues:

La cabra mansa ramonea, desatendida, por el robledalillo del monte bajo.

Don Enrique vino desde Cadalso: le daban guardia el maestre de Santiago, el arzobispo de Sevilla, sus cortesanos y más de tres mil jinetes.

Unas nubes rosadas se pintaron por los escondidos confines del río Alberche.

La cosa no fue fácil sino, más bien, dolorosa: Don Enrique confesó ante Dios y los hombres, que aquella doña Juana no fuese por él engendrada, la cual, la adúltera reina doña Juana, había concebido de otro varón y no de él.

> *Dicen que soy presumida*
> *porque soy de Mombeltrán . . .*

Un lagarto colorado y verde se asoma, por entre dos piedras, a saludar al sol.

La cosa no fue fácil sino, más bien, providencial: Don Enrique juró a la princesa Isabel por su legítima heredera.

El hacendoso escarabajo merdero buscaba, entre la yerba seca, su acomodo.

El vagabundo piensa que, sin el encuentro de los toros de Guisando, España no hubiera sido España. (V, 467–68)

[The gentle goat, untended, browses in the oak grove of the scrubland.

King Henry came from Cadalso: he was escorted by the Grand Master of Santiago, the Archbishop of Seville, his courtiers, and more than three thousand horsemen.

Some pink clouds appeared above the outline of the Alberche River.

The episode was not easy, but painful: Henry confessed before God and his fellow men that young Princess Joan had not been fathered by him and that the adulterous queen, Joan, had conceived her by another man.

> *They say how arrogant I am*
> *For I come from Mombeltrán . . .*

A red and green lizard appears, between two stones, and greets the sun.

The episode was not easy, but was providential: Henry swore to recognize Princess Isabella as his legitimate heir.

The busy dung beetle was looking in the dry grass for some business.

The vagabond thinks that, without the meeting at the bulls of Guisando, Spain would not have been Spain.]

Then the vagabond ponders (again, his weighty thoughts alternating with the description of the habitual activities of some of Nature's creatures) on how the course of history might have been different (the discovery of the New World, the fate of Granada, even the fate of Nebrija's grammar) if the Guisando encounter had not come about (V, 468–69). Indeed, just to drive home the point, he acknowledges that Henry had subsequently tried to wriggle out of the solemn undertakings.[14] Nevertheless, the agreement held and several centuries later the vagabond was to make his pilgrimage, via some of the historically most significant parts of Old Castile, to a spot that symbolically marks the starting point of modern Spain. On an altogether more prosaic level, the vagabond's arrival here and his ruminations on the place and its associations signal the rapid winding down of the account, which comes to a conclusion some ten pages later.

OLD STONES IN OLD CASTILE

In *Judíos, moros y cristianos*, the narrative of history is handled in a sporadic fashion, with the insertion at appropriate points of allusions, accounts, or anecdotes dealing with the developments, settings, and protagonists of the cultural and political evolution of Old Castile. The occasional nature of such material is understandable in that Cela was composing a travel work and not a history book. Indeed, what is much more consistently apparent throughout this account, as the vagabond makes his way along the roads, by the rivers, through the towns and villages, and even across some of the mountains of the area, is how much the impression of the physicality of these parts of Old Castile is conveyed. Features of the natural environment have a powerful influence on the vagabond's route, from the opening pages of the first chapter, entitled "Del puerto de Navacerrada al Duero" [From the Navacerrada Pass to the Douro], in which the vagabond heads northeast along the lower slopes of the Sierra de Guadarrama and the Sierra de Ayllón until he reaches the Douro River at San Esteban de Gormaz. Chapter 2, "Veinte leguas del Duero" [Twenty Leagues along the Douro], sees him following the river, through Aranda de Duero and as far as Peñafiel. In the next three chapters, two of which are largely given over to descriptions of Segovia and Avila, the vagabond's route is influenced by chance (for example, a car ride) and by the desire to see places of some historic note, rather than by the course of a famous river or the presence of inhospitable terrain. However, with chapter 6, "Del Sacro Tormes, dulce y claro río" [From the Sacred Tormes, a Sweet, Clear River], he deliberates, in a relaxed kind of way, on where the Tormes rises and then proceeds to construct his own account of the first "two or three" leagues of the river's existence (V, 373–78).

The penultimate chapter, "Gredos, espalda de Castilla" [The Gredos Range, the Backbone of Spain], contains a good deal of highly detailed material on excursions in the central part of the Sierra de Gredos and also includes the vagabond's crossing of the mountains from Bohoyo to Candeleda (a distance of some twenty-five kilometers), via the lakes of the Cinco Lagunas and in the shadow of Almanzor, at 2,592 meters the highest peak in the range (V, 422–30). This kind of demanding physical activity is hardly something that the vagabond of *Del Miño al Bidasoa* could be imagined engaging in. However, in *Judíos, moros y cristianos*, this crossing, more or less at the high point of the mountain range that in *Andanzas y visiones españolas* Unamuno terms the "espinazo de Castilla" [the backbone of Castile] (p. 16), represents for the vagabond an intimate, physical contact with the ruggedness and natural grandeur of Old Castile, and contrasts with the earlier focus on the historical and cultural heritage of the area covered.

Yet the geographical, even geological physicality that marks much of Cela's third travel book is balanced by constant references to those monuments that stand as reminders of the religious and political history of Old Castile: churches, convents, monasteries, and castles. Throughout *Judíos, moros y cristianos* the vagabond constantly notes the many "ermitas" [wayside chapels] scattered around the countryside and occasionally found in towns. He nearly always gives their dedication—for example, "la ermita de la Virgen de Hontanares" [the chapel of the Virgin of Hontanares] (V, 149) and "la de San Isidro" [the chapel of San Isidro] (V, 239)—and at one point he observes that there are many of these modest places of worship dedicated to the "Santo Cristo del Humilladero" [Holy Christ of the Boundary Cross]: "En Torrecilla hay otra de igual devoción. Y en Cabezuela, también. Y en Fuente el Olmo. Y en otros muchos pueblos de Castilla" [In Torrecilla there is another one with the same dedication. And also in Cabezuela. And in Fuente el Olmo. And in many other towns and villages of Castile] (V, 232). Yet there is never any physical description of the buildings concerned and only occasionally a line or two of supplementary information regarding the history or religious connections of a particular site.

In the case of some churches, their presence is simply noted, with no more than a spare, descriptive comment. Thus in San Esteban de Gormaz the vagabond mentions "dos o tres iglesias de estilo románico" [two or three churches in Romanesque style] (V, 265); Fuentidueña has "una iglesia parroquial remendada y de cierto empaque, la de San Miguel" [a patched-up parish church with a certain presence, the church of San Miguel] (V, 220–21), while in Segovia he passes the night sleeping against the walls of San Marcos and merely notes that some claim it to be the oldest church in the city (V, 265). When he reaches Arévalo (which has several notable churches) the vagabond mentions the presence of one, but does not name it, and later decides to sleep by the walls of another, running through the list of which one it might be as he beds down for the night (V, 323–24).

However, on other occasions the vagabond provides at least a short piece of fact or anecdote about the churches he comes across. This is most often seen in chapters 4 and 5 (the Segovia and Avila sections) where, as might be expected, he spends a substantial amount of time roaming around these two cities and taking in streets, squares, and buildings. Typical of these brief notes or pointers is the information that Segovia's church of San Sebastián was where coiners used to gather in the fifteenth, sixteenth, and seventeenth centuries, since there was in those days a Royal Mint in the same square (V, 274). Mention is made that the city's church of the Santísima Trinidad was probably built in the twelfth century on the remains of a Mozarabic temple (V, 276); there is reference to the fact that the church of San Andrés suffered fire damage to its tower in 1943 and that repairs were completed three years later (V, 285), and it is noted that the multihued and graceful church of

San Martín has, unusually, its tower built over the nave (V, 288). In contrast, the church of Santiago in Avila is described as large and not very artistic, and is simply remarked on as the burial place of two formidable and famous warriors (V, 347). The city's Santo Tomé is described as ugly and lifeless but is also identified as the church where the young St Teresa once listened to a tirade from a thoroughly bad preacher (V, 358), while the chapel of Mosén Rubí de Bracamonte is cited solely with reference to the fact that Bracamonte's father, a nobleman and alderman of Avila, was executed for opposing Philip II's demand for a tax on the city to help pay for his military campaigns. The narrator goes on to discuss the origins of the clergyman's name and the father's title, and concludes with the pronouncement: "Robin, en la langue d'oïl, el francés medieval, vale tanto como Robertito, y Rubí o Rubín son usos castellanos de Robín" [Robin, in *langue d'oïl*, medieval French, is the equivalent of Robertito, and Rubí or Rubín are Castilian versions of Robín] (V, 360–61).

A notable exception to the vagabond's unwillingness to dwell on the appearance or contents of places of worship comes with the description of the church at Barco de Avila, which is remarkable for its accumulation of detail and interesting for its concluding note of indignation and despair. After a succinct account of the church's pleasing appearance, "es sólida y hermosa, de bella traza románica y de satisfechas proporciones" [it is solid and beautiful, of fine Romanesque design and with satisfying proportions] the narrative moves to the interior of the building:

La iglesia de Barco de Avila esconde, en su sacristía y en sus penumbrosos rincones, viejos tesoros de mérito: un Cristo, negro y amargo, que sobrecoge el corazón; varias tablas góticas y flamencas; un tríptico italiano; un relieve de alabastro, también italiano, diz que de Benvenuto Cellini; un crucifijo de marfil; una dulce imagen de la Virgen y el Niño; las tallas de artístico palo de la antesacristía; las rejas platerescas, los férreos candelabros renacentistas, los atriles, la custodia, el cáliz, el copón. Como para compensar de tanta nobleza y tanta antigüedad, un Sagrado Corazón de Jesús y una Virgen de Fátima de purpurina, yeso y mazapán, pregonan, desde el altar mayor, el mal gusto y la insolvencia artística del señor cura párroco. (V, 392)

[In the sacristy and the shadowy nooks of the church of Barco de Avila are hidden old, valuable treasures: a black, suffering Christ, that makes one's heart skip a beat; various Gothic and Flemish panels; an Italian triptych; an alabaster relief, also Italian, and supposedly by Benvenuto Cellini; an ivory crucifix; a delightful image of the Virgin and Child; the wooden carvings before the sacristy; the plateresque screen, the iron, Renaissance candelabras, the lecterns, the monstrance, the chalice, and the pyx. As if to compensate for so many noble antiquities, a Sacred Heart of Jesus and a Virgin of Fatima, made of plaster and marzipan and covered in metallic powder, proclaim, from the high altar, the bad taste and artistic bankruptcy of the parish priest.]

Then, immediately after this sudden change of tone, comes the *cri de coeur*: "Al vagabundo, que ama a España sobre todas las cosas, le duele ver que a España, desde hace trescientos o cuatrocientos años, se la vienen merendando, sin tregua ni piedad, la estulticia, la soberbia y la socarronería" [The vagabond, who loves his country above all else, is distressed to see that for three hundred or four hundred years, foolishness, arrogance, and cunning have been, relentlessly and mercilessly, gnawing away at Spain] (V, 392–93).

While the churches and chapels that the vagabond comes across in the provinces of Segovia and Avila are normally the subject of the barest of architectural or artistic description, the cathedrals of the two provincial capitals fare little better. In Segovia a modest paragraph mentions that the old cathedral of Santa María was destroyed during the revolt of the *Comuneros* (1520–21) and that some of its religious decorations were transferred to the new cathedral, which was begun in the mid 1520s (V, 282–83). A little later come three brief paragraphs that include mention of the height of the cathedral's present tower and the fact that the even taller, original tower, was struck by lightning; an acknowledgment of the building's Gothic style; reference to the fact that the Jewish girl who became known as María del Salto is buried there, and the literary information that when in 1558 the cathedral was first used as a place of worship, part of the local celebrations involved performances of the plays of Lope de Rueda. The only hint of what the interior is like comes with the sparse and sweeping sentence: "La catedral, por dentro, es solemne y fría, artística, penumbrosa y sobrecogedora como todas las catedrales castellanas" [Inside, the cathedral is solemn and cold, artistic, gloomy, and scary, like all Castilian cathedrals] (V, 286).

With his slightly more extensive description of the cathedral of Avila, the vagabond makes it clear that while he is not indifferent to cathedrals, he cannot get enthusiastic about them and, in any case, prefers monuments that are less showy and grandiloquent (V, 357). In fact, at a later point in the narrative, he admits that the solemnity of cathedrals frightens him (V, 446). Nevertheless, the vagabond comments at some length on the fortresslike appearance of the cathedral of Avila, on a number of its feature that suggest that it was developed to withstand a siege, and on the general martial spirit that the place seems to exude. Indeed, understanding and forgiveness do not appear to be messages that this building imparts: "La catedral de Avila es posible que—salvo milagro de Dios, que todo lo puede—sirva menos para ayudarnos a pensar que el judío que ardió en la hoguera también tenía un alma. O que al que nos ofende, debemos responder con el perdón" [It is possible that the cathedral of Avila—save for some miracle from almighty God—is unlikely to help us realize that the Jew who was burned at the stake also had a soul. Or that we should forgive those who wrong us] (V, 356–57). Then, after a digression on cathedrals in general and on the sorts of old stones that he *does* like, the vagabond mentions the differences of opinion over who was the master builder of this cathedral, observes that the west façade was spoiled by eighteenth-century restorers, and also describes the portal on the north façade as "bella y poética" [beautiful and poetic]. Subsequently, there is a brief, matter-of-fact listing of a few aspects of the interior of the building:

El interior de la catedral de Avila también es muy meritorio. El retablo del altar mayor tiene dos docenas de tablas de Berruguete, Borgoña y Santa Cruz. El escultor Vasco de Zarza y el platero García Crespo, cincelaron el alabastro y la plata. La catedral de Avila está muy bien de muertos ilustres, enterrados con solemnidad: el sepulcro del Tostado, los de los obispos don Sancho, Domingo Xuárez y Roelas, el del chantre don Tacón y el de doña Beatriz Básquez, son muy visitados. Sobre la puerta del claustro luce un gracioso San Cristobalón, antiguo de setecientos años. (V, 358)

[The interior of the cathedral of Avila is also very fine. The reredos of the high altar has two dozen panels by Berruguete, Borgoña, and Santa Cruz. The sculptor, Vasco de Zarza, and the silversmith, García Crespo, were responsible for the alabaster carving and silver work. The cathedral of Avila is well endowed with illustrious dead, solemnly buried: the tomb of El Tostado, those of the Bishops Don Sancho, Domingo Xuárez, and Roelas, that of the precentor, Don Tacón, and that of Doña Beatriz Básquez have many visitors. Above the door to the cloister, a splendid, seven-hundred-year-old St Christopher is displayed.]

In *Judíos, moros y cristianos* there are approximately 120 references to buildings currently or formerly used for public worship or occupied by religious communities. About one third of these references are to convents and monasteries, and the overwhelming tendency of the vagabond to describe churches from the outside, and briefly, or simply to mention them in connection with a historical event or personage, or an anecdote, is repeated when it comes to the houses of religious orders. Indeed, the vagabond's treatment of convents is even more restricted to matters of location and association than is the case with churches. It is often simply a question of, for example, a passing reference to a convent in Peñaranda de Duero that serves as one reminder, among others, of the faded importance of the town (V, 180); a convent in Segovia that is near one end of the aqueduct (V, 268) and a Franciscan house that is close by the other end of the structure (V, 274); a convent near to where Antonio Machado lived in the city (V, 277), or a convent of the Order of St Clare that was previously a church and, before that, a synagogue (V, 287).

Sometimes, when the vagabond does refer to the features of a religious house, it is done in a scathing fashion. At the convent of Discalced Carmelites in Segovia, he ridicules the excessively ornate catafalque over the resting place of St John of the Cross (as if erected, he notes, in praise and memory of Ramsis II or Nebuchadnezzar) and is quite open about the place's lack of aesthetic appeal and the principal reason for this: "Este convento, aparte de sus recuerdos, no tenía ya mucho que ver y, desde la última y desdichada reforma, tiene aún menos que ver todavía" [This convent, apart from its memories, never used to have much to offer and, since the last, unfortunate refurbishment, offers even less]. The vagabond then goes on to utter a more general condemnation and also expresses his own weary indifference: "El vagabundo, en su peregrinar, ha visto ya tantas barbaridades y tantas herejías que ya ni se indigna" [In his wanderings, the vagabond has seen so many awful things and so many abominations that he no longer gets worked up about them] (V, 264).

As the vagabond makes his way around Avila, there are, of course, frequent references to convents associated with St Teresa's life and works: the convent where the young Teresa de Cepeda studied (V, 347); the house where she was born and which is now the convent of Santa Teresa; the convent (Teresa's first foundation) where she brought a child back to life; the house, now a convent, where St Teresa planned her reforms, or the convent where she received St John of the Cross and other holy men who were later to be canonized (V, 350–52). Elsewhere, the association is signaled between a particular religious house and other famous individuals. Thus, there is reference to the monastery of Santa Cruz la Real in Segovia, where the Inquisitor General, Torquemada, was once prior (V, 266); in Arévalo, the ruined monastery of San Francisco is pointed out as the place where the Bishop of Avila, Alonso de Madrigal, popularly known as "El Tostado" and who was a prolific author and fierce opponent of Torquemada, studied grammar as a youth (V, 318); in Madrigal de las Altas Torres the vagabond notes the palace, now an Augustinian convent, where Isabella of Castile was born (V, 326), or, and here the connection has literary rather than historical weight, there is mention of the monastery near Olmedo that once harbored the murderer whose ignoble actions were dramatized in Lope de Vega's *El caballero de Olmedo* (V, 304).

The churches and convents of Old Castile that the vagabond passes by and notes, now and again pauses at, but seldom enters, are only very occasionally judged on their artistic or architectural merits. Several times the point is made that he is not attracted to churches and cathedrals, and in Avila the wayfarer confesses to not being knowledgeable when it comes to old buildings, admitting that "no es hombre entendido en monumentos" [he is not an expert in monuments] (V, 337). Indeed, taking into account this lack of both enthusiasm and expertise, it is understandable that the vagabond tends to impart snippets of information about the exterior or interior of a place of worship in an altogether perfunctory manner. The numerous mentions in Cela's third travel book of churches, convents, and other religious establishments are not there to permit the vagabond to display his architectural knowledge and artistic appreciation, but rather seem to serve as constant reminders of the earlier triumph of Christianity and its enduring presence in these parts.

That victory and longevity was, of course, achieved by force and secured by strength, a strength that was most obviously manifest in the castles and other fortifications that were constructed in the wake of Christian gains. In later centuries more castles were built, this time as affirmations of local dynastic interests or in response to struggles between the Christian kingdoms. These strongholds, together with fortified towns and cities, are more vividly *sites* of history than churches and cathedrals, in that they much more readily evoke images of battle, war, and the control of territory. But while churches and fortified towns, for obvious religious, commercial, and social reasons, are still very much scenes of present-day activity, castles serve almost entirely as signposts to the past. As Ortega y Gasset observes in his 1927 essay, "Notas del vago estío," which contains a good deal of material on the significance of castles: "The castle represents what is not modern, in its absolute form" (p. 568).

Throughout *Judíos, moros y cristianos*, Cela presents castles as part of the landscape, in the distance or close by, and vestiges of the past. Very often they are no more than ruins. In the first three chapters, after the passing reference to the Moorish castle at San Esteban de Gormaz as being "en ruinas" [in ruins] (V, 165), it begins to look as though the vagabond is plotting his way past tumbledown stones, and sometimes not even these. In Castillejo, for example, there is not much more remaining than the site where the Templars' castle used to be (V, 171). However, he is soon back on the track of decay with the "ruinoso castillo" [dilapidated castle] of Peñaranda (V, 180); another "ruinoso castillo" in Castrillo de Duero that belonged to the Duke of Osuna (V, 201), and the "vetusto y ruinoso castillo" [ancient and dilapidated castle] of Fuentidueña (V, 220). But with this last-mentioned stronghold at least a little history is revealed about the location: the reader is informed that the Marquess of Villena was imprisoned in Fuentidueña's castle and also that Alfonso VIII withdrew to it after winning the battle of Las Navas de Tolosa.

Hereafter in the narrative, castles are normally presented in terms of their association with the leading figures and episodes of Castilian history, although occasionally one or two famous outsiders merit a mention. Not unexpectedly, there is rarely a visit within and usually little architectural description of a stronghold: at the castle of La Mota in Medina del Campo, the comment is made that the vagabond "no entiende mucho de arquitecturas" [does not know much about architecture] (V, 305). Indeed, when he reaches the town of Cuéllar, the man who is giving him a car ride for this part of the journey proposes a visit to the castle. The passenger's response is to suggest a look at the outside and no more, adding that there is not much to see inside. However, as if in compensation, there follows a general description of the castle's appearance; mention of how it compares to the nearby, magnificent castle of Coca; observations on its character, location, and views; some details on its construction and, finally, a historical footnote:

> El castillo de Cuéllar es más sobrio, menos elegante y dibujado que el castillo de Coca, más militar, más misterioso y peleador, quizás; por lo menos, en su apariencia. De grandiosos, por ahí se andan los dos. El castillo de Cuéllar corona el cerro sobre el que se levanta el pueblo, y desde él se ven, con buena vista y cielo limpio, las torres de Segovia, a naciente, y las de Olmedo, a poniente. El castillo de Cuéllar es fortaleza roquera, con planta cuadrilonga, de fábrica de mampostería y flanqueado por cubos que parecen cada cual de su padre y su madre, con arco árabe defendido por dos garitas y sólida torre cuadrada. El castillo de Cuéllar levantó pendones por la Beltraneja, en su guerra contra Isabel. (V, 303)

> [The castle of Cuéllar is more restrained, less elegant and detailed than the castle of Coca, more warlike, more mysterious and combative, perhaps; at least, in its appearance. Concerning their impressiveness, in these parts both are outstanding. The castle of Cuéllar crowns the hill on which the town rises, and with good eyesight and on a clear day, you can see from it the towers of Segovia in the east and those of Olmedo in the west. The castle of Cuéllar is a fortress built on rock, rectangular in shape, of masonry construction, flanked by identical round turrets, and with a Moorish archway defended by two bartizans and a solid, square tower. The castle of Cuéllar raised its standards for Joan of Beltraneja in her war against Isabella.]

Elsewhere, a stronghold's association with historical characters is brought out. Thus, the castle at Turégano is mentioned, albeit briefly, mainly in the context of its use as a harsh prison for Antonio Pérez and a venue for a meeting between King John II of Castile and Don Alvaro de Luna (V, 253). On the other hand, almost two hundred words are devoted to the castle of La Mota, with the focus on the building's connection with Queen Isabella, Joan the Mad, and even Cesare Borgia, who escaped from his imprisonment there (V, 305). The ruined castle of Arévalo is mentioned simply in terms of who was imprisoned there, summoned there, born there, and lived there—an impressive tally of monarchs, princes, and other aristocrats but which amounts to little more than a list of twenty or so names and titles (V, 318). Fortunately, this kind of itemization of historical characters is unusual. Equally rare, and rather more interesting, is the attempt to combine history and narrative creativity. Thus, when the vagabond reaches the town of Mombeltrán, he muses in a somewhat flippant tone on the place's connection with Henry IV and Beltrán de la Cueva, and on entering the castle (a rare occurrence) he proceeds to evoke the amorous notes of a lute, the sound of tiptoeing through the galleries, and even pictures a tryst between the king's favorite and the queen (V, 448–49).

Throughout *Judíos, moros y cristianos*, churches, convents, and castles are presented as an inescapable feature of the urban and rural landscapes of Old Castile. They are noted in the distance, passed close by, and occasionally entered. Their physical condition ranges from solid and imposing to tumbledown, or perhaps little more than the site where a building once stood. But above all, these places are rarely presented in terms of their architectural or artistic qualities. Instead, they are often introduced as the locations of the conflicts and dramas of the past, and are also physical reminders of the triumph and establishment of Christianity – not that the narrator ever makes this last point explicitly. Overall, these buildings and stones reflect the cultural and political history, as well as, presumably, the spirit of Old Castile.

FURTHER SIGHTS, SCENES, AND INTERESTS

While buildings connected with religion and those associated with warfare and secular power are monuments that evoke the history of Old Castile and indicate the gestation of modern Spain, the descriptive material in Cela's third travel book is by no means restricted to such solemn architecture. Nowhere is this more apparent than in chapter 4, which is almost wholly given over to the account of the vagabond's stay in the city of Segovia. While in this chapter there are even more references to churches, convents, and so on, than there are in the Avila section of chapter 5, in Segovia the vagabond wanders, in a rather more leisurely manner than in Avila, through various quarters and the streets and squares of the old town. Here mention is made of a number of houses or even grander secular buildings of particular interest. However, the Alcázar is dealt with in a brief and unenthusiastic way and it is the city's Roman aqueduct that particularly captures the interest of the vagabond. With facts, figures, and history, and interrupting the commentary to digress on a building or thoroughfare, he traces it from where it begins in the newer part of Segovia to its final arches, some eight hundred meters away, in the old city (V, 268–74).

But though the vagabond presents the aqueduct as the historical and architectural glory of Segovia, on a more personal note he seeks out, describes, and spends the night in the modest boardinghouse where Antonio Machado stayed for thirteen years. This episode, a moving example of a literary pilgrimage in which the vagabond describes Machado's modest bedroom, gives some account of the poet's artistic and other acquaintances in Segovia, and then, in a thoroughly melancholy state, spends the night in the dining room of the boardinghouse, is one of the most poignant and vivid sections of the whole work (V, 277–81).

Yet, not all of the descriptive material in *Judíos, moros y cristianos* is concerned with famous places and buildings, or places connected with famous figures. Thus a scene in the waiting room of a country railway station seems to consist largely of the postures of a group of rural types:

La sala de espera de la estación tiene encharcado el suelo de losetas de cemento. El vagabundo, sobre el largo banco de tabla, se busca su acomodo entre un zagal segador y una campesina que intenta dar de mamar a un niño que grita sin entusiasmo alguno, sólo por hacer la cusca al próximo.

En la sala de espera de la estación hay otras cinco personas: un viejo que dormita con la apagada colilla entre los labios; una señorita de pueblo con el pelo teñido de rubio y su mamá, que casi no puede respirar dentro del corsé; un hombre de mediana edad que mira para la bombilla, y un cura flaco y meditabundo que hace, de vez en cuando, un raro guiño con la boca y con la nariz. (V, 176)

[The waiting room in the station has a floor covered with cement tiles. The vagabond sits on the long, plank bench between a young reaper and a peasant woman trying to suckle a baby who is screaming without any enthusiasm, but simply to annoy the person alongside.

In the station's waiting room there are five other people: an old man dozing with an extinguished cigarette butt between his lips; a young, working-class girl with her hair dyed blond and her mother, who can hardly breathe in her corset; a middle-aged man who is looking at the lightbulb, and a thin, pensive priest who, from time to time, pulls an odd face with his mouth and nose.]

Elsewhere, in Medina del Campo, the vagabond witnesses the activity that a new day brings:

> Cuando la luz se hizo ya y la calle comenzó a bullir, el vagabundo, con sus mejores razones a cuestas, asomó los hocicos al aire de Medina. Un can de negras lanas y cara de fraile, hoza, igual que un jabalí, en un montoncito de basura. Desde un balcón de pobre y misteriosa traza, un niño se cisca sobre el mundo, con un infinito y desentendido gesto de desprecio. Las campanas de las iglesias y de los conventos llaman, con su dolida, con su quejumbrosa voz, a su clientela de beatas. Un mozo arrea una tunda regular a una mula esquelética y desvencijada, llena de blanquecinas mataduras en carne viva. Una niña modosita y amarga, una niña que cree que es pecado sentir que el breve seno se le despierta, cruza con un albo y blando paquete bajo el brazo. Unos feriantes zamoranos—vinateros de Toro, tratantes de Villalpando, molineros de Guarrate—marchan, presurosos, camino de la estación del ferrocarril. (V, 308–9)

> [When it was already light and the street began to stir, the vagabond, having come to, poked his head out into the air of Medina. A black dog with the face of a friar is rooting around, just like a wild boar, in a small pile of garbage. From a poor and strange-looking balcony, a young boy is crapping on the world, with an infinite and indifferent look of scorn. The bells of the churches and convents are calling, with their sorrowful and plaintive sound, to their pious clientele. A lad is giving a beating to a skeletal, broken-down mule, its hide covered in whitish sores. A young, demure, and sullen girl, a girl who thinks it is a sin to be conscious of her dainty breasts, crosses the street with a soft, white package under her arm. Some traders from Zamora—wine-merchants from Toro, dealers from Villalpando, millers from Guarrate—hurriedly head toward the station.]

However, the obvious problem with this last example of descriptive writing is that, with its self-conscious style and indications of omniscience, it smacks of fictional narrative. Once the vagabond has disappeared from view, this becomes the kind of passage that could be found in Cela's fiction.

In other parts of *Judíos, moros y cristianos*, the descriptive writing can be much more tranquil and bucolic, occasionally poetic, or even excessively sentimental. The following passage is from the early pages of the work:

> Entrando el vagabundo en la comunidad de Ayllón, las nubes rojas y largas de la tarde empezaron a dormirse sobre los bosques. El esquilón de un buey suena, a lo lejos, cadencioso y gentil, igual que el esquilón de una mansa ermita perdida en un castañar, mientras el corazón del vagabundo, a los pri-

meros claros de la luna, se va llenando, poco a poco, como el pilón de una fuente sosegada, de una ternura infinita. (V, 150)

[As the vagabond entered the community of Ayllón, the long, red clouds of the evening were starting to settle over the woodlands. In the distance, an ox's bell sounds, rhythmically and delightfully, like the bell of a humble hermitage hidden away in a chestnut grove, while, with the first moonlight, the vagabond's heart gradually fills, like the basin of a gentle fountain, with an infinite tenderness.]

And much later, in the closing pages of the narrative, a goatherd in sentimental mode and setting reveals the vagabond's sharp ear and acute vision. Or perhaps this is simply another example of the author indulging in poetic license:

A lo lejos canta, con una vocecilla quebrada y triste, un zagal pastor de cabras—abarcas a los pies, zamarra en bandolera, camisa de botón y once años pegados a los lomos—, y por el cielo cruza, como en un telón bíblico, la campesina cigüeña, que vuela pausadamente, igual que un ave sagrada, un ave santa. (V, 477–78)

[In the distance, singing in a sad, faltering little voice, there is a young goatherd – sandals on his feet, a sheepskin over his shoulders, a button-up shirt, and eleven years old – and, as in a biblical backdrop, a rural stork crosses the sky, flying slowly, like a sacred, holy bird.]

While in his two earlier travel books, Cela provides ample evidence of his interest in the geography of road and river systems, there is nothing in *Viaje a la Alcarria* or *Del Miño al Bidasoa* to match the survey, in chapter 6 of *Judíos, moros y cristianos*, of the first ten to fifteen kilometers of the Tormes River. Indeed, this material is produced not primarily as part of the travel narrative, but rather as an attempt to write "una descripción no literaria, sino real y verdadera" [not a literary description, but a real, factual one] (V, 374). This is intended to remedy the lack of any such existing geographical description. The result is a methodical, detailed, and occasionally poeticized account of the course of the Tormes from where it is thought to rise to where, having been joined by many tributaries, it reaches the vicinity of Bohoyo (V, 374–78). Yet such an exhaustive mapping of the early stages of the river appears to be a relatively modest, and successful, narrative parenthesis when compared to the almost tediously detailed description of the various tracks and routes to the peak of Almanzor and the nearby lakes (V, 408–19). Even the inclusion of detailed sketch maps cannot prevent this section from lapsing into a kind of guidebook style commentary that is both tiring and confusing.

In other parts of the narrative, there are rather more manageable descriptions of river and road systems, sometimes given from a truck as it rumbles along, or from a car, and on one occasion, as he enters Aranda de Duero, the vagabond even manages to bring together in two paragraphs an account of local river, road (although briefly), and rail systems (V, 182). Together with a certain interest in the presence and style of bridges (structures that permit the orderly intersection of road, rail, and river), Cela's third travel book reveals a continuing interest in river and road networks as clear reminders of both the natural and human geography of a region.

The work also returns to a theme passed over in *Del Miño al Bidasoa* but which had been central in *Viaje a la Alcarria*—the contrasting fortunes of the inhabitants of the area visited. There are, as was seen earlier, frequent pointers in the narrative to the dilapidated state of many of the churches, convents, and castles of Old Castile, or to town walls that are the worse for wear or have even ceased to exist. Yet, in addition to such indicators of the decline or abandonment of buildings and other structures, there are frequent reminders of the decay of whole villages and even of some towns. *Judíos, moros y cristianos* contains many references to abandoned areas and villages, so-called *despoblados*, and the vagabond even offers his own interpretation of the term: "Despoblado, según quiere entender el vagabundo, es voz que, más que por desierto, quiere valer por desierto que, en tiempos, no lo fue" ["Despoblado" according to the vagabond's understanding, is a word that means more than just "desolate" and indicates a desolate place that in bygone times was not] (V, 170). Hereafter, these *despoblados* are noted, usually in ones and twos, but sometimes in clusters, such as in the mountainous terrain to the north of Sepúlveda. The vagabond observes that in these parts: "Navares de Ayuso colecciona despoblados—Casares, Castillejos, San Cristóbal y Valdellanos" [Navares de Ayuso collects abandoned villages—Casares, Castillejos, San Cristóbal, and Valdellanos]. He mentions three more on his way to nearby Urueñas, and then, as he heads away from there, notes with dismay another three: "El vagabundo, a poco de salir de Urueñas, deja a la diestra, y a varios cientos de pasos de su camino, a Castrillo de Sepúlveda, con su encinar del monte Viejo y, ¡ay!, otros tres despoblados" [Not long after leaving Urueñas, the vagabond passes on his right, a few hundred paces from the road, Castrillo de Sepúlveda, with its oak woods on Mount Viejo and, oh, another three abandoned villages) (V, 239).

Yet, while some hamlets and villages have been abandoned, a number of towns are also seen to have suffered, although not quite so drastically, the march of time and changes in circumstances. Peñaranda de Duero, in the province of Burgos, is described as once having been "más de lo que hoy es" [more than what it is today] and is then referred to as one of "estas viejas ciudades muertas y señoriles, gloriosas, militares y olvidadas" [these old, dead and noble cities, glorious, warlike, and forgotten] (V, 180). The case of Pedraza, in the province of Segovia, is presented in a more striking and detailed manner. It is first described by the vagabond as a large, half-empty town and he then proceeds to elaborate on this:

> Pedraza es pueblo de aire militar y derrotado, de digno y pobre ademán, de altanera traza e inhóspita y misteriosa realidad. En Pedraza—Pedraza de la Sierra, le llaman algunos—hay setenta, ochenta, quizás cien casas deshabitadas. Según el censo, Pedraza no tiene muchas más. Pedraza, en tiempos, fue villa de quince mil almas. Hoy tiene menos de doscientas, no llegan a ciento cincuenta. (V, 249)[15]

> [Pedraza is a town with a warlike yet defeated air, with a dignified and needy appearance, with a proud posture and an inhospitable and mysterious reality. In Pedraza – some call it Pedraza de la Sierra – there are seventy, eighty, perhaps a hundred uninhabited houses. According to the census, Pedraza does not have many more occupied houses. In former times, Pedraza was a town of fifteen thousand souls. Today it has fewer than two hundred, not even 150.]

Turégano, too, exhibits the faded glory so typical of many towns of Old Castile. It is likened to Pedraza and to so many other Castilian towns that were once a lot more significant than they are nowadays. It is yet another product of "este inmenso mundo de fiera lucha y de lenta y despiadada agonía que son los pueblos de Castilla la Vieja, rebosantes de dignidad y agobiados de dorados o de férreos recuerdos" [this vast world of ferocious struggles and the slow and merciless decline of the towns of Old Castile, brimming with dignity and weighed down by golden or iron memories] (V, 252–53). While such sentiments recall those expressed by the traveler in Pastrana, in the closing stages of *Viaje a la Alcarria*, they chiefly stand as acknowledgments of the decay of small towns whose whole being and vigor depended on wars to fight or territory to defend, and who were unable to adapt and sustain themselves once lands were secured and hostilities had become a thing of the past.

Nevertheless, some towns and cities did manage to adjust and prosper. There is no suggestion in the Segovia and Avila sections of Cela's third travel book that these two important cities are anything but comfortable or, indeed, thriving. Nor is there any indication that the larger towns the vagabond passes through or stops in are suffering economic stagnation or social hardship. Indeed, he occasionally mentions the prosperity of a particular place. Thus, after initially describing Aranda de Duero as "pueblo importante y grandón, polvoriento, rico y, a su manera, progresista" [an important, solidly built town, dusty, rich, and, in its own way, progressive], the vagabond mentions the attractive and well dressed local young women, in their fashionable shoes and silk stockings, and he notes that in Aranda "se ve en seguida que hay pesetas" [you can see right away that there is money] (V, 182). He then observes that the town has some good architecture, a variety of other attractions, including two markets a week, and concludes: "Aranda es un pueblo que ya tiene bastante con todo lo mucho que tiene" [With the many things that it does have, Aranda has plenty] (V, 184). Elsewhere, the vagabond comments that Barco de Avila "es pueblo próspero y de calles anchas y bien dibujadas" [is a prosperous town with wide, well laid-out streets] that also has fine houses (V, 386–87).

However, these and other indications of comfort and prosperity in many of the towns and cities visited need to be contrasted with indications of hardship and even poverty in the villages of Old Castile. In the opening chapter of *Judíos, moros y cristianos*, as the vagabond makes his way into the district of Ayllón, he comments on the hunger in the hamlet of Alquité and notices hardship in other villages of the area. In the same vein, he later notes of the villages which lie about twenty-five kilometers to the south east of Peñafiel: "Todos estos pueblos que van pasando, unos más chicos y otros menos chicos, parecen sacados de la misma pobre y agostada y yerma matriz" [All these villages going by, some a bit larger than others, seem to have come from the same poor, withered, and barren womb] (V, 233). Elsewhere, there is the observation that in these villages, where the youngsters ask him if he is a peddler, they do not have a penny to call their own. These are forgotten, dusty places besieged by Nature, shortage, and penury: "Pueblos a los que bate el lobo, y el rayo, y la sequía; pueblos que han olvidado el color de la hartura y que siguen ignorando el de la felicidad" [Villages assailed by wolves, lightning, and drought; villages that have forgotten what it was like to have plenty and which live unacquainted with happiness] (V, 328–29).

But such gloomy conclusions do not indicate the total picture of life in the rural areas visited by the vagabond. The narrative contains occasional mentions of the crops grown in a particular area, vegetable cultivation elsewhere, or the presence of vineyards or grazing land. Parts that are especially productive, such as the lands around Roa (in the province of Burgos) Turégano (Segovia), Piedrahita and Candeleda (both in the province of Avila) are highlighted and the local produce is detailed, often with enthusiasm. In the case of Candeleda, the vagabond notes that the place is thriving. He also reveals that the area attracts young migrants from Avila, Toledo, Cáceres, and Salamanca, and lists the local crops: "En Candeleda se cría el tabaco y el maíz, el pimiento para hacer pimentón y la judía carilla, sabrosa como pocas" [In Candeleda they grow tobacco and sweet corn, peppers for making cayenne pepper, and spotted French beans, which are tastier than most]. It is then mentioned that lemon, orange, and almond trees abound in the area, and that everywhere there are pinewoods and fig, chestnut, and olive groves. Finally, the vagabond lists the flora of the land around Candeleda, which includes, the reader is informed, nard and jasmine (V, 430–31).

Yet these pockets of productive land, with their busy communities, are few and far between on the route that the vagabond takes through Old Castile. Indeed, they stand out amidst the much more frequent indications of rural hardship or poverty: poor ground yielding a little cereal, scrubland providing for a few animals, and the many references to deserted areas and abandoned villages. Thus the kind of contrast in rural fortunes that was depicted in *Viaje a la Alcarria* is again revealed in Cela's third travel book, but this time the geographical scale is vaster and the overall picture is bleaker.

In *Judíos, moros y cristianos*, the vagabond's normally sparse descriptive technique is deployed to show towns and monuments, and also to give repeated indications of inhospitable landscapes and social hardship, which are occasionally contrasted with areas of plenty and apparent prosperity. But whatever kind of place or scenery is being described, his approach is mainly fact-based with, from time to time, personal responses and interpretative asides. However, the vagabond sometimes lapses into a kind of perfunctory quantification and itemization that smacks more of the catalog than the literary description. This kind of technique is seen, for example, with what amounts to an inventory of Aranda de Duero. This lists and gives brief comments on the town's two chapels, its six woods (one of which displays five shades of green), four rivers with their three bridges, one hundred [*sic*] young girls who have similar looks and dress in a like fashion, two avenues of Lombardy poplars, two market days a week, two fairs a year, parish registers in which are listed seven famous sons of Aranda, and so on. In fact, the paragraph that catalogs the many features of Aranda contains seventeen sentences: the first begins with the name of the town and the next sixteen all begin with what comes to be a monotonous and mechanical "Y" [And] (V, 183–84).

Elsewhere, such enumeration is used to describe the twenty or so trades and crafts associated with the townspeople of Peñafiel (V, 208), the dozen and a half famous figures of history connected with the castle of Arévalo (V, 318), and, rather more prosaically, the many different goods on sale at the market of Barco de Avila (V, 388) or the various kinds of animals and insects to be found in the area of Candeleda (V, 432–33). But at least such catalogs have local connections and provide a certain amount of local color. In contrast, it is difficult to see the point of the kind of itemization indulged in when, for example, the vagabond sits by the road outside Segovia's old quarter and records the passage of three cars, five trucks, eight wagons, twelve bicycles, fifteen horses, eighteen mules, twenty peasants, and an infinite number of silent, courting couples, hand in hand (V, 265).

The narrative also includes several lengthy examples of the kind of enumeration that does not suggest roadside observation but smacks instead of research carried out after the completion of the journey. When, for example, the vagabond decides that he wishes to pass through Peñaranda in order to touch the *picota* (a stone pillar, often ornamented, that served as a kind of pillory and gibbet) on which, he states, so many vagabonds had been quartered, he uses the opportunity to launch into an account of which provinces have the most *picotas* and where fourteen surviving ones are to be found in the province of Burgos (V, 179–80). And when, a little later, he decides to pass through Castrillo de Duero, the vagabond mentions the presence of the words *castro* and *castrillo* (in old Spanish, "fort" and "small fort") in place names and proceeds to list each of the forty or so instances of their use in the provinces of Old Castile, province by province (V, 199–200). Then, in the closing stage of his journey, the vagabond notices on some houses in Lanzahita the sign used by vagrants to denote where alms are readily given to those in need. The narrative subsequently includes illustrations, with brief commentaries and appropriate dialogue, of a dozen and a half other signs that reveal to itinerants information about the disposition of the inhabitants of a particular place and also offer advice to those on the road (V, 453–61). This type of survey has a certain curiosity value and shows yet another aspect of the vagabond's fund of knowledge. Yet it adds little to the picture of the place or area that is being passed through and instead suggests a writer indulging himself.

OTHER KINDS OF NARRATIVE MATERIAL AND TECHNIQUES

One of the most obvious points of contrast between Cela's third travel book and the first two is the way in which the account of the journey through Old Castile is peppered with references to works of literature and writers—from the *Poema de Mio Cid* to Pío Baroja, who died in 1956, the year of the publication of *Judíos, moros y cristianos*. There are also observations on painters, from El Greco to Ignacio Zuloaga. Indeed, in the early pages of the first chapter the thought is conveyed that in the recent past the writers and painters who had the most perspicacious understanding of Castile were non-Castilians: Unamuno, Azorín, Baroja, Antonio Machado, and Zuloaga, with the two madrileños, José Solana and Ortega y Gasset, being included on the grounds that Madrid is a city set apart from the region of Castile (V, 137–38). Hereafter, the literary and artistic references largely involve associations with a particular location. For example, in the early chapters mention is made of the connection between Baroja's *Aviraneta, o la vida de un conspirador* (1931) and Aranda de Duero (V, 184), as well as that between Cervantes's *Rinconete y Cortadillo* and the coat of arms of Roa (V, 186). There is reference to the fact that the Plaza Mayor and castle of Sepúlveda were the subjects of paintings by Solana and Zuloaga (V, 240); a mention that these two artists, as well as Ramón de Zubiaurre, painted scenes of Turégano (V, 254), and there is a reminder that Zuloaga bought the castle at Pedraza and converted its keep into his studio (V, 250).

However, it is with the chapters that focus on Segovia and Avila that references to works of literature and to writers are most frequent. Apart from the already mentioned pilgrimage that the vagabond makes in Segovia to Antonio Machado's old boardinghouse, Segovian connections are also made with Unamuno, *Don Quixote*, Lope's *Jerusalén conquistada*, Victor Hugo, Baroja's *Camino de perfección*, Lope de Rueda, *El Buscón*, the young Lope de Vega, Jorge Manrique, and others. On route to Avila, the vagabond quotes Lope de Vega on the once fertile area known as the Moraña, and then, as he passes through Madrigal de las Altas Torres, he mentions that El Tostado, that most prolific of writers, was born there and spent his last, unhappy years in the town. There is also a reminder that this was the place where Fray Luis de León died (V, 324–26).

The section on Avila takes up over half of chapter 5 and is dominated, as one might expect, by reminders of the figure of St Teresa. However, there is still room for reference to impressions of Avila from Azorín, Unamuno, and Solana (V, 331), a reminder of *El coloquio de los perros* (V, 332), mention of the inspiration for one of Lope de Vega's plays (V, 334), and of the city's associations with St John of the Cross (V, 352). In the last three chapters references to works of literature, writers, or painters are fewer. There is passing mention in chapter 6 of Fray Luis, Antonio Machado, Garcilaso de la Vega, and one or two others, and when in the same chapter the vagabond explores Piedrahita he notes that Manuel José Quintana and Juan Meléndez Valdés stayed in the

Palace of the Dukes of Alba and that Goya completed some paintings and drawings while in residence there (V, 382). Then, as the narrative nears its end with the arrival of the vagabond at the stone bulls of Guisando, it is observed that there are two references in *Don Quixote* to the bulls, and the vagabond also muses on the use made of these stone sculptures in Lorca's lament for his bullfighter friend, "Llanto por Ignacio Sánchez Mejías" (V, 472–74).

But while there are frequent references in Cela's third travel book to writers and to specific works of literature, the narrative itself also contains numerous indicators that it, too, is a piece of literary creation and not simply a log book or descriptive account of a journey. The description of countryside, towns, and cities is regularly punctuated by sketches or scenes that may not be factually based, but which certainly inject an element of drama, humor, or simple human interest into the narrative. Examples of such interludes include the encounter with the old beggar in Roa, who regales the vagabond with his record of and commentary on the history of the town (V, 186–98); the meeting and suggestion of companionship with the traveling salesman, Quintín Jumilla (V, 202–05), and the lengthy episode of the vagabond's aching tooth, its ritualized and brutal extraction by the phlebotomist, Fabián Remondo y Larangas, and the subsequent travel and companionship of the two men, interspersed with Don Fabián's storytelling (V, 216–33). There is also the encounter with the knifegrinder who is obsessed with the conflagrations he has seen in Castile (V, 255–58); the story of the simian, bullfighting bootblack, El Gran Merejo (V, 350–53), and the meeting with the young shepherd, his tales of wolves, and then the vivid, interpolated narrative of a wayfarer being stalked and killed by a wolf (V, 395–403).

Yet the most exuberantly stylized passage in the work, with its section of rhyming prose followed by alternating salutations and floral descriptions, comes when the vagabond cheerfully makes his way through the colorful fields of flowers around Lanzahita:

> El vagabundo, por Lanzahita, el pueblo de los meloneros, entre huertas de curioso mimo y flores de aromas y de colores prolijos, saluda, como un resucitado, a la niña que salta, a la mujer que canta, al hombre que trajina, al viejo que camina, al cura que pasea, al perrillo que husmea, al niño que se mea desde el alto pretil, y a la guardia civil.
> —Buenos días, niña salerosa.
> Por Lanzahita, se alumbran alhelíes de cinco colores.
> —Buenos días, mocita galana.
> Y rosas fragantes y lirios azules.
> —Buenos días tenga usted, señora.
> Y claveles rojos y azucenas blancas.

—Buenos días, hermano.
Y aúreas florecitas misteriosas.
—Buenos días, abuelo.
Y lirios morados.
—Buenos días, padre.
Y flores de altar.
—Salud, canes nutridos, gatos que no conocéis la tiña.
Y yerbas de rústicas veterinarias.
—Buenos días, jovencito meón, deja algo para luego.
Y altas matitas de albahaca para quien apunte mejor.
—Buenos días, señor cabo . . .
—Buenos días, buen hombre . . . (V, 452–53)

[By Lanzahita, the village of the melon growers, amidst neatly tended fields and flowers of many fragrances and colors, the vagabond greets, like a reinvigorated man, the girl who is skipping, the woman who is singing, the man who is carting, the old fellow who is walking, the priest who is strolling, the dog who is sniffing, the child who is peeing from the parapet, and the civil guard.
"Good morning, charming young girl."
In Lanzahita, wallflowers are blooming in five different colors.
"Good morning, elegant young lady."
And fragrant roses and blue irises.
"I wish you a good morning, madam."
And red carnations and white lilies.
"Good morning, brother."
And mysterious little golden flowers.
"Good morning, grandfather."
And purple irises.
"Good morning, father."
And altar flowers.
"Good health, well fed canines and mange-free cats."
And rustic, veterinary herbs.
"Good morning, young pisser, save a little for later."
And tall clumps of basil for whoever can aim better.
"Good morning, corporal . . ."
"Good morning, my good man . . ."]

With its repetitive structure, narrative tone, rhymes, and associations, this passage is certainly one of the most glaring indications of the creative writer revealing himself a little too enthusiastically in *Judíos, moros y cristianos.*

On an earlier occasion, in Barco de Avila, the vagabond had indulged in an altogether different kind of contrived description, this time seeking a comic effect. In a tavern, the huge and aptly named Treintarrobas [Thirdofaton] is seen tucking into a dish of roast kid. He then lets out the most explosive and alarming belch that the vagabond has ever heard. The reaction described is vivid but also thoroughly overdrawn:

El macho de reclamo aleteó, espantado, en su jaula de caña. El perro que tan bien ensayado tenía su piadoso gesto, salió huyendo despavorido como alma que lleva el diablo. Un gato rubio se cayó del estante en que dormía. La señorita del calendario, a pesar de estar retratada sobre cartoné de primera calidad, palideció. (V, 389)

[Horrified, the decoy bird beat its wings in its bamboo cage. The dog with the well rehearsed look of supplication, shot off, terrified, like a bat out of hell. A white cat fell from the shelf on which it had been sleeping. And even though the young woman on the calendar had been printed on top-quality backing, she turned pale.]

On many other occasions in Cela's third travel book, the reader is given striking reminders that the vagabond is engaged in much more than the assembling, ordering, and delivery of descriptive or even dramatic material. On regular occasions throughout the account, he indulges in the self-consciously controlled and sometimes heavily stylized presentation of his material. He also includes encounters with a number of bizarre individuals who Cela may or may not have come across on the road. Unlike *Del Miño al Bidasoa* and *Primer viaje andaluz*, the Castilian travel book contains no "Censo de personajes" indicating which characters are drawn from reality and which are literary creations. But in any case, *Judíos, moros y cristianos*, like *Del Miño al Bidasoa*, has moved a good way beyond the author's claim that the task of the travel writer is solely to tell and show things just as they are.

CONCLUSION

In *Por la Europa católica* (1902), Emilia Pardo Bazán describes some of her travels through Belgium, France, and Portugal as well as visits to three regions of Spain: Castile, Aragón, and Catalonia. Commenting on the historic buildings of Zaragoza, the Galician author laments the demolition, in 1894, of the famous Torre Nueva and, casting her mind back to earlier visits to the city, she recalls the striking appearance of the ninety-meter, leaning tower and also reflects on how different Spain might have been had the Moors and the Jews not been expelled from the country:

It was a strange tower, which preserved in its elegant and delicate decorations visible reminders that Christian, Jewish, and Moorish craftsmen had worked together on it. The blend of Gothic and Arab styles in the beautiful tower seemed to symbolize what Spain could have been if, instead of casting them out, we had known how to amalgamate and fuse the conquered races with our own.[16]

Despite its title, no such *cri de coeur* is to be found in *Judíos, moros y cristianos*. Indeed, Ricardo Senabre's assertion that Américo Castro's ideas on the remarkable coexistence in the peninsula of the three races and Cela's admiration for Castro are factors that "loom large" in this travel book, seems to owe more to Cela's acknowledged regard for Castro and to the title of the narrative than it does to the thrust or content of the work.[17] Robert Kirsner's observation that, with the publication of *Judíos, moros y cristianos*, "Cela establishes himself as a historian, and in particular as a partisan of Américo Castro's concept of Spanish history,"[18] is, to say the least, somewhat harsh on professional historians. In this narrative, Cela's approach to history deals mainly in the currency of names, dates, facts, and historical anecdotes, and the work can only really be considered partisan in terms of the title it bears. In almost every respect, this title is less a description of the themes and content of *Judíos, moros y cristianos* than a bow of homage to Castro and an acknowledgment of Cela's subscription to his thesis. It is difficult to see how the substance of the book is anything more than a very restricted reflection of a title which, as D. W. McPheeters gently notes, "is a little misleading."[19]

Although J. M. Castellet sees "the weight of history" as the most striking feature of *Judíos, moros y cristianos* (p. 23), in his brief assessment of the book he makes no mention of Américo Castro. However, both Castellet and Senabre do suggest links between Cela's view of Castile—its towns, monuments, and landscapes—and those of the writers of the so-called Generation of 1898. Certainly, the author's third travel book is about Old Castile. This is clearly signaled in the prologue, with its constant preoccupation with definitions, interpretations, aspects, and experiences of Castile, and especially of Old Castile. Once the text is underway, the principal visual and descriptive concerns are with the presence, the physicality of the region: its mountains, rivers, areas of wilderness, as well as its man-made structures (churches, castles, bridges, villages, towns, and cities). In addition, a good deal of space is found for Old Castile's rich historical, artistic, and religious associations.

Of course, the buildings and towns described often tell a story of wars, struggle, power, religion, settlement, success, and decline. In other words, they suggest the narrative of a historical, cultural, and social process. And although Cela pays some attention to aspects of the lengthy conflict between Christians and Muslims, he is just as interested in the reminders of the dynastic struggles taking place in Old Castile during the fifteenth century. But in the end, and despite the almost constant testimony in the work to the ravages of time, faded glories, and the long-lost dynamism of a past that produced cathedrals and castles, what is judged to have come out of this historical process is something that crystallized in September 1468 at the site of the stone bulls of Guisando and subsequently developed into the nation state of Spain. Thus, if in 1956 members of the establishment bristled when they saw the title of Cela's latest travel work, their apprehension or indignation would have been largely unjustified. They certainly could have read the book without experiencing many moments of agitation and would surely have nodded with approval when, in the closing pages, Cela dramatically evokes the figure of the youthful Isabella the Catholic.

7
History and the Arts: *Primer viaje andaluz*

AN EARLIER JOURNEY

IN CHAPTER 5 IT WAS POINTED OUT THAT MUCH OF THE APPARENT itinerary of *Del Miño al Bidasoa* drew on a half dozen of Cela's twenty-eight *Pueblo* articles of September–November 1948. The last piece used for source material for the second travel book was originally published on 20 September 1948 and showed Cela in Santesteban (Navarre), visiting the Residencia Martín M. de Espronceda. The corresponding section of *Del Miño al Bidasoa* describes Dupont and the vagabond passing through Santesteban and subsequently parting company a few kilometers away, near the French border, with the vagabond walking on for a while before deciding to spend the night under the stars.

After the publication of the *Pueblo* article showing the author at Santesteban (the thirteenth piece to appear in the series) another fifteen articles came out in the newspaper during the following six weeks. The first four of these fifteen appeared in *Pueblo* on 21, 22, 23, and 24 September 1948 and were later collected in volume 6 of Cela's *Obra completa* with the notation that *Primer viaje andaluz* had its origins in these four travel pieces.[1] The first of these four articles (which have a total length of some sixty-five hundred words) describes in a detailed and relatively leisurely fashion how Cela made his way from Santesteban, through Pamplona and then Vitoria to the next holiday residence on his schedule, in Sobrón (Alava). This journey south to Pamplona and then westwards across Navarre and the Basque country (covering a distance of about 180 kilometers) forms the geographical framework for the first two chapters of *Primer viaje andaluz*. The reference in the opening paragraph to the departure of Dupont therefore provides an almost seamless join with the closing scenes of *Del Miño al Bidasoa*. Hereafter, the traveler, once again styled as the "vagabond," traces the route to Sobrón first described in the *Pueblo* article of 21 September 1948.

Yet it is not solely the route of the *Pueblo* piece that is incorporated in the first two chapters of the 1959 travel work. In the same way that a good deal of the content of *Del Miño al Bidasoa* rehashed or reworked a significant portion of the *Pueblo* articles, so chapters 1 and 2 of the Andalusian travel book include a substantial amount of the newspaper material, often with only minor changes. A couple of comparisons will serve to illustrate the degree to which Cela has drawn on his 1948 account. On one occasion in the opening pages of *Primer viaje andaluz*, the author indulges in some remodeling that achieves three changes in a short passage: he incorporates a correction (and, in so doing, pokes a little fun at himself), changes the protagonist from a car passenger to a walker, and also manages to add a little drama and poetry to his material:

Pueblo article	*Primer viaje andaluz*
Por detrás de Armendoz sube el viejo monte Abartón; Armendoz es un pueblecillo situado a la izquierda del camino, con sus casas, altas y aisladas, rodeadas por el verde maíz. (VI, 666)	Por detrás de Almandoz—lugar que el vagabundo sabe que algunos, por no saber, escriben Almendoz y aun Armendoz—sube el viejo y verdinegro monte Abartón, poblado de sombras y de recuerdos. Almandoz es pueblecillo colocado a la izquierda del hombre que camina con la espalda en Francia, lugar con las casas altas y aisladas, como en Guipúzcoa, y rodeadas por el tibio y majestuoso maíz. (VI, 33)
[Behind Armendoz rises old Mount Abartón; Armendoz is a village located on the left of the road, with its tall houses standing apart and surrounded by green sweet corn.]	[Behind Almandoz—a place the vagabond knows that some, who know no better, spell as Almendoz and even Armendoz—rises the old and dark green Mount Abartón, full of shadows and memories. Almandoz is a village located to the left of a man walking away from France, a place with tall houses standing apart, just like in Guipúzcoa, and surrounded by aloof, majestic sweet corn.]

A little later, the author uses two brief scenes from the *Pueblo* piece as a frame into which he inserts additional description and observation, this time on one of his favorite topics:

Pueblo article	*Primer viaje andaluz*
La carretera en Echarren, cruza por en medio del pueblo, entre gallinas,	La carretera, en Echarren, cruza por en medio del pueblo, entre gallinas,

carros y niños pequeños. A la salida, sobre la fachada de una casa, se ve el escudo del pueblo, hecho en cerámica. (VI, 668)

carros y niños pequeños. Echarren es pueblo de muchas venas de agua y de próvidas fuentes. Por Echarren pasa el río Burunda, saltarín y crecido. A la salida de Echarren, sobre la fachada de una casa, se ve el escudo del pueblo, hecho en cerámica. (VI, 46)

[In Echarren, the highway passes through the middle of the village, through hens, carts, and small children. On the way out, on the front of a house, is the village's ceramic coat of arms.]

[In Echarren, the highway passes through the middle of the village, through hens, carts, and small children. Echarren is a village with many underground streams and abundant springs. The Burunda River, which is swift and swollen, runs through Echarren. On the way out, on the front of a house, is the village's ceramic coat of arms.]

In general, what the author does here and in later parts of *Primer viaje andaluz* is to build, often quite extensively, on a line or two taken verbatim or almost intact from the newspaper material. However, after the first two chapters such borrowings become increasingly sporadic. The reason for this is simple. The three *Pueblo* articles of 22, 23, and 24 September constitute just forty-five hundred words and describe in a speedy and somewhat sketchy manner Cela's car journey from Sobrón to the residence at El Puerto de Santa María (Cádiz), a distance, the reader is informed, of just over eleven hundred kilometers. In the first of these pieces, Cela describes a route that took him from Sobrón to Madrid and thence to Aranjuez, Ocaña, and Madridejos. The *Pueblo* article of 23 September covers the journey from Puerto Lápice, through Valdepeñas, Las Navas de Tolosa, Bailén, and as far as Córdoba. The following piece recounts the drive from Córdoba to Ecija and then nonstop through Seville before heading south for Jerez de la Frontera, and on to El Puerto de Santa María.

In the journey recorded in the *Pueblo* articles, Cela's route from the north of Spain to the province of Cádiz is largely the itinerary that will be followed in much of *Primer viaje andaluz*. However, there are two significant differences between the route described in the four *Pueblo* pieces and that taken in the Andalusian travel book. The first of these is that in *Primer viaje andaluz* the vagabond does not follow the main route between Bailén and Córdoba, but bypasses Bailén, with a southerly detour to Córdoba through Ubeda, Jaén, Lucena, and Montilla. And whereas in the *Pueblo* account Cela heads south after driving straight through Seville, in *Primer viaje andaluz* the vagabond leaves this city (having spent a number of days there) and heads west toward Huelva and the Portuguese border.

A final couple of points should be made concerning the relationship between the four *Pueblo* articles and the travel book they spawned. The *Pueblo* pieces of 21, 22, 23, and 24 September 1948 describe what appears to be a journey lasting about four days: through part of northern Spain and then southward, presumably staying overnight in Madrid, before heading south again, with an overnight stop in Córdoba and then driving on to El Puerto de Santa María. In *Primer viaje andaluz*, on the other hand, the account is of a journey that apparently lasts (including a significant stopover in Seville) more than six weeks. Thus, although the *Pueblo* itinerary is largely followed in the travel book, it is drastically slowed in pace and substantially expanded in description, detail, and narrative invention.

The brisk pace of the last three of the four *Pueblo* articles drawn on for *Primer viaje andaluz* means that these particular pieces present little more than fleeting impressions of people and places as, after Sobrón, Cela was driven south to the province of Cádiz. Indeed, some of these brief images from the 1948 trip are transplanted, usually with little or no attempt to reflect the late 1950s setting of the fourth travel book. For example, seemingly a decade or so after 1948, Aranjuez is almost identically presented as just as colorful and well cared for, and with the waters of the Tagus retaining their same rich hue:

Pueblo article	*Primer viaje andaluz*
Aranjuez es un oasis umbrío y versallesco en medio del páramo. El Tajo va casi de color esmeralda, los jardines están floridos y bien cuidados y la arquitectura aparece en orden. (VI, 676)	Aranjuez es un oasis amable y versallesco en medio del páramo. El Tajo va casi de color esmeralda, los jardines están floridos y bien cuidados y la arquitectura aparece en orden. (VI, 84)
[Aranjuez is a shady and Versaillesque oasis in the midst of the bleak plains. The Tagus flows almost emerald in color, the gardens are flowering and well tended, and the buildings are in good order.]	[Aranjuez is a pleasant and Versaillesque oasis in the midst of the bleak plains. The Tagus flows almost emerald in color, the gardens are flowering and well tended, and the buildings are in good order.]

In Puerto Lápice (also known as Puerto Lápiche) the appearance of the houses, supposedly a decade later, still catches the vagabond's eye. However, the revamped passage in the travel book implies that there is something enigmatic about Puerto Lápice, makes mention of how it suffered in nineteenth-century conflicts, adds a few details about the scene captured, and also injects a note of mundane drama with the suggestion that the local women do not appear to be enjoying the task they are engaged in:

Pueblo article

Puerto Lápiche es un pueblecito antiguo, de buenas casas, con rejas en las ventanas. Bajo el sol, unas mujeres enjalbegan las bardas de un corral. (VI, 679)

Primer viaje andaluz

Puerto Lápice es un pueblecito curioso, de buenas casas, con rejas en las ventanas y en los balcones. En la guerra de la Independencia fue arrasado y durante las luchas civiles del siglo XIX, los carlistas le pegaron fuego. Unas mujeres sin edad enjalbegan, también sin entusiasmo, las altas tapias de un corral de adobe. (VI, 99)

[Puerto Lápiche is a very old village, with good houses that have grilles at their windows. In the sun, a group of women are whitewashing the walls of a yard.]

[Puerto Lápice is a strange village, with good houses that have grilles at their windows and on the balconies. In the War of Independence it was devastated and during the civil conflicts of the nineteenth century the Carlists set fire to the place. A group of women of indeterminate age are unenthusiastically whitewashing the high, adobe walls of a yard.]

In effect, by taking such pieces from the *Pueblo* articles and then using them, sometimes with slight modifications and on other occasions with considerable additions, the author is not only reworking earlier material, he is also possibly revealing that he made no subsequent visits to the locations in question. The Andalusian narrative, which Cela finished writing in the summer of 1959, is in fact given an approximate chronological setting of the late 1950s. Thus, mention is made of the death of the South African poet and Hispanophile, Roy Campbell (VI, 267), who committed suicide in 1957; in Moguer, the vagabond visits the grave of Juan Ramón Jiménez (VI, 335), who died in 1958, while in Niebla there is reference to a windstorm that destroyed more than twenty houses just two years earlier, in 1957 (VI, 330). So, taking into account the travel book's reliance for much of its itinerary on the 1948 articles, its reworking of some of that material, its opening presented as a practically seamless continuation from the parting of the ways with Dupont at the end of *Del Miño al Bidasoa*, and the inclusion of other excursions and experiences—all this means that the narrative sources of

Primer viaje andaluz straddle a period of ten or so years. Yet the material incorporated from the *Pueblo* pieces is hardly ever modified to reflect the passage of time. A rare indication of change of circumstances does however occur when, in the travel book, the vagabond notes that the mining town of La Carolina, near Las Navas de Tolosa, is not as prosperous as it used to be:

Pueblo article	*Primer viaje andaluz*
En La Carolina, un pueblo minero, grande y rico, se entra por un paso a nivel sobre el ferrocarril de vía estrecha y se sale por otro. (VI, 681)	La Carolina, a poco andar de las Navas, es pueblo minero y grande y menos rico de lo que fue, al que se entra por un paso a nivel sobre el ferrocarril de vía estrecha. (VI, 121)
[La Carolina is a large, prosperous mining town, which you enter by a grade crossing over the narrow-gauge railway and leave by another one.]	[La Carolina, not far from Las Navas, is a large mining town that is not as prosperous as it once was, and you enter it by a grade crossing over the narrow-gauge railway.]

All in all, then, these reused passages of descriptive material simply take a scene as it was captured toward the end of one decade and transplant it, normally with a few stylistic modifications or descriptive insertions, to a period some ten years later. As is the case with *Del Miño al Bidasoa*, such reworking or rehashing is not footnoted in any editions of *Primer viaje andaluz* and it is only in the *Obra completa* that this source material is acknowledged and displayed in the appropriate appendix. Accordingly, readers who come to Cela's second and fourth travel works in editions other than those of the *Obra completa* are given no indication of the extent to which *Del Miño al Bidasoa* draws on the *Pueblo* articles of 1948 or of how the Andalusian travel book incorporates a noticeable amount of out-of-date descriptive material from the newspaper pieces.

GETTING THERE

It is not until the early part of chapter 4 (that is, after some eighty pages, or a quarter of the whole account) that the vagabond actually sets foot in Andalusia. As was noted in chapter 3, at the beginning of *The Old Patagonian Express*, Paul Theroux notes that "the going is often as fascinating as the arrival" (pp. 11–12), and, indeed, there are several facets of the first eighty pages of *Primer viaje andaluz* that are particularly interesting from the point of view of "going" or "getting there." In the first place, Cela spends the first two chapters (some forty pages) rounding off the journey that had been developed in *Del Miño al Bidasoa*. Not only does the narrative of *Primer viaje andaluz* pick up exactly where and when the 1952 work had left off, chapters 1 and 2 also serve as a kind of postscript to it by bringing to a conclusion the vagabond's journey across the north of the country.

But after the north, where next for the vagabond? Theroux suggests that it is useful to know the motive for any journey undertaken, and with regard to this particular point the narrative of *Primer viaje andaluz* becomes utterly fanciful. Chapter 3 begins with the vagabond at the Ebro River, tired of the roads of northern Spain. During the course of the next five pages he decides that Castile will not be his next destination, since he has already traveled there, and so he sits down in order to seek advice from his guardian angel. This soon comes, in the form of a birdcall that repeatedly exhorts him to head south. At first fearful, since he is a northerner who regards the south as colorful, dazzling, exotic, and incomprehensible, the wayfarer ponders until, after more urging from the mysterious adviser, he is persuaded and is soon enthusing at the prospect of the blue skies and blue mountains of Andalusia.

So, it is on the basis of this embarrassingly contrived scene that the vagabond decides to make his way to the south. He has, so it would seem, no grand geographical or cultural quest. Once the decision has been made, he reveals no more than a sense of excitement and anticipation at the thought of exploring a part of Spain that he regards as "rara y hermética" [strange and inscrutable] (VI, 76). However, something altogether more mundane than voices from above or visions from within is introduced to transport the vagabond to the threshold of his land of marvels. Nearby, as good fortune would have it, he comes across a truck heading for Córdoba and so his journey to the south is greatly hastened. Just as in *Del Miño al Bidasoa*, a truck serves to repeat the speed, and also excuse the lack of descriptive detail, of that early part of the new travel book that draws on the car ride of the *Pueblo* articles.

The half dozen pages of the *Pueblo* articles of 22 and 23 September 1948 that record, with some haste, the car drive from near Sobrón to Madrid, and thence to Venta de Cárdenas, are transformed in *Primer viaje andaluz* into thirty-two pages describing the vagabond's truck journey from more or less the same point of departure—and following the same route—until, at Venta de Cárdenas, he chooses to walk the few remaining kilometers into Andalusia. In both versions of the journey from north to south, the section from Sobrón to Madrid is mentioned in a few lines, with no physical description of any features of this 350-kilometer stage. But whereas in the two *Pueblo* pieces the drive from Madrid southward to Venta de Cárdenas is largely described in terms of relatively brief observations on the appearance of towns passed through, the sight of the occasional individual or activity, the look of the countryside, or the picture presented by a river or some distant mountains, in chapter 3 of *Primer viaje andaluz* considerable extra bulk is given to the account of this journey. The *Pueblo* trip from Madrid to Venta de Cárdenas is expanded from an original half dozen pages to more than thirty by the introduction of a few short, dramatic episodes or scenes, the inclusion of the occasional geographical digression, and, especially, by the evocation of the historical and literary associations of certain buildings and towns.

The brief narrative scenes that are developed from time to time in the third chapter of the travel work can even stem from something mentioned in passing in one of the *Pueblo* pieces. So, when Cela leaves Madridejos on the 1948 trip, there is a three-line description of the car overtaking a cyclist who is laboring up a hill (VI, 678). Eleven years later, this brief reference to the struggling rider becomes a one-page account in which the vagabond and the truck driver discuss whether to offer a lift to the cyclist, draw level with him, make their offer, and then have it politely declined as the cyclist explains that he is exercising in an attempt to shake off a cold. They drive on, acknowledging that all kinds of therapy should be respected (VI, 98–99).

Some fifty kilometers further south, in Manzanares, Cela had stopped in 1948 for a bite to eat at a place that had been pointed out to him but which, it transpired, had no ordinary red wine. This information was given some three lines (VI, 679). However, in *Primer viaje anda-luz* it spawns two consecutive scenes. In the first, the vagabond and his driver, having asked a passerby where they can get something to eat, are treated by the local know-all to a bombastic encomium of a nearby establishment. Once in the place, they find it to be shabby, cold, charmless, and with the look of an unfriendly bar. To cap it all, their request for two glasses of red comes to nought when they are informed by the smug owner that he sells only quality wines and so cannot oblige them. Consequently, the two men leave and end up in a bar of their own choosing, where they eat and drink well at a reasonable price (VI, 100–2). In this way, a single sentence from one of the *Pueblo* articles is developed into a narrative sequence in the Andalusian travel book. What, of course, remains unclear is the degree to which these scenes in *Primer viaje andaluz* might be relating events that actually occurred in 1948 but were not, for any number of reasons, included in the newspaper account, or whether what is narrated in these parts of the 1959 travel work is partly a fictional elaboration, or even a total creation.

Elsewhere in chapter 3, Cela returns to one of his enthusiasms when he introduces material that gives a brief description of the origins and destinations of the three (apparently foul-smelling) streams that converge on Getafe, south of Madrid. However, the half dozen lines used to chart this local network are nothing compared to the six pages which, beginning with a brief, passing reference (echoing that in the *Pueblo* account) to the dry bed of the Amarguillo River in Madridejos, pursue a detailed description of the rivers, lakes, and streams that form part of what is termed the "intricate cobweb" radiating from the mysterious Guadiana River. So here, a one-line reference in the 1948 account has been lengthened to a couple of slightly more descriptive lines in *Primer viaje andaluz,* and these, in turn, have been used as the point of departure for an extensive and complicated documentation of a river system (VI, 91–97).

In this description of the waters that have some connection with the Guadiana, there is also mention of the literary associations of the river, with references to Lope de Vega, Cervantes, and the Andalusian poet Juan Rufo. In addition, the lexicographer Sebastián de Covarrubias is brought into this part of the narrative, as is the historian, Pedro de Medina. Indeed, the third chapter introduces the kind of historical and cultural material that will emerge as such a prominent feature of the last three-quarters of *Primer viaje andaluz.* Therefore, from the unlikely vantage point of a truck laden with the personal belongings of a family moving to Córdoba, the narrative is punctuated with information and observations concerning a variety of monuments, historical figures, and historical events associated with locations on the road south, as well as mentions of literary and other figures of importance in Spanish culture, from the Golden Age to the mid-twentieth century.

Thus, there are passing references to the ruins of the castle at Pinto, the location of the castle of Monreal, the elegant castle at Manzanares (described as being full of tales of heroes and knights), and to the occasional wayside chapel. Elsewhere en route, relevant information is given when the truck passes through a place in which a famous person was born or died. So, the reader is informed that two famous sons of Valdemoro were the theologian, Fray Alonso de la Cruz, and Philip II's architect, Juan de Castro. Yepes, "con su pretérito solemnidad; con su presente miseria" [with its past solemnity and its present poverty] (VI, 85), is pointed out as the birthplace of Gonzalo de Yepes, a weaver by trade and the father of St John of the Cross, and also the town where Fray Diego, Prior of the Escorial and confessor to Philip II, was born. Tembleque, too, produced famous churchmen, including Bishops of Milan and Malta, and a confessor to another Hapsburg monarch, this time Philip IV. Infantes was the birthplace of a saint, Tomás de Villanueva, and was also where Francisco de Quevedo died, the writer described by the vagabond as the man who "manejó la herramienta del idioma castellano como nadie jamás lo hiciera ni jamás nadie lo volviera a hacer" [handled the tool of the Castilian language as nobody had ever done before, or would ever do again] (VI, 105).

On other occasions in chapter 3, reference is made to the fact that the Princess of Eboli was imprisoned in Pinto (an observation accompanied by a reminder of the wayfarer's earlier association with the famous historical figure during the Pastrana stage of the Alcarria trip) and, as Ocaña is passed through, there is a substantial digression on some of the town's many historical associations, from Roman times to the War of Independence. Indeed, on several occasions during the journey south, the sites of encounters with Napoleon's forces are identified and information is given on the participants in or the outcome of these actions. In a similar vein, there are several references to places that figured in the Carlist wars, culminating at the close of chapter 3 with the account of the terrible atrocities that were committed at Viso del Marqués and Calzada de Calatrava (both to the west of the route being followed) and which, the vagabond notes, are painful to write about.

In addition to the historical data and commentary included in the account of the drive south (at least some of which comes as information supplied by the vagabond to the driver), the third chapter also contains a noticeable number of references to writers that are triggered by a scene or a setting. Thus, the poverty that the vagabond witnesses on the southern outskirts of Madrid reminds him of the creations of Baroja and also of those of the painter and writer, José Solana. Shortly after, as the truck passes by Getafe, Juan Bautista Amorós (Silverio Lanza), who lived and died there, is recalled. So, too, are the gloomy titles of some of his fiction and his link with Alejandro Sawa. Elsewhere, people or places make the vagabond think of Bécquer, Lupercio Leonardo de Argensola, and Calderón. The Guadiana River, as was mentioned earlier, evokes thoughts of Cervantes and gives rise to brief, pertinent extracts from the work of Lope de Vega and Juan Rufo. Later, as the vagabond muses on the beauty of the women of Santa Cruz, he recalls Antonio Machado's description of the women of La Mancha.

Chapter 3 of *Primer viaje andaluz* is a functional and fairly brisk account of the journey from northern Spain to within a few kilometers of the borders of Andalusia and which brings the narrative, a quarter of the way into the work, to a location where, in fact, the vagabond acknowledges that his account should really have started (VI, 109). Although the chapter does not quite carry the reader to Andalusia, it still gives a clear foretaste of the narrative approach and thematic concerns that will become evident once the vagabond begins his journey through the southern region.

The Andalusian Itinerary

It was pointed out in chapter 2 that Cela has frequently stated his dislike of cities and has also mentioned escape from the city as an important motive for traveling. Yet as was seen in *Judíos, moros y cristianos*, the vagabond's time in Segovia takes up most of chapter 4 while his stay in Avila constitutes just over half of the following chapter. Consequently, it comes as no surprise to find that in *Primer viaje andaluz* the vagabond should also spend time exploring many of the cities of the south. Indeed, as he is about to enter Córdoba, he even becomes a little defensive on this point, confessing: "En esta su descubierta andaluza, el vagabundo, incluso forzando un poco sus principios, va a meterse—ya se viene metiendo—por las ciudades. También, a su manera, va a contarlas—ya las viene contando" [In this, his Andalusian expedition, the vagabond, bending his principles a little, is going to enter—he has already been entering—cities. Also, in his own way, he is going to describe them—he already been describing them] (VI, 171).

The vagabond's journey from Venta de Cárdenas takes him through the gorge of Despeñaperros and thence more or less south via Linares, Ubeda, and Jaén. After Jaén, he moves ever westward, but in what is often a looping, rather than a direct course, to the Portuguese border. Thus, he travels southwestward to Linares and Puente Genil, before heading north to Montilla and Córdoba. After Córdoba, he follows the Guadalquivir as far as Palma del Río, then undertakes a substantial southern loop through Ecija, Marchena, and Carmona, before heading north once again to join the Guadalquivir at Lora del Río and subsequently traveling the road that follows the valley of the river through to Seville. The journey from Seville to Huelva includes a detour, through Almonte, to the coast, and then back north before approaching Huelva via Niebla, Moguer, and Palos de la Frontera. After Huelva, the vagabond heads northward along the valley of the Odiel River, as far as Gibraleón, turns southwest to Cartaya and Lepe, and then strikes out for Ayamonte on the Guadiana, which marks the border between Spain and Portugal, and also the end of the journey.

Chapters 4 to 7, which contain the Andalusian scenes of this travel work, show the vagabond passing through hamlets, villages, towns, and cities in what is presented as a period of just over five weeks. In this section of the narrative, he pauses in most of the towns and all the cities en route and usually supplies a moderately detailed description of the features and associations of these places. Thus, Jaén, Ecija, Osuna, Carmona, and Sanlúcar la Mayor are each accorded five or six pages, while Montilla, Palma del Río, Castilleja de la Cuesta, Niebla, and Moguer merit three or four apiece. Huelva and Córdoba are somewhat more generously treated, with ten and sixteen pages respectively. However, Seville (including Triana) accounts for a hefty seventy pages, or getting on for 30 percent of the material of the four Andalusian chapters. Thus the vagabond's trip to southern Spain and thence through much of a region initially touted as remarkable, dazzling, proud, strange, and mysterious (VI, 76), eventually climaxes in the lengthy account of the principal city of southern Spain and the time spent there. Indeed, once the reader has absorbed the two Sevillian sections of chapter 6, "La más bella ciudad" [The most Beautiful City] and "Triana, capital del cante" [Triana, Capital of Flamenco Singing]—which between them are longer than any of the other chapters in the work—then the journey to and through Andalusia can be seen, with hindsight, to have been mainly a pilgrimage to Seville. A pilgrimage that subsequently develops into a homage to that city, its history, and cultural associations. Certainly, after this penultimate chapter the narrative momentum of *Primer viaje andaluz* gradually peters out as the vagabond makes his way toward the frontier with Portugal in the anticlimactic last phase of the journey.

PLACES THAT SPEAK AND THOSE THAT SING

Although Cela's fourth travel book opens as if it were the sequel to *Del Miño al Bidasoa*, it is, with its similarities of focus and structure, much more the narrative successor to the 1956 work, *Judíos, moros y cristianos*. In the Castilian travel book, the vagabond certainly seems to be illustrating, as was previously pointed out, Butor's notion of the travel narrative as a pilgrimage to places that "tell us of our history and ourselves" (p. 61). With the Andalusian account, on the other hand, the quest seems to be more restricted. Here, the vagabond goes to explore a region of his country that he regards as distinctively different from the rest of Spain. Yet in his descriptions of the cultural legacy of Andalusia, he comes to focus far less on those manifestations that were the product of Moorish or Hispano-Arabic civilizations than on those that proved to be an essential and enduring part of the evolving, modern Spanish culture.

Soon after the vagabond sets foot on Andalusian soil, he arrives at Las Navas de Tolosa and there indulges in an account of the background to and the course of the historic battle that took place in 1212 and in which the armies of Aragón, Castile, and Navarre, along with the assistance of French knights, inflicted a crushing defeat on the Almohads. In the corresponding *Pueblo* article, Cela had simply described the celebrated place as follows: "Las Navas de Tolosa, en un sitio ideal para hacer la guerra, es un pueblecito pequeño. A la puerta de una casa cuatro hombres juegan al mus rodeados de veinticinco o treinta mirones" [Las Navas de Tolosa, in an ideal location for doing battle, is a tiny, little place. At the door of one of the houses, four men are playing cards, surrounded by twenty-five or thirty onlookers] (VI, 681). In the travel book, however, the material relating to this famous site is expanded to over four pages that detail events leading up to the battle and also include a brief re-creation of the engagement. Immediately after, attention is switched to the rather more prosaic pursuits of the group of men playing cards and being watched by others. Now, the time of day is specified, there has been a slight change of location, and while the numbers are the same the spectators are this time described as "silent," as if in contrast to the din and frenzy of the battle that has just been described: "Son las nueve del día y en Las Navas de Tolosa, a la puerta de una cantina, cuatro hombres juegan al mus rodeados de una nube de veinticinco o treinta mirones silenciosos" [It is nine in the morning, and in Las Navas de Tolosa, at the door of a bar, four men are playing cards, surrounded by a crowd of twenty-five or thirty silent onlookers] (VI, 120).

Henceforth, the conflicts as well as the artistic and architectural legacies of Andalusia's Muslim past figure only sporadically in the account. Certainly, in Priego de Córdoba, the vagabond entertains himself by rehearsing how the town had frequently changed hands during the period of the *Reconquista*, until it was finally secured for the Christians in 1409. And when, a little later, he finds himself in the area of Cabra, he recalls it was thereabouts that the Cid defeated the Moors of Granada, along with their ally, the Count Don García Ordóñez. Once the vagabond reaches Córdoba, though, he deals with the Mezquita, once the principal mosque of western Islam, in a few lines, in the sketchiest of terms, and feels thoroughly uncomfortable as he spends some brief moments inside the building. He explains that such grand monuments do not suit him and notes that his response to the Escorial or Burgos cathedral is just the same (VI, 172).

In fact, the two days that the vagabond spends in Córdoba, and which are described in sixteen pages of narrative, are largely given over to walking the streets and squares of the place. Unfortunately, much of this material amounts to little more than a guided tour of the city, with the vagabond pointing out churches, convents, chapels, and palaces, and sometimes noting their treasures or their associations with the famous. Elsewhere, a street or a square is linked with a well-known figure, a tradition, or a historical episode, and there are also frequent references to connections between the city, or its particular quarters, and famous writers. Not surprisingly, Luis de Góngora comes to the fore, but García Lorca, George Borrow, Théophile Gautier, Duque de Rivas (like Góngora, a son of Córdoba), Lope de Vega, Azorín, Valera, Baroja, Cervantes, and Campoamor are also conjured up. In addition, there are allusions to the city's powerful connections with bullfighting and note is taken of the street where the most famous of bullfighters, Manolete, was born.

The bars of Córdoba frequently figure in the description of the vagabond's stay in the city (in one establishment he has a particularly tasty lamb stew and provides the recipe) and then, during his second evening there, he is taken to hear *flamenco* music. This generates some observations on the characteristics of local *fandangos* and *soleares*. And while there is only a page or so describing the music of Córdoba, it is worth noting that this amounts to double the space accorded to the city's Mezquita.

On the other hand, a few kilometers outside Córdoba the vagabond visits the ruins of the Umayyad palace city of Medina Azahara, outlines the history of the various buildings, notes events that took place in the caliphate of Córdoba during the late tenth century, mentions the wonders of the architecture, evokes the luxury and splendor of the place in its heyday, and also relates how, what has been called a "unique monument,"[2] was sacked and largely destroyed by the Berbers in 1010 (VI, 187–89). A little later, and before leaving the valley of the Guadalquivir to head south toward Ecija, the vagabond passes through Palma del Río and notes that this Christian town had also been sacked during the *Reconquista*, this time by the Moorish king of Granada.

Despite such observations on the monuments of Muslim Spain or mentions of episodes of the *Reconquista*, the historical flavor of the Andalusian chapters of Cela's fourth travel work is largely provided by the inclusion of material on characters or incidents of the period spanning the fourteenth to the nineteenth centuries. These references to the players and episodes of history are, as was noted earlier, usually prompted by associations with a particular place. So in Martos, near Jaén, the vagabond recalls that at the nearby cliff, Ferdinand IV had the two Carvajal brothers put to death in August 1312 and notes how, before they died, the condemned men cited the king to die within thirty days. He adds that King Ferdinand died exactly thirty days later. At the castle of Almodóvar, near Medina Azahara, mention is made that it was here that King Peter I, the Cruel, of Castile (1350–69), kept his treasure and also imprisoned Doña Juana de Lara, before eventually having her executed. Later, in Carmona, some thirty kilometers east of Seville, the vagabond lists historical figures and incidents associated with the town during the reign of Alfonso XI (1312–50) and after the death of Peter the Cruel.

In Córdoba, there is reference to a spot where Columbus apparently prayed, while later, when the vagabond reaches Palos, he observes that not only did Columbus set sail from this (now landlocked) town in August 1492 but that Hernán Cortés returned here from Mexico in May 1528. Shortly after, as he makes his way toward Huelva, he comes to the place where Columbus fitted out his three caravels and pictures the bustling scene. He also identifies the spring from which the ships were watered, comments on its cool, plentiful, clear, and healthy water, and then proceeds to wash himself in it before setting off for Huelva (VI, 339–40). In the 1960s, Nina Epton found herself at the same spot. However, her description of the spring is rather different from that contained in *Primer viaje andaluz*:

> Two small boys interrupted their play to take us down to the Arab fountain to the right of the main road on the way to Moguer, hidden among a clump of trees, where the navigators provided themselves with water for the voyage. It must have been fresher then than it is now or they would probably have died of typhus. I found it despoiled by litter, an old rubber tyre and weeds.[3]

After his references to Columbus and Cortés, the vagabond makes hardly any allusions to historical events of the next three centuries, preferring instead to reserve his asides and observations for places having connections with the War of Independence and the Carlist Wars. There is mention of the part played by the men of Alcaudete at the battle of Bailén (1808) and in the vagabond's tour of Seville there is a reference to the fact that, during the French occupation, Marshal Soult lodged in the Archbishop's Palace. In addition, it is noted that two patriots who fought against the French are buried in the Patio de los Naranjos of Seville's cathedral. Then, just before the vagabond gets to Niebla, he gives an outline of the town's history, from when it was probably founded by the Phoenicians to the time that the castle was blown up by Marshal Soult's troops.

Although *Primer viaje andaluz* contains a half dozen or so passing references to the Spanish Civil War (including the vagabond's sharp retort when asked by the truck driver on which side he fought during the conflict), there are scarcely any other allusions to historical or political events of the twentieth century. Indeed, the vagabond's interest in historical process, fact, or detail hardly gets beyond occasional mentions of the Carlist Wars of the nineteenth century. In the first three chapters there are a few, brief references to the Carlist conflicts, culminating in the pained acknowledgment of the atrocities committed at Viso del Marqués and Calzada de Calatrava. Of course, in the Andalusian chapters of the narrative there is less scope for commenting on what were, principally, northern civil wars and there are just a couple of observations on the Carlist commander, Miguel Gómez. One of these describes how, during a six-month period in 1836, Gómez led a force of three thousand men around the peninsula, plundering as they went: from Alava, through the Asturias and Galicia, on to León and then La Mancha, before taking Córdoba, moving on through Extremadura, setting up camp in Ronda, and then heading north for Burgos before returning to headquarters at Orduña. According to the vagabond, Gómez arrived back with more men than he started out with, and throughout his immensely profitable swing around Spain was pursued by Generals Espartero and Narváez (VI, 146). Later in the account, when he reaches Palma del Río, the vagabond mentions that this town, too, had fallen victim to the ravages of Gómez and his Carlist troops.

The figure of Miguel Gómez had first caught the vagabond's attention when he came upon the soldier's birthplace, the small town of Torredonjimeno, nearly twenty kilometers west of Jaén. This technique of identifying famous Spaniards who either started or finished life in the places that the vagabond passes through (and which was used in chapter 3) is also employed throughout the Andalusian chapters of the account. Thus, the reader learns that Manolete died in the Linares bullring and that St John of the Cross died in Ubeda, while in Priego mention is made that the explorer, Alonso Carmona, and Niceto Alcalá Zamora, the first president of the Second Republic, were both born there. As the vagabond goes through Jauja he expresses his admiration for the famous brigand born there in 1805, popularly known as *El Tempranillo*; Cabra is identified as the birthplace of Juan Valera, while La Rambla was where the former Prime Minister, Alejandro Lerroux, was born. In the ancient town of Ecija it is revealed that the first Bishop of Athens was born locally, as were the Jew, Juzeph, the finance minister of Alfonso XI; the Golden Age writer, Luis Vélez de Guevara; the explorer, Rafael de Aguilar (who, the reader is informed, founded Nueva Ecija in the Philippines); the musician, Juan Bermudo, as well as, the vagabond adds, many more famous Spaniards. When he gets to Castilleja de la Cuesta, just to the west of Seville, the vagabond confesses his admiration for Hernán Cortés, who died in disgrace in this small town.

But while the events of the past and the leading figures who shaped those events are often evoked as the vagabond makes his way through Andalusia, he is also constantly aware, as indeed he was in *Judíos, moros y cristianos*, of the monuments and debris of the past, of the physical reminders of the region's cultural and political history. Often, monuments are seen in association with their connections with history or historical figures: for example, events that took place within the walls of a castle or the part a fortress played in a conflict of long ago, or who is buried in a particular church or cathedral. Such associations bring these inanimate monuments to life by involving them in part of a historical, social, and even dramatic process.

Unfortunately, the vagabond is also capable of indulging in an unashamed cataloguing of churches, chapels, castles, towers, and ruins as he moves along the road or around a town. So, in the early stages of the journey through Andalusia, he lists the palaces and churches of Ubeda or some of the fine buildings of Baeza, with maybe a few words of comment on their appearance. He mentions the castles, towers, and ruins of Torre del Campo, and as he looks down on Lucena he notes and comments in the briefest of terms on its castle, palace, church, and convents.

When he arrives in Ecija, on the other hand, the vagabond starts with a summing up of the architectural delights of the ancient town: "En Ecija, el vagabundo vio muy nobles palacios y muy bellas torres" [In Ecija, the vagabond saw very noble palaces and very beautiful towers]. A few lines later, he adds that here everything "huele a pretérito" [smells of the past] (VI, 205). Then comes a tour of the place, with brief comments on the squares, churches, towers, and palaces. But it is the sight of the residences of the once-powerful aristocratic families that brings the visitor back to thoughts of faded glory and to the appropriate lines of Jorge Manrique's *Coplas por la muerte de su padre* [Couplets on the Death of his Father]. Nevertheless, amid the architectural splendors of Ecija and despite the vagabond's meditations on the presence and power of the past, he still manages to include a one-page recipe for a culinary speciality of the town, "Huevos a la flamenca" [Eggs Flamenco].

Yet the six-page account of Ecija, or even the earlier sixteen pages devoted to Córdoba, are modest narrations when compared to the seventy pages dedicated to Seville—including thirty to the Triana district of the city. Before entering Seville, the vagabond recalls how it had been perceived by the local poet, Fernando de Herrera (for its size), by Ortega y Gasset (for its dazzling appearance), by Pedro Salinas (for its indescribable light), and by Cervantes (for its immensity). He then enters the city, parts company with his old friend from the Alcarria trip, the traveling salesman, Martín, and notes quite simply: "Se echó a callejear" [He started to walk the streets] (VI, 230–38).

Chapter 6 of *Primer viaje andaluz,* which begins with the vagabond on the road to Ecija and is subsequently largely devoted to his stay in Seville, is entitled "El soberbio teatro del mundo" [The Great Theater of the World], one of Lope de Vega's descriptions of the city. It is undoubtedly intended to be the climax of the Andalusian travel work. The forty-page central section of this hundred-page chapter (by far the longest in the book) shows the vagabond reaching Seville, very much in awe of the city before him, already conscious of its beauty, its luster, its uniqueness, and what he terms its "mysterious history." Thus, already overawed by Seville even before he begins to make his way around the city, he sets out to describe its streets and buildings.

Yet, the ensuing description of streets and monuments, while indicating the history and itemizing the treasures of the place, does not really convey what was initially heralded as the wonder of Seville. Indeed, the vagabond's account of the city is occasionally prosaic and at times reads like the catalog of an impressively stocked museum. Now and again an anecdote or an aside is included, but in general the approach is brisk and guidebook like. So, on his tour he lists the churches that he comes across, sometimes commenting on their style, or mentioning their treasures or who is buried within their walls, or occasionally recounting an aspect of their history. In this way the reader is informed, for example, that the church of San Luis is baroque and circular in construction; San Román is a Mudejar church and the painter Juan Sánchez de Castro is buried there, while the church of San Lorenzo contains the sculpture of Christ called "Jesús del Gran Poder" [Jesus of the Great Power], which is taken out at 2 A.M. on each Good Friday morning to provide a spectacular and moving sight. Apparently, one of this church's former chaplains died at the age of 120 (from a fall) and had, some twenty-one years before his death, sailed off to the Indies. Elsewhere, the church of Santa María Magdalena is simply described as baroque and showy, and is reported as being well endowed with paintings and sculptures, although no details are given. San Esteban, on the other hand, has paintings by Zurbarán of Saints Peter and Paul, is a blend of Romanesque and Mudejar styles and, around the turn of the century, some thirteenth-century Moorish tiles were found in the church. Finally, after giving a little description of the university church, the vagabond mentions that here, amidst many of the high born, the Bécquer brothers are buried, and he even throws in a little gossip concerning a possible affair between Gustavo Adolfo's wife and a brigand from the mountains of Soria.

A number of the convents and monasteries of Seville are accorded similar narrative treatment: sometimes an observation or two is made in passing and occasionally a slightly fuller (but never extensive) commentary is given. So, when he arrives at the convent of Santa Clara, the vagabond mentions that it was built in the Mudejar style and that later remodeling was well executed. He notes that there is a reredos by José Martínez Montañés in the convent's church and also multicolored tiling there. In the grounds, he tells how the founder buried herself alive to escape her pursuers, how grass immediately grew over the spot, and notes that she emerged safe and sound once the king's henchmen had left. Mention is made of aspects of the history of the nearby monastery of San Clemente and there is an indication of some of its treasures, as well as a warning of its poor and precarious state. Subsequently, the vagabond points out a convent that Queen Isabella was especially fond of, Madre de Dios de la Piedad (although there is no mention that she founded the convent, in 1496), while a little later he observes that the best thing about the convent of San Leandro are the candied egg yolks (yemas) that the nuns make and sell. Although the recipe is apparently a jealously guarded secret, the vagabond proceeds to offer a possible method, involving the use of holy water, for the confection of what is described as "pasto angélico y manjar excesivo para el amargo paladar del hombre" [angelic nourishment and excessive sustenance for the bitter palate of man] (VI, 253). Such an accolade does not, however, prevent him from buying a dozen yemas, which he scoffs before leaving the premises. No other items of information are given about the convent of San Leandro.

Elsewhere on his tour of the city, the vagabond takes in some of Seville's secular landmarks. When he sees the Museo Provincial de Bellas Artes, he describes it as the second most important art gallery in Spain, but with the best collection of works by Murillo and Zurbarán. However, he does not go in to see the paintings and informs the reader that this is because ever since he was thrown out of the Biblioteca Nacional he has been rather wary of official centers of culture. The Casa de Pilatos, described as "ostentosamente rica y abigarrada y, aunque parezca paradoja, también airosa y señorial" [ostentatiously sumptuous and polychromatic, and although it seems paradoxical, it is also elegant and majestic] (VI, 252), is briefly presented as a palace regarded by Sevillians as the original residence of Pontius Pilate and not, as tradition has it, a copy. To reinforce this suggestion of the locals' bizarre belief, the vagabond mentions the account of a French visitor who, when he was shown over the palace, claimed that a maid pointed out to him where Peter sat as he denied Christ. At the Alcázar there is some description of the gardens, a list of Spanish monarchs from medieval times to the twentieth century who had some involvement with developing and altering the complex, and then, interspersed between reminiscences with an old friend now employed there, the vagabond gives a few, brief indications of some of the finer decorative work carried out over the centuries.

After lunch with his friend, the vagabond makes his way over to the Casa Lonja, which he describes as a noble building. There follows a brief account of how it came to be designed by the architect of the Escorial, Juan de Herrera, as a commodity exchange for merchants previously trading in the cathedral precincts and of how, some two hundred years later, in the 1780s, it was transformed into the Archivo General de las Indias. Finally, the vagabond makes his way to the Hospital de Santa Caridad, located between the Casa Lonja and the Guadalquivir River, and which was established in the late seventeenth century for the poor and elderly sick. Apart from giving a little history of the site where the hospital stands, this visit to the building that the vagabond describes as being inhabited by death, focuses almost entirely on the figure of the founder, Don Miguel de Mañara. Apparently a reformed debauchee who was mistakenly regarded by some as the model for Tirso's Don Juan, Mañara came to devote his life to religion and good works and, according to the vagabond, clothed himself in mock humility. After mentioning the portraits there of Mañara by Valdés Leal and Murillo, the visitor quotes the epitaph on his tomb: "Aquí yacen los huesos y la ceniza del peor hombre que ha vivido en el mundo" [Here lie the bones and ashes of the worst man to have lived in the world] (VI, 271). However, the vagabond derides the pride and arrogance of someone who would so distinguish himself from the rest of the human race.

In view of the vagabond's oft-repeated dislike of large, religious buildings and his reluctance to enter such places, it comes as something of a surprise to find that the most extensive amount of description (over four pages) accorded to any of Seville's impressive monuments is that devoted to the city's cathedral. Initially, he does not make it clear that he will enter the cathedral precincts, merely stating that he is going to recount something of what he knows about the place. He comments on the huge size of the church, the third largest in Christendom, its foundation in 1402 and completion just over one hundred years later, the various portals and their characteristics, the Patio de los Naranjos, and aspects of doorways and decorations. Then, as an indication that he did in fact enter the cathedral, the vagabond mentions what impressed him most of all within the building. He cites two wooden sculptures by José Martínez Montañés, one of the Virgin, with eyes almost closed and known as "La Cieguecita" [The little, blind Virgin], the other, the so-called "Niño mudo" [The mute Christ-child], as well as a crucifix by the same sculptor. In addition, he names the painting of St Jerome by Jerónimo Hernández, the tomb of Alfonso X, the Wise, and the embalmed remains of his father, Ferdinand III, the Saint, who in fact recaptured Seville in 1248. The vagabond then adds very casually that the other features of the cathedral's interior can be found listed in guidebooks.

A little earlier, when contemplating the Giralda, the vagabond had made some preliminary remarks on the origins, construction, and significance of the tower. He described it as being "de impar elegancia, de singular belleza" [of unequaled elegance, of exceptional beauty] (VI, 257) and then noted how easy it was to understand why it had inspired so many poets. Hereafter, he quotes appropriate passages from Lope de Vega, Salvador Rueda, Juan Ramón Jiménez, Gerardo Diego, and Fernando Villalón. He then goes on to recall that in *Don Quixote* (part 2, chapter 14) the Knight of the Wood revealed that his damsel, Casildea, had enjoined him to challenge the (five-meter) bronze figure of Faith that serves as a weather vane (*giraldilla*) atop the tower:

> "Once she ordered me to go and challenge that famous giantess in Seville called La Giralda, who's brave and strong and made of bronze and, although she never moves from where she stands, is the most changeable and inconstant woman in the world. I came, I saw her and I conquered her, and I made her remain settled and steadfast, because for over a week only the north wind blew."[4]

The Giralda, then, unlike the cathedral, is largely presented in terms of its more famous literary resonances. In fact, the literary motif had already become prominent in the previous chapter. There, as he begins to make his way through the province of Córdoba, the vagabond comes across a solitary olive tree and recalls two lines from Antonio Machado's poem "Olivo de camino" [Roadside olive tree] and then, when he stops for a drink and reflects on the evils of watered wine, a couple of apposite lines from Lope de Vega are quoted. In Lucena, the vagabond notes that Luis Barahona de Soto was born there and mentions that in *Don Quixote* Cervantes refers to him as a "divine" writer. After Lucena, he sleeps by the road to Benamejí and there recalls the four Heredia cousins of Lorca's "Muerte de Antoñito el Camborio" [Death of Antoñito Camborio]. Later, approaching Puente-Genil, the vagabond quotes seven lines of verse from Antonio Machado's brother, Manuel, which describe the white and sky-blue appearance of the small town.

In view of these literary references, it is hardly surprising that Lorca's *Romancero gitano* [Gypsy Ballads] should be returned to when Cabra is reached. Here the vagabond recalls some of the words of the mortally wounded young man of the "Romance sonámbulo" [Somnambulistic ballad] and then, as he gets closer to Córdoba, he quotes a stanza from another of Lorca's mysterious and haunting poems, the "Canción de jinete" [Song of the rider]. In between the inclusion of these two brief extracts from the poetry of Lorca, the vagabond notes that in the peaks above the town of Cabra is to be found the cavern of Cabra. He then proceeds to list some of the works of literature that refer to this famous geological feature: these include Juan de Padilla's *Los doze triumphos de los doze Apóstoles* [The Twelve Triumphs of the Twelve Apostles], Luis Vélez de Guevara's *El diablo cojuelo* [The Lame Devil], and Cervantes's *El celoso extremeño* [The Jealous Extremaduran]. Mention is also made of how, in *Don Quixote*, another of the labors requested of the Knight of the Wood by Casildea was that he should descend into the cavern and then report back to her on everything he had seen there.

This motif of the richness of Andalusia's literary connections (in terms of the region's wealth of native writers and its frequent use as a setting by authors from other parts of Spain) continues as the vagabond makes his meandering way to Seville. Thus in Ecija there are separate mentions of *El diablo cojuelo* and the novel's author, who was a native of the town, while a little later, as he and his old acquaintance from the Alcarria trip, Martín, approach Seville and stop for a drink in Cantillana, it is recalled that Vélez de Guevara claimed that the devil lived in this place. And finally, before they reach Seville, the two men pass through Alcalá del Río where, the vagabond explains, Estebanillo González had lunch and dinner, and also stole a young goat.

As might be expected, when Seville is eventually reached its literary connections are given due weight. Of course, as the city of birth of painters such as Velázquez (described by the vagabond as the most beautiful painter the world has seen), Murillo, and Valdés Leal, as well as being where Zurbarán and the sculptor José Martínez Montañés worked, it is understandable that the plastic arts should be given full recognition, even though this sometimes comes in the form of an inventory. Fortunately, the city's literary connections, far less visible and accessible than its monuments and plastic arts, are not subject to the kind of catalog-style presentation that is occasionally used for buildings, paintings, and sculptures. Indeed, the vagabond is nearly always much more at home with writers and their literature than he is with architecture and works of fine art.

Reference has already been made to how, when the vagabond reaches Seville, he cites those qualities of the city that most impressed various Golden Age and modern authors, and it was also noted how a number of writers had reacted to the Giralda. At other times during his tour of Seville, the vagabond comments on, for example, the building in which the poet he admires most, Antonio Machado, was born and mentions the burial places of Bécquer and the altogether less worthy, Baltasar del Alcázar—"poeta de lo peor y más indigesto—¡ay, *La cena*!" [one of the worst and most indigestible poets—oh, *The Supper*!] (VI, 253).[5] However, his principal literary focus is to reveal what certain writers thought of Seville, its buildings or districts, or how such buildings and areas figured in their lives or in their works.

Accordingly, the vagabond tells how Cervantes used to enjoy viewing the rooftops of Seville from the tower of the church of San Marcos, while at the Casa Lonja he recalls that Luis Vélez de Guevara, alluding to the fact that its architect (Juan de Herrera) also designed San Lorenzo del Escorial, mockingly referred to the Sevillian building as "lonja del pernil de San Lorenzo" [a slice of St Lawrence's haunch] (VI, 269). But in particular, the vagabond is keen to evoke those parts of the city that figure in works of literature. When he reaches the Calle de Bustos Tavera he suggests that it was on events that took place hereabouts that the play *La Estrella de Sevilla* [The Star of Seville] was based, and as he sits down for a rest in the Alameda de Hércules the vagabond is reminded that it was here that Marcos de Obregón came, in Vicente Espinel's novel of 1618, to recover from the fight in the Calle de las Armas. At the bullring, the vagabond recalls that nearby there had once been the two districts of El Compás and La Mancebía, both demolished in the eighteenth century, and which had such vivid literary and picaresque connections. Later, as he walks alongside the Guadalquivir and looks at the ships against the background of the Triana district, he is reminded that it was from here that Quevedo's Don Pablos sailed to seek good fortune in the New World.

In his journey around the old center of Seville, the vagabond conveys not only the historical and artistic richness of the city but also the wealth of its literary associations. Such an approach, which obviously reveals the vagabond's narrative priorities (in Córdoba and Seville, for example, he pays precious little attention to the inhabitants of these places), also suggests that he is the possessor of a great depth of historical and artistic knowledge. Although some of this material could have been acquired or consolidated along the way, much of it may well have been inserted at the time of composition. Indeed, during the later stages of his Triana account the vagabond acknowledges jotting down *part* of what he had learned in his time there. But whatever the procedure adopted, the end result is that Seville is presented almost wholly for its historical, religious, artistic, and literary presence and legacy. The city is certainly not described in terms of its inhabitants and their activities.

Once the vagabond has completed his lengthy commentary on Seville, he crosses the Guadalquivir, spends five days in the Triana quarter of the city and there gives a fairly detailed account and analysis of the other great aspect of Andalusian popular culture, the *cante flamenco*. At the beginning of his assessment of the various forms of flamenco singing, the vagabond states that Triana and Jerez are the capitals of the *cante*. He then describes spending five days touring the bars of Triana, listening to the various kinds of *cante*, writing down examples, commenting on their geographical origins and subsequent history, comparing different forms, and mentioning exponents and interpretations. The whole exercise becomes a dissertation of some twenty or so pages, interspersed with references to the *fictitious* Señorita Gracita Garrobo (with whom the vagabond is supposed to have stayed while in Seville) and her family and friends.[6] Thus, he begins with the *cante jondo*, noting that this category consists of the *caña*, the *polo*, the *seguirilla*, the *gitana*, the *soleá*, the *debla*, and the *martinete*, and then considers these various types. For example, one page is devoted to the *martinete*. Its two different forms are mentioned, with an illustration of each as well as information concerning the best interpreters of the *martinete* and where they perform. There are then two pages on the *caña*, described as "la madre de todos los cantes" [the mother of all flamenco styles] (VI, 279). Here there is mention of famous, past exponents and an observation on how, among others, Manuel de Falla, Lorca, and Ignacio Zuloaga were responsible for the resurgence in popularity, after some fifty years of decline, of this and other forms of the *cante jondo*. The *polo*, described as the "little brother" of the *caña*, merits half a page, while the *seguirilla*, with the inclusion of various examples and mention of a number of interpreters, is dealt with in a page and a half. Comparable space and approach is dedicated to *soleares*, and so on.

With this kind of treatment, in which the vagabond attempts to convey and explain the intricacies and delights of the *cante flamenco* as he trawls through the bars of Triana, losing all sense of time and also consuming a good deal of wine, the reader gains some flavor of the district (especially in the opening part of the Triana section) and receives a useful introduction to *flamenco* songs and singing. But it also has to be acknowledged that the Triana visit becomes a rather specialized catalog with, after the four or five preliminary pages, hardly any sense of movement. Although the main part of chapter 6 is principally a progress around the center of Seville, at least it has a varied focus and frequent changes of pace. The Triana episode, on the other hand, despite the fascinating, well ordered, and no doubt carefully researched material it contains, brings to an end the Seville phase of *Primer viaje andaluz* on something of a repetitive and anticlimactic note.

TRUTH AND TALES

The way in which the vagabond constantly reveals his knowledge of history and his interest in literature emphasizes the Andalusian travel book's thematic links with *Judíos, moros y cristianos*. And with *Primer viaje andaluz* there is also a gradual continuation of the process whereby the vagabond, sometimes rather coyly, acknowledges who he really is, his profession, and also recalls parts of his earlier travels. There are references to the fact that he is a Galician, who comes from Padrón, is called Camilo, and whose birthday falls on 11 May. On top of this, the vagabond mentions that he has walked Castile and the north of Spain; he refers to his earlier association with the shade of the Princess of Eboli in Pastrana; in Lora he comes across Martín, the traveling salesman he first met in the Alcarria in June 1946, and rides on his scooter as far as Seville. In La Guardia the vagabond talks of a horrifying story he has already dealt with in one of his earlier travel accounts (in fact, in *Judíos, moros y cristianos*) and while in Cabra, the birthplace of Juan Valera, he refers to the nineteenth-century novelist as a "colleague," although more illustrious than himself.

Yet, despite these indications that the vagabond is the author Camilo José Cela, he is also quite capable (as he was in *Del Miño al Bidasoa*) of giving misleading information about his situation and his person. So, in Navarre he lies to another vagabond that he has not eaten a hot meal for some days. He mentions a girlfriend he once had, but she turns out to be one of the fictitious creations of *Primer viaje andaluz*. In Montilla, when asked if he is selling colored prints of the Virgin Mary, the vagabond says that he is, but has sold out. He tells a passerby in Córdoba that he is on a pilgrimage, the result of a vow made when his son was taken captive by the Moors (although at least on this occasion the deceit is acknowledged to the reader). While visiting Ecija he informs the reader that in Maracaibo he married a black woman who bore him nine sons, only three of whom survived and who achieved musical fame as "El Trío Cartago" [The Carthage Trio]. The vagabond then cheekily adds that this is a story "que no hay por qué traer aquí" [that there is no need to go into here] (VI, 204).

Setting aside such lighthearted fibs and fantasies, a more serious question concerning the veracity of events recounted in *Primer viaje andaluz* is posed by the fact that, as was the case with *Del Miño al Bidasoa*, the narrative contains a number of fictitious characters (acknowledged in the "Censo de personajes" found in the first and some later editions, but not the *Obra completa* version) with whom the vagabond becomes involved in what are, presumably, fictitious scenes or episodes.[7] Mention has already been made of the fictitious Garrobo family of Seville who, the reader is told, provide a room for the vagabond and help him with his contacts in Triana. Earlier in the narrative, Don Jacinto Camarón, the poetaster whom the vagabond seeks out in La Carolina, only to be rebuffed when he finds him, turns out to be a creation of the author's imagination. Similarly, after giving a factual and fairly detailed description of Osuna, the vagabond then encounters the fictitious spinster, Doña Mencía Corrales, a rather sad and vulnerable figure who is obviously very taken with him. He charms her (but lies about why he is heading for Seville) and between them they play out a touching little episode. Subsequently, there are several more invented characters, including the young Rocío Barragán Donaire, who sings to the vagabond, and Paulo Mampoy, a black flamenco singer and aspiring bullfighter with whom he spends an evening in Moguer. Shortly after, in Huelva, the vagabond is invited to eat with Señorita Cinta Coronado, yet another literary creation, this time a procuress with a massive backside who tells him about her family and her skill at procuring for high-class gentlemen.

The vagabond's supposed encounters with these invented characters bring to the narrative moments of drama, humor, or human interest. Yet they also raise the question of the degree of veracity of the already conflated account. To be sure, the fictitious characters are identified in the "Censo," but how reliable is the description of many of the incidents and episodes in which the vagabond was alone or was involved with unnamed individuals who do not always figure in the cast of characters? For example, in the scene where the vagabond upset the young nanny in Vitoria and was briefly questioned about this by the local police, or in the lengthy and entertaining episode concerning the old silver coin that he found and the way he subsequently managed to exploit an innkeeper's lust for the piece—how much is fact and how much is fiction? How factual are the descriptions of the heavy drinking sessions that the vagabond engages in at Moriles and also Montilla, and when, after indulging for many hours in a bar in Palma del Río, he sees a bull on the road ahead of him and promptly falls head-first into the drainage ditch, how much of this is a faithful record of what happened? Or was it simply inserted for comic effect? And in Sanlúcar, did the vagabond really spend a couple of hours working as an assistant to the fakir, Tortajada? According to the "Censo," Tortajada was indeed a real person. However, the reader is asked to take on trust the fact that the vagabond became part of his act for a short while.

This issue of narrative reliability and the fact that Cela readily acknowledges that some of the characters introduced are his own inventions serve as vivid reminders that the author is also a novelist. Indeed, in *Primer viaje andaluz* Cela displays certain stylistic techniques that are common to the earlier travel works as well as to his fiction. One of the hallmarks of his prose style is the use of anaphora, and when, on their way south, the vagabond and his driver stop in Manzanares, part of the description of the place consists of a series of scenes captured in various of the town's small squares and presented in a thoroughly self-conscious manner:

> En la plazuela de Marcote, un maestro carretero se aplica a las viejas artes de la carretería. En la plazuela de Rosado, un maestro confitero cubre, con una tarlatana verde, el mazacote dulce de la carne de membrillo. En la plazuela de la Virgen de Gracia, un maestro tejedor mide los colores y sus fuegos y sus intensidades a la luz del día. En la plazuela de Toledo, un maestro de escuela toma café. (VI, 102)

> [In the Plazuela de Marcote, a master carter is engaged in the ancient arts of carting. In the Plazuela de Rosado, a master confectioner is covering the sweet mass of his quince jelly with a piece of green tarlatan. In the Plazuela de la Virgen de Gracia, a master weaver is gauging colors, and their brightness and intensity, in the daylight. In the Plazuela de Toledo, a schoolmaster is drinking coffee.]

This kind of technique, and there are numerous examples of anaphora in *Primer viaje andaluz,* suggests polishing in the writer's study rather than a wayfarer on the road jotting down what he sees and preserving this simply and accurately for the reader. Moreover, in this particular passage, how does the vagabond know that the man having a coffee in the Plazuela de Toledo is a schoolmaster? Did he talk to him, is he guessing from his appearance, or is this simply an example of the inventive novelist intruding in a travel narrative?

Another technique, employed earlier by Cela in *Judíos, moros y cristianos* and on which he often relies in the Andalusian travel book, is that of alternating between banal, present-day comments or scenes (sometimes with a crudely comical flavor) and items or features of historical significance. Thus, at one stage in Ocaña, the account shifts between references to important moments in the town's history, the sight of a little boy picking his nose, and the attempts of a dog to mount a much larger bitch. The passage climaxes on a note that suggests pain and humiliation on a personal level and also in national terms:

> En el toma y daca de la Edad Media, don Nuño Pérez, maestre calatravo, cedió la villa de Ocaña, al cambio de la Alcobera, a los caballeros de la orden de Santiago. Hay quien dice que Ocaña fue feudo santiaguista por privilegio real. Un niño barrigón pega mocos en la pared, concienzudamente. Don Juan II y don Enrique IV celebraron cortes en Ocaña. En medio del trajín, un perro canijo hace los inútiles posibles y los ilusionados imposibles por montar a una perra flaca y grandullona. En Ocaña se hizo la jura del príncipe don Miguel, nieto de los Reyes Católicos. El niño que se daba al arte de pegar los mocos a tresbolillo, suspendió sus industrias por atender — atónito y pasmado — a los fallidos esfuerzos amatorios del perrillo ruin. La

madre, sin previo aviso, le pegó un capón. En la guerra de la Independencia, a los españoles, por estas trochas, nos tocó llevar más que un pandero. (VI, 86–87)

[In the cut-and-thrust of the Middle Ages, Don Nuño Pérez, Grand Master of the Order of Calatrava, ceded the town of Ocaña, in exchange for the Alcobera, to the knights of the Order of Santiago. There are those who say that Ocaña was a fiefdom of the Order of Santiago by royal concession. A pot-bellied boy is diligently sticking bits of snot on the wall. John II and Henry IV held court in Ocaña. Amidst the hustle and bustle, a scraggy dog is making useless, optimistic attempts to mount a skinny, oversized bitch. In Ocaña, Prince Michael, the grandson of the Catholic Monarchs, took the oath of allegiance. The boy who was dedicating himself to making patterns with his bits of snot, ceased his activities to concentrate—with astonishment and wonder—on the unsuccessful amatory efforts of the squalid dog. Without any warning, the mother cracked the boy around the head. In the War of Independence, we Spaniards took a drubbing in these parts.]

In Sanlúcar, the narrative alternates between the instructions of Tortajada, the fakir, to the vagabond, his new assistant, and the listing of important moments in the history of the town, from Roman times to the nineteenth century. And later, when the wayfarer gets to Palos de la Frontera, references to the famous sons of the town and its historical connections with Columbus and Cortés are interspersed with mentions of a variety of seafood dishes to be sampled there.

Such techniques are, of course, far removed from Cela's early proclamations that travel writing should do no more than describe things as they are. However, elsewhere in the account the vagabond can also show that he is capable of conveying a simple, vivid picture. Thus, he describes a rural scene outside Ocaña as follows:

Dos burrillos peludos y cenicientos, dos burrillos de la gastada y artesana color de la plata vieja, aguantan, en medio del ancho páramo, el sol a pie firme: heroica y olvidadamente plantados como estatuas o como pacientes olivos llenos de resignación. Las ovejas de los rebaños—el mirar triste, los cueros sucios y, en el lomo, el brochazo de almagre—están inmóviles, jadeantes, la boca entreabierta, muertas de sed. Entre los carros de mulas aparece, de cuando en cuando, alguna pesada galera de cuatro ruedas. (VI, 88–89)

[Two small, shaggy, ash-colored donkeys, two small donkeys that are the worn, craftwork colour of old silver, are standing still in the middle of the broad plain, enduring the burning sun, heroically and forlornly planted like statues or patient olive trees, full of resignation. Flocks of sheep—with doleful expressions, dirty fleeces and, on their backs, a daub of red ochre—are motionless, panting, their mouths half open, absolutely parched. Among the mule carts there appears, from time to time, a heavy, four-wheeled wagon.]

And elsewhere, on the road between Ecija and Osuna, the vagabond paints a brief, simple scene that depicts a combination of landscape and human activity, into which he then inserts himself:

> Por los campos se ven arder las rastrojeras; el fuego que las consume lo cuida, con un palo en la mano, un campesino de gesto casi animal. Un ciclista de chaquetilla corta y sombrero cordobés, pedalea sin demasiadas ganas mientras va fumando un purito. Un carro marcha completamente tapado por un toldo que por detrás le llega hasta el suelo, como una cortina. Hace calor y el vagabundo, por ver de cobrar fuerzas y el ánimo bastante para seguir, se sienta al borde del camino, en una sombrita no más que suficiente. (VI, 212–13)

> [Stubble can be seen burning in the fields; the fire is being controlled by a peasant with an animal-like look and a stick in his hand. A cyclist, wearing a short jacket and a Córdoba hat, is pedaling along without too much enthusiasm, smoking a cigar. A passing cart is completely covered by a tarpaulin which, at the back, reaches to the ground like a curtain. It is hot, and the vagabond, trying to regain sufficient strength and spirit to carry on, sits down at the side of the road in a barely adequate patch of shade.]

In other parts of the narrative, the vagabond sometimes employs his descriptive energies in an altogether more prosaic, factual, and systematic manner. He lists the impressive variety of crops growing in a particular part of Navarre or, in another area of the region, details the different species of trees being destroyed by industrial pollution. And when he reaches Andalusia, mention is made, for example, of the productive land around Cabra and the different crops grown there; details are given of the produce of the fertile land beside the Guadalquivir at Almodóvar del Río, while at Sanlúcar the vagabond marvels at the richness of the land surrounding the town and the variety and quality of the local produce. Although such catalogues might not be lyrical or compelling, at least they are in keeping with the author's notion of travel books as principally works of geography and his proclaimed approach of simply recording what he sees.

Conclusion

As has been noted, although *Primer viaje andaluz* starts as a continuation of the journey described in *Del Miño al Bidasoa*, the Andalusian

travel book is, in effect, the thematic successor and companion piece to
Judíos, moros y cristianos. The works of 1956 and 1959, both acknowledged conflations of several trips around the areas described in the narratives, are very much cultural pilgrimages to the key regions in the
historical and artistic development of modern Spain. But whereas
Judíos, moros y cristianos is an account built around a pair of hefty, central pillars, the tours of Segovia and Avila, the Andalusian book lacks
the balance and symmetry of its predecessor and has much more of a
piecemeal structure.

As in *Judíos, moros y cristianos*, the vagabond is presented as something of a rogue, but one who is also the possessor of a wealth of historical, artistic, and literary knowledge. In addition, he exhibits a keen
interest in etymology and botany, and also enjoys, for example, listing
Basque place names or interesting street names found in Seville or in
nearby Castilleja de la Cuesta. Conversely, the vagabond shows no
more than passing interest in social conditions or in evidence of economic decline or hardship. There are in *Primer viaje andaluz* occasional
indications of poverty or suffering, but these observations normally
come without any kind of explanation or sense of concern. Indeed, at
such moments, the tendency is for the vagabond to register what he sees
and then quickly move on to another topic. So, as he makes his way
through Navarre, following the Araquil River, he notes:

> Por Yabar, con un paso a nivel y su buen puente — también sobre el río Ara-
> quil —, aparecen las casas de adobe, huellas de la morisma y la miseria. Hu-
> arte-Araquil, en una vega hermosa y a la sombra del monte Aralar o de San
> Miguel — con la basílica de San Miguel in Excelsis —, es pueblecillo no
> grande y cargado de historia. (VI, 46–47)

> [In Yabar, with its grade crossing and fine bridge — over the Araquil — there
> are adobe houses, the sign of a Moorish past and also of poverty. Huarte-
> Araquil, in a beautiful plain and in the shadow of Mount Aralar or San Mi-
> guel — with its basilica of San Miguel in Excelsis — is a little town laden with
> history.]

The vagabond also refers to abandoned villages in Navarre and
Alava, and later, heading south, he mentions the poverty to be seen on
the outskirts of Madrid. Here, unusually, he expresses a word or two of
compassion. But thereafter, as he continues southwards, the vagabond
names, in a dispassionate manner, the derelict villages that his truck
passes by. Once in Andalusia, and on foot, he alludes to the fact that in
La Carolina the mining industry is in decline but then, still in the same
town, gives a good deal more attention to the preparation of the sauce
for a fish that is being cooked for him. In Carboneros, though, which

lies just to the south of La Carolina, the reader is informed that several mines have closed and the town's menfolk have headed for Catalonia in search of work. Here, the vagabond allows himself a low-key protest as he briefly laments the fact that in these parts there is nothing available for anyone who wants to do an honest day's work. And when he gets to the province of Córdoba, he again mentions migration, this time by those who have given up trying to make a living out of the soil and have uprooted and moved to Catalonia and the Asturias. In between these references to economic migration, the vagabond observes that in the mining town of Linares there is evidence of both hunger and prosperity. However, here he also comments in general terms on the misery that mining brings and even voices some indignation at the plight and treatment of those miners who have been poisoned by the lead they once dug for.

Yet these indications of decline, deprivation, and even injustice are sporadic and need to be balanced against the occasional, specific reminders of economic well-being. In *Primer viaje andaluz*, a general impression is created, more by implication than through assertion, that in social and economic terms things are generally comfortable. Although scattered throughout the account there are occasional (no more than a couple of dozen) indications of social problems, such instances of deprivation constitute a minuscule part of the narrative. Indeed, on this point it is instructive to make comparisons with two Spanish travel works that were published just a year after *Primer viaje andaluz*: Juan Goytisolo's *Campos de Níjar* and *Caminando por las Hurdes*, by Antonio Ferres and Armando López Salinas. A comparison of these narratives with Cela's fourth travel book (while, of course, bearing in mind that the other three authors describe particular areas known for their poverty) will serve to underscore just how little concerned Cela was with socioeconomic matters. There is no disguising the fact that in the Andalusian narrative the author gives a good deal more space to eating, drinking, and a half dozen recipes than he does to the manifestations and causes of social hardship. Nevertheless, even the detailing of such pleasurable pursuits and culinary interests is still only a minor aspect of this travel book. Once the vagabond sets foot in Andalusia, the account becomes principally a celebration of a distinctively different region of Spain and its mightily impressive and influential cultural legacy.

8

Geography and a Changing Landscape:
Viaje al Pirineo de Lérida

IN AN AUTOBIOGRAPHICAL ESSAY PUBLISHED IN 1962, CELA MENTIONS that in August 1956 he went on a walking trip around the Pallars Sobirà, the valley of Arán, and the Alto Ribagorza, all in the Lérida section of the Pyrenees. He also states that he traveled in the company of Felipe Luján, the writer Josep María Espinàs (Luján's son-in-law), and his friend and fellow Galician, the physician José Luis Barros. The author adds that though he has detailed notes of the journey he has yet to write up an account of the visit.[1] In fact, Cela began drafting what was to be his fifth travel work in July 1963 and completed the task in February of the following year.[2] The account of the Pyrenean trip first appeared in the newspaper *ABC*, in forty-seven installments, between 5 October 1963 and 7 June 1964. The first edition in book form was published by Alfaguara (Madrid) in January 1965, with the full title, *Viaje al Pirineo de Lérida: Notas de un paseo a pie por el Pallars Sobirà, el valle de Arán y el condado de Ribagorza* [Journey to the Lérida Pyrenees: Notes of a Journey on Foot through the Pallars Sobirà, the Valley of Arán, and the County of Ribagorza].

The route taken by the traveler (who is described throughout the narrative as the *viajero*, a term Cela had not used since *Viaje a la Alcarria*), including detours both short and lengthy, roughly resembles the top and two sides of a square that is slightly tilted to the right. The top length runs more or less parallel with, and twelve to fifteen kilometers inside the Pyrenean border, while the two side pieces of the square point approximately in the direction of the city of Lérida and its surrounding area, some 120 kilometers to the south. The account of the journey is divided into three parts, corresponding to the three sides of the "square," with each focusing on a particular area and phase of the trip: "Primer País. El Pallars Sobirà" [First Landscape. The Pallars Sobirà] (114 pages); "Segundo País. El valle de Arán" [Second Land-

191

scape. The Valley of Arán] (107 pages), and "Tercer País. El condado de Ribagorza" [Third Landscape. The County of Ribagorza] (53 pages).

The whole journey appears to take about three and a half weeks and, interestingly, but perhaps not unexpectedly, the traveler presents himself throughout as a lone wayfarer, although he does, from time to time, find some company (including a dog that befriends him) as he makes his way from place to place along roads and rustic tracks. The three companions with whom Cela set out in August 1956 are not mentioned in the narrative. In the opening pages of the work, the traveler describes how *he* took the train from Barcelona to Pobla de Segur and thereafter he gives no indication that the visit to the Lérida Pyrenees was made in company. Indeed, even though the first edition in volume of *Viaje al Pirineo de Lérida* is dedicated to the three men concerned (and that dedication appears in subsequent editions), there is no indication that these were, in fact, the author's traveling companions on the trip. Readers would be none the wiser unless they were acquainted with the information given in the 1962 essay. But the most significant aspect of the omission of reference to the three other men is that, as with *Viaje a la Alcarria*, the account of the trip falsely presents an independent traveler.

PYRENEAN LANDSCAPES

It is worth recalling that in the dedication preceding the account of the journey described in *Viaje a la Alcarria*, Cela suggests that his intention was simply to record what he saw, since it was a work of geography rather than a novel. With *Viaje al Pirineo de Lérida* there is a far stronger sense of the physical geography of an area than in any of Cela's other travel works. The itinerary takes the traveler through valleys, besides rivers, over high ground, through mountain passes, and around lakes, all of which are resolutely and carefully recorded. Overall, there is in the account a predominance of material dealing with the geography (in the sense of the principal physical features, both natural and man-made) of that part of the Pyrenees visited. Indeed, shortly after his arrival in Pobla de Segur, and before beginning his walking tour, the traveler sets out the geographical limits of the Pallars area. He differentiates between the location of the Pallars Sobirà and its neighbour to the south (which will not be on his itinerary), the Pallars Jussà, emphasizes the mountainous topography of the area to be covered, and also indicates the location of the two other areas that will be walked during the trip, the valley of Arán and the county of Ribagorza:

El Pallars es el país que forman las cuencas del Flamisell y del Noguera Pallaresa hasta la sierra del Montsec (el pico Montsec, según el mapa militar de España, llega a los 1.678 ms. de altura). Al norte de las sierras de San Gervás y Boumort queda el Pallars Sobirà (pico San Gervás, 1.834 ms.; pico Boumort, 2.070 ms.), capital Sort. Al sur de los montes dichos queda el Pallars Jussà, capital Tremp, que comprende los valles de Pobla de Segur y de Salàs de Pallàs y las concas de Tremp y de Isona. Pallàs es la forma anticuada de Pallars. El Pallars Sobirà limita: al norte con Francia, al este con Andorra y el Alto Urgel y al oeste con el valle de Arán y el Alto Ribagorza. El Pallars Jussà linda: a levante con la cuenca del Segre y a poniente con la del Noguera Ribagorzana. (VI, 389)

[The Pallars is the area formed by the basins of the Flamisell and the Noguera Pallaresa up to the Sierra of Montsec (Mount Montsec, according to the military map of Spain, reaches a height of 1,678 meters). The Pallars Sobirà , with its capital Sort, is to the north of the Sierras of San Gervás and Boumort (Mount San Gervás, 1,834 meters; Mount Boumort, 2,070 meters). To the south of these mountains is the Pallars Jussà, with its capital Tremp, and which takes in the valleys of Pobla de Segur and Salàs de Pallàs, as well as the basins of Tremp and Isona. Pallàs is the old form of Pallars. The Pallars Sobirà stretches to France in the north, to Andorra and Upper Urgel in the east, and in the west to the valley of Arán and the Upper Ribagorza. The Pallars Jussà borders on the basin of the Segre in the east and that of the Noguera Ribagorzana in the west.]

This verbal sketch-map of the area is soon followed by an account of the historical origins of the county of Pallars, going back to the days of the Spanish March of Charlemagne's second Frankish dynasty. It is noted that "la historia de los condes de Pallars arde con la Edad Media y, como la Edad Media, es tumultuaria y confusa" [the history of the Counts of Pallars burns bright by the time of the Middle Ages, and like the Middle Ages it is tumultuous and confused] (VI, 391). There then follows a description of how the last Count of Pallars, Hugo Roger III, in his struggles with his father, John II of Aragón, threw in his lot with Prince Charles of Viana (the half brother of Ferdinand of Aragón and to whom Isabella had once been promised) and perished for his troubles. Subsequently, Ferdinand sold off all the belongings of the Count of Pallars to the Count of Cardona and converted the county of Pallars to a marquisate. As an update, the traveler notes that in the late nineteenth century Catherine of Aragón and Sandoval, the Marchioness of Pallars and Duchess of Cardona, married the eldest son of the Duke of Medinaceli and, in effect, the Pallars-Cardona dynasty was swallowed up by the ducal house of Medinaceli (VI, 391–92).

Yet if the power and titles of the scions of the Counts of Pallars disappeared with the passing centuries, the name of the area certainly survived, as did, of course, its rivers, valleys, mountains, and lakes, as well as the local towns, monuments, and typical trees and plants. These are the features of the Pallars Sobirà (and the bordering valley of Arán and county of Ribagorza) on which the traveler will focus in his trip of August 1956. As was suggested earlier, the route chosen for his journey around the Lérida section of the Pyrenees that lies to the west of Andorra largely follows the roads that accompany the principal rivers of the area. He does occasionally leave the river valleys to cut across country or visit highland lakes, but for the most part the traveler follows a course that takes him to the towns and villages that are dotted along the main rivers of the district: the Noguera Pallaresa, the Noguera de Cardós, the Garona, and the Noguera Ribagorzana.[3]

In earlier chapters, it was mentioned that Cela's travel books often include descriptions of river systems, and it is no surprise that this interest should once again be revealed in an account set in a part of the country with abundant rivers, streams, and lakes. So, for example, when the traveler arrives at the San Mauricio lake in the Aigüestortes national park, he gives a vivid and complicated description of the connecting river system and lake system:

Al extremo sudoeste del lago hay una cueva frente a la que desemboca el torrente del Portarró, que engorda con las aguas del Subenulls, que ruedan de sur a norte, y con las del Ratera, que caminan de norte a sur. El torrente del Portarró viene, tal como dice, del portarró o puertecillo de Espot, donde se parten las aguas de las vertientes de los dos Nogueras: el Pallaresa, en el camino de Roma (o de la Meca), y el Ribagorzana, en el camino de Compostela (o de Nueva York). El torrente de Subenulls nace en el pico de Subenulls y se remansa en los dos estanques de Subenulls, el Superior y el Inferior; la verdad es que el torrente de Subenulls no se gastó la hijuela en imaginaciones ni bautismos. El torrente de Ratera se escurre desde el tuc o pico de Ratera y el estany Glaçat, o helado, que rebrilla en la coma de Ratera; al estany Superior de Ratera van las aguas de la coma y de la estanyola de Crabes; al Inferior, que recibe todas las anteriores, caen las de la coma y el estany de Amitjes, y las de la coma del Abeller o del abetal. A medio camino del estany Inferior de Ratera y del lago de San Mauricio, saltan las aguas por la cascada de Ratera que se presenta de pronto, en un respiradero del pinar. (VI, 473)

[At the southwest end there is a cave, in front of which the River Portarró, having taken in the waters of the Subenulls, which flows from south to north, as well as those of the Ratera, which runs from north to south, flows into the lake. The name Portarró comes, so they say, from the *portarró* or small pass of Espot, where the waters of the two Nogueras part and fall in different directions: those of the Pallaresa heading for Rome (or Mecca) and those of the Ribagorzana flowing toward Santiago de Compostela (or New

York). The River Subenulls rises on Mount Subenulls and forms the two Subenulls tarns, the Upper and the Lower; the truth is that the River Subenulls did not show a great deal of imagination or energy. The River Ratera runs down from Mount Ratera and from the Glaçat, or frozen tarn, which lies in the Ratera glacier; the waters from the glacier and from the tarn of Crabes flow into the Upper Ratera tarn, while the Lower Ratera tarn, as well as receiving the previously mentioned waters, is also fed by the Amitjes glacier and tarn, as well as by those of the Abeller (or firwood) glacier. Halfway between the Lower Ratera tarn and the Lake of San Mauricio, the waters cascade over the Ratera waterfall, which suddenly appears in a break in the pinewoods.]

There are other descriptions of this type, although none quite as finicky as this. And although the narrative contains numerous mentions of the presence of rivers, lakes, tarns, and waterfalls, these are usually part of the account of what the traveler witnesses as he moves along, rather than the above kind of map-style indications of the courses of rivers or the location of lakes in the area.

For example, having set out from Pobla de Segur, negotiated the defile of Collegats, and admired the elegant and sedate waterfall of Argentería, the traveler looks ahead of him, up the valley through which runs the Noguera Pallaresa:

Pasada la Argentería, el valle se abre y se pinta de color de esmeralda, el río se remansa y baja la voz, y el sol—igual que un carnero loco—se revuelca sobre la húmeda yerba de los prados. A mano derecha y más allá del río negrea el bosque de Morreras, de abetos mansos y amables, que se pierde a lo lejos, por el monte arriba. (VI, 399)

[After Argentería, the valley broadens and takes on an emerald hue, the river runs calmer and quieter, and the sun—like a mad ram—wallows in the damp grass of the meadows. To the right, and beyond the river, the woods of Morreras appear black, with their gentle and pleasant fir trees, and climb away up the distant hillside.]

And in the closing stage of his trip, the traveler encounters an even more splendid and tranquil example of the beauty of unspoiled Nature when he takes in the valley of Biciberri—an area that shows no signs of human habitation and which, he muses, must appear as it did at the time of the Creation. Here, the description is more poetic and idealized than in the previous example, and the response even more admiring. In addition, since he is nearing the end of his journey, the traveler reveals a certain sense of fulfillment and finality:

El viajero, entre cascadas rumorosas, flores bellísimas y abetos de color gris tierno, empieza a andar, de cara al sol que nace y dando la espalda al Noguera Ribagorzana, con el ánimo reconfortado por el silencio y su disfrute en paz y buen sosiego. El bosque se va espesando, diríase que con solemne conciencia de que lo hace, a cada paso del viajero, mientras que por el aire, como un anuncio de la confianza, vuela — solitaria y displicente como una reina — la elegante y brava y poderosa paloma torcaz. El bosque del vallecico de Biciberri quizás sea el más selvoso y natural, el más romántico y recoleto de todo cuantos rincones se lleva andado el viajero en su paciente tobogán pirenaico. (VI, 619–20)

[Amid burbling waterfalls, beautiful flowers, and soft, gray firs, the traveler starts to walk, facing the rising sun and with his back to the Noguera Ribagorzana, with his spirit comforted by the silence and enjoying the peace and utter calm. The forest gets denser — it could even be said that it does so with a studied awareness of what it is doing — with every step the traveler takes, while flying through the air, like a proclamation of optimism, and alone and serene as a queen, goes the elegant, valiant, and powerful ringdove. The forest in the little valley of Biciberri is perhaps the most sylvan and natural, the most romantic and tranquil of all the nooks that the traveler has wandered around in his unhurried, Pyrenean ramble.]

On other occasions, however, the visitor reports on how man has modified the natural setting for his own benefit. Thus, near the power station of Torrassa he notes with some pangs the way the banks of the Noguera Pallaresa have been reinforced by stones that are imprisoned beneath steel mesh and so are no longer part of the natural environment:

Las piedras de los muros de contención del río están sujetas por gruesas redes metálicas de fiero trazo carcelario; el viajero, al verlas, se imagina que las piedras presas son como tiburones muertos: un día violentísimos y poderosos, y hoy no más que pesados. (VI, 466)

[The stone pitching of the river's containing walls is held in place by heavy, metallic netting that has an ugly, custodial appearance to it; as he looks, the traveler imagines that the imprisoned stones are like dead sharks: once extremely dangerous and powerful, and now just dead weight.]

In addition, the traveler occasionally mentions the wild flowers and herbs that thrive in these parts. So, as he follows the Noguera Pallaresa through the valley of Aneu he lists a whole variety of medicinal herbs (as well as their applications) that grow in the area — although without actually stating that he saw them with his own eyes. Elsewhere, on the other hand, the traveler takes note of the flowers in the meadows around a mountain refuge in the valley of Arán:

En las praderas que enmarcan la borda del Ticolet se pintan, entre la verde yerba, la anémona violeta y blanca, la azul campánula, la genciana de color de oro y el níveo y aromático narciso. Y sobre las más viejas y acariciadas rocas, trepa, con sus rositas blancas y montaraces, la indiferencia casquivana y silvestre del té de monte. (VI, 511)

[In the meadows surrounding the Ticolet refuge, adorning the green grass are violet and white anemones, blue bellflowers, gold-colored gentians, and snow-white, sweet-scented narcissi. And climbing the oldest and most welcoming rocks is the mountain tea, with its small, white, wild roses and carefree, rustic indifference.]

But, of course, the area visited is not just occupied by rivers and lakes, tree-covered hills and rugged peaks. Nor is it solely the habitat of wild flowers and herbs. There are also human settlements, which are often seen to blend with and nestle comfortably in their unspoiled surroundings. So, in the final part of the narrative Barruera is pictured at the tranquil center of an idyllic scene:

El caserío de Barruera luce rodeado de praderas verdes en las que se pinta la amapola y canta el grillo su solitario sentimiento; el arroyo Calvó, que baja del coll Gelada, por encima de Erillavall y entre fresnedas y robledales, cae al Noguera de Tor por Barruera, al norte de las casas y sin mojarlas. (VI, 643)

[The hamlet of Barruera appears amid green meadows in which poppies are blooming and crickets are chirping their solitary note; the stream called Calvó, which, passing through ash groves and oak woods, comes down from Gelada Hill, above Erillavall, flows into the Noguera de Tor at Barruera, to the north of the houses and so without making them damp.]

And Llesp, about eight kilometers downstream, set beside a lake and amidst meadows, orchards, and groves of trees, is tiny yet quietly self-sufficient:

Llesp guarda (y también regala) verdes variados, entonados, diversos. El caserío se mira en las quietas aguas de su embalse y se enseña entre praderas y pomaradas, peraledas y nocedales, fresnedas, choperas, robledales, hayedos y una huertecilla humilde y suficiente. Llesp tiene quince o veinte casas y mil truchas a punto de la sartén. (VI, 647–48)

[Llesp contains (and also displays) diverse, harmonious greens. The hamlet is reflected in the still waters of the reservoir and is surrounded by meadows and apple orchards, pear orchards and groves of walnut trees, ash groves, poplar groves, oak woods, beech woods, and a small but adequate market garden. Llesp has fifteen or twenty houses and a thousand trout awaiting the frying pan.]

However, not all the villages and towns of the Lérida Pyrenees are quite so blessed in their setting or charming in appearance, especially some of the larger ones. Llavorsí, at the confluence of the Noguera Pallaresa and the Noguera de Cardós, and almost surrounded by water, is described as having a distinctly unprepossessing air about it:

Es un pueblo negro y con cara de pocos amigos, un pueblo de aire fosco y centinela, agazapado, flexible y militar. Llavorsí parece un viejo lobo receloso que hubiera bajado a despiojarse al río (o a lavarse, en las aguas del río, la mordedura del cepo de hierro). (VI, 429)

[It is a dark town, with a sullen look about it, a town with an aggressive, vigilant appearance, crouching, lithe, and warlike. Llavorsí is like an old, suspicious wolf who has gone down to the river to delouse himself (or to wash in the river's waters the gash from an iron trap.)]

Similarly, Valencia de Aneu, which is described as being located in an intimidating and rugged landscape, seems to have taken on the unappealing characteristics of its surroundings: "Valencia de Aneu es caserío áspero y violento, fiero e hirsuto como la garduña. En Valencia de Aneu, hasta la iglesia tiene un aire bélico y feudal" [Valencia de Aneu is a rough, wild hamlet, as fierce and shaggy as a marten. In Valencia de Aneu, even the church has a bellicose, feudal appearance] (VI, 496).

So, although the traveler often describes landscapes and scenery that are majestic, beautiful, or just charmingly attractive, it is also apparent that not every setting or place is presented as another facet of some kind of earthly paradise. Indeed, a feature of *Viaje al Pirineo de Lérida* is the way the narrative indicates how, in a variety of ways, earlier inhabitants left their mark on the area. Also revealed is the way in which, during the 1950s, parts of the district had become the site of substantial construction projects while other locations were witnessing the development of tourism and its associated amenities.

HUMAN PRESENCE OVER THE CENTURIES

While a strong sense of geography and detailed descriptions of the natural environment determine the structure and furnish much of the content of Cela's fifth travel book, the Pyrenean narrative also reveals the visitor's consciousness of the area's history and his awareness of the architectural and artistic legacy of that past. In addition, it discloses his concern at the way modern life has brought about changes that have altered the character, and to some degree the appearance, of parts of the Lérida Pyrenees.

From time to time, the traveler exhibits a sound knowledge of the history of this part of Spain. As was noted above, attention is drawn to the rise and fall of local ruling houses during the Middle Ages and reference is made to some of the dominant figures and significant struggles of various phases of the medieval period. At the beginning of his account, as the traveler set out to explore the Pallars de Sobirà, he observed that the county of Pallars was as old as the Carolingian Spanish March and also made a number of allusions to the fact that Charlemagne's Frankish counties had included much of modern Catalonia.[4] Elsewhere, there are several mentions of Charlemagne (including the thought, when the traveler sees a fellow wayfarer carefully delousing himself, that the poetic-looking stranger is killing the descendants of those lice that once camped in the emperor's warlike locks).

In addition, there are occasional allusions to Moorish incursions into this part of the peninsula, while the final part of the narrative contains a brief account of the fate of the county of Ribagorza from the ninth century until it was annexed by Sancho III of Navarre at the beginning of the eleventh century. It is also pointed out that in the same century the Counts of Pallars seized the domain of Erill in the valley of Bohí. Yet the struggles for territory and power in these parts were not confined to the Middle Ages. The traveler observes that Les Bordes, in the valley of Arán, had been fought over at various times, from as far back as the thirteenth century to as recently as 1944, and also notes that Bossost, about eight kilometers up the valley, felt the effects of the Carlist Wars during the nineteenth century.

However, much more frequent than the accounts of conflicts over the centuries are references to the monuments, and even debris, of history: churches, chapels, and monasteries, whether sound, crumbling, or in ruins. The area visited, unlike the locations of much of *Judíos, moros y cristianos* or the Andalusian section of *Primer viaje andaluz*, contains no great, historical towns or cities rich in architecture, art, or historical and literary associations. Nevertheless, with *Viaje al Pirineo de Lérida*, the old buildings, or their remains, that the traveler comes upon largely serve as reminders that, however isolated certain parts might be, the area has seen many centuries of human settlement and development.

Yet, despite its turbulent history, the Lérida section of the Pyrenees is not a land bristling with castles or fortified towns. During his journey, the traveler indicates only a handful of castles, including, as he makes his way along the valley of the Noguera Pallaresa, the abandoned castle at Malmercat and the ruins of the one at Vilamur. The fortress at Sort has served as the local cemetery since the nineteenth century and the traveler observes: "El castillo de Sort es un muerto habitado por la muerte. El castillo de Sort es un viejo soldado que, por la cuesta abajo del tiempo, paró en enterrador" [The castle of Sort is a dead man inhabited by the dead. The castle of Sort is an old soldier who, traveling down the slope of time, ended up as a gravedigger] (VI, 417).

In effect, the monuments that the wayfarer most often notes as he moves around are chapels, churches, and religious houses. Indeed, in the early part of his journey he indicates that monasteries have fared particularly badly in these parts. Near the Argentería waterfall he comes upon the tumbledown Cistercian monastery of San Pedro de las Malesas and a little later, at Gerri, he points out that the parish church of San Félix has been built from the remains of a neighboring monastery. The church is consequently described as: "Construcción parásita del abandonado monasterio, muro que vive y se nutre de los muertos y gloriosos restos de las piedras que fueron y ya no son" [A parasitic structure made out of the abandoned monastery, with walls constructed from the dead and glorious remains of stones that once were and now no longer are] (VI, 402).

The churches and chapels of the area are usually given just a simple acknowledgment of their presence and their name. Yet on some occasions, as with the case of the recycled stones at Gerri, the traveler adds an observation or two on the appearance of a building or on its contents. Thus, in the valley of Arán, he comments that the church of San Esteban, in Betrén, is one of the loveliest in the whole valley and suggests that Viella does not possess a church that is as elegant, illustrious, or graceful. However, he goes on to mention the comparisons that experts make between this church and San Miguel in Viella, and then gives a brief description of the interior of San Miguel and its bell tower, although it is not clear whether these are his own observations or are gleaned from elsewhere. A little later, the chapel of Mont-Corbizón is mentioned for its eye-catching, Roman funeral stone or *stela*, while in Bossost the twelfth-century church is described as having a sober appearance, apart from its "progressive" clock lodged in the bell tower. And, in the final section of the account, the traveler praises the slender, graceful bell tower of the church of Santa Eulalia in Erillavall, although he laments the fact that two important twelfth-century images have been taken from the church to an art museum in Barcelona.

On a different note, in Escalarre, toward the end of the first stage of the journey, the traveler comes across a priest about to celebrate mass in an empty church. Much later, in the closing pages of the account, he is drawn to the venerability and simplicity of the church of San Juan Bautista in Bohí. It is not, he suggests, as graceful as the one in Erilla-vall, yet he muses that it reflects the surrounding landscape and goes on to mention his liking for such unassuming and calm places of worship that quietly serve the needs of the local community:

La iglesia de San Juan Bautista de Bohí es más modosa y sin afeites, más acorde con el escueto y sobrio puro paisaje en el que se alza. Al viajero le resultan especialmente amables estas olvidadas piedras sin pretensiones pero rebosantes de silenciosa intimidad y de mansa unción, en las que las gentes se bautizan humildemente, se casan sin dar tres cuartos al pregonero y asisten, con muy contenida compostura, al funeral por el padre al que se le acabó la cuerda, casi a la chita callando, después de haber dado un oficio y una escopeta y un saco con cien duros dentro, a cada hijo. (VI, 641–42)

[The church of San Juan Bautista in Bohí is more modest and without frills, more in harmony with the plain, sober, and bare landscape in which it stands. The traveler is particularly fond of these forgotten stones that are unpretentious, yet brimming with quiet intimacy and soothing ritual, in which people are unceremoniously baptized, get married without making a great fuss, and, in a completely composed manner, attend the funeral of the father who, without letting on, had reached the end of his tether, but only after he had given a trade, a shotgun, and a bag containing five hundred pesetas to each son.]

There is also the occasional sighting of an abandoned church or the ruins of a chapel, and even indications that some former places of worship are now used for altogether demeaning purposes. Thus, in Artíes, about eight kilometers to the east of Viella, the visitor is pained to find that a thirteenth-century church is being used as a storehouse for cement, bricks, and building tools, while a nearby abandoned chapel serves as a shelter for livestock. The discovery of these two places causes him unhappiness and he is also indignant that Spaniards should treat "their own history" (VI, 535) with such apparent disrespect.

The traveler had begun his inventory of the religious buildings encountered on his tour of the Lérida Pyrenees with mention of three ruined monasteries: two abandoned to the elements and one having had its stones recycled to build a church. In dramatic style, he completes his account of the journey with a description of how the monastery of Labaix, dating back to at least 771, which had been abandoned with the disentailment of 1835 and was subsequently set fire to, was in 1956 being gradually engulfed by the waters of the Escales reservoir. Now, once again imperiled, this time by the requirements of hydroelectric technology, it is described as having the appearance of an old ship broken on coastal rocks, whose strength, maintained over so many centuries, had finally given out on its last voyage.

The scene of the waters of a reservoir lapping against the historic hulk of an ancient monastery ends *Viaje al Pirineo de Lérida* on a graphic and sentimental note that suggests, not for the first time in the work, that progress and modern ways have taken their toll on the natural and architectural heritage of the area. In the case of the monastery of Labaix, the disentailment of 1835 brought to an end the religious function of the house, while the fire of the same year inflicted serious damage on the structure. Over a century later, the development of hydroelectric schemes simply began a new phase in the destruction of the building. Indeed, throughout the narrative the traveler frequently airs the view that the district, subjected to the depradations of modern development and exploitation, is steadily having its character changed for the worse.

During the course of his journey, the visitor notes three principal aspects of economic life in the Pyrenean section of the province of Lérida: the loss of traditional local industries, the expanding presence of new activities, mainly connected with the creation of hydroelectric schemes, and the burgeoning tourist trade. At an early stage of the trip, as he makes his way through the valleys of the Pallars de Sobirà, he mentions the decline of iron-ore mining in the aptly named Vall Ferrera, as well as the fall in the number of iron works and foundries in Llavorsí. A few kilometers away, near the entrance to the Vall Ferrera, he comments on the ruins of the once-busy wool factory at Tirvia and then, a little later, returns to the subject of the local iron industry, noting that until the turn of the century there were eighteen charcoal fired iron mills in the Vall Ferrera. Areu, in the most northerly part of the same valley, is described as having seen its population fall by at least 70 percent since the closure of its ore mines resulted in the miners leaving for France in search of work. Later, in the valley of Arán, Les Bordes is presented as a dying town (although here the traveler seems to be thinking as much in psychological as in postindustrial terms), while in this same section of the narrative it is mentioned that the village of Canején, which had eight hundred inhabitants at the beginning of the century, now has fewer than 150, and has no doctor or pharmacist.

Yet such indications of the decline or disappearance of traditional industries and the resultant depopulation need to be balanced against evidence of the survival of some mining activity in certain areas, a bustling logging industry, and, above all, the construction work associated with the generation of hydroelectric power. Thus, when he is in Bossost, in the northwestern corner of the Lérida Pyrenees, the traveler notices that there are many Andalusians in the town and comments that while

some of them are working in the local zinc sulphide mine, most are employed as laborers at the power stations under construction in the area.
He goes on to add: "Los andaluces, desde que descubrieron que se
podía salir del país y ganar jornales más decentes, no paran quietos"
[Since they discovered that they could leave their region and get decent
wages elsewhere, the Andalusians will not keep still] (VI, 589). Indeed,
he pays a visit to the bustling Café del Centro, which he describes as "a
kind of Andalusian Consulate General" (VI, 589), and where the mi-
grant workers gather to play dominoes, sing, and talk of the Sevillian
soccer club, Real Betis.

Although there are occasional references to tree felling and the
changing methods of the logging industry, it is the construction work
associated with dams and power stations, and the presence of large
numbers of southern workers that catch the traveler's attention. As he
leaves Escaló on the Noguera Pallaresa, he notes the cabin that in earlier days provided accommodation for the men who guided the rafts of
cut timber down the river to the sawmills (a task since taken over by
road transport) and which is now occupied by men from Murcia, Almería, Jaén, and Huelva who are employed as laborers at the Torrassa
power station. A little later, on the road to Esterri, he sees what he calls
murcianos, earth-moving in preparation for the construction of a dam,
but points out that most of the men engaged in this dusty, spectacular
operation are not actually from Murcia, but mostly from various parts
of Andalusia. The adjective *murciano*, the traveler observes, is used in
this area as a catchall term for construction laborers. On leaving Esterri, he spots a group of badly designed, ridiculous looking, wooden,
prefabricated houses for the families of men working on one of the
nearby power stations, while at Viella he comes across five or six bars
where, from time to time, *flamenco* music can be heard and where, apparently, there is occasional trouble involving the Andalusian workers.

Another incursion that reflects how this part of the Pyrenees is having its economy boosted and its character changed is that involving vacationers and other leisure seekers, such as anglers and mountaineers.
Throughout the first two sections of *Viaje al Pirineo de Lérida* there are
frequent mentions of the presence of these visitors, with comments that
are sometimes matter-of-fact, but often disparaging. At the starting
point of his tour, Pobla de Segur, the traveler pays some attention to
the tourists there and subsequently indicates that Llavorsí is swarming
with visiting anglers—who are perceived as arrogant, showy types who
bring along their unappealing families. There are vacationers in Ribera
de Cardós, but about whom the traveler has nothing to say, whereas
at the Torrassa reservoir he notes that at around 9 A.M. some elegant,
fashionable, city types show up to bathe.

It is apparent that as the traveler continues his journey he becomes increasingly intolerant of vacationers and also scornful when it comes to the tackier side of the tourist trade. Thus in Espot, several kilometers to the west of the Noguera Pallaresa and described as a vacation center, he sees big-bottomed, betrousered young women, men in shirtsleeves and wearing suspenders, fat women in chintz dresses, and youngsters listening to transistor radios and sipping vermouth. Indeed, the traveler indignantly pronounces that while Espot, the gateway to the famous lake country of Lérida, is as noble and old as any other Pyrenean town, it is being sullied by tourism, which brings with it the artificial grime of the cities. However, a little later he refers to the litter that *some* tourists leave behind and, in fact, he is not scathing about all visitors to the area: he indicates his respect for visiting mountaineers, for pursuing their sport quietly and without fuss.

Although it is made clear that vacationers come to the area not only from other parts of Spain but also from France, it is presumably with the French tourists in mind that local shops are seen to stock tasteless souvenirs that have almost nothing to do with the area. In Viella, the traveler sees mementoes on sale that he describes as falser than Judas and which he then proceeds to list: castanets, *banderillas*, tambourines, and dolls dressed variously as bullfighters, civil guards, priests, Andalusian women, and so on. While he accepts the importance for Spain of the souvenir industry, he nevertheless wonders, rather idealistically, why tourists do not satisfy themselves with something local and natural, such as a twig, the blade of a fern, or the petal of a flower. Indeed, just to drive home the point of how the commerce of tourism can vulgarize aspects of Spanish life and culture, when he is in Bossost the traveler reflects on how he preferred the hillier, upper part of the valley of Arán since it was "todavía no hollado por la turbamulta de los turistas" [as yet untrampled by the tourist mob] (VI, 587). He then describes a group of French visitors buying leather wine bottles decorated with pictures of bullfighters or gypsy women wearing flounced dresses. One of the tourists, a young priest, is clicking castanets, a girl is playing at bullfighting with her father, and all this amidst cries of "¡Viva España!" When a nun in the group gives the wayfarer some of the bread she is distributing, he thanks her for her charity and then offers to be photographed looking suitable grateful or, if she prefers, putting on the expression of somebody from an underdeveloped country (VI, 587–88).

But while tourists may be regarded as unsightly, noisy, untidy, tasteless, and patronizing, their personal impact on the environment is presented as intrusive rather than overwhelming. And although the facilities provided for them, especially the new hotels and souvenir shops, do not have the same physical impact on the area as the major construction projects that the traveler encounters during his journey, he does, nevertheless, become increasing irritated by the evidence of tourism and what he perceives as its harmful influence on the character of various places.

In addition to such concerns, it is also suggested that the cultural and artistic heritage of the Lérida Pyrenees is being undermined in a less visible but equally relentless way. It is not simply a matter of building materials being stored in a church or livestock kept in a chapel. He also laments the neglect and apathy of Spaniards that can allow, for example, the thousand-year-old monastery of San Pedro de Burgal to fall to the ground and condemns the vandalism that sweeps away a Romanesque chapel or removes a menhir marking the center of a valley. Furthermore, and echoing sentiments expressed in the Pastrana section of *Viaje a la Alcarria,* the traveler voices his indignation that cultural treasures, some of which have been in the same location for many centuries, have been transferred to city museums. Thus, the eight-hundred-year-old Romanesque paintings in Estahón's church of Santa Eulalia were taken to a museum in "the city," "embalsamadas igual que momias" [embalmed just like mummies] (VI, 453). Two images, sculpted in the twelfth century, had apparently been removed from Erillavall's parish church and deposited in an art museum in Barcelona, while paintings from the churches of Santa María and Sant Climent in Tahull, as well as, it is scornfully noted, everything that the civil servants managed to get off the walls of these two churches, also ended up in the same city. When reflecting on such official plundering, the visitor maintains the thrust of the arguments he used in Pastrana to protest at this practice and expresses his thoughts with the same vehemence:

Al viajero, estas depredaciones que se hacen en nombre de la cultura y de la conservación de las obras de arte, le dieron siempre muy mala espina. A los regidores de los museos no suele importarles el arte en sí, el temblorcillo o el aleteo del arte, sino su clasificación, su ficha policiaca: esto es esto, esto es lo otro, esto es lo de más allá, procede de tal sitio, es de tal fecha, se supone obra de Fulano o de Mengano, tiene tantos por tantos centímetros, etc. Los museos son algo muerto, algo que va contra la natural ley de las cosas. (VI, 453).

[The traveler has never liked this pillaging that is carried out in the name of culture and in the name of the conservation of works of art. The administrators of museums do not usually care about art itself, the thrill or the wonder of art; they are interested in its classification, its police record: this is this, this is that, this is the other thing, it comes from such-and-such a place, dates from such-and-such a time, it is assumed to be the work of so-and-so or

what's-his-name, and is of such-and-such a size, etc. Museums are dead
places that go against the natural order of things.]

Shortly thereafter, and with reference to another painting that had
ended up in Barcelona, the reader is reminded that such actions are a
national rather than a regional problem. Here, a provocative shaft is
aimed at the whole notion of centralism:

Cataluña no se libra del mal que atenaza a España entera, el centralismo, y
engorda a su capital, Barcelona, a expensas de todo el Principado. Al viajero
le gustaría ver a las capitales más flacas y a los pueblos más vivos y lozanos.
(VI, 457)

[Catalonia is not free from the disease that afflicts the whole of Spain, centralism, and fattens its capital, Barcelona, at the expense of the entire princi-
pality. The traveler would like to see leaner capitals and livelier, healthier
provinces.]

Then, toward the close of the narrative, in Erillavall, he again drives
home his point in a bold fashion as he makes reference to the pieces that
were removed from the local church: "Al viajero le duelen en el alma
estos peculados legales, inmorales e impolíticos que se hacen en nombre
del derecho administrativo y volviendo grupas a la historia y a su liberal
fluir" [These legal but immoral and discourteous peculations, which are
carried out in the name of administrative right and run counter to the
free flow of history, really grieve the traveler.] (VI, 638–39).[5]
Throughout the narrative, then, the neglect, misuse, and destruction
of the architectural and other heritage of the area, as well as the dis-
persal of art treasures to distant museums, are observed and lamented.
Similarly, the traveler's awareness of the intrusions of concrete, steel,
tarmac, and man-made reservoirs into a sparsely populated, majesti-
cally beautiful, and largely unspoilt part of Spain is also a noticeable
aspect of his account. New buildings and other construction projects
are occasionally encountered during the journey, and are sometimes described in a matter-of-fact way. But usually they provoke reactions that
indicate concern or disapproval. And while, from time to time, he registers his disquiet at the intrusive presence of power stations, it is not
until the closing stages that a considered judgment is offered on the
massive hydroelectric projects, completed and in progress, that mark
and even scar many of the areas visited. The economic, social, and envi-
ronmental impact and implications of these schemes provide the focus
for the climax to *Viaje al Pirineo de Lérida*.
In the early part of the journey, the traveler's reactions to concrete
intrusions are relatively low-key. Thus, in the national park of Aigüest-

ortes he suggests that the concrete barrier that has turned the natural lake of San Mauricio into a reservoir will look rather better once it has some shrubbery growing on it. He also questions whether the highway and other man-made legacies belong in a national park, and adds a little later that he does not like the postcard kind of stillness of reservoir waters. Subsequently, in the valley of Arán, the visitor mentions that Artíes has a "una fábrica de luz, muy aparente y moderna" [a light-factory that is very visible and modern] (VI, 534) and soon reveals his sadness at how the town appears to have been turned into a construction site. Further up the valley, he observes that the new buildings outside Viella disfigure the countryside. Later, near Bossost, he points out a power station rising in front of the rustic serenity of Mount Montlude. Then, in his second trip to Aigüestortes, this time to the western part of the national park, the traveler notes a small power station and reiterates his position that in such parks there should be no highways nor any buildings for recreational, industrial, military, or religious purposes.[6]

In the closing stages of his journey, the traveler arrives at the reservoir of Cardet and reflects on the way in which the generation of electricity has become such an important feature of the county of Ribagorza. He acknowledges that electricity is a necessary, useful, and clean product that does not grow on trees, and confesses that he can admire the engineering feats involved in generating hydroelectric power and in exploiting other resources. However, he emphasizes that he dislikes the visible consequences of such activities and notes that in his account he has not usually described what he terms "los paisajes que, adobados en cemento, parió la industria" [the cement-bedecked landscapes that industry has given birth to] (VI, 645). Recognizing that it is pointless trying to stop progress and unable to claim that the hydroelectric projects in these parts are unnecessary, he nevertheless believes that those who design and locate these schemes should try to display some kind of aesthetic sensitivity when introducing technological developments into the natural environment. Indeed, a little earlier, with reference to what he saw as the unsuitable location of a modern chapel in the Aigüestortes national park, the traveler had stated that there should exist a relationship between architecture and its landscape, and he had gone on to make the point that architecture was itself landscape. Now, summarizing his thoughts on the aesthetic implications of the many hydroelectric installations that he has seen in the Lérida Pyrenees, he suggests that, at the very least, designers and builders could have engaged in a little more cosmetic landscaping of the constructions and been rather more willing to conserve historical monuments and preserve the natural character of the locations affected.

Finally, when he arrives at Pont de Suert the traveler experiences yet another offshoot of the development of hydroelectric power schemes in this northern section of the province of Lérida: the boom town. Noting that Pont de Suert's population had risen from five hundred to three thousand in the previous six years, he refers to it as "la próvida fuente de los kilowatios" [the bounteous source of kilowatts] (VI, 653) and "una inmensa mina de luz" [an immense light mine] (VI, 654). He then presents it as a prosperous, busy, booming town, with Andalusian workers from Baena, and full of jeeps, motorcycles, trucks, transistor radios, distinguished-looking gentlemen, and nannies to care for the children of the better off. The new part of town has well laid out streets and clean (although monotonous-looking) dwellings, and a modern, functional, and attractive church. But the traveler wonders whether Pont de Suert can continue to develop as a town? When the hydroelectric work has finished will the Andalusians pack up and move on in search of more work, having thereby treated the place as a camp, or will they stay and grow with the town? After such meditations on the present character of Pont de Suert and considerations on its future (he also hopes that the town will be robust and bold enough to withstand the eventual advent of what he terms "atomic energy") the traveler heads a few kilometers south. There he ends his trip, in a motorboat, on the Escales reservoir, contemplating the water lapping at the stones of the ancient, ruined, and engulfed monastery of Labaix.

OTHER INTERESTS AND OBSERVATIONS

Despite the above comments, Cela's fifth travel book is far from being simply an account of the wonderful scenery of the Lérida Pyrenees that is punctuated by denunciations of the excesses of the hydroelectric and tourist industries, or criticisms of official pillaging of the artistic heritage of the area. Nor, for obvious reasons, is the work the kind of homage to Spain's history and culture that the two preceding travel narratives had been. Indeed, the main things that the traveler focuses on and appreciates during his tour of the Lérida Pyrenees are the beauty and at times grandeur of the rivers and valleys that he follows, and the delights of the hills that he climbs. Other pleasing sights that he witnesses range from delicate, attractive flowers to the imposing presence of the mountains.

But some altogether different aspects of the area also arouse the traveler's interest and cause him satisfaction and enjoyment. When he pauses in towns and villages he often shows a keen interest in local festivities and other customs, as well as in the beliefs or legends associated with particular communities or locations. In Gerri, for example, he notes that on the third day of the town's main festival the *morisca* is danced. He then describes how this is a kind of pantomime, playing out the liberation of a Christian princess from the clutches of a Moorish king, in which the spectators have the real fun when they pelt the participants with sweets and sugared almonds and, in an attempt to make the dancers lose their step, fire their guns into the air. Subsequently, when the traveler is in Sort, he mentions the left-arm dance, the *esquerrana* (apparently invented by a minstrel for a count who had lost his right arm) and gives a brief description of the movements involved. In Rialp, he notes the traditional *cambra*, or distribution of food and drink, and also mentions some of the local carnival festivities. However, much later, in Canejón, when the traveler recalls the old St John's Eve pageant that used to take place he expresses his sadness that such ancient customs are dying out.

At the ruins of the Benedictine monastery of Santa María del Monestir, he recounts the story of the Count of Pallars who, saved from drowning, failed to fulfill a vow that he made to the saint and as a result was struck blind. Then, when the wayfarer comes to the chapel of San Mauricio in the national park of Aigüestortes, he mentions the legend of the two hunters who, for an act of impiety, were turned into the twin mountains of the Encantats and which, he notes, were first scaled in 1912 — by a Spanish priest. Passing through the valley of Arán, the traveler describes certain local funeral customs. Here, he notes, the chief mourner is normally not someone connected with the bereaved family. Furthermore, if the deceased is a woman, then the chief mourner will be a widow from these parts. The reader is also informed that the bereaved parents of an adult son or daughter do not attend their offspring's funeral but instead stay at home to pray and receive visitors.

Yet while the details of local dances, festivals, legends, and even mourning rites are carefully noted by the traveler, he also derives a great deal of enjoyment (as, indeed, he does in the earlier travel works) from his food and drink. Of course, in one or two places that he arrives at the visitor is unable to find any nourishment and on a couple of occasions he is served very poor food. Nevertheless, most of the time he eats and drinks well during the journey, although without indulging in drinking sessions of the kind that occur from time to time in *Del Miño al Bidasoa* or *Primer viaje andaluz*. At the beginning of his trip, the trout that the traveler has for his supper in Pobla de Segur (fried, he states, as if by an angel) is the first in a series of culinary pleasures that will permeate the account of the journey and which are often described in great detail. Subsequently, in Tornafort, he sings the praises of Señor Gasset's *xolís*, an extremely long sausage made, it is explained, from the head, neck, and ribs of the pig. He then goes into some detail concerning the way two different kinds of *xolís* are made, before apparently consuming about nine meters of the sausage, together with bread, salad, and wine. All this is rounded off with sheep's-milk cheese.[7]

This prodigious appetite is revealed a number of other times during the trip. In Rialp, the traveler breakfasts on lamb chops and wine, comments on the way chops should be cooked and then asks for more, while in Alíns, the capital of the Vall Ferrera, he takes what is mischievously termed a "teeny, light lunch" of trout, chops, and cherries (VI, 442). Before sunrise, in Escart, he breakfasts on fried eggs, fried potatoes, fried *chorizo*, and even asks for fried bread. But then a few hours later, not far from the San Mauricio lake, two kindly ladies give the wayfarer what he regards as a fairly unappetizing cold lunch and which he describes in the following way: "Pollo frío (algo seco), tortilla de patata (con el aceite ligeramente rancio) y filetes empanados (no muy tiernos). ¡Menos da una piedra!" [Cold chicken (a bit dry), Spanish omelette (cooked in slightly rancid oil), and tenderloin in pastry (not very tender). Better than nothing!] (VI, 474). However, he is right to be at least grudgingly thankful for what he gets here since, a couple of days later, as he makes his way along the valley of Aneu, he stops in the hamlet of Escalarre just before seven in the morning and finds that the local inn is unable to provide him with anything to eat. In vain he inquires after ham, eggs, rabbit, and tomatoes. There is not even any coffee.

Yet such deprivations are rare. Later in the journey, the note of hedonism is resumed when the traveler lists the many good and varied items that he has for lunch in a small hotel in Salardú (fried eggs, ham, wine, bread, more fried eggs, *chorizo* and *salchichón*, pork chops, another bottle of wine, more bread, cheese, apples, coffee, and brandy). It is little wonder that, after such an impressive display of his ability as a trencherman, he should ask the owner if he might be permitted to take a *siesta* somewhere in the establishment. And during the brief incursion that the traveler makes into France, there is a description of the lunch he has in the three-star restaurant in Cier-de-Luchon and details of the "memorable" meal that he dispatches in another three-star location, this time in Bains-de-Barbazan. Once back in Spain, though, he resorts to his less sophisticated eating habits when he orders "a dozen or a dozen and a half" lamb chops for lunch in Bossost. Francisco Umbral recently observed that in Cela's travel works can be found "a detailed description of how people eat in Spain, or rather, how they used to eat in those days, for nearly all that has changed."[8] Certainly, on many occasions in his Pyrenean trip the visitor shows that while his legs might be faltering his appetite and enjoyment of local food remain undiminished.

However, the traveler's interest in food and drink is not restricted to the act of consumption. From time to time he also describes the content of local dishes or the characteristics of local produce. Thus in Areu, a small, shrinking village in the Vall Ferrera, he lists, in a light hearted fashion, the assorted animal and vegetable ingredients of *escudella* and describes how the other local stew, *confitat*, is prepared in two earthenware pots, each containing particular parts of the pig, and is served from both according to taste (one of the pots contains the snout and the ears), with fried potatoes and tomato sauce. The traveler then describes and enthuses over the locally produced sheep's-milk cheese and the local raspberries. Then, after drinking three glasses of *ratassía*, the liquor of the area, he gives a highly detailed account of how it is produced in the Pallars district. Elsewhere in the narrative, there are also occasional instructions for the preparation of certain dishes, as when a few days later, in Lladorre, he notes how the owner of the restaurant there, Florencio Lladós, kills, keeps, cooks, and serves trout. However, he does point out that when Lladós is in a bad mood he apparently refuses to dish up his trout and eats them himself. Fortunately, he was happy with the world on the day the traveler chose to turn up at his establishment.

But in addition to displays of the wayfarer's prodigious appetite and the revelation of his more theoretical interest in food and beverages in *Viaje al Pirineo de Lérida*, the Pyrenean narrative also indicates a continuing interest in linguistic matters. In the closing chapters of *Del Miño al Bidasoa*, as the vagabond and Dupont make their way across the provinces of Vizcaya and Guipúzcoa, there is hardly any acknowledgment of the existence of the Basque language. This is no doubt less an indication of the author's anxiety to avoid a sensitive cultural and political issue than the result of the fact that the original journey had been made at speed and within the linguistic insulation of a car. On foot in the Lérida Pyrenees, however, the traveler does find time for the occasional comment or even lengthy observation on the etymology of the names of rivers, valleys, areas, and individual places. He also gathers together a list of some twenty place names of Basque origin in the district, and observes that the dialect found in the valley of Arán (where, he notes, Gascon, French, Catalan, and Castilian are also spoken) is Gascon in origin. Moreover, he muses on Catalan words and Catalan spelling and pronunciation, Old Catalan orthography, and Catalan and Castilian versions of names. Indeed, the traveler goes on to air his views on the issue of bilingualism, a phenomenon that he sees as involving an incomplete knowledge of two languages. He also makes the bold suggestion that Catalan as well as Castilian should be taught in the schools of Catalonia. However, it should be pointed out that he proposes this solely in order to improve the quality of Castilian used by Catalans. Then, having stated his love for Castilian and his respect for Catalan or any other language, the traveler gives his view of the role of the Castilian language in contemporary Spain:

> El castellano es la lengua que los españoles no castellanos—que formamos legión y somos mayoría—admitimos como común y apta y suficiente para entendernos entre todos; la denominación de lengua oficial—aunque lo sea—es impopular y le perjudica en el afecto de los no castellanos. (VI, 618)

> [Castilian is the language that non-Castilian Spaniards—we are legion and in the majority—accept as common, suitable, and adequate for us to understand each other; designating it the official language—although it is—is unpopular and makes non-Castilians less willing to accept it.]

All in all, Cela's fifth travel book reveals a greater sense of landscape, and of geography, than the preceding works. It is, of course, the natural, physical attractions of the Lérida Pyrenees that would have enticed Cela (and his traveling companions) to the area in the first place. Yet, as has been noted, *Viaje al Pirineo de Lérida* is not simply an account of the visitor moving through, admiring, and recording the splendors of the natural environment. Although for obvious reasons the work does not contain anywhere near the amount of the cultural and historical freight found in *Judíos, moros y cristianos* and *Primer viaje andaluz*, it nevertheless exhibits a certain awareness of and interest in the medieval history of the Lérida Pyrenees and the surrounding areas, and the way in which dynastic rivalries and opposing armies determined the political and social boundaries of an area already marked by formidable physical barriers. In addition, Cela's penultimate travel book comes to focus on the way in which contemporary man is also imposing himself on the landscape: with the presence of tourists and all the logistic requirements of the leisure industry and, in particular, with the reshaping and even disfiguring of the physical environment for the development of hydroelectric schemes. Both kinds of intrusion were by-products of the gradually accelerating modernization and increasing prosperity of Spain during the late 1950s. Almost thirty years after his trip to the Lérida Pyrenees Cela made a return journey to the Alcarria and discovered that the modernization process had been largely completed. Back in the Alcarria, he also witnessed and experienced a more extensive range of mixed blessings offered by the new and generally affluent Spain.

9

Postscript: *Nuevo viaje a la Alcarria*

The Traveler and his Entourage

At one point in arturo barea's introduction to the 1953 english translation of *La colmena*, the exiled writer states of the young Cela
who made his way around the Alcarria district in 1946: "A shabby traveller on foot with a rucksack, he was accepted by people as a man, not
as a writer from the big city" (p. 14). This observation is, however,
partly the product of sentimental speculation. In fact, there is photo-
graphic evidence that the traveler of 1946 was casually, but quite
smartly dressed. The close-up photograph used for the frontispiece of
the first edition of *Viaje a la Alcarria* (Madrid: Revista de Occidente,
1948), which shows Cela sitting at the roadside taking notes, also reveals that he is wearing a shirt that bears a "C.J.C." monogram. This
photograph was reproduced a few years later along with another which
shows a very well turned-out traveler, in the company of Quico and his
donkey, on the excursion to the Tetas de Viana.[1]

The existence of such photographs is, of course, an indication that
Cela was accompanied by a photographer. As was mentioned in chapter
4, the title page of the first edition states "(Fotos de Karl Wlasak)"
[Photos by Karl Wlasak] and the edition contains fifty black-and-white
plates, nearly all with captions taken from an appropriate part of the
text. Subsequently, Cela was to acknowledge that Wlasak and also
Conchita Stichaner accompanied him on his trip (IV, 171n). This admission clearly raises questions concerning both the presentation and content of *Viaje a la Alcarria*. Indeed, the fact that the presence of Stichaner
and Wlasak is not even hinted at in the text of the travel book should
also serve as a reminder that Cela's account reveals only what the author wanted to transmit to the reader.

Barea's observation on how Cela was "accepted" by the people he
came across is an assumption not always backed up by the evidence of
the text. Indeed, Barea gives no indication that he has any extratextual
information on this matter and he is, presumably, indulging in senti-

mental conjecture concerning the way in which the people of the Alcarria, with their "dignity" (p.15), generally treated the young visitor from Madrid. Certainly, the picture that the travel work shows is almost entirely one that reveals an unknown and seemingly unimportant outsider, interested in seeing something of an area and its people, who is received by the locals in a variety of ways—with warmth, indifference, suspicion, and even occasionally with hostility.

Thirty-nine years later Cela returned to the Alcarria. However, this time he swept into the area in a blaze of publicity, with a hefty entourage, and as a famous author, Senator, and television celebrity. Sponsored by *Cambio 16*,[2] the sixty-nine-year-old Galician was scheduled to revisit many of the towns and villages that he had stayed in or passed through in 1946. He was also going to stop at some of the places that he had bypassed on the earlier trip. The area to be covered was more or less the same, except that, of course, some dramatic physical changes had affected the district since the 1940s, the most spectacular of these being the construction of the huge Buendía and Entrepeñas reservoirs, which had been completed in 1956.

But if the Alcarria had witnessed some significant changes since Cela's visit of 1946, so too had the circumstances and stature of the author. The opening two chapters of *Viaje a la Alcarria* had presented the young writer as a rather solitary figure, planning his journey and subsequently setting out by walking through a gloomy and somewhat depressing urban landscape to the Atocha station and thence by train to Guadalajara. In contrast, the first two chapters of the account of the 1985 journey show the author flying into Madrid, staying in a hotel (where he gives interviews for television and the press), dining with his friends from the Casa de Guadalajara and then, the following day, being seen off by a couple of dignitaries as he sets out for Guadalajara and the Alcarria in a chauffeur-driven Rolls-Royce.

In the original trip, and setting aside casual acquaintances with whom he had traveled along for a while, the author had been in the (unmentioned) company of two other people. Now, in June 1985, he was part of a veritable cavalcade, consisting of Oteliña (his young, black, female, American driver), a pair of minstrels, a cohort of six or eight cars, and a tour bus. When, early in the narrative, the traveler (in this work referred to throughout as the *viajero*) orders his driver to pull over so that there can be roadside music and dancing, the convoy comes to a halt and a while later a passing motorist slows down for what he assumes to be the scene of an accident.[3] Elsewhere in the narrative, it transpires that the author's entourage is being followed by a group of gypsy peddlers who are anxious to take commercial advantage of the crowds that gather whenever the various vehicles stop in towns and villages (p. 153).

Yet this cavalcade that crisscrossed the Alcarria for ten days was not simply a brash publicity gimmick for *Cambio 16* or an exercise in self-promotion by the aging writer. Certainly, the flamboyant style of the operation invited judgments such as that of José María Martínez Cachero, who described it as "a great advertising stunt" which the author thoroughly enjoyed (p. 125). In effect, when it was suggested to Cela that the second Alcarria journey was undertaken amidst a good deal of hype, the author agreed but noted that the magazine (and future publisher) was responsible for this aspect of the trip.[4] Yet while Cela appears to have been a willing participant in the razzmatazz surrounding the return journey to the Alcarria and the schedule devised for him, he alone was responsible for the account of the trip. And although his record of the occasion often reveals a certain levity that accords with the festive and celebratory nature of much of the procession through the Alcarria, it is also a frequently sober reflection on how places and society have changed over the years. In addition, it is a fascinating and occasionally moving reminder of locations, incidents, and people associated with the journey of June 1946.

FÊTING THE CELEBRITY

In the opening chapter of Cela's first travel work the traveler-figure is presented as a young writer, surrounded by the books in his study, thinking about a walking trip and then tentatively planning his tour around the Alcarria. As in all the subsequent travel books, the protagonist is described in the third-person singular. In this way he is constantly in view in the account, operating at one remove from the narratorial voice and also being cast in the role of participant in the action rather than simply a narrator-observer. The protagonist is also kept at arm's length from the figure of the author, despite the fact that, scattered throughout the first five travel books, there are increasing indications that the traveler-figure is indeed Cela, or at least a version of the author. However, with *Nuevo viaje a la Alcarria* the reader is presented with a conflation of author, narrator, traveler, and public figure who is greeted and fêted during his procession through the area that he had endowed with literary immortality.

In the course of the visit of June 1946, the young wayfarer had experienced a few difficult moments—when he was on the receiving end of rudeness or other kinds of hostility, or when he became involved in tricky situations. Indeed, he had even mentioned in passing the fact that he had been locked up for a day and a night on the orders of one of the local mayors. Now, thirty-nine years after that visit and that unseen incident, the traveler is given red-carpet treatment wherever he stops or stays. In the account of the 1946 journey, he mentions coming across only three or four mayors and notes that he was particularly impressed by those of La Puerta and Pastrana. At the start of the 1985 trip, on the other hand, he is guest of honor at a lunch in Guadalajara attended by most of the mayors of the Alcarria district. Thereafter, as he moves around, he is welcomed by nearly twenty mayors in the various towns and villages. Moreover, in Moratilla he notes what fine hosts and guides the local mayors are turning out to be, and recalls that in his previous visit they were, with a couple of exceptions, his worst enemies, apparently even worse than the Civil Guards (p. 234).

But not only is the traveler now escorted around towns and villages by the local dignitaries. His whole visit to the Alcarria is punctuated by formal lunches and dinners at which he is the guest of honor, and where, back to a familiar theme, he often acknowledges how good the food is. He sometimes details the full menu, and occasionally gives the recipe for a dish he particularly enjoys. Even when he eats with friends rather than with the local worthies he continues to reveal his hearty appetite and love of good food. The only suggestion of culinary weariness comes when, toward the end of the journey, he finds that he is to dine yet again on the customary, done to a turn, lamb.

Yet official lunches and dinners are not the only way in which the traveler's status is recognized during his tour. In Guadalajara, and then later in Caspueñas, he presides over panels making literary awards. Receptions are organized in his honor, his progress is monitored by various reporters, he receives telegrams from as far away as Paris, he is recognized, photographed, applauded, and greeted by musicians and crowds. People travel to the towns and villages of the Alcarria to see or meet him. He is photographed and his autograph is sought: in Sacedón more than two dozen young Civil Guards, each with a copy of *Viaje a la Alcarria*, are waiting to have these signed by the author. Finally, there are constant visual reminders of the visit of 1946 (and the subsequent fame of the traveler) in the form of the tile plaques that indicate places he visited or where he stayed, and which contain brief, apposite quotes from the first travel book.

Michel Butor talks of travelers leaving their traces in the towns that they pass through: "So many registers signed, checks cashed, mementos inscribed." He goes on to observe that "to leave a trace of our passing is to belong to a spot" (p. 68), subsequently claiming that even if there is no book that records the journey, there will always be some kind of "trace" or "recording of the travel" (p. 69). What Cela's 1985 return trip to the Alcarria does is use, as a series of almost ritualistic markers or reference points, the very public and intertextual "traces" of fifteen or so of the tile plaques that were put up in 1976 to commemorate the thirtieth anniversary of the first tour.

These plaques, the first of which is encountered on the street wall of the saddlery in Guadalajara, are an obvious reminder (and confirmation) of the visit of 1946. Also, with their short extracts from *Viaje a la Alcarria*, they serve as a graphic and physical link between person, place, and text. That person is normally just the author-traveler himself, as is indicated in the inscription on the plaque at the inn where he stayed in Torija during the first visit: "C.J.C. durmió en esta casa el 6 de junio de 1946. La cama es de hierro, grande, hermosa, con un profundo colchón de paja" [C.J.C. slept in this house on 6 June 1946. "It is a large, fine, iron bed, with a deep, straw mattress"] (p. 45). Occasionally, though, the plaque may include reference to a local character mentioned in the first travel work, as is the case with the one outside Julio Vacas's former shop in Brihuega: "En esta casa hablaron de todo C.J.C. y su amigo, el amo, el 7 de junio de 1946. Mi nombre es Julio Vacas, aunque me llaman Portillo" [In this house, C.J.C. and his friend, the owner, talked about everything on 7 June 1946. "My name is Julio Vacas, though they call me Portillo"]. And then, as if to underscore the conflation indicated on many of the plaques between "C.J.C." and the *viajero*, the narrative continues: "El viajero ya no volverá a hablar jamás con su amigo Julio Vacas, alias Portillo, por culpa de la muerte" [The traveler will never again talk with his friend Julio Vacas, alias Portillo, death has seen to that] (p. 80).

So these plaques (some of which, it is pointed out, have been replaced, removed, or damaged) serve as indicators of Cela's fame and also as an affirmation, indeed confirmation, of the whereabouts of the traveler at various stages of the journey of June 1946. However, the frequent references to and quotations from these commemorative tiles are more than just a reminder to the reader that the traveler is revisiting places and specific sites encountered in 1946. The plaques also become a reinscription of parts of the earlier narrative within the new account: a type of paralleling intertextuality as well as a kind of ritualistic (even narcissistic) series of self-referential indicators. Furthermore, these tile texts, systematically inspected and inserted in the account of the 1985 visit, draw together Cela the author and the traveler-figure in a rather more restrained and literary way than the fêting and fanfares laid on for Cela the celebrity.

Figures from the Past

Nuevo viaje a la Alcarria is not, however, just an account of adulation, feasting, and self-indulgence. Throughout the narrative there runs a much more personal, intimate leitmotif: the process whereby the traveler renews contact with some of those he first met during the 1946 visit, makes the acquaintance of relatives or friends of others, recalls those who have gone to live elsewhere, and, of course, reflects on those who have died during the intervening years. The moments dedicated to these people, living or dead, and who are associated with specific places, episodes, or incidents, reveal a reflective and compassionate side to the traveler. Furthermore, the encounters with individuals directly or indirectly connected with the first trip, as well as the memory of others, often provide touching pauses that contrast with the bustle and even frivolity that mark a good deal of the 1985 visit.

The most unexpected and interesting reunion with a surviving character from *Viaje a la Alcarria* takes place in Torija. Here the traveler suddenly finds himself in the presence of Armando Mondéjar López, the freckled, redheaded, thoughtful boy who in June 1946 walked with him for a while along the road to Taracena (IV, 54–59). Now a canon at the cathedral of Burgo de Osma (Soria), he had gone to Torija in order to pay his regards to Cela, who was delighted by this chance meeting and the opportunity to find out what had become of Armando during the intervening years (pp. 49–50). Far less animating is the subsequent encounter in Gárgoles de Abajo, where the traveler talks briefly with Francisca, the unnamed, attractive young maid in mourning dress who had served him lunch at the inn there in 1946. Now he notes that, despite the passing of so many years, Francisca's appearance still reveals a certain Moorish dignity. For her part, she simply comments rather tritely that she has seen her famous visitor on television (p. 123).

Later in the trip, when he gets to Casasana, the traveler is reunited with Felipe el Sastre. In 1946, the young man had loaded his donkey, Lucero, with the wayfarer's luggage and then accompanied the visitor to Sacedón. Felipe is now treated as an old friend (p. 180). Subsequently, in Pastrana, at the same inn where he stayed previously, he encounters the doctor, Francisco Cortijo Ayuso. The Don Paco of *Viaje a la Alcarria* was deputy mayor in those days and was described as "un hombre joven, atildado, de sana color y ademán elegante" [a spruce young man, with a healthy complexion and an elegant bearing] (IV, 230). Thirty-nine years later and now retired, the physician nevertheless retains his impressive air. This is conveyed with the author drawing closely on the earlier description: "Don Paco ya no es joven pero sigue atildado en el vestir, de sana color en la faz y porte elegante" [Don Paco is no longer young but he is still smartly dressed, with a healthy countenance and an elegant appearance] (p. 240).

Also in the account of the return journey, the traveler comes across some individuals whom he met or saw in 1946 but who, interestingly, do not figure in the narrative of that trip. These include Don Leo in Pareja (pp. 171–72), Arturito in Casasana (pp. 180–81), and, in Tendilla, Tío Quiterio and Andrés Rodrigo (pp. 224–25). Elsewhere, there are updates on some of the characters of the earlier account who have sinced moved to other parts. So, it transpires that the woman who ran the bar in Taracena and the ten-year-old girl there had both moved to Reus many years previously (p. 42). The barber of La Puerta, Pablo Balcón (who actually lived in El Olivar), had gone to Alcalá de Henares, while the mayor of La Puerta was now living in Madrid (pp. 148–49), as was the former mayor of Pastrana (p. 243). Also in Madrid were María and Elena, the two girls that the traveler fell foul of in Pareja in a tantalizing episode that, some forty years on, is still not explained (p. 171).

In addition to these reminders of people encountered in 1946, the second Alcarria narrative also includes meetings between the traveler and relatives of individuals either presented in *Viaje a la Alcarria* or met during that first trip but not recorded in the narrative. Among these are Pedro Montes, the son of the previous owner of the saddlery in Guadalajara (pp. 36–37), and the centenarian husband of the unnamed Durón woman, now dead, who in 1946 gave the traveler a bowl of sheep's milk (p. 153). And, evoking a less touching, though rather more graphic scene, the son of the small boy who, thirty-nine years before, peed "gloriosamente, desafiadoramente" [gloriously, defiantly] (IV, 176) from a balcony in Pareja, introduces himself when the author arrives in that town. The boy's father, it transpires, now almost fifty, is alive and well. Finally, making a more decorous connection with the 1946 visit, the traveler meets the daughter of the woman, now deceased, who owned the inn where he stayed in Pastrana but who did not, in fact, receive a mention in the first travel book.

But by far the most poignant reminders of the many years that have elapsed between the first Alcarria journey and the elderly author's procession of June 1985 come with the frequent references to the demise of so many of those whose acquaintance he first made thirty-nine years earlier. And while the first dedication in the 1986 travel book is to the memory of Gregorio Marañón, who had died in 1960 and to whom, of course, the account of the first Alcarria trip was dedicated, the second dedication that prefaces the text of *Nuevo viaje a la Alcarria* is to the ordinary people that Cela came across in his visit of 1946 and had since died. This brief acknowledgment begins: "A los amigos de mi primer viaje que se fueron quedando en la monótona y cruel estacada de los muertos. De todos hablaré a su tiempo y en su lugar" [To those friends of my first journey who ended up in the monotonous and cruel stockade of the dead. I will speak of them all at the appropriate time and place] (p. 10). Accordingly, the traveler's arrival at the Casa Montes saddlery in Guadalajara begins a somber compilation of many of those who figured in the narrative of the original journey and were no longer alive, and makes occasional mention of the deaths of certain individuals met in 1946 but not included in the account.

When the traveler reaches the familiar saddlery in Guadalajara, the reader is informed of the fate of the earlier owner and his son: "Daniel . . . murió hace ya algún tiempo, hace veinticinco años largos: descanse en paz. Su hijo Daniel, el niño al que el viajero llamó Luisito de la otra vez, también murió: descanse en paz" [Daniel . . . died some time back, twenty-five long years ago: rest in peace. His son Daniel, the boy whom, on the first journey, the traveler called Luisito, also died: rest in peace] (p. 36). Later, at the inn at Torija, the style is repeated: "Marcelina García, el ama del parador, ya ha muerto: descanse en paz. Su hija Segunda Paniagua, la mujer que preguntó al viajero—hace casi cuarenta años—si iba a tomar vino, ya ha muerto: descanse en paz. Saturnino Catalán, el marido de Segunda, ya ha muerto: descanse en paz" [Marcelina García, the innkeeper, has died: rest in peace. Her daughter, Segunda Paniagua, the woman who asked the traveler—almost forty years earlier—if he wanted any wine, has died: rest in peace. Saturnino Catalán, Segunda's husband, has died: rest in peace]. Here, there is a kind of postscript, mentioning that, from time to time, Saturnino would clean the commemorative plaque on the front of the inn and, indeed, had tried to give the traveler the fine iron bed on which he had slept there in 1946 (p. 45). In Cifuentes, the traveler speaks admiringly of Don Niceto, the priest who had recovered his church's alabaster pulpit from a Madrid museum, and who died in 1955. Here, he also mentions the fate of Arbeteta, giving his real name: "El Arbeteta que se dice es don Emeterio y murió en el 63, descanse en paz" [Arbeteta, who was really Don Emeterio, died in 1963, rest in peace] (p. 107). Further on, in Trillo, he notes the circumstances of the death of Quico, his young escort to the Tetas de Viana, who was killed more than twenty years earlier, hit by a truck as he was relieving himself at the side of the road, whereas in La Puerta the traveler simply records the fact that Wenceslao, who took him in his cart to Budia for sixty *pesetas*, had also died.

Sometimes, though, the visitor of 1985 has no hard information and can only speculate on the likely fate of some of those he met in 1946. As his car drives away from Brihuega, he recalls with affection his encounter there with the old man, Jesús, and his donkey, Gorrión, and reflects on their probable fate: "Los dos habrán muerto ya, sin duda, descansen los dos en paz, pero lo más probable es que a ninguno de los dos les haya echado nadie de menos" [Without a doubt, the two of them are dead by now, may they both rest in peace, but the most likely thing is that nobody has missed either of them] (pp. 97–98). And near Cifuentes, he finds himself more or less in the area where he came across another of his companions of the road in the 1946 visit, the altogether dotty peddler, Mierda, and wonders whether he has survived the years: "El Mierda puede que haya muerto, el camino está lleno de trampas y calamidades; en este caso, descanse en paz. También puede que no haya muerto, el camino también está cuajado de remedios y purificaciones" [It is possible that Mierda has died, the road is full of traps and disasters; if so, may he rest in peace. It is also possible that he has not died, the road is also full of cures and purges]. Then, after mentioning that this man, who trusted nobody but the Pope, was about his own age, the traveler muses that he really would like to know what has become of him (p. 120).[5]

At times, however, the visitor shows much less concern or curiosity and may even resort to a rather perfunctory, abbreviated approach to the deceased. For example: "Su padre fue don Faustino, q.e.p.d., que era el alcalde que habiá de la otra vez" [His father was Don Faustino, R.I.P., who was mayor at the time of the other visit] (p. 117), and: "Librada es hija de Carmen Gabarda, q.e.p.d., la hermana de Fabián, q.e.p.d., el que fue consejal de Casasana" [Librada is the daughter of Carmen Gabarda, R.I.P., the sister of Fabián, R.I.P., the one who was a councillor in Casasana] (p. 152).

Throughout *Nuevo viaje a la Alcarria* there are scores of such references to those the traveler met in the Alcarria in 1946 (and others he got to know on later visits) and who had died in the thirty-nine years spanning the two journeys around the area. These recollections are sometimes moving and sometimes simply factual. Occasionally the updates, with their accompanying invocations, can seem a little matter-of-fact, almost as if the traveler is simply tying up loose ends. However, now and again, he does pause to reflect on the inevitability and naturalness of death, and on his own difficulty in reporting the loss of his friends. Thus, after mentioning the death of the priest, Don Niceto, he notes: "El viajero sabe que el uso que tiene el género humano de desaparecer es ley de vida a la que no cabe substraerse pero, pese a todo, no se acostumbra a sembrar de amigos difuntos el recuerdo" [The traveler knows that the habit that human beings have of disappearing is a fact of life that cannot be circumvented, yet, in spite of everything, it is difficult getting used to recalling dead friends] (p. 107). And, still in Cifuentes, when he reveals that the packsaddler, Félix Marco Laina, died in 1970 and that the sick boy he saw there, reading Hans Christian Andersen stories, had died in 1950 or 1951, the traveler acknowledges that his account of this return journey is something of a somber, painful recital: "Esto de andar recontando muertes es algo que le gusta poco al viajero, bueno, quiere decir que no le gusta absolutamente nada, que no le gusta ni pizca" [This business of going around tallying deaths is something that the traveler does not much like. Indeed, he does not like it at all, not one little bit] (p. 109).

THE TEXT OF 1948: ERRORS AND OMISSIONS

While the itinerary of the 1985 visit, the stopovers and celebrations, the renewal of acquaintances, the roll call of the deceased, and the commemorative plaques all serve as reminders of the journey of 1946 and the subsequent published account, the narrative of Cela's second trip does, from time to time, shed some interesting light on certain other aspects of the text of 1948. Here, it is worth recalling that in the dedication that prefaces the first Alcarria trip, Cela states that he had jotted down everything that he saw on the visit and that, since he was writing geography rather than fiction, he was obliged to tell the truth. Quite obviously, it would not be possible for the traveler to note down *every- thing* he saw during the journey or include all of his on-the-road experiences in the published account. So it comes as no real surprise to find that, as was noted above, among the survivors from the 1946 journey encountered in *Nuevo viaje a la Alcarria,* and also amidst the tally of the deceased that permeates the 1986 narrative, mention is made of the names of individuals who do not figure in the earlier travel book. In addition, the record of the 1985 journey also corrects some minor factual errors and, even more interesting, gives the occasional indication of a degree of self-censorship exercised in the account of the first trip.

The edition of *Viaje a la Alcarria* contained in volume 4 of Cela's *Obra completa* (1965) has copious footnotes indicating textual variants in previous versions of the work, as well as a few clarifications and updates. With *Nuevo viaje a la Alcarria* Cela takes a further opportunity to set the record straight on a number of erroneous details regarding people and places mentioned in the 1948 narrative. So, in the body of the text, the reader is informed, for example, that the little boy at the saddlery in Guadalajara was called Daniel and not Luisito (p. 56), and that, nearing Brihuega in 1946, what the traveler took to be the Ibarra Palace was, in fact, that of Don Luis (p. 72). Also, the German mountaineer who lived on the outskirts of Trillo had a route named after him in the Sierra de Guadarrama, not in the Sierra de Guadalajara (p.129), while the

Francisco Pérez associated with the inn at Sacedón and who was described as deceased in the first travel book, did not, in fact, die until
1960 (p. 194). Then, in the closing stages of the narrative, it is pointed
out that the Visigothic ruins of Recópolis are to the east of the Tagus
River and not, as was indicated in *Viaje a la Alcarria*, on the western side
(p. 259).

The correction of these details does of course provide some useful,
factual tidying up. However, these amendments are much less interesting than, for example, the brief inclusion in *Nuevo viaje a la Alcarria* of a
recalled local perspective on the traveler's presence in 1946 or the author's acknowledgment in the 1986 narrative of material omitted from
Viaje a la Alcarria and the reasons for such omissions. Let us first consider the implications of the snippet of additional information concerning one scene in the original journey. In Pareja, the retired veterinary
surgeon, Don Leo, recalls the traveler's arrival thirty-nine years earlier
at the same hostelry where the surgeon finds himself in June 1985:

—Me acuerdo perfectamente de aquel día, me acuerdo como si hubiera sido
ayer. Yo estaba en esta misma taberna tomándome unos chiquitos con el
médico cuando se presentó él con una señorita rubia, creo que era extranj-
era, sí, tenía que ser alemana o sueca o inglesa, y nos preguntó por el camino
de Casasana. Venía hecho una pena, una verdadera lástima, daban ganas de
socorrerlo con un real, iba con las alpargatas rotas y con un traje muy ajado
de caqui, parecía un uniforme de miliciano; si me lo permite, hasta le diría
que iba sucio, bueno, casi sucio. Estaban los dos agotados porque venían
andando desde Budia. Hay quien dice que también venía otro con ellos, pero
yo no lo vi. (p. 172)

["I remember that day perfectly, I remember it as if it were yesterday. I was
in this same bar, having a drop or two with the doctor when he appeared
with a young blonde lady, I think she was a foreigner, that's right, she must
have been German, or Swedish, or English, and asked us the way to Casasana. He was a sorry sight, in a dreadful state, you really felt like helping
him out, his espadrilles were torn and he was wearing a crumpled khaki
uniform, like that of a militiaman; if I may be permitted, I'd even say that
he was dirty, well, a bit dirty. They were both exhausted, since they'd
walked here from Budia. Some say that there was another person with
them, but I didn't see anyone else."]

The accuracy of this account (which was made to a third party) appears to be confirmed by the traveler's comment that Don Leo has a
good memory, while the participation of Don Leo in the events of 1946
is confirmed when it is noted that he is the one who spoke with Fabián
Gabarda's mother in Casasana (p.172). However, there is no indication

in the text of *Viaje a la Alcarria* of Don Leo's presence in either Pareja or Casasana. Indeed, the original narrative carries a somewhat different version of the traveler's arrival in Pareja, describing a solitary and rather more stately appearance, and one which certainly does not give the reader a picture of an apparently distressed, grubby figure entering the bar, along with Conchita Stichaner. Thus the inclusion of Don Leo's recollection serves as an indication that there is a significant difference between the reality of the traveler's condition and actions when he reached Pareja in June 1946 and the narrative presentation of the scene in question.

On the issue of material omitted from *Viaje a la Alcarria*, the account of the 1985 visit refers to several episodes not included in the first travel book. However, the two most fascinating pieces of new information concern the figure of Tarsicio Salvador and also the traveler's claim of an amorous liaison that took place in Trillo. Apparently, the traveler met the rather roguish Salvador on his excursion to the Tetas de Viana, and observes that since he deliberately chose not to mention him in the original Alcarria book, he will now make amends. The reason for the earlier omission is, apparently, that Salvador was being pursued by the authorities and was possibly involved in the resistance movement (pp. 130–31). Concerning his romantic adventure in Trillo, the traveler announces that he had a passionate fling with a good-looking local widow. However, he refuses to reveal her name and refers to her instead as Doña Martirio Ejea (p. 133).

But undoubtedly the most intriguing silences in the first Alcarria book involve the lack of reference to the large-scale destruction inflicted on some parts of the area in 1937, during the Battle of Guadalajara. In the first travel narrative there are fifteen or so brief references or allusions to the civil war that had ended just over seven years before Cela's first tour of the Alcarria. However, a third of these are no more than temporal indicators of the "before the war" or "after the war" type. On another occasion, the subject of the conflict is alighted on when the traveler tells Armando Mondéjar López stories about the struggle, stories which apparently leave the boy wide-eyed. Interestingly, when Armando enquires if he was wounded in the fighting, no reply is given (IV, 57). Later in *Viaje a la Alcarria*, when the traveler gets to Brihuega, the small town at the heart of the Battle of Guadalajara (8–22 March 1937), he transcribes the content of the marble plaque commemorating the bicentenary of the battle that took place there in December 1710, during the War of the Spanish Succession, and notes some shrapnel damage to the tablet (IV, 78–79). Also here, three different inhabitants do no more than allude to the bombing and strafing of March 1937 when they refer to how things were "antes de la aviación" [before the aircraft came], while one of them expresses delight as he recounts that it was here that the Italian troops first took flight (IV, 81–98). Subsequently, there is passing mention of a bomb-damaged church tower in Cifuentes (IV, 117); a Civil Guard refers, in a light manner, to the "Glorioso Movimiento Nacional" [Glorious National Movement] (IV, 173);[6] Felipe el Sastre tells the traveler that he and a close Galician friend were both wounded on the same day, fighting in the Sierra de Alcubierre (IV, 199–200);[7] a number of songs being sung by a group of maids on the bus from Sacedón to Tendilla have associations with the war or its aftermath (IV, 216–17), and a friar in Pastrana mentions the vandalism of the "reds" when they occupied the town (IV, 237).

Such references and allusions, noticeable for their brevity and infrequency, are also interesting for their restraint and lack of detail. The Guadalajara offensive, a significant action of the early phase of the war, was intended to complete the Nationalist encirclement of Madrid, and is described by Raymond Carr as "largely an Italian affair."[8] Of the more than forty thousand troops assembled for the push, around thirty-five thousand were Italians of the so-called Corpo di Truppe Volontarie (CTV), supported by about eighty Italian light tanks and a similar number of Italian aircraft.[9] The offensive began on 8 March 1937 and two days later Brihuega was taken by units of the CTV. This was followed by the fall of Trijueque, and by 13 March the Italians had reached Torija, some fifteen kilometers from Guadalajara. This was the limit of the Nationalist advance.

The previous day a snowstorm had prevented Nationalist aircraft from taking off from their improvised landing strips and this allowed Republican planes, which were operating from purpose-built runways, to bomb and strafe Italian positions and columns at will. On that same day Trijueque was recaptured and so too was the Ibarra Palace, the derelict building misnamed by the traveler in *Viaje a la Alcarria*. In fact, in André Malraux's novel, *L'Espoir* [Days of Hope] (1937), the third and final part of which largely deals with the Battle of Guadalajara, there is some description of the fighting for the Ibarra Palace.[10] Yet this engagement, in which the forces of the CTV inside the building were attacked by their fellow countrymen of the Garibaldi Battalion, as well as by French and Belgian units of the International Brigades, was merely a small part of the advance of the Republican forces on nearby Brihuega.

According to official Republican sources quoted in the Madrid newspaper, *El Socialista*, of Friday 19 March 1937, the previous Tuesday afternoon a squadron of fifteen aircraft dropped 360 bombs on enemy positions in Brihuega and the surrounding area, and then flew low to machine gun Italian and other Nationalist troops. A little later, the report continues, another squadron of bombers, escorted this time by forty-five fighter planes, bombed the same targets for an hour. The fighters then fired some twenty-five thousand rounds at insurgent troop positions in this area.[11] However, the air attacks of 16 March on Brihuega were a prelude to the even heavier assault of two days later. Hugh Thomas reports that at 1:30 P.M. on Thursday 18 March Brihuega was attacked by more than a hundred Republican aircraft. This was followed by artillery fire. Thomas then describes the final assault and the hasty retreat of the Italian forces:

> At two o'clock, Lister's and Cipriano Mera's two divisions, with seventy of Pavlov's tanks, attacked, the one in the west, the second in the east, aiming to encircle the town. They had almost achieved this when the Italians received orders to retreat. They did so, so fast that the action was almost a rout, down the only road still open. The pursuit continued for several miles. (p. 602)

The recapture of Brihuega marked the end of the Nationalist offensive in the Guadalajara area. The action lasted a further three or four days as the insurgents were pushed back to a position that restricted their territorial gain to a maximum of about eighteen kilometers over a front line of approximately seventy kilometers. The price the Nationalists paid for this relatively modest advance was heavy. Raymond Carr is cautious when assessing the importance of the outcome of the Guadalajara campaign, suggesting that "it was not a great victory either in terms of prisoners and equipment taken or territory recaptured," and seeing it as "a moral as much as a military triumph" (p. 164). Although acknowledging the limitations of the Republican victory, Paul Preston signals the wider implications of a battle that "finally broke Franco's determination to win the war at Madrid and imposed upon him a momentous strategic *volte-face.*" Preston adds that the capture of documents showing that many of the Italians were regular soldiers revealed to the world "the Nationalist lie that they were all volunteers" (p. 235). Furthermore, the defeat at Guadalajara was a personal humiliation for Benito Mussolini, and Thomas notes that "the discomforture of the previously overweening Italian ally" was not unwelcome to Franco and his high command (p. 604). Finally, Ramón Tamames points out that the Republican victory was significant for many in the international community since it showed for the first time that Fascism was not invincible (p. 279).

It was through the heart of the site of this campaign that Cela had wandered in June 1946. His account does, of course, include a whole chapter (the only one in *Viaje a la Alcarria* totally focused on a single town or village) describing his stay in Brihuega, the town at the center of the battle and the recapture of which had marked the moment of Republican victory. Even so, in an area and a place where memories and damage would have been relatively fresh, no attempt is made in the 1948 Alcarria book to elaborate on the military operations of the Battle of Guadalajara or indicate the local damage and suffering that would have resulted. In chapter 4 of the first travel book, simply entitled "Brihuega," references to the campaign are sparse and largely oblique, while in other parts of the work allusions to the war are equally infrequent and usually vague. The conclusion to be drawn from this remarkably restrained approach must presumably be that the author was mindful of the censor or that he found the recent conflict too painful to review in his narrative.

Many years later, when Cela came to write the account of the 1985 journey, the possible intervention of the censor would no longer have been a factor. Also, it is likely that the author's own sensitivity to the conflict, as well as that of others involved, would not have weighed so heavily in his considerations. But whatever the reasons, with *Nuevo viaje a la Alcarria* the traveler is substantially and dramatically more descriptive and specific when he does refer to the hostilities of 1936–39, and particularly to local actions, than he was in the first Alcarria travel work. Although in the account of the 1985 trip there are only a dozen or so references or allusions to the civil war, these are for the most part much more informative with regard to actions in the Guadalajara campaign and more precise and graphic when it comes to the destruction caused by the fighting.

When, at the start of chapter 3, the traveler's old comrade-in-arms, Iñigo Taragudo Méndez, turns up in the city of Guadalajara, the war is largely dealt with through a series of reminiscences about various colorful characters that the two men came across during their military service. However, toward the end of these recollections the traveler inserts a note of pain and indignation as he reflects on the fact that, in all probability, he will never again see this old companion who managed to survive what he calls "la vesania de quienes les empujaron a liarse a tiros para nada" [the insanity of those who forced them to start shooting at each other, all for nothing] (p. 41). No such sentiments were aired in *Viaje a la Alcarria* and, in fact, it was not until the late 1950s and the 1960s that Cela began to reveal in his writing the resentment he felt at the carnage and senselessness of the war.[12] Indeed, in *San Camilo, 1936,* which deals with the opening days of the civil war, the author uses the brief dedication of the novel to express his bitterness at all foreign involvement in the conflict.

Yet, as was noted earlier, the presence of Mussolini's forces in the

Battle of Guadalajara receives only a passing, dismissive reference in the first Alcarria book. However, when, nearly four decades later, Cela wrote the account of the return trip, this aspect of the Guadalajara campaign, although developed in the narrative, is dealt with in a factual rather than judgmental manner. So, on finding himself in the vicinity of the palaces of Don Luis and Ibarra, the author mentions that the front was here and shortly after notes that in these parts the Italians of the Garibaldi Battalion gave a hiding to their fellow countrymen of General Roatta's army (pp. 73–74). Subsequently, when the traveler is in nearby Brihuega, he makes his excuses and moves away from two retired locals who are cheerfully regaling him with the details of the positions of the German and Italian battalions of the International Brigades and of the four divisions of Roatta's opposing forces: "—Pues enfrente estaban los Camisas Negras de Rossi, los Llamas Negras de Coppi, los Flechas Negras de Nuvolari [*sic*] y la división Littorio de Bergonzoli, todos a las órdenes del general Roatta. ¡Se armó un buen cacao!" ["So, facing them were Rossi's Blackshirts, Coppi's Black Flames, Nuvolari's [*sic*] Black Arrows, and Bergonzoli's Littorio Division, all under the command of General Roatta. It was a real set-to!"] (pp. 90–92).[13]

But where *Nuevo viaje a la Alcarria* departs most noticeably from the limited and restrained treatment accorded to the Civil War in the first travel book is in the references to the local destruction caused by the hostilities. In chapter 5 of the 1948 work, as the traveler, old Jesús, and his donkey pass through Masegoso, the village is simply described as "grande, polvoriento, de color plata, con algunos reflejos de oro a la luz de la mañana, con un cruce de carreteras" [large, dusty, silver-colored, with a few golden reflections in the morning light, and with a crossroads] (IV, 106–07). However, in the second Alcarria narrative there are graphic indications of the damage sustained there in 1937, some evidence of which Cela would certainly have seen in 1946. So, with reference to the loss and recapture of the place, the reader is informed: "A Masegoso le dieron dos pasadas durante la guerra civil, una al pelo y otra a la contra, y lo dejaron como la palma de la mano, lo plancharon y lo tuvo que reconstruir la dirección general de Regiones Devastadas" [During the civil war they gave Masegoso two sweeps, one with the nap and the other against it, and they left it like the palm of your hand; they flattened it and the Office for Devastated Regions had to rebuild it]. Shortly after, and just to emphasize the point, the traveler adds: "A la vieja iglesia y a la picota las barrió la desbocada ventolina de la guerra, que no dejó títere con cabeza por todo el contorno" [The old church and the *picota* were swept away by the gusts of war, which destroyed everything in the area] (p. 102).

In fact, whereas in *Viaje a la Alcarria* the only confirmation of serious war damage to the fabric of an old building or monument comes at the close of chapter 5, with the reference to the tower of the parish church of San Salvador in Cifuentes that was rent by a bomb, the second Alcarria book contains a number of mentions of the damage (and also the looting) suffered by local churches during the hostilities. In June 1946, when he was almost midway between Torija and Brihuega, the traveler had seen to the south of the road the church tower and houses of Fuentes de la Alcarria, but had not made the detour to visit the village. This was remedied in 1985 when, among other things, he noted that the wayside shrine had disappeared during the war and also observed that the church suffered extensively as Republicans and Italians, between them, wrecked everything. Later, in Cifuentes, he once more mentions the bomb damage to the tower of San Salvador, but now adds that the church's magnificent treasures, including paintings, were looted during the conflict. Then, in Sacedón, he notes that the fine-looking parish church is empty, having been ransacked in the war by those he terms "los enemigos de la religión" [the enemies of religion]. However, in order to provide some kind of balance and also show that the twentieth century and nonbelievers have no monopoly of such acts of vandalism, the traveler also recalls that, during the nineteenth-century dynastic struggles, the same church was set ablaze by the Carlists, "los amigos de la religión" [the friends of religion] (pp. 192–93). In *Nuevo viaje a la Alcarria*, then, the traveler finally acknowledges the extent of local war damage—something that he would have been well aware of in his trip of June 1946, but chose not to portray in the first Alcarria narrative.

THE NEW ALCARRIA AND THE NEW SPAIN

The account of Cela's 1985 trip to the Alcarria, then, serves as a reminder of, a point of comparison with, and a supplement to, the narrative of 1948. However, if the theme of the past, in the shape of revisits, reminders of the war, personal recollections, and reunions is a dominant feature of *Nuevo viaje a la Alcarria*, so too is the theme of the present, with constant indications of how the Alcarria and Spain have changed during the period spanning the two trips.

In the first of the three dedications that preface the narrative of *Nuevo viaje a la Alcarria*, Cela explains that this second Alcarria travel work is being dedicated to the late Gregorio Marañón in recognition of the fondness that he showed for travel accounts dealing with "nuestra vieja España" [our old Spain] (p. 8). Yet, while in the new travel book Cela constantly evokes the relatively recent past and in so doing also gives a steady testimony to the passage of time, it cannot be claimed, by any stretch of the imagination, that he is seeking to rediscover and reveal any kind of "old" Spain. Indeed, one of the principal and constant features of *Nuevo viaje a la Alcarria* is the way in which it bears witness to the new Alcarria and the new Spain.

As was mentioned in chapter 4, when Cela undertook his journey around the Guadalajara section of the Alcarria in June 1946 France had, on 1 March of that year, closed her border with Spain. Also, the country was shunned by most member states of the United Nations and many members of that organization were seeking to intensify the international isolation of the Franco regime. Paul Preston points out that in response to such pressures: "Franco's propaganda machinery was working frantically to persuade the Spanish people that Spain was the victim of an international siege" (p. 559). Thirty-nine years later, when Cela retraced much of his original route, he traveled through a Spain that was heavily Europeanized and culturally and politically very much part of the international community. It was now a democratic country with a society that was relaxed and enjoying a prosperity that was a far cry from the hardship suffered by so many back in 1946. Indeed, a prominent feature of *Nuevo viaje a la Alcarria* is the way in which these changes are reflected in a work that is a testament to the commercial and cultural face of the new Spain, with the elderly traveler chronicling the inescapable aspects of a thoroughly westernized Spanish society and also indicating both the benefits and disadvantages of progress and consumerism.

In each of the Alcarria travel books, the second chapter describes the preliminary stage of the trip, the journey from Madrid to Guadalajara, with the 1948 version showing the young traveler making his way on foot, before first light, through a gloomy and depressing urban landscape to the Atocha station and thence by train to Guadalajara. In *Nuevo viaje a la Alcarria*, the corresponding phase of the journey shows the traveler being seen off from his hotel by a couple of dignitaries and then, in the comfort of his limousine, musing on how the prostitutes of yesteryear are being supplanted by transvestites touting for business. Hereafter, as he is driven through the capital and then on to the road to Guadalajara, he observes the new, sprawling Madrid. After a while, he takes in the changes to the landscape between the capital and his first destination, all the time reminiscing about locations as they once were and old acquaintances associated with the places he now glides through.

Overall, the environment experienced at this stage by the chauffeured traveler is both intimidating and depressing. In contrast to the indications in chapter 2 of *Viaje a la Alcarria* of the harsh conditions confronting many of the inhabitants of 1946 Madrid, what the traveler now witnesses as he heads through the capital and out toward the Alcarria are the features and trappings of an industrialized, mechanized, and commercialized society. Thus, as he makes his way out of the center of Madrid, the traveler notices the imposing and variously colored road signs and then big, busy highways, such as the M-30: "Con sus cinco o seis carriles de automóviles que pasan cagando centellas y ensuciando el aire" [With its five or six lanes of cars that go along shitting out sparks and dirtying the air] (p. 25). But in spite of such sentiments, he refuses to use his air-conditioning, preferring instead to inhale air from the outside, regardless of the fact that it is contaminated by the city's dust, factory chimneys, sweating bodies, and car emissions. In this way the author sweeps along, noting the Pegaso factory, the low-flying aircraft making their way in and out of the Barajas airport, the functional and impersonal buildings of multinational companies, glossy advertising on the billboards, and bland, discolored buildings that engulf the highway. He reflects on the mediocrity concealed beneath the slick commercial messages and, when he realizes that he has not seen a single bird since leaving Madrid, he muses that "este paisaje desorientado es la negación del orden de la vida; esto parece Europa" [this disorientated landscape is the negation of how life should be; this looks like Europe] (p. 29). Yet it is not just "Europe" that appears to have impressed its character on this part of Spain. Elsewhere, as he pulls away from the capital, the traveler sees gaudy, fast-food outlets that look as if they belong in Arizona, while new housing developments at Alcalá de Henares remind him of the suburbs of Los Angeles.

After a brief stopover in a rapidly modernizing Guadalajara, with its now confusing road network, pedestrian zones, and young women in tight jeans, the traveler spots a car scrapyard on the outskirts of the city, and when he gets to Torija he realizes that he has not caught sight of a single mule since leaving Guadalajara, which provokes the wry comment: "Algo debe estar cambiando en el país" [Something must be changing in the country] (p. 44). Hereafter, as he makes his way around various towns and villages of the Alcarria, he sees constant evidence of a late twentieth-century, consumerist society: less dramatic or threatening than huge trucks hurtling along busy highways or the polluted air of big cities, but just as indicative of the new Spain.

In various parts of the narrative there are reminders of the omnipresence of television and of the popularity of American television shows. Vans advertising electrical appliances can be seen everywhere and in Cifuentes the traveler notes all kinds of electrical goods on sale. He also mockingly suggests that "authentic" Japanese, plastic statuettes of Our Lady of Fatima are available. "University" sweatshirts are on sale, and in Almonacid he sees mothers in jeans and boys wearing T-shirts that advertise merchandise or places. The local girls, on the other hand, are neatly dressed in pleated skirts. The traveler comes across bars with American names or American-style interiors, furnished with table football and fruit machines. In Brihuega, he and four female companions go to a "pub" and order Irish coffees. Budia has "pubs" and discothèques, while Cifuentes, too, has a disco (that is occasionally frequented by attractive, female vacationers) and also a "whiskería" [whiskey bar].

But as well as prosperity, consumerism, and new tastes in food, drinks, and leisure, the traveler also indicates other changes in social behavior, with a number of references to the presence of punks, hippies, and (on a more spiritual plane) members of Hare Krishna. Some social attitudes and roles are also seen to have changed. While mention is made of younger women wearing pants or jeans, the traveler also acknowledges that there are now female doctors, pharmacists, vets, mayors, and also a town clerk. He even ventures to suggest to his female driver that, before the year 2010, women will be allowed into the priesthood. On the subject of the Church, he observes that priests are friendlier than they used to be. However, in Pastrana, where the traveler notices an up-to-date loudspeaker system in a church, he comments somewhat disdainfully: "Ahora los curas tienen que ayudarse de la técnica porque los crían con pelargón, ahora ya no es como antes y usan micrófono" [Because of their pampered upbringing, priests now have to resort to technology; things have changed and they use microphones] (p. 245). Furthermore, when in the same town he comes across four young Spanish girls with the altogether untraditional names of Vanesa, Deborah, Samanta, and Noemí it seems as if this is another area in which the Church is adapting to modern ways. But he dismisses this modern laxness with children's names as the product of liberal trendiness and even scoffingly suggests that the girls concerned have two cousins of their own age who go by the names of Melisa and Desiré Borrego Tamajón.

Yet while many aspects of present-day life just surprise or irritate the traveler (he even laments the fact that rubbish is not as appealing as it used to be), the account of the 1985 trip also contains reminders of some of the more threatening features of late twentieth-century living. So, when he catches sight of the Instituto Leprológico [Leprosy Institute] near Trillo, he reflects on various diseases that have been terrible scourges over the centuries and predicts that AIDS, and not nuclear energy, is on the way to becoming the curse of the twenty-first century. Later, he mentions the drug rehabilitation center at Hontanillas but observes with some skepticism that nearly all those who attend for treatment revert to their former dependence when they get back to the city. And in Pareja, noticing that on this visit there are no storks to be seen flying over the place, the traveler readily suggests that biocides are responsible for the disappearance of these birds. Indeed, he comments on chemical additives in food, and elsewhere denounces the use of insecticides and pesticides for the damage that these agents do to the wrong targets: killing birds and animals; harming children; poisoning crops, fruit, and vegetables; and generally destroying wildlife in the water and on land. Certainly, he acknowledges, people are waking up to the dangers of these practices, but he also recognizes that there is still much to do in this area.

On the positive side, however, mention is made that Hontanillas, now a ghost village, belongs to the Instituto para la Conservación de la Naturaleza (Institute for the Conservation of Nature), as does Torronteras, with its resident ecologists. And although the traveler accepts that society is beginning to respond, albeit tardily, to man's careless and at times reckless exploitation of the environment, he is also gratified to note the attempts to remedy the past neglect or damage suffered by the monuments and artifacts of former ages. He mentions the preservation work undertaken to date by the association of Amigos de Brihuega (Friends of Brihuega), the almost completed and extremely successful restoration of the Palacio del Infantado in Guadalajara, which was seen as a ruined shell in *Viaje a la Alcarria,* the rebuilding of the castle at Torija, and the slow but thoughtful restoration of the Palacio Ducal in Pastrana. On an altogether smaller scale, the author is heartened when he is shown the elegantly restored, fourteenth-century books in Hueva.

In addition to these encouraging signs of concern for both the natural environment and the historical and cultural legacy, the traveler points out that there are some altogether more mundane indicators of progress and rising standards of comfort. Bars and restaurants have clean lavatories, there are many good inns with hot, running water, the houses now get piped water, and people have domestic appliances to make life that little bit easier. All in all, then, in the mid-1980s the towns and villages of the Alcarria largely convey a sense of well-being and of general prosperity. At the same time, though, occasional reference is made to villages that have been abandoned and to the declining population of certain towns. For example, there is mention of almost deserted villages near Brihuega, of people leaving the land around Huetos, of abandoned hamlets near Gualda, and of empty villages in other parts. It is also pointed out that Casasana, with a population of four hundred in 1946, now has a mere eighty inhabitants, Auñón has fallen from a population of more than one thousand after the civil war to fewer than three hundred, while Pastrana, with three thousand inhabitants after the war, has around thirteen hundred in the mid-1980s.

Yet these examples of abandonment and decline are balanced by mention of the fact that the village of Moranchel is being rebuilt to accommodate workers from the nearby nuclear power station; Almonacid is prosperous because of tourism and the proximity of another nuclear generator; Durón, now with eight kilometers of beach in its municipality, is a prosperous-looking tourist center, while El Olivar, described in the account of the 1946 journey as "un pueblo miserable, perdido en la sierra" [a wretched village, lost in the hills] (IV, 165), is now a community of artists and a retreat for those seeking peace and quiet. Indeed, while *Nuevo viaje a la Alcarria* frequently indicates the physical changes that have taken place in the area between 1946 and 1985, particularly the creation of huge reservoirs and the construction of dams, viaducts, nuclear power stations, roads, and housing developments, the narrative also brings to light the widespread presence of leisure seekers and vacationers. Summer tourism, mainly developed in the wake of the adaptation of the reservoirs for bathing, sailing, and other water sports, is indicated with passing references to the tourists in the area and also with mention of hotels and holiday apartments. Local properties are even being purchased by foreign families.

In his first travel work, Cela memorably describes the Alcarria as *"un hermoso país al que a la gente no le da la gana ir"* [*a lovely area that people do not want to visit*] (IV, 27). With the journey of 1985, the traveler shows a district playing host to considerable numbers of summer visitors and clearly no longer off the beaten track. In addition, the impression of psychological and geographical isolation that informs the account of the first Alcarria journey is replaced in *Nuevo viaje a la Alcarria* by a marked and sustained sense that, for better and for worse, both the Alcarria and Spain have been fully integrated into modern, Western society and their people transformed accordingly. Although in the first dedication to *Nuevo viaje a la Alcarria* Cela makes reference to "old Spain," what he presents in the second Alcarria narrative, and feels ambivalent about, is a prosperous, more comfortable, more relaxed, more westernized, and brasher "new Spain."

ROUNDING THINGS OFF

In an interview published in early 1990, Cela justified his flamboyant conduct in *Nuevo viaje a la Alcarria,* mentioned how much he enjoyed himself during the 1985 trip, and stated that the only thing that the second Alcarria book had in common with the first one was the location. *Nuevo viaje a la Alcarria*, the author noted, was not intended to be a second part, but simply another book with the same setting.[14] Yet this suggestion is either a little disingenuous or, possibly, a tongue-in-cheek response. Certainly, the opening words of chapter 2 of the second Alcarria work: "El viajero no se levanta al alba" [The traveler does not get up at daybreak] (p. 19), are a lighthearted reminder of the Cervantine echoes of the opening of chapter 2 of *Viaje a la Alcarria:* "La del alba sería" [It was around daybreak] (IV, 35). But setting aside its literary implications, this chapter opening is also a humorous rejection, by an elderly traveler, of the Spartan requirement of making an early start to a journey. (In *Viaje a la Alcarria* the young traveler had, of course, gone on to say that he had got up even before dawn.) In fact, the "La del alba sería" formula is repeated in chapter 2 of *Judíos, moros y cristianos* (V, 165), while the second part of *Viaje al Pirineo de Lérida* begins with the variation: "Faltaba aún mucho para ser la del alba" [It was still a long time to daybreak] (VI, 501). However, in the early pages of *Nuevo viaje a la Alcarria* the traveler acknowledges that he has time on his hands. Accordingly, he gets up from his hotel bed at a leisurely 8:30 or 9:00 A.M.

For the June 1985 return journey to the Alcarria he was, of course, provided with the comforts that age and status had earned him, including a chauffeur-driven limousine. Consequently, although the return journey traces much of the route of 1946, the pace of travel is clearly very different. As a result of this, the account of the trip is not as unhurried as that of 1946 and the descriptions of the rural landscape are less detailed than was the case with *Viaje a la Alcarria*. In *Notes from a Small Island* (1995), the American author, Bill Bryson, observes that he did not enjoy his tour of the Cotswolds because he used a car for this part of his journey around Britain, and he comments: "You are so sealed off from the world in a moving vehicle and the pace is all wrong."[15] Certainly, with *Nuevo viaje a la Alcarria*, as the traveler moves around in his Rolls-Royce and is constantly catching sight of things and observing their presence, it comes as no surprise to find that he is normally restricted to the briefest of notices, in effect verbal snapshots, of passing images. Indeed, during the periods in which he is being driven from place to place the narrative is largely composed of dialogue, banter, memories, anecdotes, as well as brief observations and pieces of information that provide fast-moving background material on locations, inhabitants, aspects of local history or geography, and so on. And in between the driving come the stops: the revisiting of towns, villages, and buildings, the renewal of acquaintances, the official functions, escorted tours, and the general fêting of the famous guest.

However, here a note of caution is necessary. Cela's narrative shows the traveler constantly being honored, applauded, and treated with great respect and affection. But this is, of course, very much the author's version of the journey and of the receptions experienced en route.

In chapter 3, mention was made of Michael Jacobs's account of how, in the summer of 1991, the gardener at the Royal Textile Factory in Brihuega had been critical of Cela's travel-writing methods. He also told the British writer that people in the area did not have much regard for the famous man. Subsequently, Jacobs adds that a librarian in Trillo had also criticized the Galician's literary approach (although in the vaguest of terms) and goes on to note that the director of the local Leprosy Institute became angry when Cela's name cropped up, observing: "He treated this region very badly." After this rather general condemnation (which fails to specify which of the two Alcarria trips is being referred to, presumably the second), the director turned his attention to Cela's attempted balloon trip over the Tetas de Viana—which did not succeed in its flamboyant mission and ended in a crashlanding in an isolated spot. Here, the medical man notes rather grumpily that the thwarted expedition caused "a lot of trouble" (p. 83). It also caused some resentment in a different quarter. Francisco Umbral mentions that the Italian photographer, Gigi Corbetta, who was part of the press party on the 1985 Alcarria trip, told him that he had pulled Cela from the crashed balloon and led him several kilometers to safety. Corbetta complained to Umbral that Cela had made no reference to this in the account (p. 99). But to return to the British writer: Michael Jacobs notes that it was not until he reached Pastrana that a kind word for the author came his way: "For the first time in my whole stay in the Alcarria, I heard someone say something complimentary about Cela: 'He's a great writer, a bit too strong in his language perhaps, but a great writer'" (p. 85). However, Jacobs quickly learned that the priest who uttered this accolade was none other than the Don Licinio who had been responsible for the erection in 1976 of the commemorative tile plaques signaling notable points in the first Alcarria journey and who, indeed, is referred to in *Nuevo viaje a la Alcarria* as a friend of the author and an "hombre cultivado" [cultured person] (p. 245).

There is, then, another side to this or any other travel narrative, one that the reader is not normally given access to and, quite possibly, one that the traveler does not see. Certainly, what the reader is presented with in *Nuevo viaje a la Alcarria* is a travel narrative that reveals the author's perception and selection of events: one that for the most part, records a series of warm receptions and guided walkabouts in the towns and villages of the Guadalajara section of the Alcarria. These functions and strolls are linked by the on-the-road sections of the account. Here, interspersed with snatches of description, snippets of information, opinions, adages, anecdotes, lists of nicknames, and so on, the traveler engages in general chitchat with his driver, or with any other occupants of the Rolls-Royce who may be present for part of the journey. Sometimes, it seems as if he is simply talking to himself. And despite the tally of the deceased that becomes such a prominent feature of the narrative, as well as other acknowledgments of the unwelcome changes that the years have witnessed, the overall tone of Cela's sixth travel work is generally cheerful, occasionally frivolous, and sometimes salacious or crude. By its very nature, though, this account is also heavily self-indulgent and often reflects a journey that has all the trappings of a public revel. This is nowhere more evident than in the flight in the hot air balloon.

Yet, despite the levity and carnival spirit that mark many of the scenes and actions of *Nuevo viaje a la Alcarria*, and the sober moments when the traveler sees unappealing changes or mentions the demise of so many of those he met in 1946, there is one additional, solemn aspect of Cela's last travel work that merits attention. While the second Alcarria narrative soon develops into the record of a public homage to Cela the writer and celebrity, it also reveals the author's own constant and almost ritualistic reverence for those who have passed along the roads before him. In chapter 2 of *Judíos, moros y cristianos* the reader is quietly informed that the traveler wishes to visit Peñaranda de Duero "para tocar la picota en la que tantos vagabundos habrán sido descuartizados" [so that he can touch the *picota* on which so many vagabonds must have been quartered] (V, 179). He then goes on to discuss the location of *picotas* in various provinces of Old Castile.

The word *picota*, unsatisfactorily translated into English as "pillory" and sometimes "gibbet," signifies a stone column, originally located on the outskirts of towns and villages. The *picota* sometimes served as a place of execution or lesser punishment, and was also used to exhibit the body, or perhaps just the head (on the spike or blade occasionally found on the column's capital) of an executed criminal. Also, convicted criminals could be shackled to the column. Part of the intention of such displays was to serve as a warning not only to local people but also to travelers passing through a town or village.[16]

When Cela made his first trip to the Alcarria, he appears to have taken no especial interest in these grim, although sometimes ornate, stone columns. As he came into Cifuentes in 1946 he certainly noted the hill outside the town that was formerly used for executions and expressed a regret that the fearful silhouette of the *rollo* (frequently used as an alternative term for *picota*) no longer stood on the hilltop. He rather ghoulishly added that "hubiera hecho muy hermoso" [it would have looked splendid] (IV, 108). However, in the second Alcarria narrative he makes a point of seeking out these somber reminders of a bygone age. When they are no longer standing, he tries to find out what became of them.

Not long after leaving Guadalajara, when he gets to Torija, the traveler comes across his first *picota* of the 1985 trip, noting that it is a well-preserved, solemn, and handsome-looking one. Unfortunately, though, it has been turned into a street lamp, a modern fate, he comes to learn, that has also befallen the *picotas* of Fuentes de la Alcarria, Ruguilla, and Peñalver. The structure found in Cifuentes is described as being well-preserved and is even surrounded by a small garden, while the ones at Valderrebollo, Alhóndiga, and Hueva have carved-stone skulls or heads adorning them. And in spite of its use for street lighting, the *picota* at Ruguilla has the classic blade on its capital. Elsewhere, however, in Brihuega, Alocén, Moratilla, and Almonacid, the *picotas* are badly damaged or in disrepair. The traveler also notes that Masegoso's was destroyed in the civil war, that of Chillarón del Rey had simply gone, while the Albalete *picota* was removed when road widening took place.

There is mention of local *picotas* in nearly every chapter of *Nuevo viaje a la Alcarria* and it is possible that the author's interest during the second Alcarria visit in these structures, with their grim associations, is no more than the rekindling of an erstwhile enthusiasm. When the traveler bumps into a friend from Fuentenovilla, a village *not* on the itinerary, the only information given about that particular place (which lies some fifteen kilometers to the southwest of Pastrana) is that it has the most beautiful *picota* in the whole of the Alcarria and that a drawing of it was published in a famous Spanish magazine more than a hundred years earlier (p. 241).[17] Yet, the concern with *picotas* that is pursued in the second Alcarria journey would seem to be much more than a renewed curiosity in an old interest. The seeking out of *picotas*, in towns and villages, soon turns into a kind of pilgrimage: an unstated act of homage paid by one old traveler to unknown and perhaps ill-fated wayfarers of earlier times.

The notion of pilgrimage undoubtedly makes a strange bedfellow for some of the flamboyant and even frivolous activities recounted in *Nuevo viaje a la Alcarria*. But, as has been pointed out, the work does have its sobering aspects, notably the traveler's recollections of those who had died since the 1946 trip. Indeed, despite the frequent levity and self-indulgence that marks the account of the second tour of the Alcarria, and setting aside the suspicion that the principal motives for the 1985 journey were quite likely a combination of the publisher's eye for a good, commercial opportunity and the author's appetite for self-promotion, *Nuevo viaje a la Alcarria* is in many ways the most personal and most moving of Cela's travel narratives. In addition, the account of the 1985 trip, the least "geographical" of his works, rounds off the author's travel writing with a certain sense of both continuity and completion. It also sounds an unmistakable valedictory note and, last but not least, reveals a wary recognition that a new Spain has finally emerged.

Conclusion

AN ACCEPTABLE DEFINITION OF A TRAVEL BOOK MIGHT BE AS FOLLOWS: "A prose narrative that is presented as a factual account of a journey." Yet, as Patrick Holland and Graham Huggan remind us, travel accounts should not be taken at face value. Although Holland and Huggan overstate their case, the caution they advise still needs to be heeded by anyone approaching the genre:

> Travel writing emerges as a practical art of dissimulation, conscious of itself as at once generically elusive and empirically disingenuous, deliberately dissembling, unclear. Travel narratives, like their writers, tend to conceal as much as they reveal: their "factual" disclosures are screens for cannily structured fictions.[1]

Also, according to Holland and Huggan, the unreliability of these accounts serves to allure the reader: "The ambiguity surrounding travel narratives—the uncertainty, at given moments, of whether the writer is telling us the truth—is part of their appeal; the stories they tell are no less compelling if they happen to be mendacious" (pp. 7–8).

With regard to the issue of whether or not the reader is attracted by uncertainty over the authenticity of the narrative material, Holland and Huggan are, again, exaggerating their claims. Nonetheless, what is indisputable is that over the years and, indeed, over the centuries, many instances have come to light of travel writers indulging in artistic license, ranging from substantial fabrication to small-scale embellishment. What travel writers do not normally do, though, is reveal to their readers where they have taken liberties with the realities of a journey. Apparently, Bruce Chatwin told the writer Michael Ignatieff that he had counted up the lies contained in his travel book, *In Patagonia* (1977), noting: "It wasn't, in fact, too bad: there weren't too many."[2] And while Chatwin's biographer, Nicholas Shakespeare, acknowledges that the author embroidered, reshaped, and added details to the Patagonian narrative, he also justifies this on the grounds of artistic enhancement and literary creativity: "He tells not a half-truth, but a truth-and-a-half. His achievement is not to depict Patagonia as it is, but to create a landscape called Patagonia" (p. 318). However, the fact remains that Chatwin, like most travel writers, chose not to address his readers on matters of accuracy and reliability.

With Cela, the disclosure of narrative additions, omissions, and reshaping is handled in ways that are sometimes brought to the attention of the reader at the time of first publication and on other occasions indicated in a rather more roundabout and less immediate fashion. So, the first editions of *Del Miño al Bidasoa* and *Primer viaje andaluz* included, at the end of each narrative, an alphabetical list of all characters and in which fictitious personages were identified. Rather less boldly, a footnote in the *Obra completa* version of *Viaje a la Alcarria* (published seventeen years after the first edition) acknowledges that Cela made the trip in company, while tucked away in an autobiographical essay published in the United States is the revelation that on the Pyrenean journey recounted in *Viaje al Pirineo de Lérida* the author was not, in fact, alone but was one of a small group.

With regard to other ways in which the published accounts of journeys do not accurately reflect the experiences and circumstances of the trips that provided the raw material for these, Cela has used a variety of approaches to shed light on his methods. For example, not until the appearance in 1965 of the *Obra completa* edition of *Del Miño al Bidasoa* did the author reveal that the *Pueblo* articles of 1948 had provided the inspiration (not to mention a good deal of the source material) for the 1952 travel account. Similarly, with the *Obra completa* version of *Primer viaje andaluz*, which was published in 1968, nine years after the first edition of the Andalusian narrative, Cela notes that some of the other *Pueblo* pieces of 1948 provided the genesis of this, his fourth travel book. Yet while *Del Miño al Bidasoa* and *Primer viaje andaluz* are both acknowledged in their *Obra completa* editions as conflations, this is not the case with earlier, or subsequent, single-volume editions of these narratives. On the other hand, the fact that Cela's third travel book, *Judíos, moros y cristianos*, is also a composite work is indicated in all editions by the simple device of the author indicating at the end of the account (of what appears to be a seven-week journey) that the travels described in the text took place at various times between 1946 and 1952.

A final point concerning the issue of the authenticity of Cela's travel narratives needs to be made. This involves the highly visible (yet not strikingly obvious) ploy adopted by the author to distinguish between his three single-journey accounts and the three composite narratives. The author uses the style *viajero* [traveler] to describe the protagonists of the former, whereas the term *vagabundo* [vagabond] is employed in the conflated accounts. Therefore, in Cela's travel books these two different labels for the wayfarer are not used to denote distinctive "philosophies" of traveling. They are simply indications of different approaches adopted for the composition of a particular narrative: one method that readers and critics would regard as authentic and another, the conflation, that many would consider to be at best a questionable kind of travel narrative and at worst a literary masquerade.

But whichever type of artistic chassis Cela uses for a particular travel work, he still manages to deliver a good deal of factual and descriptive material that is presented as a faithful account or honest perception of the physical geography of areas visited, of the architectural and other features of towns and cities, of the literary and artistic associations of places stayed in or passed through, and of linguistic, historical, and other aspects of local, regional, and national culture. Some of his encounters and experiences occasionally come to irk and even pain the traveler. But more often they reveal the pleasure that he derives from seeing the way things are or from knowing how things once were or came to be.

In a discussion of motives and responses in accounts of journeys through foreign parts, Chloe Chard comments: "A conspicuous absence of enjoyment is, in fact, recognized within travel writings themselves as a major deficiency."[3] This sweeping judgment, made with regard to excursions abroad, certainly could not be applied to Cela's domestic travels which (unlike those, for example, of Goytisolo) frequently reveal contentment and quite often delight in response to what the traveler comes across, finds out, or is anxious to reveal to the reader. Such expressions of enjoyment are not, of course, confined to the context of the magnificence of Nature, impressive locations, inspiring literary associations, or the sites of momentous historical episodes. Cela's traveler also derives and conveys a good deal of pleasure from much more modest and worldly experiences. These include companionship on the road, looking at attractive females, hearing a good yarn, having a little fun at the expense of somebody else, meeting an interesting character and, last but not least, enjoying good food and drink, often in prodigious quantities. The traveler is not just an inquisitive, observant, knowledgeable, cultured, and occasionally concerned wayfarer: he can also be a witty, coarse, fun-loving, ogling trencherman.

In critical assessments of travel writing, it is often suggested that an important aspect of the journey is the process whereby the protagonist's geographical progress is paralleled by a personal journey of self-discovery. Mark Cocker, for example, observes that travel books "narrate discoveries of self through their [authors'] experiences of place" (p. 253). This notion of the self-discovering wayfarer is, I suspect, somewhat overblown, to the extent that it has become rather a cliché in criticism of travel accounts. Certainly in the case of Cela, there is no indication in his observations on travel, or evidence from his travel works, that the protagonist's acquisition of self-knowledge is an important aspect of a journey. The author seems content to project the figure of the traveler, with all his faults, talents, and idiosyncrasies; to reveal his interests, anxieties, likes and dislikes; and simply let the reader take him as he comes.

The concern that Cela's traveler sometimes discloses about things that worry or even infuriate him does of course indicate that the author's much proclaimed policy of remaining a detached observer and recorder is forgotten when the protagonist is sufficiently stirred or provoked. Similarly, the unacknowledged company that Cela had during the first Alcarria trip and on his tour of the Lérida Pyrenees, not to mention the periods of companionship that are revealed in most of the travel narratives, all tend to belie the suggestion that one of his main reasons for taking to the road was a quest for solitude. Furthermore, while Cela's identification of the fictitious characters appearing in two of his travel works comes as a refreshingly honest admission from someone working in the genre, this, along with the acknowledgment that three of the narratives are conflations of a number of journeys, makes the pronouncement in the dedication of *Viaje a la Alcarria* on fact, fiction, and travel literature ring rather hollow. Indeed, in view of the "missing" companions in at least two of the narratives and the stitched-together journeys in three others, the somewhat bizarre conclusion has to be drawn that, despite its commercial resonances and razzmatazz, its almost vulgar projection of the author-as-celebrity, its garishness, and exuberance, *Nuevo viaje a la Alcarria*, which can also be a perceptive and touching narrative, is in fact the most authentic of Cela's travel works. Furthermore, with appealing geographical symmetry (back to the Alcarria) and a sense of chronological completeness (the end of one era and the beginning of another) the last of Cela's travel books neatly rounds off a series of narratives in which, over a period of almost four decades, the author presents an attentive view of many aspects of postwar Spain. This view, as I have frequently noted, is seldom that of a social critic. Certainly, the travel books contain, with varying degrees of emphasis, some recognition of social contrasts and economic change. But Cela largely presents his country in terms of its geographical presence, historical and cultural heritage (including food and drink), as well as, in the last two works, its economic transformation. These are the areas on which the author and his traveler-figure largely focus, and which appear to matter most to both of them.

Notes

CHAPTER 1. INTRODUCTION

1. Freya Stark, "The Philosophy of Travel," in *Views from Abroad: The Spectator Book of Travel Writing*, ed. by Philip Marsden-Smedley and Jeffrey Klinke (London: Paladin, 1989; repr. 1990), pp. 3–6 (p. 6).

2. Colin Thubron, "Chuckles along the Littoral," *Times Literary Supplement*, 4 Jan. 1985, p. 6.

3. Susan Sontag, "Model Destinations," *Times Literary Supplement*, 22 June 1984, p. 699.

4. Paul Fussell, introduction to *The Norton Book of Travel*, ed. by Paul Fussell (New York and London: W.W. Norton & Company, 1987), pp. 13–17 (p. 13).

5. Percy G. Adams, *Travel Literature and the Evolution of the Novel* (Lexington: University Press of Kentucky, 1983), p. 188.

6. Mark Cocker, *Loneliness and Time: British Travel Writing in the Twentieth Century* (London: Secker & Warburg, 1992), p. 6.

7. Michael Kowalewski, "Introduction: The Modern Literature of Travel," in *Temperamental Journeys: Essays on the Modern Literature of Travel*, ed. by Michael Kowalewski (Athens and London: University of Georgia Press, 1992), pp. 1–16 (p. 7).

8. Paul Fussell, *Abroad: British Literary Traveling Between the Wars* (New York and Oxford: Oxford University Press, 1980), p. 203.

9. Quoted in Santiago Henríquez-Jiménez, *Going the Distance: An Analysis of Modern Travel Writing and Criticism* (Barcelona: Kadle Books, 1995), p. 22.

10. José Saramago, *Viagem a Portugal* (Lisbon: Círculo de Leitores, 1981).

11. Imogen Stubbs, "The Undiscovered Road," in *Amazonian: The Penguin Book of Women's New Travel Writing*, ed. by Dea Birkett and Sara Wheeler (London: Penguin Books, 1998), pp. 198–230.

12. Edward Marriott, "Travels of the Mind," *The Times*, Metro Section, 30 May 1998, p. 20.

13. Claude Lévi-Strauss, *Tristes Tropiques*, trans. by John Russell (New York: Atheneum, 1968), p. 90.

14. J. B. Priestley, *English Journey*, 3rd edn (London: William Heinemann in association with Victor Gollancz, 1937), pp. 61–62.

15. Philip Dodd, "The Views of Travellers: Travel Writing in the 1930s," in *The Art of Travel: Essays on Travel Writing*, ed. by Philip Dodd (London: Frank Cass, 1982), pp. 127–38 (p. 131).

16. Antonio Ferres and Armando López Salinas, *Caminando por las Hurdes*, Biblioteca Breve, 153 (Barcelona: Seix Barral, 1960), p. 9.

17. Juan Goytisolo, "Tierras del sur" [Lands of the South], in *Obras completas*, vol. 2, *Relatos y ensayos* (Madrid: Aguilar, 1977), pp. 1035–56 (p. 1040). This piece also appears in Goytisolo's essays on literature and culture, *El furgón de cola* (1967).

18. Goytisolo undoubtedly exaggerates the social content of Brenan's book. For a

discussion of this and other aspects of the way in which the two writers portray the province of Almería, see my "Two Views of Almería: Juan Goytisolo and Gerald Brenan," *Revue de Littérature Comparée*, no. 260 (Oct.–Dec. 1991), 429–46.

19. Miguel de Unamuno, *Andanzas y visiones españolas*, Colección Austral, 160 (Madrid: Espasa-Calpe, 1955), p. 113.

20. Francisco López-Barxas, 'Entrevista a Camilo José Cela' [Interview with CJC], *Insula, Monográfico Extraordinario Dedicado al Premio Nobel de Literatura 1989*, nos. 518–19 (Feb.–Mar. 1990), 77–80 (p. 77).

21. Miguel de Unamuno, *Por tierras de Portugal y de España*, Colección Austral, 221 (Madrid: Espasa-Calpe, 1976), p. 126.

22. J. M. Castellet, "Iniciación a la obra narrative de Camilo José Cela" [Introduction to the Narrative Writing of CJC], in J. M. Castellet and others, *Camilo José Cela: Vida y obra—Bibliografía—Antología* (New York: Hispanic Institute in the United States, 1962), pp. 7–50 (pp. 11–12).

23. Francisco Olmos García, "La novela y los novelistas españoles de hoy" [The Novel and Spanish Novelists of Today], *Cuadernos Americanos*, no. 119 (July–Aug. 1963), 211–37 (p. 232).

24. José Ortega y Gasset, "Tierras de Castilla: Notas de andar y ver," in *El Espectador* (Madrid: Biblioteca Nueva, 1950), pp. 53–62 (p. 54). "De Madrid a Asturias, o los dos paisajes: Notas de andar y ver" is included in the same collection (pp. 335–58).

25. Camilo José Cela, *Nuevo viaje a la Alcarria*, Colección Ave Fénix, 171/3 (Barcelona: Plaza & Janés, 1994), p. 8.

26. Joanne Shattock, "Travel Writing Victorian and Modern: A Review of Recent Research," in *The Art of Travel: Essays on Travel Writing*, ed. by Philip Dodd, pp. 151–64 (p. 152).

27. Paul Theroux, *Fresh-Air Fiend: Travel Writings, 1985–2000* (London: Hamish Hamilton, 2000), p. 347.

.

CHAPTER 2. CELA'S VIEWS ON TRAVEL

1. "Los libros de viajes," in Camilo José Cela, *Obra completa*, vol. 10, *Glosa del mundo en torno: Artículos, 2 (1944–1959)* (Barcelona: Destino, 1978), pp. 228–30 (p. 228).

2. *Viaje a la Alcarria*, in Camilo José Cela, *Obra completa*, vol. 4, *Viajes por España, 1 (1948–1952)* (Barcelona: Destino, 1965), p. 28. All subsequent page references to *Viaje a la Alcarria* will be to this volume and edition, and will be given in the text.

3. "Nota a la segunda edición," in Camilo José Cela, *Obra completa*, vol. 4, pp. 509–12 (p. 511).

4. "Prologuillo para escolares ingleses" [A brief prologue for English students], in Camilo José Cela, *Viaje a la Alcarria*, ed. by Philip Polack (London: Harrap, 1961; repr. of 1975 unabridged edn, 1979), pp. 21–23 (p. 23).

5. "Nota a la cuarta edición," in Camilo José Cela, *Obra completa*, vol. 4, pp. 513–15 (p. 514).

6. Prologue to *Judíos, moros y cristianos*, in Camilo José Cela, *Obra completa*, vol. 5, *Viajes por España, 2 (1952–1958)* (Barcelona: Destino, 1966), pp. 123–31 (p. 129). All subsequent page references to *Judíos, moros y cristianos* will be to this volume and edition, and will be given in the text.

7. "El calendario del corazón" [The heart's calendar], in Camilo José Cela, *Obra completa*, vol. 6, *Viajes por España, 3 (1959–1964)* (Barcelona: Destino, 1968), pp. 377–82 (p. 380).

8. *The Norton Book of Travel*, ed. by Paul Fussell, p. 13.

9. Camilo José Cela, *Obra completa*, vol. 7, *Tres novelas más (1951–1955)* (Barcelona: Destino, 1969), p. 343.

10. "Visita de la ciudad," in Camilo José Cela, *Obra completa*, vol. 10, pp. 28–31 (p. 29).

11. "Otra vez la ciudad," in Camilo José Cela, *Obra completa*, vol. 10, pp. 32–34 (p. 34).

12. "El campo, la ciudad, el campo . . . , esa margarita," in Camilo José Cela, *Obra completa*, vol. 10, pp. 60–63 (p. 62).

13. "Con la mochila al hombro y una paz infinita en el corazón," in Camilo José Cela, *Obra completa*, vol. 4, pp. 9–16 (p. 10).

14. "Breve nota para médicos y farmacéuticos" [A brief note for doctors and pharmacists], in Camilo José Cela, *Obra completa*, vol. 4, pp. 536–38 (p. 537).

15. "Andar por andar y, de paso, ver," in Camilo José Cela, *Obra completa*, vol. 10, pp. 523–26 (p. 526).

16. In his essay "A Disturbance of Memory on the Acropolis" (1936), Freud states that during his school days he had doubts that he would ever get to Athens, and observes: "It seems to me beyond the realms of possibility that I should ever travel so far—that I should 'go such a long way.' This was linked up with the limitations and poverty of our conditions of life. My longing for travel was no doubt also the expression of a wish to escape from that pressure, like the force that drives so many adolescent children to run away from home. I had long seen clearly that a great part of the pleasure of travel lies in the fulfillment of these early wishes, that is rooted, that is, in dissatisfaction with home and family." Quoted in Dennis Porter, *Haunted Journeys: Desire and Transgression in European Travel Writing* (Princeton, NJ: Princeton University Press, 1991), p. 196.

17. "Mensaje a los vagabundos," in Camilo José Cela, *Obra completa*, vol. 10, pp. 520–22 (p. 521).

18. "[Posible] despedida del camino, con veinte años más y tres arrobas de sobra" [(Possible) farewell to the open road, twenty years older and eighty pounds too heavy], in Camilo José Cela, *Obra completa*, vol. 6, pp. 371–74 (pp. 372–73).

19. "La Mancha en el corazón y en los ojos (*Elegía a lo que no se tiene en las manos*)" [La Mancha in one's heart and in one's eyes (*Elegy to what is not in one's grasp*)], in Camilo José Cela, *Obra completa*, vol. 10, pp. 582–92 (p. 582).

20. Introduction to *Primer viaje andaluz*, in Camilo José Cela, *Obra completa*, vol. 6, pp. 21–23 (p. 21).

21. "Materiales con los que cualquier sabio tratadista hubiera podido componer un prólogo" [Materials with which any wise treatise-writer would have been able to compose a prologue], in Camilo José Cela, *Obra completa*, vol. 6, pp. 25–30 (p. 28).

22. Quoted in José María Martínez Cachero, "Camilo José Cela, viajero por España" [CJC, traveler through Spain] , *Hispanística XX*, 8 (1990), 119–32 (p. 129).

23. "La confusa andadura de un libro sencillísimo" [The confusing course of a very simple book], in Camilo José Cela, *Obra completa*, vol. 4, pp. 21–23 (p. 21).

CHAPTER 3. THE APPROACH TO THE ALCARRIA

1. Emilia Pardo Bazán, *Por la España pintoresca: Viajes*, Colección Diamante, 32 (Barcelona: Antonio López, 1895), pp. 102–03.

2. See Camilo José Cela, *Obra completa*, vol. 4, *Viajes por España, 1 (1948–1952)*, p. 510n.

3. Hugh Thomas, *The Spanish Civil War*, 3rd edn, rev. and enlarged (Harmondsworth: Penguin Books in association with Hamish Hamilton, 1977), p. 929.

4. Sacheverell Sitwell, *Spain* (London: B. T. Batsford, 1950), p. 50.

5. Michel Butor, "Travel and Writing," in *Temperamental Journeys: Essays on the Modern Literature of Travel*, ed. by Michael Kowalewski (Athens and London: University of Georgia Press, 1992), pp. 53–70 (p. 61).

6. Most of the preceding details concerning the publication of *Viaje a la Alcarria* are taken from Camilo José Cela, *Obra completa*, vol. 4, 509n–10n.

7. Gérard Genette, *Paratexts: Thresholds of Interpretation*, trans. by Jane E. Lewin (Cambridge: Cambridge University Press, 1997), p. 125.

8. V. S. Pritchett, *Marching Spain* (London: The Hogarth Press, 1988), p. viii.

9. Gerald Brenan, *The Face of Spain*, Penguin Travel Library (London: Penguin Books in association with Hamish Hamilton, 1988), p. 9. The books referred to here are Brenan's *The Spanish Labyrinth* (Cambridge: Cambridge University Press, 1943) and *The Literature of the Spanish People* (Cambridge: Cambridge University Press, 1951), and Gamel Woolsey's *Death's Other Kingdom* (London: Longman & Co, 1939).

10. Raymond Carr and Juan Pablo Fusi Aizpurua, *Spain: Dictatorship to Democracy*, 1st paperback edn (London: George Allen & Unwin, 1981), p. 52.

11. Paul Preston, *Franco: A Biography* (London: HarperCollins, 1993), pp. 569, 585.

12. Paul Theroux, *The Old Patagonian Express: By Train Through the Americas* (London: Penguin Books, 1980), p.11.

13. Ted Walker, *In Spain* (London: Secker & Warburg), 1987, p. 221.

14. Jonathan Raban, "Better Half," *The Sunday Times*, section 6, Travel, 8 June 1997, p. 7. Raban's *Passage to Juneau: A Sea and Its Meanings* was published in 1999 (New York: Alfred A. Knopf; London: Picador). In the book, the account of Raban's stay in Prince Rupert makes no mention of the altercation between the two women.

15. Roger Fowler, *Linguistics and the Novel*, New Accents (London and New York: Methuen, 1977; repr. 1979), pp. 91–92.

16. Camilo José Cela, *Obra completa*, vol. 6, *Viajes por España, 3 (1959–1964)* (Barcelona: Destino, 1968), p. 109. All subsequent page references to *Primer viaje andaluz* will be to this volume and edition, and will be given in the text.

17. For a concise account of Murguía's beliefs and activities, see Justo G. Beramendi, "La Galicia de Murguía," in Manuel Murguía, *Galicia*, ed. by Justo G. Beramendi, Extramuros, 8–9, 2 vols (Vigo: Edicións Xerais de Galicia, 1982), I, i–xli. For a different perspective, see Catherine Davies, "Rosalía de Castro's Later Poetry and Anti-Regionalism in Spain," *Modern Language Review*, 79 (1984), 609–19.

18. The novel was published in Britain in 1927 under the title *Fiesta*.

19. Ernest Hemingway, *Fiesta: (The Sun also Rises)* (London: Pan Books, 1949; repr. 1963), p. 89. Interestingly, Hemingway tells how when he showed a draft of *The Sun Also Rises* to the writer Nathan Asch, the latter dismissed it as a travel book. See Kowalewski, p. 2.

20. See, for example, Hugh Thomas, pp. 609n. 1, 689n. 2, 698–99.

21. Ernest Hemingway, *Fiesta*, trans. by José Mora Guarnido and John E. Halisner (Barcelona: José Janés, 1948).

22. Azorín, *La ruta de Don Quijote*, ed. by José María Martínez Cachero, Letras Hispánicas, 214, 2nd edn (Madrid: Cátedra, 1988), p. 77.

23. Pritchett suggests that the penultimate stanza (which he appears to think is the last) contains "the essence of the Spanish genius" (p. 7).

24. Arturo Barea, introduction to Camilo José Cela, *The Hive*, trans. by J. M. Cohen in consultation with Arturo Barea (London: Victor Gollancz, 1953), pp. 7–16.

25. Américo Castro, "Algo sobre el 'nihilismo' creador de Camilo José Cela," in *Hacia Cervantes*, 2nd edn (Madrid: Taurus, 1960), pp. 386–90 (p. 387).

26. Barry Jordan, "The Emergence of a Dissident Intelligensia," in *Spanish Cultural Studies. An Introduction: The Struggle for Modernity*, ed. by Helen Graham and Jo Labanyi (Oxford: Oxford University Press, 1995), pp. 245–55 (p. 245).

27. Alonso Zamora Vicente, *Camilo José Cela: (Acercamiento a un escritor)*, Biblioteca Románica Hispánica: VII, Campo Abierto (Madrid: Gredos, 1962), pp. 93–95.

28. Robert Kirsner, *The Novels and Travels of Camilo José Cela*, University of North Carolina Studies in the Romance Languages and Literatures, 43 (Chapel Hill: University of North Carolina Press, 1963), p. 102.

29. Paul Ilie, *La novelística de Camilo José Cela*, Biblioteca Románica Hispánica: Estudios y Ensayos, 65, 3rd edn (Madrid: Gredos, 1978), p. 251.

30. José María Martínez Cachero, "Camilo José Cela, viajero por España," *Hispanística XX, Camilo José Cela: Nuevos enfoques*, 8 (1990), 119–32 (p. 123).

31. Robert Kirsner, "La persistente presencia de la Guerra Civil Española en la obra de Camilo José Cela," *Hispanística XX, Camilo José Cela: Nuevos enfoques*, 8 (1990), 69–80 (p. 73).

32. Robert Kirsner, "La España de *Viaje a la Alcarria*," *Insula, Monográfico Extraordinario Dedicado al Premio Nobel de Literatura 1989*, nos. 518–19 (Feb.–Mar. 1990), 42–43 (p. 42).

33. José María Pozuelo Yvancos, introduction to Camilo José Cela, *Viaje a la Alcarria*, Colección Austral: Literatura, 131 (Madrid: Espasa-Calpe, 1990), pp. 9–56 (p. 9).

34. Michael Jacobs, *Between Hopes and Memories: A Spanish Journey* (London: Picador, 1994), p. 79.

35. Camilo José Cela, *Journey to the Alcarria*, trans. by Frances M. López-Morillas (Cambridge and London: Granta Books in association with Penguin Books, 1990).

36. Sarah Kerr, "Shock Treatment," *New York Review of Books*, 8 Oct. 1992, 35–39 (p. 35).

37. John Butt, "God-botherer," *Daily Telegraph*, Weekend Section, 17 Feb. 1990, p. xviii.

38. Harry Eyres, "Spanish Stroller," *The Times*, 10 Feb. 1990, p. 38.

39. James Wilson, "Stepping back to Spain in an Old Pair of Shoes," *The Independent*, 25 Sept. 1993, p. 47.

CHAPTER 4. CAPTURING THE PRESENT

1. Ramón Tamames, *La República. La era de Franco*, Historia de España Alfaguara, vol. 7, 11th edn (Madrid: Alianza/Alfaguara, 1986), p. 424.

2. William Cullen Bryant, *Poetical Works* (New York: D. Appleton and Company, 1883), p. 21.

3. See William Cullen Bryant, *Letters of a Traveller. Second Series* (New York: D. Appleton and Company, 1859).

4. The second epigraph that Cela uses, two lines from the *Poema de Mío Cid* in which the Alcarria is mentioned, was not included until the *Obra completa* edition of *Viaje a la Alcarria*.

5. *The Novels and Travels of Camilo José Cela*, p. 102.

6. In a report published in late February 1946, one of the European correspondents of the *New York Times* wrote that in Spain inflation was "spiraling slowly upward," mentioned that food was "extremely short," and stated that there were also shortages of coal and fertilizer. The reporter also noted that "everyone now depends on the black market, where prices are enormously higher" (C. L. Sulzberger, "Inflation Pushing Spain into Strikes," *New York Times*, 23 Feb. 1946, p. 7).

7. In June and July 1981, two Guadalajara journalists, Salvador Toquero and Santiago Barra, retraced a good deal of Cela's 1946 itinerary. Their account of this journey appeared under the title *Buscando a Cela en la Alcarria* (Guadalajara: The Authors, 1982). The declared aim of Toquero and Barra was to contact any of the surviving inhabitants of the Alcarria mentioned in Cela's first travel book and to see if they remembered the author's visit and knew about the book (pp. 9–10). During the course of their trip it was indicated to the journalists that Cela was accompanied by a man and a woman, a couple, both assumed to be German (pp. 61–62). Toquero and Barra regarded this as an important discovery and in so doing revealed that they were unaware of Cela's admission of 1965 on this point. What they did learn of particular interest was that Wlasak and Stichaner were, apparently, locked up with Cela (in Budia) (p. 62), that Wlasak, who may have been Austrian, had been a photographer at the German Embassy in Madrid during World War II, and that Stichaner may have been Portuguese or had some Portuguese connection (pp. 178–81).

8. "Notas del vago estío," in *El Espectador*, pp. 555–610 (p. 566).

9. *Por la España pintoresca: Viajes*, p. 100.

10. The Pastrana tapestries depict scenes from Afonso V of Portugal's successful Moroccan crusade of 1471, which culminated in the seizure of Tangier. For a useful description of the six tapestries (which were subsequently returned to the town), see H. V. Morton, *A Stranger in Spain* (London: Methuen & Co, 1955), pp. 63–66.

11. Emilia Pardo Bazán, "El viaje por España," *La España Moderna*, no. 83 (Nov. 1895), 76–97 (p. 90).

12. See Preston, pp. 557–58.

Chapter 5. Fact and Fiction

1. Nina Epton, *Spain's Magic Coast: From the Miño to the Bidassoa* (London: Weidenfeld and Nicolson, 1965), pp. 3–4.

2. *Del Miño al Bidasoa: Notas de un vagabundaje*, in Camilo José Cela, *Obra completa*, vol. 4, *Viajes por España, 1 (1948–1952)* (Barcelona: Destino, 1965), p. 253. All subsequent page references to *Del Miño al Bidasoa* will be to this volume and edition, and will be given in the text.

3. For further information on the principal features of this pilgrimage-festival, see Jorge-Víctor Sueiro and Amparo Nieto, *Galicia: Romería interminable* (Madrid: Penthalon, 1983), pp. 201–05.

4. "La carambola por tablas y el espíritu de chamarilero" [A Carom off the Cushions and the Spirit of the Gambler], in Camilo José Cela, *Obra completa*, vol. 4, pp. 247–49 (pp. 247–48).

5. Cela spent the summers of the years 1947 to 1950 in Cebreros. See his essay, "Recuerdo en paz la tierra por la que anduve . . ." [I Remember with Tranquillity the Land that I Walked through . . .], in *Obra completa*, vol. 5, pp. 115–18 (p. 115).

6. *The Novels and Travels of Camilo José Cela*, p. 129.

7. *Del Miño al Bidasoa: Notas de un vagabundaje* (Barcelona: Editorial Noguer, 1952).

8. See Juan Goytisolo, *En los reinos de taifa*, Biblioteca Breve (Barcelona: Seix Barral, 1986), pp. 23–25.

9. Abigail Lee Six, *Goytisolo: "Campos de Níjar,"* Critical Guides to Spanish Texts, 59 (London: Grant & Cutler, 1996), p. 56.

10. Paul Theroux, *The Great Railway Bazaar: By Train through Asia* (London: Penguin Books, 2001), p. 379.

11. According to Cela, in the late 1940s he was living in straitened circumstances

(see V, 115). Consequently, it seems possible that the vagabond of *Del Miño al Bidasoa* as well as the protagonists of *Judíos, moros y cristianos* and *Primer viaje andaluz* (both of these subsequent works draw some of their material from this period) are intended to reflect these lean times for the writer.

12. In the "Censo de personajes" of the first edition it is made clear that "Don Camilo" is Cela, who is then described as the vagabond and author of "this book," and a person who occasionally pretends to be somebody else (p. 241).

13. Alvaro Cunqueiro (1911–81) and Gabriel Celaya (1911–91) (whose real name was Rafael Gabriel Múgica Celaya and who also published as Juan de Leceta) are referred to by first name only in the work, all three in the case of Celaya. However, the "Censo de personajes" confirms the identity of these two writers. It is interesting to note Celaya's politics. The day after his death, *El País* carried a tribute entitled "Muere Gabriel Celaya, poeta del antifranquismo" [Gabriel Celaya, anti-Franco Poet is Dead]. Elsewhere in the piece, Celaya is referred to as "antiguo militante comunista" (a one-time communist activist) and mention is made of the fact that in 1946 he and Amparo Gastón founded in San Sebastián the publishing house Norte, which published the work of, among other writers, Cela. The tribute also quotes Cela as saying how shameful it was that Celaya had died in poverty (*El País*, 19 April 1991, p. 30). I am grateful to my colleague, Professor Jason Wilson, for bringing this article to my notice.

CHAPTER 6. PAST AND PRESENT

1. See Preston, pp. 594–624.

2. Américo Castro, *España en su historia: Cristianos, moros y judíos* (Buenos Aires: Losada, 1948), p. 12.

3. Ramón Menéndez Pidal, *The Spaniards in their History*, translated, with a prefatory essay, by Walter Starkie (London: Hollis & Carter, 1950), p.181.

4. See Julio Almeida, *El problema de España en Américo Castro*, Monografías, 195 (Córdoba: University of Córdoba, 1993), p. 47.

5. See Joan Ramón Resina, "*Papeles de Son Armadans*, revista literaria de Postguerra," *Revista Canadiense de Estudios Hispánicos*, 12 (1987), 71–91 (p. 83).

6. José María Ridao, "Américo Castro, 25 años después," *El País*, 25 July 1997, p. 9.

7. For an assessment of the main arguments that Sánchez-Albornoz musters against Castro in *España, un enigma histórico*, see Almeida, pp. 206–23.

8. Camilo José Cela, "Relativo Curriculum Vitae" [Relative Curriculum Vitae], in J. M. Castellet and others, *Camilo José Cela: Vida y obra—Bibliografía—Antología*, pp. 79–109 (p. 100).

9. Camilo José Cela Conde, *Cela, mi padre*, Colección Hombres de Hoy, 11 (Madrid: Ediciones Temas de Hoy, 1989), pp. 192–94.

10. *The Novels and Travels of Camilo José Cela*, p. 30.

11. "Sobre España, los españoles y lo español," in Camilo José Cela, *Cuatro figuras del 98: Unamuno, Valle-Inclán, Baroja, Azorín y otros retratos y ensayos españoles*, Biblioteca Biográfica, 18 (Barcelona: Editorial Aedos, 1961), pp. 225–40 (p. 225). This essay was first published in 1959 in French and Italian journals. However it is most readily available in *Cuatro figuras del 98* and also in the collection of Cela's essays, *A vueltas con España*, Ensayos y Documentos, 42 (Madrid: Seminarios y Ediciones, 1973), pp. 17–34.

12. Pío Rodríguez, "Forty Years of Spanish Culture," *Cultures*, 8 (1982), 64–80 (p. 68).

13. See Townsend Miller, *The Castles and the Crown: Spain 1451–1555* (London: Victor Gollancz, 1963), pp. 49–54.

14. See Miller, pp. 54–56.

15. The present population of Pedraza, which has been developed as a tourist center of historic interest, is around five hundred.

16. Emilia Pardo Bazán, *Por la Europa católica*, Obras completas, 26 (Madrid: Administración, [1902]), p. 213. I am grateful to Dr Gloria Muñoz-Martín for bringing this passage to my attention.

17. Ricardo Senabre, "Camilo José Cela en la España árida," *Ínsula, Monográfico Extraordinario Dedicado al Premio Nobel de Literatura 1989*, nos. 518–19 (Feb.–Mar. 1990), 65–66 (p. 65).

18. *The Novels and Travels of Camilo José Cela*, p. 151.

19. D. W. McPheeters, *Camilo José Cela*, Twayne's World Authors Series, 67 (New York: Twayne, 1969), p. 133.

CHAPTER 7. HISTORY AND THE ARTS

1. The four *Pueblo* articles in question are described as "*las cuatro crónicas viajeras que fueron el huevo (o la idea) de este libro*" [*the four travel chronicles that were the source (or the idea) for this book*], Camilo José Cela, "Addenda," *Obra completa*, vol. 6, *Viajes por España, 3 (1959–1964)* (Barcelona: Destino, 1968), pp. 663–99 (p. 665). All page references to *Primer viaje andaluz* will be to this volume and edition, and will be given in the text.

The remaining eleven *Pueblo* articles, which appeared between 25 September and 6 November 1948, show Cela making his way from El Puerto de Santa María to Cádiz, thence to Torremolinos, Granada, Motril, Almería, Aguilas, and then back to Madrid. They are included in vol. 10 of the *Obra completa*, under the heading: "Notas para un *Segundo viaje andaluz*: Libro que no llegó a escribirse" [Notes for a *Second Andalusian Journey*: A Book that was Never Written], pp. 695–753.

2. Roger Collins, *Spain: An Oxford Archaeological Guide*, Oxford Archaeological Guides (Oxford: Oxford University Press, 1998), p. 180.

3. Nina Epton, *Andalusia* (London: Weidenfeld and Nicolson, 1968), p. 279.

4. Miguel de Cervantes Saavedra, *The Ingenious Hidalgo Don Quixote de la Mancha*, trans., with an introduction and notes by John Rutherford, Penguin Classics (London: Penguin Books, 2000), pp. 569–70. The Knight of the Wood goes on to mention that his lady also commanded him "to go and lift those four ancient stones, the great Bulls of Guisando, an exploit more suited to market porters than to knights errant." Nevertheless, he apparently complied (p. 570).

5. Baltasar del Alcázar (1530–1606) was a Sevillian poet who is mainly remembered for his light verse, often celebrating hedonism, and his epigrams. His best-known work is the 112-line poem, in octosyllabic quatrains (*redondillas*), "Cena jocosa" [The Comic Supper]. The flavor of this and some of his other lighter poetry is indicated by the opening quatrain of one of his untitled *redondillas*:

> Tres cosas me tienen preso
> De amores el corazón:
> La bella Inés, el jamón
> Y berengenas con queso.

[Three things have captured / This heart of mine: / The beautiful Inés, ham / And aubergines with cheese.]

6. As is the case with *Del Miño al Bidasoa*, *Primer viaje andaluz* has a "Censo de personajes" which lists the real, historical, and fictitious characters who appear or are mentioned in the narrative.

7. *Judíos, moros y cristianos* is the only one of the three "conflated" travel works that does not include a "Censo de personajes"—either in the first edition or in subsequent versions. Yet the Castilian travel narrative certainly has its share of singular characters who could well be the creatures of Cela's imagination rather than the product of his experiences on the road.

CHAPTER 8. GEOGRAPHY AND A CHANGING LANDSCAPE

1. Camilo José Cela, "Relativo Curriculum Vitae," in J. M. Castellet and others, *Camilo José Cela: Vida y obra—Bibliografía—Antología*, p. 98.

2. Camilo José Cela, *Obra completa*, vol. 6, *Viajes por España, 3 (1959–1964)* (Barcelona: Destino, 1968), p. 661. All page references to *Viaje al Pirineo de Lérida* will be to this volume and edition, and will be given in the text.

3. Having discussed the possible etymology of the word "noguera" in the *ABC* account of the trip, Cela includes a footnote in subsequent versions that reprints the lengthy observations on this point from a correspondent in Navarre. In addition, the author acknowledges that his original speculations were wrong and accepts the suggestion of the correspondent, José J. Montoro Sagasti, that "noguera" derives from a Basque word meaning fast-flowing river (VI, 435–37).

4. Charlemagne became king of all the Frankish territories in 771 and was crowned Emperor of the West in 800. He died in 814. Harold Livermore notes that by the middle of the ninth century the Frankish Empire "had passed its zenith" and goes on to observe that France's Charles I, the Bald, who died in 877, "finally recognized the Hispanic tradition of the counties beyond the Pyrenees and distinguished between the march of Gotia or Gothic Gaul, and the Hispanic March. This last, formed by the counties of Barcelona, Gerona, Urgel, Cerdanya, Besalú and perhaps Roussillon, came to form a separate domain, increasingly under the influence of the *comes* of Barcelona. By the middle of the ninth century this region was stabilized as a 'march,' no longer a moving frontier," *The Origins of Spain and Portugal* (London: George Allen & Unwin, 1971), p. 373.

5. It is interesting to note that in the *ABC* version of *Viaje al Pirineo de Lérida* the words "estas depredaciones" [these depredations] are used instead of "estos peculados legales, inmorales e impolíticos" (VI, 639 n. 245).

6. The traveler's thoughts on the purpose of national parks, as well as his views on what should *not* be allowed to take place in them, formed part of the text of the *ABC* version. However, in all editions in volume they are given as a lengthy footnote.

7. Cela measures his achievement as "cinco canas de Lérida de xolís" [five Lérida *canas* of *xolís*]. He describes a Lérida *cana* as being a bit less than two "Burgos yards" [varas de Burgos] and almost as much as a fathom (VI, 412).

8. Francisco Umbral, *Cela: Un cadáver exquisito. Vida y obra* (Barcelona: Editorial Planeta, 2002), p. 56.

CHAPTER 9. POSTSCRIPT

1. Camilo José Cela, "Relativo Curriculum Vitae," pp. 87–88.

2. The account of the journey was first published, under the title *Nuevo viaje a la*

Alcarria, in three instalments of, respectively, eighty, sixty-four, and sixty-four pages by *Cambio 16,* Información y Revistas, SA (Madrid, 1986).

3. Camilo José Cela, *Nuevo viaje a la Alcarria,* Colección Ave Fénix, 171/3 (Barcelona: Plaza & Janés, 1994), pp. 32–33. All subsequent page references to *Nuevo viaje a la Alcarria* are to this edition and will be given in the text.

4. Francisco López-Barxas, "Entrevista a Camilo José Cela," p. 78.

5. Here, then, the traveler notes that Mierda might be dead. Yet a footnote in the first *Obra completa* edition of *Viaje a la Alcarria* (1965) mentions the "triste fin del Mierda" [sad end of Mierda], (IV, 127n), and elsewhere there is an account of how he drowned in the Eria River, in León, while trying to catch trout. For this version of his apparent demise, see Camilo José Cela, *Los viejos amigos: Primera serie,* Colección El Espejo y La Pluma (Barcelona: Noguer, 1960), pp.16–18. It would seem that either the author has become confused or forgetful about the fate of Mierda or that the earlier account of his death was a fabrication. All this, of course, assumes that the character encountered in *Viaje a la Alcarria* and recalled in *Nuevo viaje a la Alcarria* did, in fact, exist.

6. In a decree of April 1937 General Franco ordered that all political parties supporting the Nationalist cause should be unified under the name Falange Española Tradicionalista y de las JONS. In fact, what Paul Preston describes as the "openly fascist" (p. 98) Falange Española, founded by José Antonio Primo de Rivera in October 1933, had already amalgamated with the Catholic, National Syndicalist JONS (Juntas Ofensivas Nacional Sindicalistas) in February 1934, adopting the symbol of the JONS, the yoke and arrows. The decree of April 1937 absorbed all other right-wing parties into the FET y de las JONS, thus establishing a single political grouping under the leadership of Franco. This grouping was then termed the Movimiento Nacional. See Fernando Díaz-Plaja, *La Guerra de España en sus documentos,* Libro Documento, 60, 2nd edn (Barcelona: Ediciones G.P., 1969), pp. 236–45.

7. According to some exchanges in the opening part of chapter 3 of *Nuevo viaje a la Alcarria,* Cela also fought in the Sierra de Alcubierre (p. 39). Indeed, the author has subsequently confirmed that he, too, was wounded there. See Camilo José Cela, *Memorias, entendimientos y voluntades* (Barcelona: Plaza & Janés/Cambio 16, 1993), pp. 191, 199. It is, of course, curious that the traveler should mention none of this to Felipe el Sastre. Although Cela fought with the Nationalists, there is no indication which side Felipe was on. However, the assumption would be that he, too, was fighting with the insurgents.

8. Raymond Carr, *The Spanish Tragedy: The Civil War in Perspective,* paperbound edn (London: Weidenfeld, 1993), p. 162.

9. For a detailed account of the battle, see John F. Coverdale, "The Battle of Guadalajara, 8–22 March 1937," *Journal of Contemporary History,* 9 (1974), 53–75. Coverdale's estimates of the numbers of troops and the amount of military equipment involved differ a little from those suggested by Hugh Thomas, p. 596.

10. André Malraux, *L'Espoir,* Le Livre de Poche, 162–63 (Paris: Gallimard, 1966), pp. 437–41.

11. Quoted in Díaz-Plaja, pp. 228–29.

12. See my article, "EndemicViolence and Political Balance in Cela's *San Camilo, 1936,*" *Romance Studies,* no. 3 (winter 1983–84), 31–46.

13. The Italian officers referred to here are Generals Mario Roatta, Edmondo Rossi, Amerigo Coppi, Luigi Nuvolini, and Annibale Bergonzoli. It seems that the two elderly locals, and also Cela (unless he is gently mocking them), have confused General Nuvolini with his countryman, the great motor-racing driver, Tazio Nuvolari (1892–1953), whose heyday was in the 1930s. Hugh Thomas makes precisely the same error in the early editions of *The Spanish Civil War,* but corrects it later.

14. Francisco López-Barxas, p. 78.

15. Bill Bryson, *Notes from a Small Island*, paperbound edn (London: Black Swan, 1996), p. 168.

16. An account of the history and function of the *picota* can be found in the 1907 study of the penologist, sociologist, and historian, Constancio Bernaldo de Quirós, which is reprinted in C. Bernaldo de Quirós, *La picota: Crímenes y castigos en el país castellano en los tiempos medios. Figuras delincuentes* (Madrid: Ediciones Turner, 1975).

17. There is a color plate of the Fuentenovilla *picota* in José Serrano Belinchón, *Guadalajara*, Guías Everest (León: Editorial Everest, 1991), p. 87.

Conclusion

1. Patrick Holland and Graham Huggan, *Tourists with Typewriters: Critical Reflections on Contemporary Travel Writing* (Ann Arbor: University of Michigan Press, 1998), p. xi.

2. Quoted in Nicholas Shakespeare, *Bruce Chatwin* (London: The Harvill Press in association with Jonathan Cape, 1999), p. 313.

3. Chloe Chard, "Unknown Pleasures," *Times Higher Education Supplement*, 3 August 1990, p. 15.

Bibliography

The definitive editions of the first five of Cela's travel books are those appearing in the author's *Obra completa*, which began publication in 1962. The *Obra completa* versions of these works are accompanied by prefatory notes and essays found in earlier editions. These versions also indicate all textual variants and, from time to time, incorporate updating and correcting footnote material. The first five travel books are included in the *Obra completa* as follows: *Viaje a la Alcarria* and *Del Miño al Bidasoa* appear in Camilo José Cela, *Obra completa*, vol. 4, *Viajes por España, 1 (1948–1952)* (Barcelona: Destino, 1965); *Judíos, moros y cristianos* appears in vol. 5, *Viajes por España, 2 (1952–1958)* (Barcelona: Destino, 1966); *Primer viaje andaluz* and *Viaje al Pirineo de Lérida* appear in vol. 6, *Viajes por España, 3 (1959–1964)* (Barcelona: Destino, 1968). *Nuevo viaje a la Alcarria*, not yet published in the *Obra completa*, is currently available in the collection Ave Fénix, 171/3 (Barcelona: Plaza & Janés, 1994).

To date, the only English version of any of Cela's travel narratives is *Journey to the Alcarria*, translated by Frances M. López-Morillas (Cambridge: Granta Books in association with Penguin Books, 1990). In the United States this translation is entitled *Journey to the Alcarria: Travels Through the Spanish Countryside* (New York: Atlantic Monthly Press, 1990).

Adams, Percy G. *Travel Literature and the Evolution of the Novel.* Lexington: University Press of Kentucky, 1983.

Almeida, Julio. *El problema de España en Américo Castro.* Córdoba: University of Córdoba, 1993.

Anonymous. "Muere Gabriel Celaya, poeta del antifranquismo." *El País*, 19 April 1991, 30–31.

Azorín. *La ruta de Don Quijote*, ed. José María Martínez Cachero, 2nd edn. Madrid: Cátedra, 1988.

Barea, Arturo. Introduction to Camilo José Cela, *The Hive*, trans. by J. M. Cohen in consultation with Arturo Barea. London: Victor Gollancz, 1953, 7–16.

Barra, Santiago. See Salvador Toquero.

Beramendi, Justo G. "La Galicia de Murguía," in Manuel Murguía, *Galicia*, ed. Justo G. Beramendi, 2 vols. Vigo: Edicións Xerais de Galicia, 1982, I, i–xli.

Bernaldo de Quirós, C. *La picota: Crímenes y castigos en el país castellano en los tiempos medios. Figuras delincuentes.* Madrid: Ediciones Turner, 1975.

Brenan, Gerald. *The Face of Spain*, 3rd edn. London: Penguin Books in association with Hamish Hamilton, 1988.

——— *The Literature of the Spanish People.* Cambridge: Cambridge University Press, 1951.

——— *South from Granada.* London: Hamish Hamilton, 1957.

——— *The Spanish Labyrinth.* Cambridge: Cambridge University Press, 1943.

Bryant, William Cullen. *Letters of a Traveller: Second Series*. New York: D. Appleton and Company, 1859.

———— *Poetical Works*. New York: D. Appleton and Company, 1883.

Bryson, Bill. *Notes from a Small Island*, paperbound edn. London: Black Swan, 1996.

Butor, Michel. "Travel and Writing," in *Temperamental Journeys: Essays on the Modern Literature of Travel*, ed. Michael Kowalewski. Athens and London: University of Georgia Press, 1992, 53–70.

Butt, John. "God-botherer." *Daily Telegraph*, Weekend Section, 17 February 1990, xviii.

Carr, Raymond. *The Spanish Tragedy: The Civil War in Perspective*, paperbound edn. London: Weidenfeld, 1993.

Carr, Raymond and Juan Pablo Fusi Aizpurua. *Spain: Dictatorship to Democracy*, paperbound edn. London: George Allen & Unwin, 1981.

Castellet, J. M. "Iniciación a la obra narrativa de Camilo José Cela," in J. M. Castellet and others, *Camilo José Cela: Vida y obra—Bibliografía—Antología*. New York: Hispanic Institute in the United States, 1962, 7–50.

Castro, Américo. "Algo sobre el 'nihilismo' creador de Camilo José Cela," in Américo Castro, *Hacia Cervantes*, 2nd edn. Madrid: Taurus, 1960, 386–90.

———— *España en su historia: Cristianos, moros y judíos*. Buenos Aires: Losada, 1948.

Cela, Camilo José. "Andar por andar y, de paso, ver," in *Obra completa*, vol. 10, *Glosa del mundo en torno: Artículos, 2 (1944–1959)* (Barcelona: Destino, 1978), 523–26.

———— "Breve nota para médicos y farmacéuticos," in *Obra completa*, vol. 4, 536–38.

———— "Con la mochila al hombro y una paz infinita en el corazón," in *Obra completa*, vol. 4, 9–16.

———— *Del Miño al Bidasoa: Notas de un vagabundaje*. Barcelona: Noguer, 1952.

———— "El calendario en el corazón," in *Obra completa*, vol. 6, 377–82.

———— "El campo, la ciudad, el campo . . . , esa margarita," in *Obra completa*, vol. 10, 60–63.

———— Introduction to *Primer viaje andaluz*, in *Obra completa*, vol. 6, 21–23.

———— *Judíos, moros y cristianos: Notas de un vagabundaje por Avila, Segovia y sus tierras*. Barcelona: Destino, 1956.

———— "La carambola por tablas y el espíritu de chamarilero," in *Obra completa*, vol. 4, 247–49.

———— "La confusa andadura de un libro sencillísimo," in *Obra completa*, vol. 4, 21–23.

———— "La Mancha en el corazón y en los ojos (*Elegía a lo que no se tiene en las manos*)," in *Obra completa*, vol. 10, 582–92.

———— *Las botas de siete leguas: Viaje a la Alcarria*. Madrid: Revista de Occidente, 1948.

———— "Los libros de viajes," in *Obra completa*, vol. 10, 228–30.

———— *Los viejos amigos: Primera serie*. Barcelona: Noguer, 1960.

———— "Materiales con los que cualquier sabio tratadista hubiera podido componer un prólogo," in *Obra completa*, vol. 6, 25–30.

———— *Memorias, entendimientos y voluntades*. Barcelona: Plaza & Janés/Cambio 16, 1993.

———— "Mensaje a los vagabundos," in *Obra completa*, vol. 10, 520–22.

———— "Nota a la cuarta edición [de *Viaje a la Alcarria*]," in *Obra completa*, vol. 4, 513–15.

———— "Nota a la segunda edición [de *Viaje a la Alcarria*]," in *Obra completa*, vol. 4, 509–12.

—— *Nuevo viaje a la Alcarria.* Barcelona: Plaza & Janés, 1986.

—— "Otra vez la ciudad," in *Obra completa*, vol. 10, 32–34.

—— *Primer viaje andaluz: Notas de un vagabundaje por Jaén, Córdoba, Sevilla, Huelva y sus tierras.* Barcelona: Noguer, 1959.

—— Prologue to *Judíos, moros y cristianos*, in *Obra completa*, vol. 5, 123–31.

—— "Prologuillo para escolares ingleses," in *Viaje a la Alcarria*, ed. Philip Polack, repr. of 1975 unabridged edn. London: Harrap, 1979, 21–23.

—— "Recuerdo en paz la tierra por la que anduve . . . ," in *Obra completa*, vol. 5, 115–18.

—— "Relativo Curriculum Vitae," in J. M. Castellet and others, *Camilo José Cela: Vida y obra—Bibliografía—Antología*, 79–109.

—— "Sobre España, los españoles y lo español," in Camilo José Cela, *Cuatro figuras del 98: Unamuno, Valle-Inclán, Baroja, Azorín y otros retratos y ensayos españoles* (Barcelona: Aedos, 1961), 225–40.

—— *Viaje al Pirineo de Lérida: Notas de un paseo a pie por el Pallars Sobirà, el Valle de Arán y el Condado de Ribagorza.* Madrid: Alfaguara, 1965.

—— "Visita de la ciudad," in *Obra completa*, vol. 10, 28–31.

Cela Conde, Camilo José. *Cela, mi padre.* Madrid: Temas de Hoy, 1989.

Cervantes Saavedra, Miguel de. *The Ingenious Hidalgo Don Quixote de la Mancha*, trans., with an introduction and notes by John Rutherford. London: Penguin Books, 2000.

Chard, Chloe. "Unknown Pleasures." *Times Higher Education Supplement*, 3 August 1990, 15.

Cocker, Mark. *Loneliness and Time: British Travel Writing in the Twentieth Century.* London: Secker & Warburg, 1992.

Collins, Roger. *Spain: An Oxford Archaeological Guide.* Oxford: Oxford University Press, 1998.

Coverdale, John F. "The Battle of Guadalajara, 8–22 March 1937." *Journal of Contemporary History*, 9 (1974), 53–75.

Davies, Catherine. "Rosalía de Castro's Later Poetry and Anti-Regionalism in Spain." *Modern Language Review*, 79 (1984), 609–19.

Díaz-Plaja, Fernando. *La Guerra de España en sus documentos*, 2nd edn. Barcelona: Ediciones G.P., 1969.

Dodd, Philip. "The Views of Travellers: Travel Writing in the 1930s," in *The Art of Travel: Essays on Travel Writing*, ed. Philip Dodd. London: Frank Cass, 1982, 127–38.

Epton, Nina. *Andalusia.* London: Weidenfeld and Nicolson, 1968.

—— *Spain's Magic Coast: From the Miño to the Bidassoa.* London: Weidenfeld and Nicolson, 1965.

Eyres, Harry. "Spanish Stroller." *The Times*, 10 February 1990, 38.

Ferres, Antonio and Armando López Salinas. *Caminando por las Hurdes.* Barcelona: Seix Barral, 1960.

Fowler, Roger. *Linguistics and the Novel.* London and New York: Methuen, 1977; repr. 1979.

Fusi Aizpurua, Juan Pablo. See Raymond Carr.

Fussell, Paul. *Abroad: British Literary Traveling between the Wars.* New York and Oxford: Oxford University Press, 1980.

—— Introduction to *The Norton Book of Travel*, ed. Paul Fussell. New York and London: W.W. Norton & Company, 1987, 13–17.

Genette, Gérard. *Paratexts: Thresholds of Interpretation*, trans. by Jane E. Lewin. Cambridge: Cambridge University Press, 1997.

Goytisolo, Juan. *Campos de Níjar*. Barcelona. Seix Barral, 1960.

—— *En los reinos de taifa*. Barcelona: Seix Barral, 1986.

—— *La Chanca*. Barcelona: Seix Barral, 1962.

—— "Tierras del Sur," in Juan Goytisolo, *Obras completas*, vol. 2, *Relatos y ensayos*. Madrid: Aguilar, 1977, 1036–56.

Hemingway, Ernest. *Fiesta*, trans. By José Mora Guarnido and John E. Halisner. Barcelona: José Janés, 1948.

—— *Fiesta: (The Sun Also Rises)*. London: Pan Books, 1949; repr. 1963.

Henn, David. "Endemic Violence and Political Balance in Cela's *San Camilo, 1936*." *Romance Studies*, no 3 (winter 1983–84), 31–46.

—— "Two Views of Almería: Juan Goytisolo and Gerald Brenan." *Revue de Littérature Comparée*, no 260 (Oct.–Dec. 1991), 429–46.

Henríquez-Jiménez, Santiago. *Going the Distance: An Analysis of Modern Travel Writing and Criticism*. Barcelona: Kadle Books, 1995.

Holland, Patrick and Graham Huggan. *Tourists with Typewriters: Critical Reflections on Contemporary Travel Writing*. Ann Arbor: University of Michigan Press, 1998.

Huggan, Graham. See Patrick Holland.

Ilie, Paul. *La novelística de Camilo José Cela*, 3rd edn. Madrid: Gredos, 1978.

Jacobs, Michael. *Between Hopes and Memories: A Spanish Journey*. London: Picador, 1994.

Jordan, Barry. "The Emergence of a Dissident Intelligencia," in *Spanish Cultural Studies. An Introduction: The Struggle for Modernity*, eds. Helen Graham and Jo Labanyi. Oxford: Oxford University Press, 1995, 245–55.

—— *Writing and Politics in Franco's Spain*. London and New York: Routledge, 1990.

Kerr, Sarah. "Shock Treatment." *New York Review of Books*, 8 October 1992, 35–39.

Kirsner, Robert. "La España de *Viaje a la Alcarria*." *Insula, Monográfico Extraordinario Dedicado al Premio Nobel de Literatura 1989*, nos 518–19 (Feb.–Mar. 1990), 42–43.

—— "La persistente presencia de la Guerra Civil Española en la obra de Camilo José Cela." *Hispanística XX, Camilo José Cela: Nuevos enfoques*, 8 (1990), 69–80.

—— *The Novels and Travels of Camilo José Cela*. Chapel Hill: University of North Carolina Press, 1963.

Kowalewski, Michael. "Introduction: The Modern Literature of Travel," in *Temperamental Journeys: Essays on the Modern Literature of Travel*, ed. Michael Kowalewski, 1–16.

Lévi-Strauss, Claude. *Tristes Tropiques*, trans. By John Russell. New York: Atheneum, 1968.

Livermore, Harold. *The Origins of Spain and Portugal*. London: George Allen & Unwin, 1971.

Llamazares, Julio. *El río del olvido: Viaje*. Barcelona: Seix Barral, 1990.

—— *Trás-os-Montes: (Un viaje portugués)*. Madrid: Alfaguara, 1998.

López-Barxas, Francisco. "Entrevista a Camilo José Cela." *Insula, Monográfico Extraordinario Dedicado al Premio Nobel de Literatura, 1989*, 77–80.

López Salinas, Armando. See Antonio Ferres.

Malraux, André. *L'Espoir*. Paris: Gallimard, 1966.

Marriott, Edward. "Travels of the Mind." *The Times*, Metro Section, 30 May 1998, 20.

Martínez Cachero, José María. "Camilo José Cela, viajero por España." *Hispanística XX, Camilo José Cela: Nuevos enfoques*, 119–32.

McPheeters, D. W. *Camilo José Cela*. New York: Twayne, 1969.

Menéndez Pidal, Ramón. *The Spaniards in their History*. Trans. and with a prefatory essay by Walter Starkie. London: Hollis & Carter, 1950.

Miller, Townsend. *The Castles and the Crown: Spain 1451–1555*. London: Victor Gollancz, 1963.

Morton, H. V. *A Stranger in Spain*. London: Methuen & Co., 1955.

Newby, Eric, comp. *A Book of Travellers' Tales*. London: Picador, 1986.

Nieto, Amparo. See Jorge-Víctor Sueiro.

Olmos García, Francisco. "La novela y los novelistas españoles de hoy." *Cuadernos Americanos*, no 119 (July–Aug. 1963), 211–37.

Orwell, George. *The Road to Wigan Pier*. London: Penguin Books in association with Secker & Warburg, 1986.

Ortega y Gasset, José. "De Madrid a Asturias, o los dos paisajes: Notas de andar y ver," in *El Espectador*. Madrid: Biblioteca Nueva, 1950, 335–58.

———— "Notas del vago estío," in *El Espectador*, 555–610.

———— "Tierras de Castilla: Notas de andar y ver," in *El Espectador*, 53–62.

Pardo Bazán, Emilia. "El viaje por España." *La España Moderna*, no 83 (Nov. 1895), 76–97.

———— *Por la España pintoresca: Viajes*. Barcelona: Antonio López, 1895.

———— *Por la Europa católica*. Madrid: Administración, [1902].

Porter, Dennis. *Haunted Journeys: Desire and Transgression in European Travel Writing*. Princeton, NJ: Princeton University Press, 1991.

Pozuelo Yvancos, José María. Introduction to Camilo José Cela, *Viaje a la Alcarria*, ed. José María Pozuelo Yvancos. Madrid: Espasa-Calpe, 1990, 9–56.

Preston, Paul. *Franco: A Biography*. London: HarperCollins, 1993.

Priestley, J. B. *English Journey*, 3rd edn. London: William Heinemann in association with Victor Gollancz, 1937.

Pritchett, V. S. *Marching Spain*. London: Hogarth Press, 1988.

Raban, Jonathan. "Better Half." *Sunday Times*, Section 6, Travel, 8 June 1997, 7.

———— *Passage to Juneau: A Sea and Its Meanings*. London: Picador, 1999.

Resina, Joan Ramón. "Papeles de Son Armadans, revista literaria de Postguerra." *Revista Canadiense de Estudios Hispánicos*, 12 (1987), 71–91.

Ridao, José María. "Américo Castro, 25 años después." *El País*, 25 July 1997, 9.

Rodríguez, Pío. "Forty Years of Spanish Culture." *Cultures*, 8 (1982), 64–80.

Saramago, José. *Viagem a Portugal*. Lisbon: Círculo de Leitores, 1981.

Senabre, Ricardo. "Camilo José Cela en la España árida." *Ínsula, Monográfico Extraordinario Dedicado al Premio Nobel de Literatura 1989*, 65–66.

Serrano Belinchón, José. *Guadalajara*. León: Editorial Everest, 1991.

Shakespeare, Nicholas. *Bruce Chatwin*. London: The Harvill Press in association with Jonathan Cape, 1999.

Shattock, Joanne. "Travel Writing Victorian and Modern: A Review of Recent Research," in *The Art of Travel: Essays on Travel Writing*, ed. Philip Dodd, 151–64.

Sitwell, Sacheverell. *Spain.* London: B. T. Batsford, 1950.

Sontag, Susan. "Model Destinations." *Times Literary Supplement*, 22 June 1984, 699.

Stark, Freya. "The Philosophy of Travel," in *Views from Abroad: The Spectator Book of Travel Writing*, eds. Philip Marsden-Smedley and Jeffrey Klinke. London: Paladin, 1989; repr. 1990, 3–6.

Stubbs, Imogen. "The Undiscovered Road," in *Amazonian: The Penguin Book of Women's New Travel Writing*, eds. Dea Birkett and Sara Wheeler. London: Penguin Books, 1998, 198–230.

Sueiro, Jorge-Víctor and Amparo Nieto. *Galicia: Romería interminable.* Madrid: Penthalon, 1983.

Sulzberger, C. L. "Anti-Franco Blows Shaping as Falangist Program Fails." *New York Times*, 26 February 1946, 1,4.

——— "Inflation Pushing Spain into Strikes." *New York Times*, 23 February 1946, 7.

Tamames, Ramón. *La República. La era de Franco.* Historia de España Alfaguara, vol. 7, 11th edn. Madrid: Alianza/Alfaguara, 1986.

Theroux, Paul. *Fresh-Air Fiend: Travel Writings, 1985–2000.* London: Hamish Hamilton, 2000.

——— *The Great Railway Bazaar: By Train through Asia*, paperbound edn. London: Penguin Books, 2001.

——— *The Old Patagonian Express: By Train through the Americas*, paperbound edn. London: Penguin Books, 1980.

Thomas. Hugh. *The Spanish Civil War*, 3rd edn., revised and enlarged. Harmondsworth: Penguin Books in association with Hamish Hamilton, 1977.

Thubron, Colin. "Chuckles along the Littoral." *Times Literary Supplement*, 4 January 1985, 6.

Toquero, Salvador and Santiago Barra. *Buscando a Cela en la Alcarria.* Guadalajara: The Authors, 1982.

Umbral, Francisco. *Cela: Un cadáver exquisito. Vida y obra.* Barcelona: Planeta, 2002.

Unamuno, Miguel de. *Andanzas y visiones españolas.* Madrid: Espasa-Calpe, 1955.

——— *Por tierras de Portugal y de España.* Madrid: Espasa-Calpe, 1976.

Walker, Ted. *In Spain.* London: Secker & Warburg, 1987.

Wilson, James. "Stepping back to Spain in an Old Pair of Shoes." *The Independent*, 25 September 1993, 47.

Woolsey, Gamel. *Death's Other Kingdom.* London: Longman & Co, 1939.

Zamora Vicente, Alonso. *Camilo José Cela: (Acercamiento a un escritor).* Madrid: Gredos, 1962.

Index